Histories of Art and Design
Education
Cole to Coldstream

Edited by David Thistlewood

Longman
in association with the
National Society for Education
in Art and Design

Longman Group UK Limited
*Longman House, Burnt Mill, Harlow, Essex CM20 2JE, England
and Associated Companies throughout the World.*

© Longman Group UK Limited 1992

First published 1992
Set in 10/12pt Plantin (Linotron 202)
Produced by Longman Singapore Publishers (Pte) Ltd
Printed in Singapore

British Library Cataloguing in Publication Data
Histories of art and design education: Cole to Coldstream.
  1. Education. Curriculum. Visual arts, history
  I. Thistlewood, David II. National Society for Education
in Art & Design
707
ISBN 0-582-07420-7

Contents

Illustrations

Acknowledgements

Chapter 1 was first published as MACDONALD, S. (1973), 'Articidal Tendencies', Chapter Eight of PIPER, D.W. (ed.), *Readings in Art & Design Education 2: After Coldstream* (London, Davis-Poynter Ltd), pp. 89–99.

Chapters 2, 3, 4, 5, 7, 9 and 10 were contributions to a *History of Art and Design Education* seminar held in conjunction with the Annual Conference of the NSEAD, Bournemouth, November 1988 (organisers Rachel Mason and John Swift).

Chapter 11 was first published as THISTLEWOOD, D. (1981), catalogue of the exhibition *A Continuing Process: the New Creativity in British Art Education 1955–1965* (London, Institute of Contemporary Arts).

Chapter 12 was first published as LYNTON, N. (1987), 'Harry Thubron: Teacher and Artist', in THISTLEWOOD, D. (ed.) (1987), *The Bramley Occasional Papers of the National Arts Education Archive*, Vol. 1, pp. 13–20. Much of the material on which this chapter was based — The Developing Process exhibition; Pasmore, Hudson, Hamilton and Thubron archives; The 1956 SEA Conference proceedings — is preserved in the NAEA holdings at Bretton Hall, West Yorkshire.

Chapter 13 was first published in *The Journal of Art and Design Education*, 8, 2, 1989, pp. 135–52.

We are grateful to the following for permission to reproduce photographs:
Annan, Glasgow, Fig 10; Anne Hirsh Collection, Montreal, Fig 22; Art Resources in Teaching Records, Special Collections, The University Library, The University of Illinois, Fig 7; Birmingham Art School Archive, Birmingham Polytechnic, Figs 1, 2, 3, 4; Collection of the Montreal Museum of Fine Arts, Purchase Contribution of the Government of Canada under the terms of the Cultural Property Export and Import Act and the Harry W Thorpe Bequest, Fig 20; Glasgow School of Art, Fig 12; Hamilton Art Gallery, Ontario, Fig 21; Hudson, Tom/ Leicester Polytechnic, Fig 26; Hunterian Art Gallery, University of Glasgow, Fig 11; Manchester City Art Galleries, Fig 8; Marion Richardson Archives, School of Art & Design Education, Birmingham Polytechnic, Figs 15, 16, 17; Suzanne Lemerise, Fig 19; The Hatton Gallery, Newcastle University, Figs 23, 24, 25.

Cover: *Fritillaria, Walberswick*, pencil and watercolour, 1915: Charles Rennie Mackintosh, Hunterian Art Gallery, University of Glasgow, Mackintosh Collection.

Introduction

This volume of essays explores the history of art and design education in Britain and North America within the period spanning Cole and Coldstream. Henry Cole initiated the Victorian National Course of Instruction in 1853, arguing for art and design's central role in the industrial and economic, and therefore material rather than cultural, well-being of a nation. A little over a century later – in 1960 – William Coldstream achieved academic respectability for the subject when he recommended that it be generally afforded degree-equivalance in the non-university sector of British higher education. The points of view represented by these two bald facts could not be more different: art and design as a matter of strategic economic necessity; art and design as comparable to other arts and humanities and worthy of disinterested study for its own sake. These principles have been evident throughout the history of state education in art and design, and they have affected similarly the systems operating on either side of the Atlantic. It is useful to recognise this today, and to realise that what seem to be unique problems in our present circumstances are in some sense universal. History – or rather histories – may be paradigms for contemporary practices.

When we review the range of histories represented in this volume it is difficult to ignore the obvious fact that fundamental, irreconcilable disagreements about policies, rationales and justifications have been usual. Revolution versus convention; child-centrality versus subject-centrality; the expressive versus the utilitarian – in some form or another they feature in every account of what has taken place before now.

Stuart Macdonald provides a general overview of the period in Chapter One. His 'Articidal Tendencies' is a much-quoted essay, first published in 1973. It is reproduced here both for its comprehensive scope and for the fact that – prophetic in its day – it establishes a tangible link with our contemporary experience. Philosophical disagreements are its major focus. One is the argument that has raged back and forth across the century (and the Atlantic) between the advocates of solid instruction and those of the lightest possible imposition of teaching. We tend to identify instruction with the beginning of the period and anti-instruction with somewhere nearer our own time, for example the permissive 1960s. However, as we are reminded here, students' complaints about having been left to teach themselves were as evident in Victorian art schools as they are today. Stuart Macdonald reminds us too that arguments about whether to teach or not to teach were interfused with a fundamental difference of belief as to whether art and design was an instrument of liberal or utilitarian education. If the latter, it was invariably taught systematically and methodically; if the former, it could be permitted to develop in untrammelled personal freedom of expression.

To complicate this otherwise neat division, however, there has been a consistent, awkward truth. Some of the best design (therefore utilitarian) education has resulted from courses in which students were encouraged to explore materials and methods of working them expressively. In exploring this particular theme Stuart Macdonald's implied criticism is of a failure to recognise that design may be taught effectively from a fine art basis, though he maintains that this is not necessarily true if a definition of 'fine art' is extended to embrace recent aesthetic manifestations in the art schools. It is undeniable that since he wrote this essay the tendency he perceived towards the relative demise of fine art as object, and the rise of fine art as transient event (happening) or ephemeral experience (personal environment), has increased. This further polarises utilitarian and liberal interests, and provides an excuse, if one were needed, for a form of interventionism in art and design education that deliberately draws pupils and students back to the disciplines of conceiving and shaping tangible, purposive, aesthetic artefacts.

Thus any attempt to identify historical pathways through the period in question is faced with at least three interwoven contradictions: design versus fine art; instruction versus freedom from instruction; the object versus the conceptual experience. That there are also many other dichotomies and paradoxes is evident in all the other contributions to this volume. This makes the study of the history of art and design education both exasperating and intellectually rewarding (another paradox), and also justifies a piecemeal or case study approach: the various oppositions are *so* interwoven that it is only within specific, tightly circumscribed contexts that it becomes possible to separate them for close scrutiny.

A history of Birmingham's art school in the last two decades of the nineteenth century bears evidence of another fundamental disagreement between educationalists, as to whether design is best taught through practical craftwork, realising artefacts in *actuality*, or through scholastic memorising of historic examples, celebrating renowned concepts in *idealisation*. John Swift's account is of a 'renegade' institution, resolutely concentrating on the former attitude and – to the great annoyance of officialdom – achieving much success in national competitions that were intended to measure the effectiveness of the latter. This is interesting enough for paradox hunters, but complicated even further because, as we are informed, the art school's external examiner at the turn of the century was Walter Crane, famous for his defence of craftwork principles, though in this case perturbed by the fact that 'amateurs', rather than professional art-workers, were the ones experiencing national success. There were also strong hints that amateurs (women) were working in inappropriate fields – for example, metal crafts rather than embroidery – which of course raises another perennial dispute.

That such disagreements were not confined to Britain is evident in the range of North American contributions to this volume. Diana Korzenik brings to the fore a classic difference of principle – one that was aired openly in public debate in the USA, rather than confined to academic debate as in Britain – centring on whether the quality of utilitarian design should be measured against foreign or native standard types. In the USA this was clouded with colonialism and unified all social outlooks. In Britain, on the other hand, it was clouded with issues of taste as reflected in its class structure, and was correspondingly socially divisive. However

9

(not shunning complication) we should note that it was *European* ideas about romantic individualism that provided America with its best hope of a national aesthetic identity, arising from a great collective effort to appreciate specifically American topography, nature and work.

It is hard to see contention rising from this state of affairs, but in the history of art and design education nothing is straightforward. The clouding issues here related to the Ruskinian argument about religiosity – an order in earthly things, perceptible through art, is a microcosm of an orderly heaven. Thus rejection of much authentic art and aesthetic principles on grounds of their foreign origins amounts to a rejection of belief that the love of God is universal. As Mary Ann Stankiewicz points out in Chapter Four, this attitude also creates an identity of aesthetics and morals: a host of issues thus demand attention. Cultural isolationism is simultaneously supported and brought into question. To import foreign aesthetics into the USA was to accept both perfections and imperfections into a society attempting to remain innocently pure; while to exclude foreign influences was to propose the creation of a specifically American aesthetic/moral code divorced from the rest of Christendom. It may not be surprising that such weighty responsibilities have been too much for the majority of teachers to consider bearing.

Kerry Freedman's contribution to this volume (Chapter Five) addresses a philosophical outlook that has seemed a preferable alternative for many teachers and writers in the arts and humanities. Opposing the idea of a desirable return to some original condition of social innocence and religious rectitude is that of creating new ideal conditions in a spirit of progress embracing the arts, science and all manifestations of human conduct. This is both historical (connoting the eighteenth century, the Enlightenment, and all the efforts towards social improvement by invention that this entailed) and contemporary, for growth, progress and elimination of ignorance are all crucial aspects of western thought today. Kerry Freedman's observations therefore centre on one of the most profound differences of belief within art and design education, namely whether it should be an accelerating or a braking influence on the great movement of thought and action that has fuelled political liberalism, religious dissent and scientific rationalism for the past two centuries.

In Stuart Macdonald's second contribution there are also echoes of the Enlightenment, especially of the grand design for a pan-European culture. He records the circumstances in which Glasgow became a centre of Art Nouveau in the early twentieth century, and argues that this occurred only because an art school – already inclined to baulk at a system imposed from London – was tolerant of creative aberrations even though there were no obvious criteria for evaluating them. More significantly, this chapter is about an early manifestation of an antagonism that was to become common in later years, the rolling dispute between advocates of conventional art forms and exponents of modernism. There have been no differences less capable of resolution than this twentieth-century phenomenon, so completely polarised as to commit respective adherents – in other respects presumably sane – to mutual nullification.

As in Scotland, so in Nova Scotia: in Chapter Seven Don Soucy describes how a much-protracted battle of wills was fought between conservatives and upstart modernists at the Victoria School of Art and Design, Halifax, Nova Scotia. Whereas Glasgow, briefly, maintained a modernist style in the face of external opposition, at Halifax a strong, conservative Principal manipulated a weak board of governors to neutralise potentially modernising influences within her staff. What was at issue was whether, by training pupils and students for craftwork industries that no longer existed, an institutional head could will an outmoded pattern of existence back into being. It was a highly idiosyncratic form of Utopian colonialism exported from Britain, and gives rise to the unexpected observation that generations of Canadians would have been better off if subjected to the usual sub-South Kensington conventions. As it was, the alternative scourge was a genre of landscape painting influenced by the *genius loci* of eastern Canada. Today such a challenge would seem innocuous enough, but this is to underestimate the power of polarisation in the history of this discipline.

In John Swift's second essay, a study of Marion Richardson's contribution to art teaching in the period between the two World Wars, at least three antagonistic tensions are apparent. Richardson is well-known for her advocacy of specific forms of imagery that manifest children's stages of perceptual development, rather than forms that oblige mimicry of adult conventions. Child-centrality versus curriculum-centrality is thus an evident polarity that only really became evident in British art and design education with the pioneering efforts of such individuals as Richardson. The tension between convention and modernism is also evident in her work through the fact that the spectacular results of her teaching were adopted by theorists of the avant-garde, such as Roger Fry, and comparisons made between her children's work and Post-Impressionism. As theorists maintained a wish to reconstitute a childlike vision on behalf of certain Post-Impressionists, there was an additional incentive to embrace her work. The idea that such artists were also striving for an essential, or primitive, mode of percipience was supported too by 'evidence' that the child recapitulated in early experience the 'early experience' of the human race. For this theoretical structure to seem valid, it had to be maintained that Richardson achieved her results – an authentic form of children's imagery – by encouragement but not by teaching, as this would have distorted its naturalness. She is still often cited in support of the latter side of the 'to teach' or 'not to teach' divide. As John Swift points out, however, Richardson was primarily a *teacher* who perfected unconventional curricula, and the fiction that she did not teach has prevented the subsequent emulation of her methods until now.

Irène Senécal's teaching career in Quebec was very similar to Richardson's though it began some fifteen years later. In Chapter Nine Suzanne Lemerise offers an account of Senécal's mediation between the demands of a utilitarian curriculum and her growing understanding of romantic symbolist painting and Surrealist techniques for tapping subconscious creativity. Senécal is presented here as resolving the conflicting demands of convention and enlightened philosophy, and this essay suggests that this required sacrifice (of reputation), and a willingness to bear the animosity of the avant-garde (who could not understand her loyalty to an outmoded curriculum even though her pupils had to take its examinations). Suzanne Lemerise's study is therefore primarily of risk-taking, of a teacher torn between extremes, and consequently living on her nerves. For many years Senécal had to maintain one frame of reference towards her institution and quite a different sensibility towards her own art. But the point here is that she achieved what the avant-garde cannot by definition achieve: it is a teacher's responsibility to trade with orthodoxy whereas this act is anathema to those at the forefront of aesthetic conquest.

Anne Savage was another Canadian counterpart of Marion Richardson and an admirer of her philosophy. In Chapter Ten Leah Sherman discusses the relationship between Savage's own art and her teaching, endorsing the suggestion that a teacher's personal creativity both fuels his or her teaching and is sacrificed to it. Savage was also an admirer of Herbert Read, whose book *Education through Art* (1943) she recognised as providing a rationale for her own intuitive values. Further propagation of Read's ideas by the efforts of such as Savage gave new meaning to the work of many thousands of art teachers who shunned conventions. Instead of merely assisting recreational skills (the only obvious alternative to teaching set formulae) their role was now seen as helping innate creative abilities to survive, for the sake of individual well-being but also for the health of the community.

The potential for success in this was evident in Read's version of recapitulation theory – the observation that children quite naturally give forth imagery which maintains contact with deep layers of social experience, and with times when social cohesion was the normal order. A corollary was the suggestion that certain defects of modern life – injustice, immorality, harsh competition, even war – had roots in conventional systems of education and, specifically, in the emphasis on intellectual development to the exclusion of other faculties which was visited upon children from around the age of ten. However, the elimination of conventional education – or rather its avoidance in the still largely untainted context of North America – would recover (in the old world) or ensure (in the new) individual, and also collective, social health.

Now there is yet another polarity evident in beliefs such as this: its spiritual or mythical connotations are at odds with the strictly pragmatic ramifications of an education in art and *design*. For Herbert Read and others like him, however, there was no inexplicable difficulty here. The answer lay in notions of a natural creativity – a creativity informed by impulses projected unselfconsciously from the subconscious mind into contemplative attention. The key concept was that of process dominance, the idea that an 'organic' sequence of creative actions could be set in motion, with each stage in the process informing the next. Not geared to anticipated outcomes, such activity would be unaffected by both conventions and preconceived solutions, and could therefore be considered genuinely creative in the sense of giving rise to concepts the conscious mind may unwittingly suppress. In Chapter Eleven I discuss one of the most celebrated attempts to practise such an educational philosophy, having avant-garde artists such as Paul Klee and mystic teachers such as Johannes Itten as its exemplars, and philosophical organicism as its theoretical basis.

The principal originators in this enterprise were Victor Pasmore, Richard Hamilton, Tom Hudson and Harry Thubron. In Chapter Twelve Norbert Lynton pays special regard to Thubron who, while collaborating with Pasmore, Hamilton and Hudson, must be regarded as uniquely original for reasons Norbert Lynton makes clear. He was the epitome of contradictions. A bohemian romantic, he worked for intuitive control over technics; he maintained that the fine artist was the proper driving force for science; his criterion of excellence was *aesthetic*, and he was indifferent as to whether this was evident in refined or coarsened forms. What he was sure had no place in the education of children or adolescents was sentimentality, and his robust way of letting this be known set him against those who, by the 1950s, were romanticising childhood in the belief that they were consolidating Marion Richardson's great gains.

There has of course been subsequent consolidation, but this has necessitated resolution of the polarities typified by Richardson and Thubron. It is my own view, expressed in Chapter Thirteen, that this has been achieved in the amalgamation of two professional bodies in Britain – the National Society for Art Education (NSAE) and the Society for Education Through Art (SEA) – to form the National Society for Education in Art and Design (NSEAD) in 1984. Two great and mutually exclusive traditions collided here, one having allegiance to the fundamental disciplines in art and design education, the other committed to their exploitation in the empowerment of individual pupils and students; and while the result might have been mutually destructive it has in fact created a Gestalt much greater than the sum of these two constituents. And what has occurred in the context of the NSEAD has been mirrored within British art and design education at large, ensuring that an official swing towards either of the polarities would be corrected by a change of policy towards the other. What may in one sense be interpreted as a series of decisive government acts over the past century, boldly shaping art and design education in line with some detectable but undeclared strategy, may in another sense be seen as a periodic failure of nerve. Coldstream thus becomes a late corrective for Cole; Cole is a tactic to ensure that a Coldstream may never occur. In the pursuit of a career in art and design education it is as well to be armed with a sense of *déjà vu*.

DAVID THISTLEWOOD

Chapter One

STUART MACDONALD Articidal Tendencies

> . . . the parents in England think that their children are born with an
> innate genius for landscape painting or something else. There is too
> much natural genius in this country, not enough study . . . and you
> suffer from the want of proper teaching [1].

These are the words of Vivant Alphonse Legros, who during the years
1876 to 1892 improved the standard of life drawing in the Slade School
and, indirectly, in the country beyond recognition.

Legros was astonished by the snobbish reverence for High Art in our
art schools, combined with a complete lack of sound instruction in
practical skills and academic knowledge.

Forty years on, in 1923 to be precise, Walter Richard Sickert referred
to 'an immense mob of idlers, male and female, to whom art schools
serve as a kind of day nursery' [2].

Nearly fifty years later Sjoerd Hannema, lecturer at Manchester,
asserts:

> Generally speaking, however, he [the student] is left to work out his
> own salvation. . . . There are also those tutors, particularly common
> in the field of painting, who believe, as an article of faith, that
> students cannot and should not be taught; instead, they should be
> left to 'feel their way' and 'organize their own experience' [3].

Some hundred years ago a mature student at the same school, namely
Charles Rowley, friend of Morris and the Pre-Raphaelites, wrote:

> I would ask whether there is anyone trained by the school who can
> clearly define any principle or art precept which has been
> communicated to them there during the last thirty years. The
> exception made by some was the system that might be defined as
> one of a thousand and one dots to the inch [4].

I would hasten to explain that the system of 'a thousand and one dots
to the inch' was not the Op dotting of recent years over which students
spent weeks, even months, but the stipple dotting over which Victorian
students spent months, even years.

It becomes clear if one studies the history of art education that the
present criticisms of fine art staff are not a new phenomenon. Hannema
points out that the introduction of Anti-art movements into fine art
departments has affected today's situation; but the non-analytical, non-
intellectual, non-teaching approach has always been uppermost in British
fine art departments. Hannema quotes a senior tutor saying in 1967: 'If
you want to pass this summer, paint Hard Edge'. I can remember a head
of painting in the days of Euston Road camp dominance, the NDD fifties,
those Spear–Sickert–Fitton–Minton–Pasmore (old style) days, grunting
to an assistant: 'If we want to pass more, paint Pasmore!' Mindless

imitation there has always been, from the days of cribbing the Discobolos to the Denny.

What is a completely new phenomenon in the history of art education is the contemporary articidal tendency, the death wish, the desire for the demise of the artefact, even of art itself. Before discussing this further it is relevant to go back in time. In the *History and Philosophy of Art Education* I researched in some depth the factual side of art education [5]. I would like now to trace in outline the attitudes of the government and the art teachers which have led up to the present situation.

From the start the development of public art education in Britain has been a struggle by the state to divert art schools from their overwhelming predilection for fine art towards industrial art, design, craftwork, and general art education. The periodic attempts of the government to do this have been rather half-hearted. *Laissez-faire* has operated until a situation has been reached of political or economic significance which portended embarrassing public outcry, the policy recommended by Lord Melbourne, prime minister at the time of state intervention, in the words 'God help the Minister that meddles with Art!'

During the period of the Schools of Design (1837–1852) the type of art work done in these institutions was laid down by the fine artists on the Council of the Central School and its headmasters, almost all Royal Academicians, whose brotherly object was to see that no rival institutions to their Academy would flourish. Richard Burchett, a well-indoctrinated member of the staff of the Central School, later its headmaster, said: 'We wish to teach art, but to teach it in a way that it should not interfere with that kind of art which comes within the province of the Royal Academy' [6]. In order that the Board of Trade's schools would not compete with the 'Schools of Design' of the Academy the Council laid down that the former were not schools for every kind of design, but for 'one kind only, viz. ornamental'.

The Royal Academicians' efforts against the tide were as successful as Canute's. The Board of Trade's Schools of Design were flooded by young ladies by day, and artisans by night, all seeking some knowledge of fine art. By 1849 the outcry in the press against Schools of Design which produced no designers brought about the sitting of a Parliamentary Select Committee, the eventual result of which, after a period of diversion caused by the Great Exhibition, was the reconstitution of the Schools of Design as Schools of Art under the direction of Henry Cole.

Cole persuaded politicians and public of the necessity for Schools of Art by representing them as centres of instruction for public education in drawing, declaring that 'straight lines are a national want'. Indeed Cole was highly successful both in compelling the staff of Schools of Art to superintend drawing in the elementary schools, and in converting 'twenty limp Schools of Design into one hundred flourishing Schools of Art', as he put it; but practically all the advanced students and the staff were pursuing fine art. Students were not encouraged to sit design papers, and very few did, a situation which continued until the 'nineties. To give a typical example of the state of affairs, at Manchester School of Art in 1892 there were 207 successful papers in the 3rd Grade Examinations of the Science and Art Department and only 15 of these were submitted for the only creative design paper: 'Design Ornament'. As a contrast there were as many as 46 successful papers concerned with direct or memory drawing from the cast of the Antique. Out of six national silver medals won that year three were for drapery arranged on the cast, and one for a modelled copy from the cast. Art was indeed castrated.

The lack of any education in designing for, and in, the materials of crafts had been noted by the Technical Instruction Commissioners, and in 1884 they had concluded that the Department of Science and Art should go 'so far as to award grants for specimens of applied art-workmanship in the materials themselves, as a test of the applicability of the design....' But as there had been no outcry nor pressure from the public and the manufacturers, who were prospering, and joyfully buying and selling the most hideous designs, the Government did nothing to alter public art education. The art masters directed their pupils more and more towards the Antique and away from the needs of contemporary society.

The art masters even managed to persuade the Department to divorce art from geometry, despite the fact that an acutely observant voyeur of the Society of Art Masters protested that 'solid geometry was essential for young ladies'. Short-sighted officialdom disagreed. Anyhow, this divorce was an unnecessary thing as far as the ladies were concerned. Victorian misses passed their time drawing from large cards of passion flower, wallflower, blushwort, blanket-flower, sweet scabious, maiden pink and wild teasel, according to their inclinations, or, if the art master approved of their talents, performing on canvas.

Unfortunately for the peace of mind of the government and the art masters, a group of disciples of Morris, the Art-Workers' Guild, had decided to lend a hand. These 'Art-Socialists' were greatly opposed to the public art schools being devoted to the production of drawing masters and fine artists. Working in conjunction with the London County Council (LCC) and the Trade Associations, the members of the Guild began to transform the nature of art education in London.

Lethaby, a founder member of the Guild, advocated Schools of Arts and Crafts, 'real making shops' combined with museums of contemporary and historic arts and crafts to comprise 'local centres of civilisation'. Craft classes, run as practical workshops and instructed by members of the Guild were established in the last five years of the century at Battersea Polytechnic, Camberwell School of Arts and Crafts, Regent St. Polytechnic and Shoreditch Technical Institute, and a little later at the Hammersmith School of Arts and Crafts, and the Sir John Cass Technical Institute. The greatest contribution of the LCC was the establishment of the Central School of Arts and Crafts in Regent St. in 1896 under the direction of Lethaby and George Frampton, ARA.

The art masters with their background of fine art, historic ornament, and 'design on paper' looked on these new developments with trepidation. They had been brought up to believe that fine art led design, and that design was merely a matter of passing this influence down to designers – an absurd theory still believed in, incredibly, by many art educationists. It was disturbing to hear that Lethaby and Crane were lecturing at Schools of Art and stating the opposite view, namely, that if society and the general level of design and craftwork was good, art would be good, otherwise it was rotten at the roots; also that design should be assimilated through the use of particular materials, and by studying actual objects made in those materials.

The art masters were not particularly worried as long as the Arts and Crafts movement was confined to London technical institutions, but to their alarm it spread to Schools of Art. Crane was appointed at Manchester (1893) and at the Royal College (1898), F. V. Burridge at Liverpool (1896), and Catterson-Smith at Birmingham (1903).

Crisis point in the progress of British art education was reached in the years 1910 to 1914. It had become embarrassingly obvious during the first decade of the century that the LCC Central School of Arts and Crafts was producing designers of European reputation, particularly in lettering, printing, and book production (Edward Johnston, Eric Gill, and Noel Rooke, to name a few); whereas the Royal College of Art, the senior art institution of the Board of Education, was merely producing fine art and 'design' teachers with a smattering of knowledge of the light artistic crafts. The Royal College classrooms in the period 1896–1920 would not have graced Dotheboys Hall. The situation was particularly mortifying for the Board, since all the Board's senior awards for art students, namely Royal Exhibitions, National Scholarships, and Studentships in Training were provided only for study at the Royal College.

In April 1910 the Board, exasperated into activity, appointed a Departmental Committee 'for the purpose of considering and reporting upon the functions and constitution of the Royal College of Art and its relations to the Schools of Art in London and throughout the country'. The Report of the Departmental Committee on the Royal College of Art, published in July 1911, was heavily critical of the situation. Commenting on the light crafts studied at the College, the Committee noted: 'They appeal to a limited public'. It was also stated: 'In so far as they receive a definite stylistic bent it is described as "mediaeval"'.

The Committee was so disturbed about the College's irrelevance to industrial design that they recommended 'decentralization', that 'mono-technics' should be set up in the centre of each major industry, and that a student wishing to study design for a particular industry should be given a grant to proceed to the appropriate centre. The monotechnic at Manchester would concentrate on cotton, at Bradford on wool, at Stoke-on-Trent on pottery, etc.

The masters at the Schools of Art, who had not the slightest idea of how to train an industrial designer, were aghast. The National Society of Art Masters suggested that a:

> Provincial Centre... might have a tendency to become 'tradey'
> ... and so not be an entirely desirable centre from the educational
> point of view. What it is hoped is that London will supply in its
> Arts and Crafts specialisation... The College needs a Craft School
> of an entirely practical nature...

The art masters were also quite happy to recommend that the Royal College should become 'an assemblage of studios and workshops'; then, they suggested, 'the idea of a school would disappear, the true feeling of higher apprenticeship taking its place'. In short, the art masters did not mind the Royal College becoming 'tradey', so long as they were themselves preserved from this fearful fate [7].

What the art masters feared was that the great network of small Schools of Art, built up by Henry Cole, would be drastically curtailed if large Schools of Arts and Crafts, or Industrial Design, were developed in monotechnics in the provincial manufacturing centres. Thus the National Society of Art Masters suggested to the Departmental Committee that two types of school should exist 'with equal claim for support'. The suggested types were:

  1. The older Schools ... for painters, book-illustrators, designers, modellers, and Art Teachers.
  2. The new 'Arts and Crafts' Schools established by the LCC ...

These Schools aim primarily at training the artisan and craftsman. What was so absurd about this suggestion of the art masters (or art officials, as Ashbee termed them) was that the oldest Schools were all in manufacturing centres full of artisans and craftsmen, and that the most progressive of these, namely those at Birmingham, Glasgow, and Liverpool, were all very much involved in training designers and craftsmen to design in the materials of their craft. The art masters did not wish to get involved with the testing realities of using craft materials. Students taking a 'Design' paper of the Board of Education were taught 'Applied Art' and 'the Principles of Design' as laid down at South Kensington. It is not generally understood today that 'applied art' was not applied, that is it was not applied to an object, or worked in a material. 'Applied art' was design *on paper* that could have been applied to a particular object.

The art masters for the moment won their retrograde cause. Centres for industrial design were not established, and the Board of Education's new examinations in art and design, introduced in the 1913–14 session, did not require designs to be executed in a craft material. To the delight of the art masters these examinations were grouped as Drawing and Painting, Modelling, and Industrial or Pictorial Design. The ivory tower was preserved: Industrial and Pictorial Design were paper subjects catered for by appropriately illustrated textbooks. Craft and Trade Classes were provided for artisans, and the many enthusiasts of the Arts and Crafts movement, but were distinctly optional.

The politicians and officials of the Board of Education were quite content with the outcome. Most of those who paid full fees at Schools of Art were studying fine art, a large proportion being ladies. Male students were heavily outnumbered in the day classes. In local Schools of Art the only day classes attended by adult males in considerable numbers from 1901 to 1914 were those in blackboard drawing for student teachers. Implementation of the Departmental Committee's recommendations would have involved the Board and the Local Authorities in the payment of grants to large numbers of male students studying industrial design and crafts, and expenditure on workshops and equipment. Thus it was that the art masters contributed to the Arts and Crafts movement becoming stagnant and irrelevant to the mainstream of industry and of daily life.

The final effort of the struggle to turn British art education towards industrial design and crafts, with the Central School of Arts and Crafts at its head, was made by Frederick Vango Burridge, who succeeded Lethaby as principal of that School from September 1912. He suggested to the Board of Education and the LCC that all the most advanced industrial design and craft students, including the National Scholars, should be sent to his school.

> The work of the Royal College of Art will still consist largely of fine art and training for teachers [he wrote] and such an environment has been demonstrated beyond dispute to be absolutely repugnant to the development of workers for crafts and trades.

However, despite a lengthy correspondence carried on by Burridge throughout the First World War, the situation remained as it was.

As if to prove Burridge's point, the next principal of the Royal College, appointed by the Board in 1920 to succeed Augustus Spencer, was a distinguished artist, William Rothenstein, who filled the College with a staff of talented fine artists and illustrators. Sir John Rothenstein wrote: 'In no time at all artists were appointed in place of pedagogues to teaching posts (then a startling innovation resented by the art teachers' organisation) and a generation rich in talent was gathering in the class-room: Henry Moore, John Piper, Ceri Richards, Edward Burra, Barnett Freedman, Edward le Bas, Charles Mahoney, Albert Houthuesen, Barbara Hepworth, Edward Bawden, and Eric Ravilious, to name but a few of the most talented members of it' [8].

Indeed the fine arts and illustration prospered, but, as Burridge had foreseen, industrial design was neglected, and design students were 'second best'. A design student of that period informed me that the College became nothing but a fashionable fine art shop. Certainly Eric Gill rejected an invitation from Rothenstein to join the staff in these words:

> I am not of one mind with you and the aims you are furthering at
> the College, and may I whisper it, I think there are too many
> women about [9].

Due to a slump in demand for British goods, the Board of Trade appointed the Gorell Committee which in 1932 reported adversely on the cooperation between the art schools and industry. Egged into action by the Report, the Board of Education by its Circulars 1431–2 of 1933 attempted at last to carry out the recommendation of the Departmental Committee of 1911 that a system of regional centres be established to replace the existing network system of Schools of Art. The intention was that the new Regional Colleges would not only produce 'a hierarchy ...an ordered system of art instruction leading up to a regional Art College', but also more important that they should become the local 'centres of civilisation' Lethaby had advocated which would serve local industry by providing not only class instruction, but also exhibitions.

The Council for Art and Industry, set up in 1934, did its utmost to encourage this situation. As a result the Board of Education and the Schools of Art were under pressure to encourage the designing, producing, and exhibiting of industrial artefacts and from 1935 facilities were provided by the Board for students to submit specimens of craftwork based upon examination designs.

From Gorell to the establishment of the Ministry's National Diploma in Design in 1946 was a period of increasing specialisation in designing and producing craftwork. The very name of the National Diploma in Design typifies the thinking: even painters and sculptors were taking a diploma in 'Design'. Painting itself could be taken in the industrial section, i.e., mural painting. Schools of Art in the 'forties specialised in producing mural or industrial paintings for various public buildings.

The Coldstream Report of 1961, and the subsequent activities of the National Council for Diplomas in Art and Design (NCDAD), resulted in a swing away from vocational, useful, and specialised design education, indeed away from the needs of society and towards a 'liberal' type of art education dominated by high art and tall talk. One accidental cause of this swing of the 'sixties was the large proportion of Colleges recognised by the NCDAD for Dip.AD in Fine Art compared with the number recognised for the Design areas. Naturally students applied for and expanded the recognised departments, thus more and more Fine Art staff were appointed, affecting the future structure of the Colleges. By the session 1969–70 there were 2,987 students following Dip.AD courses in Fine Art, more than twice as many as in Three Dimensional Design or in Textiles/Fashion, and nearly twice as many as in Graphic Design.

The new Diploma courses were, to quote the First Report of the National Advisory Council on Art Education (NACAE), to be 'conceived as a liberal education in art in which specialisation should be related to one of a small number of broad areas, or, to put it another way, should always be studied in a broad context'. The Committee also recommended: 'During the early stages of the diploma course the student should be given an opportunity of exploring his area of specialisation' [10].

These recommendations left the door wide open for a move back to fine art, especially to painting, an eternal tendency in our art schools. This should have been expected by the Committee members with some grasp of the history of British art education. C. R. Ashbee wrote in 1911:

> At present we have scores of mediocre schools of art, most of them turning out bad painters, discontented painters, and painters who become painters because there is nothing else to do . . . . [11]

Today [this paper was first published in 1973] I would not say that our Colleges of Art and Design are mediocre, nor that the painters in them are bad, but, because the Committee did not recommend that every student must carry out some practical work related to useful industrial design, a situation has arisen in which, while 'Liberal Studies' staff lecture increasingly on Communication with society, the practical course work has less and less to do with everyman, everyday, and everything. It is possible under the present system for a student to pass right through the course from a fine art orientated Pre-Dip. course to a final year

Painting without ever designing and completing any artefact in general use, from a representative book illustration to a common pot. In the days before Dip.AD this experience was enforced for every student by the Intermediate Examinations in Arts and Crafts. It is unfortunate that such experience has to be enforced, but it must be remembered that it was less than forty years ago, after a hundred years of struggle, that all our art schools were finally persuaded to ensure that students produced some useful artefacts for examination.

Professor Misha Black, of the Royal College, has said:

> If you want to have art education without taking into account
> industrial needs then you must accept that you won't get jobs at the
> end of it.

Professor Black's view is very unfashionable. Some would argue that the best way to develop the individual is to develop skills in some depth.

A very large proportion of Dip.AD graduates become teachers, sooner or later, but it is to be fervently hoped that this will not influence in any way the Dip.AD course in the future. Hannema in his *Fads, Fakes, and Fantasies* wrote that, since the great majority of our art students are going to be teachers 'it would be more honest, and more beneficial to their pupils, to train them as such from the beginning'.

We would be back in the dreary days of the art masters (1852–1914) when the examinations were designed to produce teachers, the most stultifying period of British art education. If anybody believes, as Mr Hannema has written, that training as a teacher would give the students 'a vitally important sense of purpose', he should compare the percentage attendance of students at Colleges of Education with that of students of art and design at Polytechnics, or he could read Dr Lomax's damning research into students' attitudes at a College of Education in Manchester. Keep the students' feet on the ground by all means, but do not deliver them into the hands of 'Education'.

Christopher Cornford writes that art students 'could be encouraged to think of teaching children as an admirable and interesting kind of job' instead of 'an absolute last ditch' [12]. True, but the hostility towards, and fear of society, which motivates dislike of teaching, of any other 'ordinary' job, even of society itself, is what needs to be banished; instead it is often deliberately encouraged. Crane, Lethaby, Gropius and Sir Robin Darwin have demonstrated by their success, that one produces a special kind of person by contact with society and industry, not by seeking escape to rarefied isolation.

Digby Jacks, on behalf of the NUS, is pressing for art education to be integrated into a comprehensive university structure. This seems to me to be the most sensible course – faculties of art and design awarding degrees. Already moves are being made towards a 'polyversity' at Loughborough. Jacks stated that the latest Coldstream Report (1970) is 'thoroughly contradictory'. Of course it is. It is well known that several members of the Committee have directly opposite viewpoints and each is catered for. Perhaps one day we will be rid of our 'national art education' see-saw.

Articidal tendencies are not only the prerogative of artists on governmental committees. Art educationists elsewhere have been busy demolishing the subject which supports them. 'Beauty' as a quality of an artefact was vaporised some years back. 'Craft', with its connotation of old-fashioned hard work, has been given short shrift. 'Artefact' is now being replaced by 'museumart'. Art education was deleted recently in favour of 'visual education'. Art itself will go shortly.

The Artscouncil Newspeak dictionary defines 'museumart' as 'any art which is not involved in living, meaningful, and dramatic activity'. Emmanuel Goldstein, the enemy of educational progress and advocate of Realspeak, has pointed out that artefacts are much more a part of the life of the People than the so-called meaningful activities sponsored by Patronart, and that it is only the most expensive of artefacts that are in galleries and museums. This retrograde has also argued that if passive paintings and sculptures are museumart, so are passive curtains, wallpaper, book illustrations, photographs, etc. To ridicule Goldstein, the Patronart ordered a Two Minutes' Hate Symposium to be provided by Liberal and Peripheral Studies Staffs at Artscouncil. At this O'Brien, the Patronart, declared that any art teacher who did not recognise that screaming, stripping, turf cutting, and car bandaging were in the van of progress would be seconded to a cell in Minitrue for an in-service stretch so that his vision and body could be extended.

To be serious, in Oldspeak, Dada is very much our father. The nude female seems the only indestructible subject of study.

Notes and References

1   (1884) *Report of the Royal Commission on Technical Instruction*, Vol. 2, p. 201.
2   EMMONS, ROBERT (1941), *The Life and Opinions of Walter Richard Sickert* (London, Faber).
3   HANNEMA, SJOERD (1970), *Fads, Fakes and Fantasies* (London, Macdonald), p. 109.
4   (1877) *Manchester Guardian* 19 February 1877, p. 8, cols 3–4.
5   MACDONALD, STUART (1970), *The History and Philosophy of Art Education* (London, London University Press).
6   *Loc. cit.* (n. 4).
7   (1911) *Report of the Departmental Committee on the Royal College of Art*, p. 56.
8   ROTHENSTEIN, JOHN (1965), *Summer's Lease* (London, Hamish Hamilton).
9   SPEIGHT, ROBERT (1966), *The Life of Eric Gill* (London, Methuen).
10 (1960) *First Report of the National Advisory Council on Art Education* (London, HMSO), p. 17.
11 ASHBEE, C. R. (1911) *Should We Stop Teaching Art?* (London, Batsford), p. 67.
12 CORNFORD, C. (1970), letter to Jean Creedy in CREEDY, J. (ed.) (1970), *The Social Context of Art* (London, Tavistock), p. 197.

Chapter Two

JOHN SWIFT The Arts and Crafts Movement and Birmingham Art School 1880–1900

This chapter addresses a selected period of the history of one specific English art school. The example of Birmingham reveals some typicality *vis-à-vis* other large art schools, but its particular location and emphasis identify it as distinctive pedagogically. The purpose here is to identify and analyse the results of that distinctiveness: the growth of executed design, the effect of this on the student body with special reference to female students, and local and national reactions.

Between 1880 and 1900 Birmingham Art School changed its location, size and financial status; there were changes, too, in the theoretical and practical education it offered. The constants were the majority of the Management Committee, its headteacher, Edward R. Taylor and the ubiquitous National Syllabus of the Department of Science and Art (DSA). The growth of the School was rapid. Within twenty years one temporarily-housed Central School and six Branch Schools [1], had developed into a new purpose-built and extended building with fifteen branch schools [2]. Student numbers grew from *c.* 1,320 in 1880 to 4,268 in 1900, with over 1,300 attending the Central School [3]. In 1880 the combined staff of the schools numbered 23, of whom most were part-time; by 1900, 87 staff were in post, over 50 being part-time. The representation of female staff had increased from 4 per cent of 23 to 9 per cent of 87, with 9 further women teaching Art to classes of female pupil-teachers [4].

The status of the School changed from one typically supported by grants from the government DSA, subscriptions and student fees, to that of a municipal art school. The changed responsibility towards the new 'owners' – the ratepayers of Birmingham, with the DSA having an examining and quality control role – led to greater independence. This was marked by more local entry scholarships, further liaison with local industries, a tendency to challenge the DSA over appropriate art and design education, and the development of the arts and crafts movement into an educational practice.

New concepts of art and design education were derived from John Ruskin and William Morris. The typical characteristics of this new-education were an amalgam of Ruskin's espousal of nature, Morris's vision of art communities, the social theories to which they both subscribed, and the reification of all of these ideas in the forms of the Art-Workers' Guild and the Arts and Crafts Exhibition Society [5]. The products of the resulting growth of 'art industries' interested many middle-class purchasers generally and in Birmingham specifically, where many of the influential industrialists, politicians and philanthropists were firm Ruskinians and collectors of late Pre-Raphaelite and arts and crafts work [6]. Given such a climate and an active arts and crafts headteacher, it is not surprising that some contentious changes in the content and methods of teaching occurred – specifically in relation to executed design.

The 'hands-on' argument for design was not new. It had been unsuccessfully attempted in the early Schools of Design, but now it was part of a widespread movement with powerful and articulate proponents. Too much designing in art schools was non-specific – designing in the abstract – with no precise outcome or materials in mind, though this had begun to change by 1880. However, an unduly heavy emphasis on historic ornament pervaded much teaching and inhibited new design ideas. It was common to find students drawing, painting, designing on paper and modelling in clay in most large art schools, but to find no evidence of crafting in other materials or any real understanding of design's technical consequences [7]. Birmingham was the art school that introduced executed design.

Despite this, Birmingham was not openly rebellious at first. As late as 1886–1887, the School of Art journal *The Art Student* reflected its Janus-like position: whilst arguing progressively more strongly for independence of standards and methods (specifically designing in actual materials) the school pragmatically continued to adhere to and be the highest medal winner in the very system it was in part challenging [8].

The progress towards executed design work was rather slow during the first ten years, as prizes, workspaces, equipment and staff were acquired. Prizes to encourage endeavour and reward excellence were common, usually given by local manufacturers, some of whom were members of the School of Art Management Sub-Committee. These were by no means exclusively for applied or executed design: many were for drawing or designs *for* materials. The latter were relatively successful in two-dimensional surface design, where no substantial technical understanding was needed [9]. The 1880–1881 Birmingham Prize List contained categories for 'designs *for* materials'; some two and some three-dimensional [10]. The first specific mention of executed designs is found in the Prize List for 1881–1882 when two students won large money prizes from the Goldsmiths' Company of London for engraving on metal and repoussé work [11]. Both were local designers who would have designed at the art school and executed at their workplace.

In 1883 plans for the new art school contained no workshops; each space was designated on traditional lines [12]. When the new building opened in 1885, the School appointed a new modelling master who happened to be a repoussé expert, attracted prizes for modelling for repoussé, and a year later proposed actual technical instruction in the area [13], which by 1887–1888 had been designated a prize category [14]. The opportunity to see work executed in the intended materials would have been more common for designers in local metalwork manufacture, but rarer for other crafts. [15]. During 1888, the chairman of the Birmingham Jewellers and Silversmiths Association (BJSA) proposed a jointly-administered special class for apprentices in the jewellery trade which the Art School Committee had approved and acted on during the same year [16]. New teachers of an arts and crafts persuasion were sought and appointed, joining a growing group of like-minded staff [17]. In 1888 when a proposal for an extension to the new school was discussed Taylor stated that if space permitted:

> it would now be desirable to teach the students how to bake and to cast their own models. Enamelling, encaustic painting and other Decorative Arts should also be fully taught in the School. It will too, probably be necessary . . . to open special classes for students engaged in certain manufactures [18].

Although the 1888–1889 prize list numbered only two examples of prizes for 'designs executed in their respective materials', 1889 was an important year in that it saw Walter Crane's Examiner's Report on the School, the Technical Instruction Act, proposals for a technical teaching class in Birmingham's jewellery quarter, and further moves to extend the existing art school building.

Crane's Report praised the School's work for its integrity within the DSA's system, its concept of design linking materials and use, and its move towards executed design through the establishment of:

> workshops . . . where students might familiarise themselves with methods and materials, and practise some of the simpler forms of handicraft, such as repoussé, metalwork, wood and stone-carving, sgraffito, mosaic, glass painting, wrought iron-work, and the like [19].

Crane's suggestions both confirmed and encouraged the Birmingham School's ambitions.

The Technical Instruction Act affected the more elementary level of the Science and Art classes, prohibiting the teaching of a trade or industry in the guise of manual instruction. It also helped to make modelling obligatory at elementary art levels, i.e., in all branch schools [20].

The success of the BJSA joint class led to a larger and more appropriate property in the jewellery quarter, where space was requested 'for teaching processes' [21]. The BJSA's willingness to fund a practice already close to the Management Committee's heart, resulted in a classroom for teaching:

> engraving, enamelling, chasing, embossing in high relief, die-sinking, applied wire ornamentation, carving, lapidary work, damascening . . . . [22]

The intention to extend the new School of Art building was taken not only in terms of increasing student numbers [23], but also to realise the implications of Crane's Report, to build on the practical tuition of metalwork students, and to extend the success of executed design work in outside competitions [24]. Nevertheless, the first report to Birmingham Council in May 1890 was cautious – room specifications being typical apart from facilities for 'casting and baking . . . for modelling' [25].

Prizes in executed design increased from 2 to 6 during 1890–1891 [26], and in March 1891 Taylor offered more radical proposals, specifically:

> proper facilities for students to carry out their designs in:
> i. Repoussé and kindred subjects, e.g., niello, chasing, etching and

engraving on metal, damascening and filigree,

ii. Enamelling: Cloisonné, Champlevé and Limoges, and

iii. Wood-carving, wood-engraving, needlework, terracotta, encaustic painting, the making of decorative cartoons, and working in fresco, tempera and sgraffito etc. [27].

Rough plans accompanied the proposals with space allotted for two art laboratories (workshops) in the basement linked with the modelling and casting rooms, and a cartoon and fresco room on the first floor [28].

The proposals echoed what Taylor had already published in 1890, and would have discussed with his friends on the various committees as his ideas had developed in the writing of *Elementary Art Teaching* [29].

The design itself can hardly be said to be completed until it is executed in the materials for which it is intended [30].

Taylor's book had argued that some executed design was almost identical to drawing and painting, being essentially two-dimensional; and that many other activities were relatively easy to learn and control [31]. He had also argued for the earlier integration of designing in the art school timetable, which he had already achieved at Birmingham [32]. Taylor became increasingly resistant to centralised authority as both his own and some of his staff's actions demonstrated later [33].

The first decade's successes, when Birmingham was the consistent DSA prize winner with design (albeit predominantly on paper or modelled) forming a significant proportion [34], were overshadowed by the results of the next ten years. Its successes elsewhere were equally significant [35].

Even before the new extension with its art laboratories opened in September 1893, executed design was well in evidence. The school programme for 1891–1892 listed *Section 6: Advanced Design*, including, 'designs executed in the materials for which they are intended', and of the 15 local prizes awarded to that category, 14 were won by female students [36]. The success of female students in local, national and outside competitions increased with the development of executed design, including repoussé work which had been intended to encourage the male artisan [37]. These results were repeated in 1892–1893 [38], and continued the following year [39]. This feature will be discussed in detail in the concluding part of the Chapter.

Before the new facilities were available, Birmingham staff and students had considerable success in the Arts and Crafts Autumn Exhibition of 1893 [40]. Rooms in the School were kept open during the summer months to enable work to be completed [41], and of 31 pieces accepted, 18 were by women, as were 6 of the 11 executed designs [42].

By 1893 staff appointments for embroidery, needlework, enamelling, and wood-engraving had been made, and equipment ordered for a wide variety of crafts [43], and the School Programme's introduction for 1893–1894 explained the new facilities, their purpose and availability [44].

In January 1894 Taylor, on the advice of his Committee, wrote to the DSA requesting the admission for exhibition and competition of executed designs for *Stages 23e and f* [45]. Perhaps Birmingham's eminent position and proven worth elsewhere [46], coupled with other pressures, in-

1   The cartoon and figure design studio where fresco, tempera, oil painting and
other techniques were studied; Birmingham Art School, *c.* 1900; Birmingham
Art School Archive, Birmingham Polytechnic.

2   Designing for gesso
work [?], a standard subject
in the male-only
housepainting and
decorating workshop;
Birmingham Art School,
c. 1900; Birmingham Art
School Archive,
Birmingham Polytechnic.

fluenced the DSA. In September the Directory was modified to allow a wide range of craft activities from 1895, but with a very curious proviso. The Department would accept for examination:

> designs carried out in various materials, such as earthenware, porcelain, glass, metal, wood, paper, leather, textiles, etc.

as long as the work was submitted:

> to fully illustrate or explain the original drawn, painted or modelled design . . . . such executed designs will not be admitted . . . when they are not accompanied by the design for them [47].

Thus whether they wished or not, art schools were obliged to continue the presentation of paper or clay designs, with the executed designs in their actual materials merely serving as illustrations or explanations. Birmingham gained the first DSA awards for executed design one year earlier than regulated for: two awards to two female students [48].

Despite these successes, Taylor was not complacent. He was prepared to criticise staff for omissions in their craft-skills vocabulary [49], and to insist that craft expertise and artistic sensitivity were insufficient in themselves: his staff had to be effective teachers [50]. The Prize List for 1895–1896 showed seven executed design categories; the Examiners' Report itemised many more in both the Central School and Vittoria Street [51]. The range was continued into the following year.

An increasing number of craft areas capable of executed design typify Birmingham's approach during 1897–1899 [52]. As craft skills grew, so did the opportunity to combine personal skills, or to collaborate with others on one object [53]. Growth and success were reflected in the DSA results [54], the proposal to build another purpose-designed branch school [55], and unsolicited comment from George Frampton:

> on the unique achievements of your school . . . it is the School that has done more for the Decorative Arts than any other in the country [56].

Attempts to open Vittoria Street School for day-release students, following the continental examples, did not meet with immediate success [57]. The local prize lists were recording large entries for executed design, and these were still dominated by female students [58].

The Examiners' Reports from 1897 to 1900 reflect the dynamic development of Birmingham – however, there were some problems over style, the type of work, and the intention of the student. In the report for 1897–1898, Wainwright criticised both local manufacturers' constraints and artificial 'artistic' finish [59]. The following year he noted a pervasive influence from art magazines, and suggested it should be controlled and counterbalanced with historic ornament. He also commented on the preponderance of personal ornament in gold, silver and jewellery. Whilst such items were not exceptional, one suspects that it was the gender of the maker that most disturbed him, a point picked up the following year by a new examiner, W. R. Lethaby [60].

He was undoubtedly impressed by Birmingham Art School [61], his arts and crafts beliefs being reflected in his support for workshops, practical designing at all levels, and the problem of finding suitable staff [62]. He deplored the DSA's system of hindering 'life and experiment', and identified Birmingham's success as a result of 'independent, liberal support', i.e., municipalisation [63].

His criticisms were concerned with the number of amateur 'prize-gainers' [64] who were winning prizes planned for artisans [65]. His solution was to make every class trade-related, i.e., specifically directed towards occupation. This would have had the effect of removing almost all of the female students from most of the executed design classes. Lethaby used the term 'amateur' in a way which leaves one with little doubt that his statement ('special classes should not be for a floating population of amateurs ... but ... should ... be for those in the trade ... and other serious students') was intended to exclude female, middle-class students; he specified that jewellery would improve if it were more vocational [66].

Taylor replied to the full report, by both agreeing and elaborating on some factors, identifying five 'trade-directed' workshops [67], and describing the new design procedures occasioned by executed design [68]. He avoided the problem of 'ladies' and 'amateurs'; I will suggest the reasons in the concluding section.

1900 was no less successful than previous years. Vittoria Street School was expanding its technical facilities, and because of its location and specialisation in metal seemed to have developed a closer relationship and faster reaction to local needs than the Central School which had far more diverse responsibilities. Executed design work was requested for the forthcoming Paris Exhibition [69] and the Glasgow International Exhibition [70]. Such exhibitions continued the policy of collaborative ventures between staff and students which was to remain typical of Birmingham in the following century.

We are now able to evaluate the growth of executed design at Birmingham, the female students' role, and some specific and general reactions to these factors. From a small beginning when students were designing in the art school and making the object at their workplace, a steady if small increase is discernible, mostly in repoussé work, until the 1890s when a burst of activity followed the opening of the Vittoria Street Branch School and the extension of the Central School a few years later.

Most of this was initially linked with the local metal trades, but much was not. Many crafts were introduced as a result of arts and crafts enthusiasm and predilection; certainly the stained-glass, mural work, and book-illustration owed much of their style and subject-matter to this source. This flavour was acceptable to many clients. The large number of illustrated books, the commissions for interior decoration and fittings including murals, glass and many other crafts, are testimony to the taste of the new, wealthy middle-class patron, especially around the Birmingham area. However, when the same style and work ethic was transposed into small or large commercial workplaces, especially in the metal trades, the reaction was less welcoming.

The effect on students varied. Apprenticed elementary students at Branch Schools would have had a little experience in executing designs, but would not necessarily have absorbed an arts and crafts ethos; the more experienced artisans and designers might have had more difficulty.

Eventually, in advanced classes, they would have been taught by staff with defined beliefs which would be unlikely to find sympathy in many workplaces [71]. From existing records and on stylistic grounds, it is clear that only three or four larger manufacturers in the local metal industry actively welcomed the Birmingham School's approach to commercial needs, and this is hardly surprising if the students took with them the typical arts and crafts aversion to machinery.

The mixture of class attendance, personal and professional needs, and the novelty of the arts and crafts emphasis affected student number, background, purpose and aspiration. Typical earlier patterns of art school students reveal a large percentage of subsidised or free elementary level pupils and evening-only artisans, with trainee teachers, teachers taking further qualifications, and people studying for pleasure, i.e., advanced classes, mostly paying full fees. Therefore, art schools had taken care to increase their advanced level student numbers, advanced examination results paying more money and many advanced students' fees being unsubsidised [72]. Many of the trainee teachers and those studying for pleasure were women. Many of them were from middle-class backgrounds and some were the daughters of local 'art industrialists'. As such they probably had a superior or at least a broader education than the typical artisan or ex-branch or Board School scholar. The 'pleasure classes' could be relatively free from the DSA's regulations: their names often reappeared on registers over long periods of time as their interests changed and their skills developed.

What is slightly unexpected is the degree of enthusiasm and success with which they embraced executed design. Whereas predictably many still-life, flower, and portrait prizes, especially in watercolour, were won by female students, it would not follow that working manually, with what could be described as trade materials, would similarly engage their interest. Whilst partly confirming Callen's findings that in general arts and crafts women worked in traditionally 'feminine' crafts, the students at Birmingham worked across a wider range, thus appearing partly to counter the socially determined and conflicting roles of 'woman' and 'artist', and 'lady' and 'work' [73].

There is a discernible growth in the number of female students winning local prizes in art and in paper-design. Until the opening of the extension, many female students were prize-winners in the traditional areas of drawing, painting and modelling, with design skills slowly evolving [74]. After 1894 special prizes were introduced for outstanding advanced art and design work, and whilst the average percentage for female art work fluctuated between 40 and 60 per cent, with a peak of 74 per cent in 1899–1900, the design prizes for paper-designing were consistently in the mid-60 percentile [75].

The growth of local prizes for executed designs from 1890 onwards reveals an even more startling progression, ranging from 40 to 100 per cent; between 1890 and 1900 female students won 74 per cent of the 157 listed awards. Outside bodies' awards repeat the tendency, e.g., the Armourers and Braziers Awards from 1890 to 1893 show female students winning 47 per cent of the executed design prizes; the Arts and Crafts

Exhibition of 1893, 54 per cent of all designs and 58 per cent of all executed designs; and the Paris Exhibition of 1901, 77 per cent of all executed designs [76].

Given this successful female student competitiveness, what crafts did they succeed in, and how closely do they conform to Callen's thesis of feminine activities?

A proportional analysis of approximately 307 different listings for executed design undertaken by female students reveals that 54 per cent were for combined metalwork and enamelling, specifically 40 per cent for a variety of metal crafts and 14 per cent for the three main types of enamelling; 28 per cent for needlework and embroidery; 7 per cent for gesso; 5 per cent for book illustration and prints, and the remaining 6 per cent spread fairly evenly over vase decoration, fan painting, grisaille (glass painting), leatherwork, and carving (usually plaster, but also wood and ivory).

There were many other activities, and the fact that female students were not mentioned in them does not necessarily indicate that they did not undertake them. Some areas were rarely undertaken at Birmingham by any student at this period, e.g., terracotta, stained-glass, mosaic,

3   FLORENCE CAMM
Portrait, watercolour, 1899; successfully submitted for *Stage 17b* of the National Competition; Birmingham Art School, *c*. 1900; Birmingham Art School Archive, Birmingham Polytechnic.

4   FLORENCE CAMM *St Francis of Assisi*, cartoon for stained glass window.
Honourable mention, National Competition, 1899. Birmingham Art School,
c. 1900. The School did not have facilities to complete stained-glass at this time,
but it is possible that this design was realised because Camm's family firm was a
major glass specialist in the locality; Birmingham Art School Archive,
Birmingham Polytechnic.

ceramic murals, poster designs, bookbinding, and metal-casting. Some
were usually practised at an elementary level, e.g., die-sinking, and
chipped metal, leaving a few areas where perhaps male-dominated trades
inhibited female acceptance, e.g., cabinet and furniture making, iron

foundry work, stone-carving, and house-painting (male only class).

The effect of Birmingham's particular emphasis on an arts and crafts practice and the success of female prize winners are not reflected in any policy changes. Whilst the School was delighted with its local, national and even international success due to its innovatory teaching of design through execution, much of which was due to its large, middle-class female student population, it made no attempt to rectify the imbalance in its staffing [77]. In 1899, 9 per cent of the Central School staff were women, and the same percentages were found in the branch schools. Only in the branch school for female trainee-teachers was it different; here nine female assistant teachers outnumbered the one male master-in-charge [78].

Whilst Wainwright's and Lethaby's comments reflected an unease at so many 'amateurs' winning so many prizes, and Lethaby's suggestion for retitling craft activities as specific trades would have decimated the number of female students, Birmingham did not respond to the suggestion. I doubt whether this was enlightenment; I suspect it was more due to the fear of losing prestige, fees, and the support of the 'art industrialists' whose daughters were part of this group.

Putting aside this not untypical reaction, the Birmingham School of Art's success was important in several other ways. Its art educational practices specifically affected the national system and other art schools, e.g., in Leicester and London; its national and international reputation influenced ideas for broader change in design teaching; and it was the midlands centre of a virile and long-lasting arts and crafts movement.

Taylor was to retire in 1903, the DSA regulations were to be replaced and simplified, and the Birmingham School of Art was set to move towards a further development of arts and crafts activities under the guidance of its next headmaster. The end of the century must have seemed an apposite time to look back at the success of the new city – a sense of self-congratulation was present. Great achievements there had been, the art school being one of the most significant, but 'biggest and best' are hard terms to live up to, and arguably the seeds of later problems had already been sown. The supporters on the city's coat of arms, redesigned for 1889, were Art and Science, reflecting the pride of a city which saw itself as advanced in technical, scientific and artistic activities. The adoption of an anti-machine philosophy by its art school could not be sustained in the new century.

Notes and References

1 'Central' referred to the more advanced teaching, 'branch' to the more elementary – thus the branch schools fed the central school. In 1880 all the branch schools consisted of rented rooms in Birmingham's School Board elementary schools.

2 Two were untypical in that one was jointly run by trade and another purpose-built. Vittoria Street School for Jewellers and Silversmiths opened in 1890, and Moseley Road Branch School was opened in 1899.

3 Some of the 1,300 were elementary students having gained admission by competitive scholarships offered by the School and various legacies.

33

4   (1881–1884) *Birmingham Society of Arts and School of Art Minutes* (BSASA),
    Vol. 14, p. 9; and 1897–1900 *Birmingham Municipal School of Art Manage-
    ment Sub-Committee Minutes* (BMSAMSC), Vol. 22, Appended 273–274 & 94,
    pp. 7–8.

5   The Arts and Crafts Movement generally could be described as moving away
    from established authorities and their bodies, questioning the equation
    between economic success and industrial mechanisation, and having an
    ambiguous link with social reform.

6   SWIFT, J. (1988), 'Birmingham and its Art School; Changing Views
    1800–1921', *Journal of Art and Design Education*, 7, 1, p. 14.

7   'Modelling' involved the manipulation of clay and other materials in figura-
    tive or ornamental work. Whilst the students handled the materials, they did
    not understand anything of the firing, casting or mould-making necessary
    for retention. The model would be sent to specialists and returned com-
    pleted.

8   See COND, J., 'Municipal Schools of Art', *The Art Student*, a magazine
    published by staff and students of the Birmingham Municipal School of Art,
    1886–1887, pp. 101–104; and WAINWRIGHT, W. J., 'The National Competi-
    tion 1886', *ibid.*, pp. 88–90.

9   (1881–1884) BSASA, Vol. 14, pp. 100–101. The committee judging designs
    for an encaustic ceramic tile competition for Coalville and Company in 1883
    noted that 'the nature of the designs asked for no special knowledge of the
    difficulties of construction' (adding) 'to the weight of proof that the ill
    success of art students in ordinary design, as applied to manufactures, is due
    in large measure to their want of technical knowledge ... the student must
    be brought by some means or other into close proximity with the workshop'.

10 The 'designs for specified materials' included 'certificates, wallpaper, fans,
    ... stained glass, ... jewellery, silverware', utensils, and rooms containing
    the above. Such prizes for 'designs for' continue throughout the twenty
    years under scrutiny and form an increasingly specific and numerous feature
    of Birmingham's prize lists.

11 (1881–1884) BSASA, Vol. 14, p. 58.

12 (1890–1893) BMSAMSC, Vol. 20, Appended 69–71.

13 (1885–1888) BMSAMSC, Vol. 18, p. 111. The first specialist master in
    repoussé work was Thomas Spall, a designer for Elkingtons and Company.

14 *Ibid.*, p. 268. The prize list for 1887–1888 offered a J. H. Chamberlain
    Memorial Medal for 'two designs for a door plate modelled or executed in
    repoussé'.

15 The publication of the *Art Student* helped make students' writing and
    illustration public. Whilst there is no evidence that initial ideas were
    developed through cutting/engraving and printing, the stylistic tendencies
    that were to typify the Birmingham Group in the mid-1890s were embryoni-
    cally present in the early examples of book illustrations by Arthur J. Gaskin,
    Kate Bunce, Frederick Mason and Charles M. Gere ten years earlier.

16 (1888–1890) BMSAMSC, Vol. 19, pp. 30–32, 72, 84, 100, 149. The new
    class opened at Ellen Street Branch School with a group of 95 pupils.

17 (1888–1890) BMSAMSC, Vol. 19, pp. 137, 142–143, 151–152 shows the
    lengths to which Birmingham went to attract and employ a suitable arts and
    craftsperson – Benjamin Creswick, who joined Arthur Gaskin and Sidney
    Meteyard.

18 (1885–1888) BMSAMSC, Vol. 18, Appended 294–295.

19 (1888–1890) BMSAMSC, Vol. 19, Appended 215, p. 28 and (1890–1893)
    BMSAMSC, Vol. 20, Appended 111, p. 7.

20 *Ibid.*, Vol. 19, Appended 223, pp. 4–5. Technical instruction 'shall not
    include the teaching of any trade or industry or employment ... the
    expression "manual instruction" shall mean instruction in the use of tools,
    processes of agriculture, and modelling in clay, wood and other materials'.

21 *Ibid.*, pp. 237–240.

22 (1890–1893) BMSAMSC, Vol. 20, pp. 7–12.

23 From 5 branch schools in 1884, the number had risen to 11 by 1891; the consequent pressure for places at the Central School demanded more space.

24 (1890–1893) BMSAMSC, Vol. 20, p. 6. In the Armourers and Braziers Exhibition of May, 1890, Birmingham students won 8 prizes for executed design, 3 by female students, in repoussé, engraved, etched, chased, and embossed metalwork and brasswork.

25 *Ibid.*, Appended 15, pp. 5, 8–9. The Report describes increases in numbers, Board School drawing supervision and teaching, the growing number of branch schools, the proposed opening of Vittoria Street School for Jewellers and Silversmiths, and the increase in free admissions and types of students attending as reasons for the new extension.

26 *Ibid.*, Appended 67, pp. 3–16.

27 *Ibid.*, Appended 69.

28 *Ibid.*, Appended 70 (3 sheets).

29 TAYLOR, E. R. (1893), *Elementary Art Teaching* (Chapman & Hall) (1st Ed. 1890).

30 *Ibid.*, p. 164.

31 *Ibid.*, pp. 164–166.

32 (1890–1893) BMSAMSC, Vol. 20, Appended 76–77. Taylor's view of a design-oriented school contrasts with that of the 1891 examiner, Wainwright, who wrote, 'drawing from the figure and historic ornament are the backbone of Birmingham's study'.

33 In 1894 Taylor was instrumental in having executed design placed within the National Syllabus; a few years later, Crewick, the modelling master, challenged the DSA's standards, aims, and right to dictate educational and artistic rationales to a municipal art school.

34 (1890–1893) BMSAMSC, Vol. 20, Appended 165, pp. 3 et seq. In 1891 Birmingham won 18 medals and 31 National Book Prizes. Of the total of 49, 36 were for design or modelled design, and of these 18 were won by female students.

35 *Ibid.*, Appended 165. Eight awards for executed design were won by Birmingham students, 50 per cent of which were by female students, in repoussé, brasswork and etched metalwork.

36 *Ibid.*, Appended 165, pp. 3–5.

37 *Ibid.*, pp. 157–158. The local firm of Hukin and Heath had offered five years of prizes for repoussé, to spur 'the Authorities at South Kensington ...(to)...see their way to recognise it as one of the Arts worthy of encouragement'.

38 *Ibid.*, Appended 229. Female students won 87 per cent of 15 local prizes for executed design, and 71 per cent of 5 prizes in the Armourers and Braziers Exhibition.

39 (1893–1897) BMSAMSC, Vol. 21, Appended 13, pp. 1–18, 23–25. Executed design categories were for fans, gesso, embroidery, etched and bitten metalwork, repoussé, pierced work, and enamelling. The prize list for the same period showed 81 DSA prizes, 37 for design, of which 25 were won by female students. Local prizes in executed design show female students gaining 86 per cent of the 7 categories.

40 *Ibid.*, p. 241.

41 *Ibid.*, p. 251.

42 *Ibid.*, Appended 288. Designs were executed in silver, enamel and glass, linen, embroidery, brass, etched copper, repoussé, book plates and illustrations, and wood-carving.

43 *Ibid.*, pp. 208, 233, 267, also appended 255–256. Mary Newill, Bernard Sleigh and Louis Joseph had been appointed to teach embroidery, wood engraving and enamelling respectively. New equipment had been ordered for enamelling, annealing, etching, lithography, wrought and beaten iron-work, terra cotta, glazing and stained-glass work, and carpentry.

44 *Ibid.*, Appended 276, pp. 1, 12, 25. Classes were suited for 'all classes of the community ... the main object ... is to make workmen better workmen'. The subjects were grouped to relate to local trades and the opportunity for executed design would be available to advanced and honours level students. Lithography and leatherwork were added to the 1892–1893 crafts.

45 *Ibid.*, pp. 9–10.

46 *Ibid.*, Appended 45, pp. 3–4. The *Report of the Museums and School of Art Committee* stated, 'in the opinion of the officers of the Department of Science and Art, and of the many representatives of other schools who have visited Birmingham, the School is the best and most complete in the United Kingdom'.

47 *Ibid.*, Appended 52.

48 *Ibid.*, Appended 84, pp. 14–24. Local executed design categories were ironwork, engraving on metal, repoussé, woodcarving, woodcuts, stencilling, needlework, leatherwork, gesso and enamelling; 70 per cent of which were won by female students. The DSA awards totalled 76, of which 30 were for design, 14 being won by female students. The 2 executed design awards were for a gesso design and 'an etching from nature'.

49. *Ibid.*, pp. 57–58. Taylor criticised accomplished wood engravers for their lack of modelling skills, and even enforced their retraining in order to retain their posts.

50 *Ibid.*, Appended 82.

51 *Ibid.*, Appended 113. Four from 7 executed design awards were won by female students – the areas listed were wall decoration, embroidery, enamelling, engraving on metal, leatherwork, repoussé, and wood-engraving. The examiner, W. J. Wainwright mentioned executed work in jewellery, gold and silver, repoussé, engraving and chasing, enamelling, embroidery, bookbinding, forged ironwork, lithography, wood-carving, gesso, and stencilled patterns at the Central School, and repoussé, enamelling, etching and engraving, and the customary metal-working skills at Vittoria Street.

52 (1897–1900) BMSAMSC, Vol. 22, 1897–1900, Appended 21–28. Executed designs were offered in gesso, gold, linen and thread-work, silk, enamelling in all three types, leather, chased and raised metal and repoussé in 1897–1898. Appended 282: Metal-casting (foundry), stone-carving, oil painting, drawing for book illustration, embroidery, die-sinking and gesso work had been added to the programme, and the examiner, W. J. Wainwright, noted work in arch-carving, ceramic mural work and stained-glass. Pp. 153, 180, 192–193 reveal the teaching of 'cera perduta' (lost wax casting), new equipment for refinement of enamelling, and staff being appointed, e.g. Louis Movio, metalworker, in late 1898, and May Morris, embroiderer, in late 1899, or promoted for their specific craft skills, e.g., in metalwork, enamelling and lithography.

53 *Ibid.*, Appended 134–135. An increasing number of complicated caskets, books or ornaments displayed multiple craft skills from 1897 onwards.

54 *Ibid.*, p. 206. In 1898 Birmingham won 76 awards, the highest number by far in the country, followed by New Cross and Glasgow; in 1899 it won 90 awards, 35 ahead of its nearest rival, Glasgow.

55 *Ibid.*, Appended 74. A proposal to erect a new branch school on Moseley Road in Balsall Heath was submitted in early 1898, and the school was opened in late 1899.

56 *Ibid.*, p. 108. Frampton had been invited to deliver prizes and a speech, and had reluctantly refused due to work pressure.

57 *Ibid.*, Appended 187–188, 210. Research had shown that French and German apprentices generally obtained two afternoons a week release. The system was not immediately effective in Birmingham, the numbers released being insufficient to justify the opening of the school in the day, although access to the Central School was offered instead.

58 *Ibid.*, Appended 21–28; Appended 134–135; Appended 239–240, 245. The

1897–1898 Prize List shows that of the 59 prizes awarded for design, 37 were won by female students, and all of the 19 executed designs. The 1898–1899 results show 14 of the 19 executed designs being won by female students, and those of 1899–1900 show that they won 30 of the 37 executed designs, plus 2 special medals for executed design.

59 *Ibid.*, Appended 29, pp. 6–7.
60 *Ibid.*, Appended 140, pp. 6–8.
61 *Ibid.*, Appended 246, p. 5. Lethaby wrote, 'the school stands so high as compared with other Art Schools known to me, that if my report were to be merely comparative, I would say nothing more than Birmingham stood first, or amongst the very first, in the kingdom'.
62 *Ibid.*, pp. 11–16.
63 *Ibid.*, p. 11.
64 *Ibid.*, p. 7.
65 *Ibid.*, p. 6.
66 *Ibid.*, p. 12.
67 *Ibid.*, Appended 248, p. 2. Taylor identified beaten metalwork, engraved and etched metalwork, enamelling, house-painting, and embroidery/needlework: actually he had merely given areas; Lethaby would have titled the area by occupation.
68 *Ibid.*, Appended 248, p. 4. In brief, these were the production of preliminary studies, development of one, execution of the work allowing for modification during production, and production of a finished paper-design, 'as a valuable school study' and to 'receive recognition at South Kensington'.
69 *Ibid.*, p. 255. 13 executed designs were selected, of which 10 were by women, in crafts as diverse as wood-carving, chased copper, champlevé enamel, gesso, silver repoussé, steelwork, lace, needlework, and embroidery.
70 *Ibid.*, pp. 289–291. Glasgow requested works in textiles, ceramics, bookbinding, enamels, mosaics, metalwork, and wood-carving, plus minor features of architectural details accompanied by preparatory studies and designs, 'and any other such work . . . (which will) . . . illustrate the course or courses of study pursued . . . .'
71 It is difficult to be precise – records linking students to workplaces are rare, and one would still need evidence of any short- or long-term effect.
72 Many art schools earlier in the nineteenth century had been in danger of bankruptcy; the lesson would have been learned.
73 CALLEN, A. (1979), *Angel in the Studio* (Astragal), pp. 218–221.
74 Until 1884 a maximum of 2 per cent of female students had won design prizes, although their success in pictorial art had grown from 16 to 32 per cent in four years. Whilst the percentage of overall prizes increased from approximately 30 to over 40 per cent by 1893–1894, the design prize percentage had increased to 27 per cent.
75 Birmingham awards from the DSA, although not completely documented, show a parallel growth, from 18 to 35 to 44 per cent in 1880, 1883, and 1893 respectively; the female prize-winners in design rose from zero for the first two years to 64 per cent in 1893.
76 (1881–1900) BMSAMSC, Vol. 14, 18, 19, 20, 21 and 22 – figures extracted from details of Prize Lists, Awards and other documents.
77 There had been a national financial inducement to employ young students to teach at elementary level, and/or in branch schools, but the proportion of young female students so appointed remained disproportionately low.
78 (1897–1900) BMSAMSC, Vol. 22, Appended 94, pp. 7–8.

Chapter Three

DIANA KORZENIK Foreign Ideas for American Originals: Francis Wayland Parker

Nineteenth-century experience

I view the history of education in the United States not as a stable set of goals, a given birthright of its citizens, but largely as rivalling efforts toward building a new country, building new industries and forming new citizens who matched the perceived (sometimes local, sometimes national) political and social needs of the times. Change in art education, too, should therefore be expected within this context. In the United States, we can see how each direction in art teaching, each methodology, won support when the powers-that-be perceived that a particular practice in art-making offered a possible solution to a political, social or economic problem.

In the ferment and search for new and better ideas in the latter half of the nineteenth century, writer, lecturer, and innovative school super-intendent Francis Wayland Parker developed the notion that the learner is one who is at home with behaviour characteristic of artists. Parker significantly influenced the place of art in American schools. To under-stand his theory, particularly his use of the word 'foreign', its sources and its appeal to his contemporaries, we first need a view of the landscape of art education ideas in which and from which his ideas grew.

Farming parents, say in New England, at the time of Parker's child-hood, the 1840s, would have directed their children to remove the rocks, to clear the soil. This was work that someone would have had to do and children were able to do. Anyone observing young children could have noticed that they learned concepts of 'tall' and 'short', of 'over' and 'under' as they moved things about. Sensory experience was the begin-ning of the child's mastery of concepts used in science, maths, language and art. Not only developmentally, but as members of a pre-industrial agricultural society, children learned through substances and materials.

But in the nineteenth century such knowledge was taken for granted. Schools concerned themselves with what people knew less well: how to read and how to write. So the development of the common schools concentrated on written language: both learning to express ideas in writing and learning to understand other people's ideas by reading. Schooling *was* language.

Despite this, art, the training of observation and hand skills, did find a place within public schools. American schools in the nineteenth century argued for art in terms of amazingly different objectives, each geared toward mastery of particular behaviours that people might accept within the school. I consolidate the *mélange* of objectives into four major categories or traditions, each of which I summarise: the utilitarian, spiritual, community-making and pedagogical.

Gathered within the *utilitarian* tradition are those viewing and making art practices that prepare young people for their adult work lives. Educators anticipate the jobs that the society will need done. Art-making becomes a form of work that will prepare the student to be employable. Horace Mann recommended in an 1845 issue of *The Common School Journal* that children be taught according to Peter Schmidt's drawing techniques, which promised precise, obedient, careful workers. This drawing method required students to observe prearranged blocks and then draw with their slate pencils the exact measured edges from one end of a block to another and from the corner of one block across the space to the corner of another. The power of disciplined drawing seemed worth the risk that worried Mann, that restless young hands and minds, if left undirected with their slates, might allow drawing to deteriorate into mere picture-making!

In the last quarter of the nineteenth century, the utilitarian approach dominated American schools. In Massachusetts a law was even passed, The Drawing Act of 1870, mandating not only that art be taught in the schools, but that free evening drawing classes be offered at the public expense to enable those over the age of fifteen to improve their drawing skills and thus share in the employment opportunities in the burgeoning mills. One of the problems with the utilitarian objective was that it applied to a portion of the population only. Work with the hands was relegated and therefore prized by a growing, segregated, working class. Since not all students would be working with their hands as the nineteenth century came to a close, the utilitarian art direction narrowed and acquired the stigma of manual labour.

To widen the appeal of art, a different, more *aesthetic/spiritual* approach was developed. Art instruction of its kind was purifying, pleasing and morally uplifting for its practitioners. It was good for everyone and was free of any associations with art and manual labour. Art in this new vein was for general purposes and personal improvement. Schools taught good taste and argued that art made good children even better. The 'Picture Study' movement, as this turn of the century trend was called, was marked by this aesthetic/spiritual orientation.

With the diversity of populations migrating to the United States, a third objective for teaching art emerged: *community-making*. Jane Addams and Ellen Gates Starr, amongst their many innovations at Hull House in Chicago, realised how the art and crafts of different cultures could weave a community of dissimilar people, interrelate people who lacked a common language or common holiday rituals and life cycle traditions. People taught each other the practices of their own countries by exhibiting the precious crafts they carried with them: weaving, embroidery, ceramics.

The fourth objective for studying art, I call the *pedagogical* objective because in it art-making becomes a medium of teaching across all subjects. Thinking needs object-making to be complete. The model learner needs to be an artist. Students are taught to observe and extract

5 'Anyone who can learn to write can learn to draw'; page from JOHN GADSBY CHAPMAN (1847) *The North American Dream* (New York, J. S. Redfield), a popular volume whose many editions over more than 20 years promoted American curiosity about learning to draw.

ANY ONE WHO CAN LEARN TO WRITE CAN LEARN TO DRAW

and, as writing is not taught to those only who are destined to become authors, but as forming an essential part of general education, so is drawing equally important to others besides professional artists. To write —to draw a form or figure that shall be recognised as the representative of a letter or word, is one thing; and to be able to design, draw, or write such forms, upon principles of grace and accuracy—to understand the Art of writing—is another. Thus it is also with Drawing, another mode of expressing ourselves, not less useful or necessary than that by letters

features from the world and then make something out of, perhaps, their geographical or botanical observations by drawing, painting, or modelling, using art to give form to their understanding.

Parker and art-making as a model for learning

I place the significant accomplishments of Francis Wayland Parker (1837–1902), a non-art educator, in this last tradition. This is the man of whom John Dewey wrote

6 HENRY WALKER
HERRICK *Life on the Farm*,
wood-engraving, 58.5 ×
42.0 cm, published in
Harper's Weekly, 1867.
Images such as this helped
popularise topographical
drawing techniques.

[he] more nearly than any other one person, was the father of the
Progressive education movement, a fact all the more significant
because he spent most of his educational life in public rather than
private schools – first at Quincy, Mass and then at Cook County
Normal school in Englewood Chicago [1].

Parker epitomised the pedagogical tradition. He realised that the rote
lessons of nineteenth-century schools were frustrations for children who
grew up on farms actively using their eyes and hands, and from this
experience had their minds full of ideas. Parker, even in the early days of
his teaching career, believed:

The child's preparation for reading is *not* reading. The preparation

is the acquisition of ideas from the world by means of the senses [2]
so it is not surprising that he wondered why only in art lessons were
children allowed to feel any substances in their hands and to use the
observations they witnessed with their own eyes.

Parker saw the essence of education as two processes: attention and
expression. Attention is an act of the senses and the mind. Ideas come
from looking, listening, smelling, tasting and touching. Attention is an
act of will inhibiting all 'foreign' activities from consciousness. By
attending, one holds the associations and makes new connections. In this

41

way, the self becomes active and, to use Parker's word, 'imaginative.' Parker saw the effect of attending as stimulating 'intense acts of imagination' [3]. Imagination is not some vapoury, unrealistic fantasy. It is thinking, the integration of new ideas and observations into one's current understanding.

> All education consists of the development of thought and expression. The thought must precede the expression [4].

The other process that teachers were to promote was expression itself. Once thoughts were in the child's mind, the teacher's role was to help the child express, to give form to his or her own thoughts. All modes of expression are equally usable: the speaking voice, singing voice, written language, drawing, moulding, and moving the whole body as in gymnastics.

Parker's simple plan disguises a complex vision. He believed:

> The child instinctively begins all subjects known in the curriculum of the university. He begins them because he cannot help it; his very nature impels him . . . . These quiet persistent, powerful tendencies, we must examine and continue with the greatest care [5].

The subjects the child begins are geography, geology, mineralogy, botany, zoology and anthropology, as he invents his own relationships to things in the world. Parker's pedagogy, viewed in its nineteenth-century context, provided education's answer to the question. 'Why should we not enjoy an original relation to the universe?' [6]. The artistic process furnished Parker with his instructional method for doing that. Since he believed agricultural children already had an 'original relation to the universe', though acting on the basis of their own looking and noticing of differences, it was a small leap to see how drawing or modelling, like farming, require actions and responsive modification.

Parker wrote:

> Every child has the artist element born in him: he loves to model objects out of sand and clay. Give a child a piece of chalk, and its fancy runs riot: people, horses, houses, sheep, trees, birds, spring up in the brave confidence of childhood. In fact, all the modes of expression are simultaneously and persistently exercised by the child from the beginning except writing. It sings, it makes, it moulds, it paints, it draws, it expresses thought in all the forms of thought expression, except one [7].

Parker's theory is a metaphor. The learning child becomes the working artist. Parker sees that, like artists, children give their attention to what interests them and develop 'their original relation to the universe' apart from the adult-transmitted concepts of information. Children's attention leads them to absorb and retain knowledge in their own ways. The other aspect of the artistic process, expression, also involves enjoying 'an original relation to the universe'. The object of one's own making *is* one's original response. Whereas earlier schooling made attention suffice, and repetition and memorisation served simply as evidences that the learner had heard, Parker required more: children were to give form to their ideas through expressive production.

Parker's sources for his art ideas

The art-making metaphor for general education did not grow full-blown out of the head of Parker. Even before 1872, when Parker decided to interrupt his teaching to study in Europe, he was familiar with the theories of European educators. Newspaper reports tell of his days as North Grammar School's master, when he adapted Froebel's ideas to the school year, discovering that he could use not only language, but also athletic and military drill to teach concepts to his students [8].

After seven years of success in North Grammar School, with a strong sense of himself as an educator, Parker set off for Europe for an intense period of study. Rousseau, Wordsworth, Froebel – three writers whose work echoes in Parker's own words – were likely to have occupied him. So far I find only Froebel acknowledged in a primary source [9] but since texts from Rousseau and Wordsworth seem influential, they too are discussed here.

Art

But before looking at texts Parker read, we need to look at how 'the artist' was seen, in the changing times in which these men were writing. Who was 'the artist'? What was so exciting about 'being an artist' that Romantic writers on education would use him as their model? The artist's dream was to release the significance hidden within Nature herself. The Romantic visual artist based his ambition upon a distrust of words. Words were conventional and carried tradition. Visual art could create a language independent of tradition, a natural language accessible to all. The goal was to create a natural symbolism that grew out of the artist's contact with nature. Access was through the individual's consciousness. Nature was the medium. Landscape painting, like landscape poetry, was proof that people could create their own symbols, suggesting that independence from previous traditions was possible.

Between 1790 and 1825, Romantic art's struggle was to separate art from its traditions. Visual artists opposed the hierarchies and traditions that had dominated their world. As part of the dissolution of the old order, artists courted public censure. In 1857 after the publication of *Mme Bovary* Flaubert said:

> Now I have been attacked by the government, the priests, by the
> newspapers. It is complete. Nothing is lacking for my success! [10]

One thing was missing: the attack that he was a 'child'. The charge of behaving like a child was hurled at the memory of Delacroix. In 1864, soon after the French artist's death, the French Minister of Fine Art, Nieuwerkerke, rejected any notion of the government reproducing Delacroix's work, by saying:

> Well! A ten year old child at school who did that, we would throw
> him out . . . We only encourage high class works, and all this
> [speaking of Delacroix] emanates from a demented mind [11].

In the Romantic era, the artist had become a naughty boy. By extension, the natural, unconstrained child became a myth and a route for introducing a more flexible behaviour into a rigid European society. Reformers wrote about the child. The child joined the sprinkling of people on the periphery of conventional society who, through their example, suggested a freer society.

> The most extreme statements, where romantic doctrine finds its
> purest expression in the visual arts, were often made by amateurs,
> craftsmen, eccentrics, outside the accepted centers of professional
> activity [12].

A language and sets of ideas were prepared for revolutionary writers and educators.

Rousseau

Though art plays only a part in Rousseau's many agendas for *Emile*, it faces us even in the book's first sentence. The prognosis isn't very good. There are two kinds of creators, the natural and the human.

> Everything is good as it comes from the hands of the Creator;
> everything degenerates in the hands of man [13].

Rousseau's writing on art would have intrigued Parker in terms of (i) drawing as a process for using raw sensation, responding to Nature; (ii) drawing as a manifestation of awkwardness; (iii) drawing as a reflection of stages of growth; and (iv) learning from one's own motives.

Drawing as raw sensation, response to Nature
When he writes of Emile, Rousseau says: 'His sensations are the raw materials of his ideas'. Training the senses is 'the *apprenticeship* to learning' [14]. 'Apprenticeship' is an intriguing word choice. Apprenticeships were how one learned a craft. By making sensation the basis of all learning, all ideas, Rousseau provided that bridge that Parker needed; raw sensation honed by the craftsperson is the first step. Raw sensation refined for academic thinking takes one that much further. Rousseau tells us:

> People of all ages, but children above all, wish to show signs of their
> power and activity by imitation, creation and production [15].

The exercise of sensory power and activity requires a territory; the child must have his own turf to do his own thinking and creating. Rousseau offers the garden to meet this need. Many farming families instructed their children starting in their garden. The garden is useful as a repository of sensory learning and as an alternative to book learning. Rousseau recommends not only learning from sensation, and having your own turf, but that the child actually draw. Drawing itself shall be part of the child's study:

> Children being great imitators, all try to draw. My pupil will study
> this art, not precisely for its own sake, but to give him a good eye
> and a supple hand [16].

Drawing for Rousseau was an activity by which boys might learn accurately from Nature.

Mistakenly, I believe, Rousseau includes the 'laws of perspective' as laws of and a part of Nature. As such he wants his student to know perspective. Rousseau seems unaware of the contradiction between this statement and what follows:

> I shall not send him to a drawing-master, who would only teach him to imitate imitations and to draw from copies. I wish him to have no other master than Nature, no other model than the objects themselves. He should have the original before his eyes, not the paper representing it; he should draw a house from a house, a tree from a tree, a man from a man. Thus he will be accustomed accurately to observe the appearances of bodies, and not to mistake false and conventional imitations, for genuine representations. I would even discourage his drawing from memory, till frequent observation had strongly impressed the true shape on his imagination; lest through the substitution of strange fantastic shapes for the reality, he should lose his sense of proportion and his taste for the beauties of Nature [17].

Here Rousseau announces the battle lines that have been drawn across art study ever since. Some say art should be learned directly from observation, that nature is the best teacher. Others deny that and claim that pictures come mostly from other pictures, and therefore copying and studying the art of others are prerequisites to original work. As the new romantic ideal of the artist suggested, direct observation was the route to the new man. Copying inevitably reiterated dead traditions.

Drawing as a manifestation of awkwardness

To Rousseau, the consequences of being close to Nature are worth the loss of elegance.

> I know this method will, for a long time, lead to unrecognisable daubs; ... but by way of recompense, he will certainly acquire an accurate eye and a steadier hand; he will learn to know the true relations of size and shape between animals, plants and other natural objects [18].

Here Francis Wayland Parker may have gleaned the notion that the value of art-making was as a model for *general* learning. Rousseau writes:

> My intention is not so much that he should imitate objects as that he should *know them*. I should much prefer him to be able to show me an acanthus than to be adept in drawing the leaves on a capital [19].

Drawing provides children with a basis for differentiating and recognising all knowledge.

By the early nineteenth century, awkwardness had become a learned aesthetic style. People admired awkwardness and incompleteness.

> For a number of years early in the 19th century, there was a monstrous fashion for writing fragments; hundred of writers published thousands of little clever observations. The fashion of the fragment was related on one hand to the contemporary taste for ruins, and on the other to the growing appreciation for sketches and the sketchy finish, a finish that made visible and exploited the individual brushstrokes. The fragment in the visual arts is not the result of literary doctrine but actually precedes the literary fashion in time [20].

Rousseau anticipated this trend in which awkwardness in drawing proves to be an asset. When Rousseau wrote that he would draw badly, along with his pupil, the nineteenth-century artists and writers who read him would have cheered him along.

> I shall use it [drawing] as badly as my pupil. Though I were an
> Apelles, I would appear a mere dauber [21].

Even if he were the most skilled artist of his time, he would pretend in front of Emile that he could do no better at drawing than his student. Rousseau continues to describe his method for working with Emile:

> My first sketches of a man will be like those which boys draw on the
> walls; a stroke for each arm, a stroke for each leg, and the fingers
> thicker than the arms. After some time, one of us will notice the
> want of proportion; we shall remark that a man's leg has a certain
> thickness, that the thickness varies. . . . In this progress I shall keep
> pace with him, or advance so little ahead that he can easily overtake
> me, sometimes surpass me. We shall have brushes and colors; we
> shall try to imitate appearance and color as well as shape. We shall
> color, paint, daub; but in all our daubings we shall never cease to
> watch nature . . . [22].

Rousseau asserted that he was putting the emphasis in the right place; in favour of awkwardness. Awkwardness was a sign to one's contemporaries of an impossible paradox: art, an external, visibly perceivable form, showed that external appearances didn't matter! Awkwardness was a sign of rejecting conventionality and a manifestation of an *inner* knowing. Since awkwardness needed some visible trace, the less conventional, the more fragmentary, the better.

Drawing as a reflection of stages of growth

Since learning required dynamic, interactive, responsive behaviours (of which drawing was one, of course), drawing should be useful in showing the stages and changes happening within the learner. Rousseau tells us that through drawings he captures moments in time as evidence of change:

> I would have drawings framed and covered with glass, that they may
> receive no further touches, but may remain as we left them. We
> have thus a motive for not being careless. I arrange them in order
> around the room, each drawing repeated twenty or thirty times;
> they will thus display *the progress of the artist* from the time when the
> house was a rude square, till its front and its sides, its proportions
> and its shades, are absolutely true to nature. These stages cannot fail
> to give us a constant supply of pictures . . . [23].

The art-making process, for Rousseau, externalises the child's growth and change. Rousseau tells us that drawing remains a metaphor, that 'will pass into a proverb', for all learning. The metaphor is explained in how he would frame the glass-protected drawings:

> Our first rude daubs will need to be set off by fine gilt frames; as the
> drawings improve, and the imitation [his words!] becomes more
> exact, I shall be content with plain black frames. The pictures no

longer need extraneous ornament; it would be a pity if the attention
due the picture were distracted by the frame. Hence we both aspire
to the honor of a plain frame; and, *when either of us wishes to
disparage the performance of the other, he condemns it to a gilt frame.*
Some day no doubt these gilt frames will pass into a proverb with
us, and we shall be astonished to see how many people do
themselves justice by a similar adornment of their own person [24].

Rousseau here expresses his hostility to the high art world which uses
gold frames to display its wealth. He also unconsciously condemns the
less adept child by putting his early efforts in the gold frames, the sign of
approbrium. Rousseau is mightily confused here about his own intentions; he claims to praise the beginner, and then he shames him. One
Romantic aesthetic notion here needs emphasis: the idea that when art is
better, it needs *less* glamour. With improvement and progress, simplicity
shall replace the sparkle of the gold frame.

Parker, reading all this, would have agreed that drawing was useful as
a tool for tapping sensations, for allowing the natural awkwardness and
as an index to the boy's progress in all learning. Drawing shows how the
boy makes subtler and subtler distinctions. Rousseau said what was to
become Parker's creed: 'As drawing stands to seeing, so do speech and
music to hearing' [25]. Rousseau teaches us that tutors must become
appreciators of all the child. 'Instead of teaching them our method,
we . . . study theirs' [26]. 'You will find out the whole of elementary
geometry in proceeding from observation to observation, without troub-
ling yourself about definitions, problems' [27].

Learning from one's own motives

Rousseau tells us: 'Children generally acquire speedily and certainly
whatever they are not pressed to learn' [28]. The boy is an artist/artisan,
working from his own motives and curiosity, giving form to things. The
child's work should grow out of the boy's own identification of some
need for it. Like artists, children identify their own subjects. Rousseau
describes how the boy's curiosity naturally leads him to geography,
physical sciences, etc.:

The earth is man's island and the Sun his most striking spectacle.
As soon as our ideas begin to extend beyond ourselves, our attention
will necessarily be attracted to one or the other of these two objects
[29].

'Negative education' encourages observation and activity, not the mere
acquisition of facts. From the example of geography, Rousseau sum-
marises:

Here you will see the difference between Emile's ignorance, and
other boys knowledge. They know maps, he makes them [30].

In summary, because Rousseau contradicts his own opening sentence,
proving that *not* 'everything degenerates in the hands of man' he suggested
strands of thinking about art in general learning that Francis Wayland
Parker found useful, that in time carried over into the twentieth century's
progressive education movement that grew from him.

Wordsworth

Parker would also have read Wordsworth. Even though education was not his profession, it became one of Wordsworth's themes. Born in 1770, just seven years after Rousseau conceptualised the boy's new education in *Emile*, we know Wordsworth literally applied Rousseau's 'negative education' when in the autumn of 1795, in his twenty-fifth year, he and his sister Dorothy, assumed responsibility for the upbringing of Basil Montague, a 2¾-year-old boy whose mother had died, and whose father chose to leave him with the Wordsworths while he pursued his life in London. Basil enabled them to apply *Emile*:

> We teach him [Basil] nothing, at present but what he learns from
> the evidence of his senses. He has an insatiable curiosity, which we
> are always careful to satisfy . . . directed to everything he sees; sky,
> fields, trees, shrubs, and corn . . . . Our grand study is to make him
> happy [31].

More consequential to Parker than any information we have on Basil's care was Wordsworth's example – typified in *The Prelude* [32] – of self-analysis (in Wordsworth's case examining his own childhood and the seeds of his own later development, celebrating the power of childhood, and contrasting the stages of childhood that Rousseau delineated).

Like Rousseau, Wordsworth attributes the child's growth to an inherent attraction to sensory experience. Wordsworth's 'poet of the future' anticipates Parker's philosopher-child; both envision growth born of pursuit of the child's 'soul unsubdued', born of the child's pursuit of its natural bent, its own attention and curiosity. In 1802, in the Preface to the *Lyrical Ballads*, Wordsworth describes the poet of the future, who:

> will be ready to follow the steps of the man of science – carrying
> sensation into the midst of objects of the science itself. The remotest
> discoveries of the chemist, the botanist, or the mineralogist, will be
> as proper objects of the poet's art as any [33].

This anticipates Parker's words 92 years later:

> The child instinctively begins all subjects known in the curriculum
> of the university. He begins them because he cannot help it; his very
> nature impels him [34].

Childhood for Wordsworth is a powerhouse.

> Dumb yearnings, hidden appetites, are ours,
> And *they must* have their food. Our childhood sits,
> Our simple childhood, sits upon a throne
> That hath more power than all the elements [35].

Here in *The Prelude* Wordsworth recalls his own childhood, when:

> . . . the earth
> And common face of Nature spake to me
> Rememberable things . . . . [36]

Just as Rousseau had been appalled, so Wordsworth was, by school's success in impoverishing the child, who

> . . . knows the policies of foreign lands,

Can string you names of districts, cities and towns,
The whole world over tight as beads of dew
Upon a gossamer thread [37].

Both confirmed for Parker what he had already seen in the schoolroom. All three, across time, shared feelings in common about the power of childhood and the roles of sensation and curiosity.

But where, in Wordsworth's work, do we find the artist/creator? Young Wordsworth himself is his subject in *The Prelude* – a poem almost scientifically subtitled *Growth of a Poet's Mind*. The author's self-analysis explores and gives form to how the young child, the artist-learner, metamorphoses into the adult whose lines we read.

Frail creature as he is, helpless frail,
An inmate of this active universe.
For, feeling has to him imparted power
That through the growing faculties of sense
Doth like an agent of the one great Mind
Create, creator and receiver both,
Working but in alliance with the works
Which it beholds. – Such verily, is the first
Poetic spirit of our human life . . . [38].

Further on in *The Prelude* Wordsworth writes:

But let this
Be not forgotten, that I still retained
My first creative sensibility;
That by the regular action of the world
My soul was unsubdued. A plastic power
Abode with me . . . [39].

At the age of thirty-two (in 1802) Wordsworth, recollecting the origins of his current feelings in childhood, wrote the poem that beings 'My heart leaps when I behold a rainbow in the sky . . .'. This is where, influenced by Rousseau and in anticipation of Freud, he says 'The child is father of the man' [40]. Childhood experience, more than a foundation of human life, is both treasure trove for, and a tyranny over, the life that grows from it.

Reading Wordsworth, Parker would have recognised the poet's debt to the then-new ideas of Rousseau – that childhood feelings survive into adult life, that transitions are linked, that stages must be lived for what they are and not only as a preparation for what one will become, that our past, present and future have critical interconnections, and the processes by which we learn begin from sensory and imaginative responses to Nature.

As Parker read Rousseau and Wordsworth, I also imagine him wrestling with their differences, particularly with regard to art-making in the child's growth. They placed the emphasis differently. Rousseau emphasised physical curiosity and the tactile response while Wordsworth's concern was for the child's capacity for feeling and emotional response. Rousseau could claim that every learner had senses – and hands, feet and a self – to move in space. Wordsworth could claim that all human emotions matter and every human being is capable of feeling.

Both Rousseau and Wordsworth shaped images of learning quite apart from the process of schooling:

> When I began to enquire,
> To watch and question those I met, and speak
> Without reserve to them, the lonely roads
> Were open schools in which I daily read,
> With most delight the passions of mankind,
> Whether by words, looks, signs, or tears, revealed; . . . .
> And – now convinced at heart
> How little those formalities, to which
> With overweening trust alone we give
> The name of Education, have to do
> With real feeling and just sense [41].

Parker could take what was useful from both Rousseau and Words-worth. But he needed a theorist to transform these ideas into a schooling programme. For the transition to curriculum itself, Parker needed Frederick Froebel. From newspapers we know Parker was influenced by Froebel even before he started his European study tour.

Frederick Froebel

For Froebel, again and differently, the child is an artist. With Froebel, we subtly shift from an education created for Europe, to one using Europe as a laboratory, anticipating export to the United States. Whereas Froebel saw the Old World as too constrained by its old conventions to accept his ideas, Americans such as Parker were just the receptive minds for whom Froebel hoped.

As Parker read Froebel and the other writers/educators, he eaves-dropped, as it were, on a vast conversation. All these writers themselves were engaged in agreements and disputes that mattered and shaped what they were to create. Sometimes he could recognise ideas lifted wholesale. Twenty-four years after Wordsworth compressed his vision into the few words, 'The child is father of the man', Froebel wrote: 'This is seen in the child, man as a whole . . . .' [42]

But whereas Pestalozzi, one theorist I do not examine here, found in Rousseau his fascination with training the immediate sense perceptions of the child, Froebel was much more intrigued by children's cultivation of their own curiosity, their own motives, their 'self-activity'. Froebel saw the limits of sense perception. He preferred to emphasise the child's work as finding inner connections, finding and pursuing what is attractive to himself. The mind seeks food. The child actively seeks what is nourishing for him.

> To have found one fourth of the answer by his own effort is of more value and importance to the child than it is to half hear and half understand it in the words of another [43].

Where is the artist within Froebel's text?

> God created man in his own image; therefore, man should create and bring forth like God. His spirit, the spirit of man, should hover over the shapeless, and move it that it may take shape and form, a

distinct being and a life of its own .... We become truly godlike in
diligence and industry, in working and doing, which are
accompanied by the clear perception or even by the vaguest feeling
that thereby we represent the inner in the outer ... [44].

The artist produces an external thing from inner motives. This is
Froebel's model for the child. The translator of *The Education of Man*,
W. N. Hailman, pointed out:

It has long been conceded that experience, and, primarily direct
experience, furnishes the material for human insight and conduct.
Until quite lately, however, the school has recognized this fact only
in the in-leading processes of intellectual growth. In the out-leading
processes of intellectual growth, in the expression of ideas, the
school is still satisfied with words and ignores the value of things. It
neglects the plastic expression of ideas by the hands ... [45].

Froebel observes in child play the behaviour of the sketching artist or
the clay-modelling sculptor.

The child would know himself why he loves this thing; he would
know all its properties, its innermost nature, that he may learn to
understand himself in his attachment. For this reason the child
examines the object from all sides; for this reason he tears and
breaks it .... We reprove the child for his naughtiness and
foolishness; and yet he is wiser than we who reprove him .... For
what man tries to represent or do, he begins to understand [46].

Froebel also wrote quite specifically of the evolution of drawing and of
its relation to language.

For the word and the drawing are always mutually explanatory and
complementary, for neither one is, by itself, exhaustive and
sufficient with reference to the object represented .... The faculty
of drawing is, therefore, as much innate in the child, in man, as is
the faculty of speech, and it demands its development and
cultivation as imperatively as the latter [47].

Through art-making processes the child assimilated all knowledge
across subjects.

The representation of objects by and in drawing induces and implies
clear perception, e.g. two eyes, and two arms, five fingers and five
toes .... Thus the drawing of the object leads to the discovery of
number. The repeated return of one and the same object leads to
counting ... [48].

There is in art ... a side where it touches mathematics,
understanding; another where it touches the world of language,
reason; a third, where – although itself clearly a representation of
the inner – it coincides with the representation of nature; and a
fourth where it coincides with religion. Yet all these relationships
will have to be disregarded ... in order to lead him to an
appreciation of art. Here art will be considered only in its ultimate
unity as the pure representation of the inner [49].

The purpose of teaching and instruction is to bring ever more *out* of
man rather than to put more and more into him [50].

Froebel's notion of education posits a boy who is a container for 'the inner' experience but those inner experiences only serve their purpose when the child gives form to inner feelings.

> Man is developed and cultured toward the fulfilment of his destiny and mission and is to be valued . . . by what he puts out and unfolds from himself [51].

> The life of the boy has, indeed, no purpose but that of the outer representation of his self . . . . In the forms he fashions he does not see outer forms which he has to take in and understand; but he sees in them the expression of his spirit, of the laws and activities of his own mind [52].

Conclusion

From the Declaration of Independence to the Centennial, Americans felt their economy, and indeed their society, weakened by dependency upon things and people who were foreign. Education, like houses and shelf ornaments, was dominated by foreign dependency. American schooling was one arena in which people could wrestle with, and diminish, foreign influences. One method was by seeing the child as an artist, by encouraging original, independent, natural thoughts and creations.

'The foreign', Froebel's term for alien, unintegrated information, those 'mind-killing practices' that schools imposed on their students, must have rung in Americans' ears. Schools, he tells us, are 'stamping our children like coins and adorning them with foreign inscriptions' [53]. Froebel's kindergarten could become at once a political and an educational alternative. Parker himself distrusted the 'foreign'. It undermined attention, that concentrated taking-in of experience so important to his theory. Attention, that act of will, required inhibition of all 'foreign' activities from consciousness. Parker used the word 'foreign' to condemn distraction, whatever was diverting attention.

The nineteenth-century American use of the word 'foreign' was layered with many associations. It meant formal education based upon acquiring other peoples' knowledge, particularly European. 'Foreign' was repressive, imitative, diverting of American attention. Ironically, by emulating and lifting ideas on art from European thinkers, Francis Wayland Parker came home with an American programme of intellectual independence that launched America's progressive education movement. Teaching for an 'inner knowledge', cultivating one's native attention and own curiosity, matched America's deeply-felt political disposition. Here educators had their own declaration of independence.

Notes and References

1 DEWEY, JOHN (1930), 'How Much Freedom in New Schools?', *New Republic*, 9 July 1930.
2 PATRIDGE, LELIA E. (1883), *Notes of Talks on Teaching, given by Francis Wayland Parker at the Martha's Vineyard Summer Institute, July 17–August 19, 1882* (New York, Kellogg & Co.), pp. 27–8.
3 PARKER, FRANCIS WAYLAND (1884), *Talks on Pedagogics: an Outline of the Theory of Concentration* (New York, Kellogg & Co.) (reprinted New York, Arno Press/New York Times, 1969).
4 PATRIDGE (n. 2), p. 84.
5 PARKER (n. 3), p. 23.
6 EMERSON, RALPH WALDO (1836), *Nature* (Boston, James Munro & Co.), p. 1.
7 PARKER (n. 3), pp. 22–3.
8 *Daily Mirror & American* (Manchester, New Hampshire) 8 November 1913, *Scrapbook B*, p. 176.
9 *Daily Mirror* 30 June 1914, *Scrapbook D* (*loc. cit.*, n. 8), pp. 36–7.
10 ROSEN, CHARLES and HENRI ZERNER (1984), *Romanticism and Realism: the Mythology of Nineteenth Century Art* (New York, W.W. Norton), p. 15.
11 *Ibid.*
12 *Ibid.*, p. 35.
13 ARCHER, R.L. (1964), *Jean Jacques Rousseau: his Educational Theories selected from Emile, Julie and other writings* (New York, Barron's Educational Series), p. 55.
14 *Ibid.*, p. 82.
15 *Ibid.*, p. 101.
16 *Ibid.*, p. 133.
17 *Ibid.*
18 *Ibid.*
19 *Ibid.*, p. 134.
20 ROSEN and ZERNER (n. 10), p. 25.
21 ARCHER (n. 13), p. 134.
22 *Ibid.*
23 *Ibid.*, p. 135.
24 *Ibid.*
25 *Ibid.*, p. 137.
26 *Ibid.*, p. 135.
27 *Ibid.*, p. 136.
28 *Ibid.*, p. 121.
29 *Ibid.*, p. 148.
30 *Ibid.*, p. 153.
31 WORDSWORTH, JONATHAN, MICHAEL C. JAY and ROBERT WOOLF (1987) *William Wordsworth and the Age of English Romanticism* (New Brunswick, Rutgers University Press), pp. 70–1.
32 WORDSWORTH, WILLIAM (1926), *The Prelude: or Growth of a Poet's Mind* (ed. Ernest de Selincourt) (Oxford, OUP), Book I.
33 WORDSWORTH, JAY and WOOLF (n. 31), p. 63.
34 PARKER (n. 3), p. 23.
35 WORDSWORTH (n. 32), Book V, lines 506–9.
36 *Ibid.*, Book I, lines 586–8.
37 WORDSWORTH, JAY and WOOLF (n. 31), p. 84.
38 WORDSWORTH (n. 32), Book II, lines 253–61.
39 *Ibid.*, lines 358–63.
40 WORDSWORTH, WILLIAM (1950), 'The Rainbow' in: *Selected Poetry* (New York, Modern Library), p. 462.
41 WORDSWORTH (n. 32), Book VIII, lines 160–72.

42 FROEBEL, FREDERICK (1887), *The Education of Man* (New York, D. Appleton & Co.), p. 36.
43 *Ibid.*, p. 86.
44 *Ibid.*, p. 31.
45 *Ibid.*, p. 37.
46 *Ibid.*, p. 73.
47 *Ibid.*, p. 80.
48 *Ibid.*, pp. 226–7.
49 *Ibid.*, pp. 270–1.
50 *Ibid.*
51 *Ibid.*
52 *Ibid.*
53 *Ibid.*, p. 231.

Chapter Four

MARY ANN STANKIEWICZ Barbarian or
Civilised: Ellen Gates Starr,
T. C. Horsfall, and the Chicago Public
School Art Society

Contemporary art education may be compared to a river system: several
tributaries have contributed to the flow, some of which are less well-
known or less well-travelled than others. While much of the history of
nineteenth-century art education in English-speaking countries has
focused on one mainstream, the development and influence of the
Schools of Art and Design in Great Britain and the work of Walter Smith
and other South Kensingtonians in North America and New Zealand,
there have been other streams as well. One was schoolroom decoration
and picture study, a movement that first emerged in the United States
around 1840 and continued in some form for nearly a century [1]. This
stream of art education focused not on learning how to draw or how to
design, but on learning from and about works of art. In other papers I
have examined the types of reproductions available during the middle
and late nineteenth century and the powerful influence of Ruskin's
Romantic Idealist aesthetic on American school people at the turn of the
century [2]. In this chapter I will discuss transatlantic influences and the
role of women in picture study. After a brief overview of the use of
reproductions in nineteenth-century art education, I will analyse the
influence of the Englishman T. C. Horsfall (1844–1932) on Ellen Gates
Starr (1859–1940), co-founder of Chicago's Hull House with Jane
Addams and founder of the Chicago Public School Art Society.

Reproductions of objects and pictures

Casts and flat reproductions were extensively utilised in the instructional
methods of the British Schools of Design to provide exemplars of the
best art and ornament from which students could copy [3]. Sir Henry
Cole took pride in making casts and examples of art manufactures
available to the working-class families who visited the new museum at
South Kensington [4]. In this, Cole anticipated an attitude pervasive
during the second half of the nineteenth century that reproductions were
best suited to naive viewers – children, the servant and working classes –
and that their function should be educational [5]. The first American
museums, modelled in part on South Kensington, had large collections
of casts, printed engravings and photographic reproductions as means to
educate their patrons about the variety and history of fine and applied art
[6].

Reproductions also had an important role in the education of the artist. By the early sixteenth century, apprentices in an artist's studio began their studies by copying conventionalised representations of various parts of the human body from two-dimensional models. Drawing three-dimensional models such as casts and sculpture was the next step and '[m]asters often assembled collections of casts, drawings, and prints to aid in the training of their apprentices' [7]. Drawings, prints, and paintings of artists' studios and art academies through the nineteenth century show such collections hanging on walls, resting on tables, and stored in drawers and cabinets, ready to be taken out for reference by the artist or for copying by the student. When mass art education became an issue in the mid-nineteenth century, the recently developed process of lithography was available to supplement more traditional and more linear print-making processes in reproducing works of art for students to copy. Cole utilised student skills by having the Female Special Class for Lithography copy examples of ornament onto stone for printing [8].

At the 1893 International Congress of Education held in conjunction with the Chicago World's Fair, an American woman art educator, Mary Dana Hicks, made a distinction between drawing an object and drawing from a flat copy. In the first case, the child could express his own thought about the object; in the second, the pupil was expected to 'learn the thought of a more cultivated mind and spirit concerning the object' [9]. Here we see a change in the rationale for the use of reproductions; copying not only trains the eye and hand, but somehow connects the student to the mind of the artist – even at second or third hand. This romantic belief that the character and personality of the artist were embodied in the work of art appears throughout the picture study literature. It was perhaps most vividly stated by John Ruskin, noted for his moralistic assumption that great art could only be produced by artists of noble character. A corollary assumption that the critic imaginatively recreated the artistic process in reading the work of art helped explain how contact was made between the minds of artist and viewer. While Ruskin believed that few people were destined to become artists, he did believe that anyone could learn to appreciate fine art critically.

Isaac Edwards Clarke expressed similar views in his 1885 report to the United States government on art and industry [10]. Clarke shared an expressivist aesthetic with many of his contemporaries. As he explained it, art is the expression of an idea or emotion conceived or felt by the artist with sufficient power to reproduce the idea or emotion in the viewer. Thus we have a double potential for moral benefit from observing art works and their reproductions: not only can one be inspired by the noble character of a great artist, but the message in a refined and exalted subject could also affect the viewer. For many picture study advocates, a reproduction could communicate subject matter as well as an original [11].

Clarke suggested a third way in which the art work could inspire the viewer to moral and civic virtue. In his descriptions of a coming 'Age of Display' Clarke pointed out that both publicly commissioned and privately owned works of art are part of a community's wealth. According to Clarke, one duty of those who possess power and money is to display their accoutrements, an idea that resonates with the Puritan belief that the wealthy are rich because they are good and that poverty is somehow the result of sin [12]. If wealth equals goodness then one has a duty to display that wealth and share its benefits with the less fortunate, deserving poor. In the United States, such display and sharing often took the forms of cultural and charitable philanthropy. Among the middle classes, as Thorstein Veblen argued, desire to emulate the wealthy resulted in conspicuous consumption by the middle-class housewife, she who decorated the home with the products of the Aesthetic movement [13]. While the housewife could not acquire original paintings and sculptures, she could purchase chromolithographs and plaster casts to give her parlour an air of refinement and to introduce her children to art-culture [14].

Thus, while two- and three-dimensional reproductions filled empty walls in early United States museums and provided models to copy in British and North American art schools, they performed a decorative and inspirational function in middle-class American homes. In 1840, the popular lady writer Lydia Sigourney had addressed the Connecticut Common School Convention on the perception of the beautiful:

> Why should not the interior of our schoolhouses aim at somewhat of the taste and elegance of a parlor? Might not the vase of flowers enrich the mantlepiece; – and the walls display not only well-executed maps, but historical engravings and pictures; – and the bookshelves be crowned with the bust of moralist or sage, orator or Father of his Country? [15]

Mrs Sigourney argued that exposure to beauty could refine and sublimate the character, increasing chances of future happiness; such exposure should be incorporated into the entire process of education through the beautification of schoolhouses. American educators and the public were slow to respond to Mrs Sigourney's plea. The Schoolroom Decoration movement did not reach its height until the last decade of the nineteenth century, although first stirrings had been felt in Boston in 1870 [16]. In that notable year, casts of antique sculpture purchased with private subscriptions were placed in the hall of the Girls' Normal and High School. However, development of Industrial Art Education took precedence over Schoolroom Decoration for the next two decades.

On 20 April 1892 the Prang educational publishing company held a conference in Boston on *Art in the Schoolroom: Pictures and Their Influence*. Among the speakers was Mr Tetlow, principal of Girls' High, who explained how the casts were incorporated into the educational programme of the school, and Ross Turner, an artist from Salem on Boston's North Shore. The following month, Turner led in organizing the Boston Public School Art League, a group which collected pictures for distribution to the schools. By 1896 the movement had spread so widely that an exhibition of pictures and casts suitable for schoolroom decoration was held at the Brooklyn [New York] Institute of Arts and Sciences. In 1899 Henry Turner Bailey, Massachusetts drawing supervisor, collaborated on a book which urged that school buildings be made more physically and aesthetically healthful through proper ventilation and adequate lighting, improved sanitation, and the repainting of stark white walls with pastel colours [17]. Bailey encouraged teachers to establish beauty corners, to use the best pieces of ceramics available as pots or vases for flowers, to hang pictures and display casts on shelves. Again, technology contributed to this new use of reproductions in art education. During the 1880s photographic processes of reproduction had been perfected so that half-tone prints of recognised masterpieces, patriotic portraits, and historical spectacles were available at prices schools could afford [18].

Educators influenced by Pestalozzi also adapted pictures and other objects for the education of young children. Pestalozzi had argued that learning concepts required prior knowledge of percepts or, as he called them, 'sense-impressions' [19]. As Wygant describes it, the Pestalozzian mode of instruction:

> began with the simplest elements, proceeded slowly and incremen-
> tally, and used perception through all of the senses. Vocabulary was
> developed through observation of the dimensions, the form, and the
> qualities of common objects [20].

While Pestalozzi's work influenced the development of pedagogical drawing, Wygant states that the most popular application of Pestalozzi's methods in the United States was object teaching [21]. Object or objective teaching was popularised by Edward A. Sheldon, superintendent of schools and later head of the Oswego [New York] State Normal and Training School [22]. About 1860 Sheldon had visited the National Museum in Toronto where he saw collections of pictures, charts and books from all over the world. Particularly impressed by the work of the Home and Colonial Infant and Juvenile School Society established in 1836 in London, Sheldon purchased some materials, initiated the process of curriculum change in the Oswego schools and in 1861 imported Miss Margaret E. M. Jones from the English society to teach this new system. When she left the following year, Herman Krusi, Jr., son of an associate of Pestalozzi, replaced her as teacher of the training class. Although object teaching could degenerate into the formulaic recitation of facts parodied by Charles Dickens in *Hard Times*, the approach at its best stressed learning through the senses and promoted use of two- and three-dimensional visual materials in public schools [23].

Thus we find several strands in the development of picture study: belief that reproductions were well suited to introduce naive and lower-class viewers to the world of art; respect for the authority of artistic tradition; belief (perhaps best exemplified in the writings of Ruskin) that the artist's special virtues could be conveyed to less well-endowed mortals through proximity with and observation of art works or reproductions; desire to make bare classrooms more pleasant and homelike; and a need to make ideas and concepts vivid for children whose lives lacked sensory stimulation.

Chicago Public School Art Society

Although American precedents existed, the Chicago Public School Art

7   Chicago schoolchildren holding reproductions and standing in front of stories written about each picture; Art Resources in Teaching Records, Special Collections, The University Library, The University of Illinois.

Society (CPSAS), an extension of a local women's club, was directly based on an English model. Ellen Gates Starr had met Jane Addams when both were first-year students at Rockford [Illinois] Female Seminary. After Ellen left to earn her living teaching first in rural schools then in private girls' schools in Chicago, she and Jane maintained their friendship through an intense correspondence. In 1888 the two young women visited Europe with another friend, Sarah Anderson, a teacher at Rockford. It was Ellen's first trip abroad and she relished the chance to visit cathedrals and art galleries. All three women purchased reproductions of works of art for themselves, for Rockford, and for Ellen's school. During this trip, Jane Addams formed the idea of establishing a settlement house in Chicago, based on the model of Toynbee Hall which she had visited before her return to the United States.

Toynbee Hall, founded in London's East End in 1884 by Canon Samuel Barnett and a group of university men, represented a new approach to charity. Barnett's vision of a paternalistic, but disinterested, upper-middle-class, predominantly male élite performing one-on-one charity work reflected his belief that 'the social problem is at root an educational problem' [24]. In Barnett's view the right sort of education should alleviate poverty but also contribute to social tranquillity by encouraging respect for Christian family virtues, traditional social roles, order and authority. Art played an important role in Barnett's didactic philanthropy. Beginning in 1881, Barnett and his wife Henrietta held a series of Easter art exhibitions in Whitechapel as a means to provide worthwhile leisure activities and contacts with upper-class culture for their parishioners [25]. Works of art were loaned by artists and collectors; a written catalogue made the moral content of many works explicit. The exhibit was open evenings and Sundays, a revolutionary move for a clergyman, to attract working men and women. Contemporary newspaper accounts doubted whether the 'aesthetic furniture and Japanese fans' found in Toynbee Hall would regenerate the poor [26]. Barnett himself was unsure whether the 55,000 visitors who attended one exhibition were motivated by a desire for conformity and respectability or by consciousness of the need to cultivate their relationship to the First Artist. Nonetheless, the exhibitions of *Pictures for the Poor* continued under Toynbee Hall sponsorship until 1898 when the foundation stone for the Whitechapel Art Gallery was laid.

On their return to Chicago, both Addams and Starr worked while preparing for their new endeavour. Starr continued teaching art history and appreciation at a private school; Addams, who had an independent income, did volunteer work, taught industrial art part-time at a local missionary training school, and gathered support for the proposed settlement from local women's clubs. In nineteenth-century Chicago, men's and women's philanthropies were separate. Under the ideal of *noblesse oblige* both men and women contributed to charitable and cultural philanthropy in Chicago [27]. While men initiated charities and cultural groups, women volunteers helped found asylums. While men established the Art Institute, women founded organizations such as the Society for Decorative Art, established in 1877 to provide training in art for impoverished middle- and upper-middle-class women; the Fortnightly Club, established in 1873 for intellectual and social culture; and the Woman's Club with its art study class [28]. According to Blair's feminist analysis of women's clubs, participation in such groups allowed women close contact with culture and the chance to claim literature and the arts for their sphere, 'an alternative to the acquisitive and competitive goals of men in an industrializing America' [29]. Just as women feminised culture, so they feminised some aspects of moral reform, typically those which related to women and children, extending domestic activities into social homemaking [30]. Thus, when Addams and Starr approached the upper-class women of Chicago, the mothers and older sisters of Starr's pupils, with the idea of establishing a residence for themselves in a poor neighbourhood, the Woman's Club chose to support their endeavour rather than let it become part of the male philanthropic domain. While the British settlement tended to be staffed by male university graduates, American settlements were dominated by women.

The women of Hull House were involved with art and art education even before the settlement opened its doors in October 1889 [31]. Starr hung reproductions in the freshly painted rooms and placed casts where little hands could touch them in the day nursery. She organised a lending library of reproductions, which the settlement residents expected would raise the tastes of their neighbours above printed scarves, paper flowers, and wax funeral wreaths [32]. The first addition to Hull House was a library and art gallery, funded by local businessman Edward B. Butler. When the new building opened in June 1891, Revd Barnett spoke sentimentally of the value of pictures in comforting the poor and inspiring them to recognise heroic deeds and value beauty [33].

The following year, Ellen Starr returned to England, visiting Revd Barnett and his wife and others involved in social reform. In May 1892 she visited a Mr T.C. Horsfall, a friend of the Barnetts, at Swanscoe Park, his home near Manchester. She was as impressed with Horsfall's work of supplying circulating collections of pictures to elementary schools as Ruskin had been with Horsfall's plans for a museum for Manchester's poor a decade and a half earlier.

Thomas Coglan Horsfall's concern with making art available to the lower classes first appeared in an 1877 letter to the *Manchester Guardian*, parts of which Ruskin included in Letter 79 of *Fors Clavigera*. Like Ruskin, Horsfall at this time was dismayed by the condition of contemporary art and held a romantic reverence for the art of the past. Believing

8 Nature exhibits, Horsfall Museum (n.d.). Manchester City Art Galleries (UK).

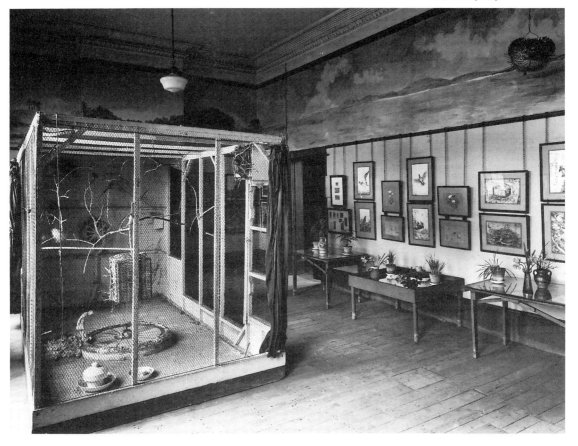

that seeing beauty regularly helps one appreciate it, Horsfall urged that common schools be beautified. He asserted that experts should select pictures and provide written labels for the working class, while recognising that members of that class rarely visited art galleries [34]. Ruskin agreed with Horsfall's desire to place pictures, casts, vases, and pretty screens in schools because he was engaged in a similar endeavour through his St George's Guild in Sheffield. However, as their correspondence developed and Horsfall visited Ruskin at Brantwood, they agreed to disagree on certain points. Horsfall admitted ignorance of form and colour, but appreciated 'noble human feeling' [35]. He deferred to Ruskin as his superior in clearly articulating right relations of art with society. Horsfall was hopeful of national progress, Ruskin convinced of national decline. Ruskin argued that perceiving order on earth was prerequisite to faith in an orderly heaven, tying art to morality. Horsfall, on the other hand, tended toward the Utilitarian argument that art was important as a means of pleasure for the masses.

This Utilitarian tendency, suggesting perhaps some familiarity with the work of Jeremy Bentham, James Mill or John Stuart Mill, grew stronger in Horsfall's writings of the 1880s. Albert Fein has discussed how disciples of Bentham:

> interpreted education to mean all those advantages formerly held by an aristocratic class living in rural isolation. An urban society needed to make available to all its citizens those means of education and leisure formerly enjoyed by the landed aristocracy – the park, the college, the library, and the museum [36].

Like James Mill, Horsfall saw education as a means to inculcate virtues such as temperance and fortitude. Early in his correspondence with Ruskin, he labelled the work of providing art and music for working classes 'cure of drunkenness' [37]. Like John Stuart Mill, Horsfall believed in the moral importance of cultivating emotions; in Horsfall's case, love of beauty.

By 1884, when he addressed the International Conference on Education in London, Horsfall could discuss the right use of works of art in elementary schools on the basis of his experience with a new museum in Manchester [38]. Horsfall's argument that pictures revealed the highest qualities of human nature to poor children suggests a lingering tie to Ruskin, but his other goals confirm his Utilitarian approach: improving taste for both workers and employers, making the working-class home more attractive, providing wholesome recreation for the working-class family, and making schools more pleasant for children and their teachers. One of Horsfall's favourite arguments for the importance of picture study was based on the pleasures of literature. He described urban children who apparently had never seen the flowers, bees, or larks referred to in school poems, or, if they had seen them, did not know their names [39].

This variation of an associationist theory of learning was a major part of Horsfall's appeal for Ellen Starr, who reported that she had begun a collection of pictures for schools in 1891, choosing pictures that could help children develop mental images of beauty in nature and architecture.

Starr brought Horsfall's ideas to Chicago, organising an exhibit of pictures for schools at Hull House in October 1892 and the Public School Art Society in April 1894. In her lecture at the exhibit, she credited Horsfall with many valuable suggestions for the picture study work, first and foremost the rationale that pictures were prerequisite to mental imagery and necessary to understand literature.

Horsfall's practical contributions included careful selection of pictures that would attract children's interest and 'direct them somewhither for profit' [40]. In Manchester, according to Horsfall, the collection included local scenery and landscapes, pictures of English flora and fauna, foreign scenes, seascapes, war scenes, religious subjects, portraits, copies of works by Turner, as well as examples of good pottery, glass, metal work and textiles, a model miniature house fitted out by William Morris and W. A. S. Benson, and casts of Greek sculpture. Original oil and water-colours, prints and photographs were included with reproductions. Two aspects of the Manchester exhibit seem unique: labels attached to provide critical commentary and descriptions of how pictures were made; and prices attached to the cheaper pictures so that the poor would know that they could afford them. The descriptive labels were supplemented by bands of 'explainers' as docents were called. Labels, the emphasis on nature, urban monuments, and portraits of admirable people were among the ideas Starr borrowed from Horsfall.

A preliminary meeting to organize 'a society whose work shall be the placing of pictures in the public schools for the promotion of art education' was held in the Chicago Woman's Club rooms on 16 April 1894 [41]. While the society's history cited the influence of the World's Columbian Exposition of 1893 as a factor in establishment of the group, continuing local arguments over the value of special subjects, such as art education, to working-class children may have contributed as well [41]. Ellen Gates Starr presided and was chosen president as well as chair of the Censorship Committee, whose task it was to approve pictures for purchase or acceptance as donations. Other committees included Ways and Means, and a School Visiting Committee, charged with visiting those schools desiring pictures to determine their suitability and to distribute the pictures. Later a Vacation School Committee was established to place pictures in summer schools, and a Label Committee to keep track of the society's pictures and label them. The CPSAS was incorporated on 30 March 1900. Less than a decade after incorporation, the society owned over 1,200 works of art, originals and reproductions, with a value of about $18,000, placed in 102 Chicago public schools and two small school art libraries. When the society celebrated its twenty-fifth anniversary year, it owned thirty original works of art out of the 2,000 pictures in use. Cases with displays of hand-crafted everyday objects were also available for loan.

Membership in the CPSAS was overwhelmingly female. In its second year, the society listed 114 members, only seven of whom were male, including John Dewey and Charles L. Hutchinson. Colonel Francis W. Parker was made an honorary member in March 1895, probably for his active support in allowing the society to decorate a room at the Cook

County Normal School. The Chicago Board of Education was also supportive; one member of the society was Ella Flagg Young, future superintendent of the city schools. Although the Art Institute was not officially affiliated with the CPSAS, sculptor Lorado Taft made Institute reproductions available at reduced prices and had his students make moulds for casts.

Although artistic merit was the society's first criterion for selecting pictures and appreciation of form and colour a major goal, art remained tied to moral and social betterment throughout the early years of the organisation. In January and February 1897, during a series of lectures in New York and Detroit, Starr explained that the goal of the movement was to provide 'free art on a purely democratic principle, the best for everybody' [43]. Members saw links between perception of beauty and civic reform, including renewed religious spirit and reduced delinquency. Horsfall had written Ruskin: 'Till churches will help many, I want museums to help a few' [44]. An unnamed member of the CPSAS declared in 1902:

> if we could have something of the Art Institute in every school
> building there would result from it a passion for social betterment –
> a future demand for more beauty in the city, and possibly there
> would arise a new kind of religious worship, a lavishing of wealth on
> schools instead of on churches as in olden times [45].

The society continued to share Horsfall's view of pictures as a kind of window revealing the creations of God and humanity to urban children and providing pleasure amid the work of school.

Like Henry Turner Bailey's book, the society's work was related to the City Beautiful movement which arose at the turn of the century. Parks and other recreational sites were developed in American cities as a means of alleviating unhealthy urban conditions, providing wholesome leisure activity, and controlling the pastimes of workers [46]. Bodily and spiritual health, sanitation and beauty went hand in hand. Horsfall had explained that the community had a duty to provide public gardens and art galleries so that citizens could fulfil their pleasant duties to themselves and their neighbours by strolling amid nature and art [47]. The CPSAS participated by placing pictures in regular and summer schools, encouraging the opening of schools as social centres, and beautifying school yards as well as classrooms. Horsfall had declared, as Starr frequently quoted, that the community decision to use art in education was in fact a decision whether the masses should be barbarian or civilised. The CPSAS opted for civilisation.

Conclusion

Reflecting the uneasy balance its British models maintained between social reform and the continuation of traditional values, the picture study movement in the United States was a class-related phenomenon in which upper- and middle-class women and men attempted to use works of art to instil desired virtues in poor, working-class, and immigrant children. Helen Horowitz has argued that the idealist cultural philanthropies of late nineteenth-century Chicago were directed primarily toward the middle classes [48]. Although policies at some cultural institutions limited access by Chicago's poor and immigrant populations, the CPSAS brought works of art to such people in their own neighbourhoods. By the 1920s, the society was bringing eighth graders to the Art Institute three times a year for systematic instruction. More than many similar groups in other parts of the country, Starr and the CPSAS sought coloured reproductions that would appeal to children. Due to Horsfall's Utilitarian influence, Starr brought a less romantic and idealistic perspective to the work than many of her cohort.

Although some proponents would claim that they wanted to elevate the taste of the lower classes without generating the desire to accumulate luxuries inappropriate to their station, in actuality development of taste was prerequisite to consumption [49]. If the lower classes did not follow the lead of those with more money and purchase consumer goods available from growing manufactures, the economy would falter. Thus the prices that Horsfall put on pictures and the miniature home in the Manchester museum were contributions to consumer education as well as art education. The many landscape pictures gave workers a chance to purchase images of the rural life they or their parents had been forced to leave to earn a living in Manchester's factories.

Although Starr reported that the work of the CPSAS was more aesthetic and less educational than Horsfall's in England, the consumerist aspect of picture study may have been an unconscious part of its appeal to a certain class of American women [50]. Their participation in clubs and philanthropies reflected their increased leisure and their role as domestic consumers and social homemakers. Ostensibly inculcating virtues such as temperance, love of beauty, or patriotism, the patronesses of picture study were actually contributing to the process of making works of art information and commodities [51]. While the women may have thought of their sphere as less acquisitive and materialistic than the domain of men, there is evidence that the social reform activities of settlement workers, and of related organisations such as the CPSAS, taught their poorer sisters to value certain goods above others. In her autobiographical novel about art and settlements, Vida Scudder, a friend of Starr's, has three working-class women explain why they appreciate the finer things offered by the settlement. They admit that they find it difficult, when hungry and worn out from working, to imagine themselves in the pictures and stories. However, at least one has decided that a plush parlour suite will not do when she establishes her own home. Instead she wants 'a wood floor and a rug, and wicker furniture stained green, and those plaster angels on my walls' [52].

Notes and References

1   The following works are among the chief picture study references. GREEN, HARRY B. (1948), *The Introduction of Art as a General Education Subject in American Schools* (unpub. dissertation, Stanford University). EISNER, Elliot W. and DAVID W. ECKER (1966), *Readings in Art Education*

(Waltham, Mass., Blaisdell). SAUNDERS, ROBERT (1966), 'A History of Teaching Art Appreciation in the Public Schools' in ECKER, DAVID W. (ed.), *Improving the Teaching of Art Appreciation* (Columbus, Ohio State University). DOBBS, STEPHEN M. (1972), 'Attic Temples and Beauty Nooks: the Schoolroom Decoration Movement', *Intellect*, 101, pp. 35–43. JONES, R. L. (1974), 'Aesthetic Education: its Historical Precedents', *Art Education* 22, 9, pp. 13–16. SMITH, PETER (1983), 'Picture Study: the Neale Report', paper presented at the National Art Education Association conference, Detroit, 28 March. WYGANT, FOSTER (1983), *Art in American Schools in the Nineteenth Century* (Cincinnati, Interwood Press/NAEA).

2 STANKIEWICZ, MARY ANN (1984), '"The Eye is a Nobler Organ": Ruskin and American Art Education', *Journal of Aesthetic Education*, 18, pp. 51–64. And STANKIEWICZ, MARY ANN (1985), 'A Picture Age: Reproductions in Picture Study', *Studies in Art Education*, 26, pp. 86–92.

3 Stuart Macdonald has described how Henry Cole dealt with the problem of finding sufficient prints and casts for students to copy, and how Cole made provision for those at a distance from London to see works from the South Kensington collection through the Travelling Museum and by means of photographs and electrotypes. See MACDONALD, STUART (1970), *History and Philosophy of Art Education* (London, London University Press).

4 MACDONALD (n. 3), pp. 180–1.

5 For examples of this point of view see the debate between the German-American chromolithographer Louis Prang and the *New York Tribune* art critic Clarence Cook over the value of chromo facsimiles reprinted in PRANG, L. (1868), *Prang's Chromo* 1, 2, April 1868, pp. 2–3; criticism of the chromo by GODKIN, E. L. (1870), 'Autotypes and Oleographs', *The Nation* 10 November 1870, pp. 317–8; and arguments over the place of casts in the new building for the Boston Museum of Fine Arts *c.* 1903–4, Reel 2493, Archives of American Art, Boston Museum of Fine Arts. The idea that highly imitative art forms appeal to less sophisticated viewers such as women and young girls has been attributed to Michelangelo by PANOFSKY, ERWIN (1971), *Early Netherlandish Painting*, Vol. 1 (New York, Harper & Row), p. 2.

6 For an example of the educational view of casts from the history of the Boston Museum of Fine Arts see HARRIS, NEIL (1962), 'The Gilded Age Revisited: Boston and the Museum Movement', *American Quarterly*, 14, pp. 545–66.

7 BLEEKE-BYRNE, GABRIELE (1984), 'The Education of the Painter in the Workshop' in *Children of Mercury: the Education of Artists in the C16th and C17th* (Providence RI, Rice University Department of Art), p. 35.

8 MACDONALD (n. 3), p. 189.

9 HICKS, MARY DANA (1984), 'Does Art Study Concern the Public Schools?', *Proceedings of the International Congress of Education of the World's Columbian Exposition, Chicago, July 25–28, 1893* (Boston, National Education Association), pp. 490–1.

10 CLARKE, ISAAC EDWARDS (1885), *Art and Industry, Part 1: Drawing in Public Schools* (Washington DC, Govt. Printing Office).

11 Art historians too have often preferred to use photographs to study iconography or to analyse details in the process of recreating an artistic personality. See BROWN, DAVID ALAN (1979), *Berenson and Connoisseurship of Italian Painting* (Washington DC, Nat. Gallery of Art).

12 CLARKE (n. 10), p. clxvii.

13 VEBLEN, THORSTEIN (1926), *The Theory of the Leisure Class* (New York, Vanguard). On the Aesthetic movement see: BURKE, DOREEN BOLGER *et al.* (1987), *In Pursuit of Beauty: Americans and the Aesthetic Movement* (New York, Metropolitan Museum of Art).

14 Catharine Beecher and her sister Harriet Beecher Stowe told American women how to furnish a parlour for $80, 25 per cent of which could be spent

on reproductions 'of really admirable pictures of some of our best American artists'. See BEECHER and STOWE (1869), *The American Woman's Home* (New York, J. B. Ford & Co.), p. 81.

15   SIGOURNEY, LYDIA H. (1840), 'On the Perception of the Beautiful', *The Common School Journal*, 2, 6, March 1840, p. 84.

16   Not only was Walter Smith hired to implement the new Massachusetts drawing law in 1870, but both Boston and New York established what would become major museums in the same year.

17   BURRAGE, SEVERANCE and HENRY TURNER BAILEY (1899), *School Sanitation and Decoration* (Boston, Heath).

18   Although inexpensive chromolithographed, coloured facsimiles of paintings were available throughout the late C19th, they were usually not judged suitable for school use. See STANKIEWICZ, 'Picture Age' (n. 2).

19   Use of pictures and objects in the education of children was a notable part of the plans for educational reform introduced by Comenius in the Seventeenth century. See ALPERS, SVETLANA (1983), *The Art of Describing* (Chicago, Chicago University Press), pp. 93–9.

20   WYGANT (n. 1), p. 79.

21   See ASHWIN, CLIVE (1981), 'Pestalozzi and the Origins of Pedagogical Drawing', *British Journal of Educational Studies*, 29, 2, June 1981, pp. 138–51.

22   DEARBORN, N. H. (1925), *The Oswego Movement in American Education* (New York, Teachers College, Columbia University).

23   DICKENS, CHARLES (1961), *Hard Times* (New York, New American Library), pp. 13–14.

24   The *Toynbee Record* (1893), quoted in MEACHAM, STANDISH, *Toynbee Hall and Social Reform 1880–1914* (New Haven and London, Yale University Press), p. 55.

25   BORZELLO, FRANCIS (1980), 'Pictures for the People' in NADEL, I. B. and F. S. SCHWARTZBACH (eds), *Victorian Artists and the City* (New York, Pergamon).

26   *The Spectator* (1884) quoted in BRIGGS, ASA and ANNE MACARTNEY (1984), *Toynbee Hall: the First Hundred Years* (London, Routledge & Kegan Paul), p. 21.

27   MACCARTHY, KATHLEEN D. (1882), *Noblesse Oblige: Charity and Cultural Philanthropy in Chicago 1849–1929* (Chicago, Chicago University Press).

28   FULLER, HENRY BLAKE (1897), 'The Upward Movement in Chicago', *Atlantic Monthly*, 80, pp. 334–547.

29   BLAIR, KAREN (1980), *The Clubwoman as Feminist: True Womanhood Redefined 1868–1917* (New York, Holmes and Meier), p. 118.

30   On the feminisation of culture see DOUGLAS, ANN (1977), *The Feminization of American Culture* (New York, Knopf). For an early twentieth-century view see BARNES, EARL (1912), 'The Feminizing of Culture', *Atlantic Monthly*, 109, June 1912, pp. 770–6. For relationships between urban life, moral reform movements and the growth of feminism see BERG, BARBARA J. (1978), *The Remembered Gate: Origins of American Feminism: the Woman and the City 1800–1860* (London and New York, Oxford University Press). The phrase 'social homemaking' is used by MATTHAEI, JULIE A. (1982), *An Economic History of Women in America* (New York, Schocken), p. 173. For a discussion of change in women's roles in the late nineteenth century see ROTHMAN, SHEILA M. (1978), *Woman's Proper Place* (New York, Basic Books).

31   STANKIEWICZ, MARY ANN (1988), 'Art Education at Hull House, 1889–1901' (unpub. paper), NAEA Conference, Los Angeles, 8 April 1988.

32   ADDAMS, JANE (1895), 'The Art-Work done by Hull House, Chicago', *The Forum*, 19, July 1895, pp. 615–6.

33   (1891) 'Chicago's Toynbee Hall', *Chicago Tribune* 21 June 1891; Jane Addams Memorial College, University of Illinois at Chicago Circle. Research

at Chicago was supported in part by a grant from the Spencer Foundation.

34 For contemporary recognition that museums are class-related see EISNER, ELLIOT W. and STEPHEN DOBBS (1988), 'Silent Pedagogy: How Museums help Visitors Experience Exhibitions', *Art Education*, 41, 4, July 1988, pp. 6–15.

35 COOK, E. T. and A. WEDDERBURN (eds) (1907), *The Works of John Ruskin*, Vol. 29 (London, George Allen), p. 216.

36 FEIN, ALBERT (1970), 'The American City: the Ideal and the Real' in KAUFMANN Jr, E. (ed.), *The Rise of American Architecture* (New York, Praeger), p. 80.

37 RUSKIN, *Works* Vol. 29 (n. 35), p. 214. For a discussion of Horsfall's contribution to a synthesis of Utilitarian and Romantic approaches to town planning see REYNOLDS, JOSEPHINE P. (1952), 'Thomas Coglan Horsfall and the Town Planning Movement in England', *Town Planning Review*, 22, pp. 52–60.

38 See HARRISON, MICHAEL (1985), 'Art and Philanthropy: T. C. Horsfall and the Manchester Art Museum' in KIDD, ALAN J. and K. W. ROBERTS (eds), *City, Class and Culture* (Manchester, Manchester University Press), pp. 120–47. For an account of student reactions to the museum in its later years, as well as extensive quotation from Horsfall on the function of his museum, see (1925) 'The Manchester Art Museum: the Story of an Educational Experiment', *The Beacon*, 3, pp. 41–51.

39 For a contemporary version of the argument that knowledge of visual art is necessary to full understanding of language and literature see BROUDY, HARRY (1987), *The Role of Imagery in Learning*, Occasional Paper 1 (Los Angeles, Getty Center for Education in the Arts).

40 STARR, ELLEN GATES (n.d.) 'The Use of Pictures in Education and the Manchester [England] System', *loc. cit.* (n. 33).

41 Papers of the Chicago Public School Art Society, University of Illinois at Chicago Circle.

42 One socialist labour leader argued that children of the working class must have access to art education and other subjects typically reserved for wealthier students in order to rise above mechanical obedience to employers. See HOGAN, DAVID JOHN (1985), *Class and Reform: School and Society in Chicago 1880–1930* (Philadelphia, University of Pennsylvania Press), pp. 99–100.

43 Newspaper clippings, Box 21, Folder 267, *Ellen Gates Starr Papers*, Sophia Smith Collection, Smith College, Northhampton, Mass. Research in the Sophia Smith College was supported by a grant from the University of Maine *Women in the Curriculum* programme.

44 RUSKIN, *Works*, Vol. 29 (n. 35), p. 217.

45 Minutes, Box 4, Folder 2, CPSAS Papers (n. 41).

46 For an overview of the ideas of the City Beautiful see WILSON, RICHARD GUY (1979), 'The Great Civilization' in *The American Renaissance 1876–1917* (Brooklyn, Brooklyn Museum), pp. 87–92.

47 CLARKE, Part II (n. 10), p. 722.

48 HOROWITZ, HELEN LEFKOWITZ (1976), *Culture and the City: Cultural philanthropy in Chicago from the 1880s to 1917* (Lexington, University Press of Kentucky).

49 See the comments of Miss Bailey of the Doreck College in CLARKE, Part II (n. 10), p. 725.

50 Report of the Chicago Public School Art Society, March 1896, CPSAS Papers (n. 41).

51 BERGER, JOHN (1972), *Ways of Seeing* (Harmondsworth, Penguin/BBC).

52 SCUDDER, VIDA D. (1903), *A Listener in Babel* (Boston, Houghton Mifflin), p. 235.

Chapter Five

KERRY FREEDMAN Structure and Transformation in Art Education: the Enlightenment Project and the Institutionalisation of Nature

Educational history includes the consideration of how concepts become institutionalised. It is important to consider how our beliefs, ideas and interests become part of the foundations of schooling because once they are institutionalised, they are recontextualised. They are no longer only a part of daily life, they are codified and become symbols for action and frameworks for new categories and organisations. Institutionalisation is a historical and cultural process. Even when the time seems relatively short, the assumptions and activities of institutionalisation are conditions of history. These assumptions and activities are part of a transformation of consciousness or mentality within a social structure which maintains constancy. This chapter will explore these characteristics of institutionalisation in order to provide an argument for the social construction of our most basic assumptions about nature and culture in art education.

History, change and constancy

A tradition of mainstream western history has been to focus upon individuals and events [1]. Historical writing has represented certain individuals as having control over larger political, economic and social situations as well as the occurrences of their lives. It has been assumed that people do certain things at particular times that 'change the course of history' and that those actions are in some way isolated from the rest of time. Actions and events are viewed as bits of time, independent of the social and historical frameworks that made them possible, and outside the cultural medium which suspends them.

The French historical school, the *Annales*, represents history in a different way. From this perspective, time is multi-layered and hierarchical, but not in the traditional sense. History is represented as having three layers or lengths of time that impinge on each other: a short period of time, which might be thought of as the time of actions or events; a middle length of time called a *conjuncture* which may be a decade to a half century in length, and the *long durations*, which are centuries and the eras of culture. Contrary to the mainstream perspective, the long durations are viewed as the most important layers of history because they provide the *structures* within which the others may occur. *Annales* historian Fernand Braudel [2] describes the long durations as locating history in a geographical context, and focuses upon a natural foundation for the development of culture. For Braudel, how we survive in relation to our physical needs, geography and the other conditions of our environment determines cultural structures. Therefore the event, or time of an individual's actions, is of least importance when understanding social life.

This perspective of history is helpful in understanding change, but rather than starting with the geographical conditions of structure to analyse art education, we may focus upon the social aspects of structure and what leads to institutionalisation. To consider institutionalisation in relation to social life, we must look at the traditions and tensions that occur as part of the overlapping of conjuncture and structure. Structure dictates constancy over time and place; it provides us with, and is reflected in, collective subjectivities or ways of thinking. Conjunctures contain changing ways of thinking about various dimensions of structure.

For these reasons, we must focus attention away from change as a 'natural' process and a generalisable condition and on to the transformation and use of a particular, cultural and historical discourse. The transformation occurs within a medium of social structure and the *structure* provides for and directs social transformation through discourse.

If we accept the importance of the peculiarities of time and place to social transformation, what within structure directs the process of institutionalisation? Sociologist Anthony Giddens [3] distinguishes between the notions of *structure* and *system*, defining 'structure' as deep and unobservable, and 'system' as surface and apparent. Institutions are a type of system, and like other systems they are behavioural models of the structures to which they belong. However, this theory does not stop the question [4]. The explanatory character of social and historical contexts, for example, the conceptions and uses of nature and culture in institutions, is diminished in Giddens's definition because they become simply patterns of behaviour. To understand institutionalisation in our culture, we must make it problematic. We must look upon our culture as an anthropologist looks at other cultures, as peculiar and informative. We must explore the sources of our structural context. In the next section, one vital source, the Enlightenment, will be considered.

The Enlightenment project: a structure for contemporary discourse

An understanding of contemporary change within a historical and cultural context may begin by focusing upon the project of the Enlightenment. A philosophical debate emerged in Europe during the seventeenth and eighteenth centuries about the character of knowledge which focused upon the attributes of nature and culture. The Enlightened perspective involved a conception of natural knowledge which had been thought masked by corrupt clergy and greedy aristocracy. It was newly believed that these authorities had constructed culture artificially and imposed it upon 'the individual' in order to maintain their positions of power. The politics of the debate focused upon the new idea that men had natural civil rights including a right to knowledge and freedom from political oppression. The Enlightenment project was to support the idea that men were freewilled and able to control their own destiny. The Enlightened man was to act progressively to improve society and to maintain individual freedom. The French Revolution and other responses to authoritarian regimes placed tradition in crisis by representing in vivid form the cultural character of politics and social arrangements.

In contrast to culture, which was assumed to be based on interests and beliefs, enlightened knowledge was considered disinterested and rational. Science focused more upon logic than empiricism because it was thought that men naturally thought logically. As scholars have recently pointed out, there were various conflicts in the Enlightenment project, which have remained part of the structure of our thought [5]. There has been a profound disillusionment voiced internationally about the limitations of reason and the new technologies of control which the enlightened vision provided in the name of natural freedom.

Consider the contradictions in the assumptions of progress and humanism in the enlightened view of women's place in nature and culture. Enlightened knowledge was not for women. The conception of nature was vital to the ways in which reason and culture were represented in relation to women. Women presented a dilemma for enlightened thought because, at one level, women were believed to be both more natural (which was better) and more uncivilised (which was worse) than men. This was thought proven by, for example, women's natural ability and assumed desire to give birth and their continual irrational and emotionally unstable state. On another level, women were supposed to socialise the natural man so that he could live in a communal situation which was newly thought opposed to his natural tendencies, but was necessary in civilised society [6]. A woman was to provide a family and home which would be dependent on a man, but also make him dependent upon her [7]. Boys and girls were to be educated differently to take on these particular roles, and children were thought of as men and women in miniature.

The example of contradictions in the structure of gender relationships may be thought of as providing support for the structuralist approach to social transformation. The individual was represented as an agent of change. To move away from the authority of the aristocracy and the clergy, each person was to be a free actor. The idea of naturally freewilled individuals contained conflict because only a certain type of person was to be considered an individual. Being an individual meant something different for different races, classes and genders.

Discourse as historical and cultural convergence

Recently, social theory has taken a perspective on change that is derived from French structuralism and post-structuralist analysis. This vision of change rejects the essentialism and logocentrism of the traditional approach to history and brings the notion of the subject as initiator of change into question [8]. From this perspective, the subject is de-centred; there is either no subject or there are groups or collective subjectivities located in certain positions in the social structure, none of which completely controls social change.

Michel Foucault, for example, is not concerned with the subject as actor [9]. Rather, he focuses upon sites of contestation in the control of knowledge and discourse. Although discourse maintains structure, and therefore promotes constancy, power arrangements shift and new social patterns emerge through discourse. Groups are excluded or included through discursive practices and those with little power are given new legitimacy by adopting a 'legitimate' discourse.

Another perspective which shifts attention from the subject views social transformation as emanating from cultural contradictions, such as those of gender discussed earlier. The primary theoretical framework providing this alternative to the traditional theory of historical change is structural marxism [10]. The debate focuses upon the notion of structure as being deterministic, where internal contradictions provide reasons for change, versus the notion that individual agents take voluntary action. From this Marxist perspective, change is determined by the economic relations of production and the proletariat is the revolutionary agent. Jurgen Habermas's theory of communicative action [11] represents social transformation as a function of linguistic structure and moral development. From this perspective, the cultural contradictions have not always been in place because they have been produced by, as well as produce, crises in advanced industrial countries which have developed complex rationalities of economic organisation [12].

The argument supporting an understanding of social transformation as crises resulting from contradictions in long-standing structures will be helpful in the discussion of art education in the following sections.

A shift in focus to systems and discourse
There is currently a debate about the relationship of individuals to structure in history [13]. Agency assumes that there are individuals who have power and who intend and act freely, independent of structural restrictions. The debate about structure and agency focuses upon the problem of de-centring the individual while maintaining the belief that what we do improves our lives. The notion of agency is problematic because we live within rule-based systems which reflect and direct collective mentalities, not our own personal being. Actions are made conceptually possible before they become reality; that is, transformation occurs through a redefinition of self which is brought on by discursive conflict. A collective subjectivity directs individuals, so that by the time they act, transformation has already begun.

The notion of agency includes the assumption that the interests and actions of individuals serve some progressive purpose and will improve their situation. However, the assumptions of progress are problematic because what improves a situation for one group often worsens it for another; people do not often know or agree upon what will be an improvement. Further, the outcomes of actions do not fulfil their purposes; actions produce unintended, and often undesirable, results. As well as beginning before an event, transformations continue past events and individuals into conflicts and oppositions to the original intent. Regardless of our actions and intentions, meanings are developed that we do not control. Discourse has a life of its own which is not tied to original intent [14].

Another perspective of the debate about structure and agency is discussed by Giddens who represents structure and agency as a duality (rather than a dualism) [15]. For Giddens, agency is inherent to structure rather than in contrast to it. Social transformation reflects values and meanings which emerge through systemic experience within structure. We do not construct meaning personally, arbitrarily or through free-will. We are bound by the way we describe ourselves and the way others describe us.

Foucault has provided an understanding of how historical representations of human beings have become mechanisms of control [16]. Foucault discusses the human sciences as being constructed through an interplay of discursive relations. Discursive practices govern action by providing structures of rationality which make certain thoughts and activities reasonable. What counts as truth is determined by the discursive relations of a particular discipline, which are shaped over time, but also exist as somewhat independent of the meanings assigned to the words and practices of any particular time.

To apply the above argument to art education, a summary is necessary:

1. Social transformations, such as institutionalisation, occur within a particular historical and cultural context. The transformation is discursive. That is, it is tied to a system of symbols and codes which result in continually redefined concepts and structural relocations.

2. Transformations, including institutionalisation, do not occur as the result of an individual or event in sequential time. Rather, time is non-linear in that we continue to exist within structures we study as the past, and our 'reforms' are only reflections of possibilities that already exist. For example, recent educational reforms reflect and legitimate social and political circumstances that have already become part of public life [17]. At present, in the United States' cultural mainstream, we remain immersed in the structure of the Enlightenment.

3. The process of institutionalisation, and what becomes institutionalised (part of which is the process), includes crises resulting from contradictions in social structure. Contradictions of the Enlightenment project are reflected in distinctions we make between nature and culture, male and female and self and others. The meanings attached to these words change and represent oppositions which are discursive, not 'natural' or 'real'.

4. In art education, as in other areas, the crises in our conceptions of nature and culture have become part of practice. The depth of the crises has been demonstrated in our field by historical study. For example, historical accounts of art education, such as those which focus on the antecedents of the current reform movement [18], and what the reform movement has responded to [19], reveal tensions in our field that reflect and reproduce the structure of our society.

In the next section, I will examine some historical uses of gender and art activities for young children. These uses of gender reflect contradictions in the conception of knowledge, human rights, and a natural self which emerged during the Enlightenment.

Conceptions of gender and Enlightened knowledge in early childhood art education

I will summarise by focusing upon a debate about nature and culture which emerged during the Enlightenment. The debate produced, as well as reflected, political and social crises. The idea of human rights emerged in response to social control by the church and aristocracy. The authoritative power of these institutions, which was previously assumed a divine right and considered the natural order of things, was challenged by a new conception of nature which represented men as free and previous authorities as unnatural, cultural traditions.

Jean Jacques Rousseau articulated the new view of nature, and a perspective of education, parts of which became institutionalised. His conception of a natural educational process contained conflicting depictions of society and the self. For example, Rousseau believed that nature had been corrupted by social change which had reduced the differences between men and women. Rousseau assumed that the sexual attractiveness of women to men was based on their social differentiation. To reduce those differences was a threat to society [20].

Rousseau believed that men naturally seek an existence independent of social relationships and considered the arrangements of a family unit inherently unnatural. The socialisation of men was considered unnatural but necessary to transform them into good citizens. This was the responsibility of women. Women were to socialise men by becoming dependent upon them, and by making men dependent upon women, thus establishing an interdependence Rousseau believed to be the foundation of society. For this process to occur, Rousseau maintained that women must be as different from, and as attractive to, men as possible.

To promote gender differences, boys and girls were to be educated differently. In *Emile*, Rousseau described an education that would protect boys from socialising forces until it was appropriate for romantic love to emerge. Both genders were to develop an understanding of the 'natural' tendencies of men to be independent and of women to be social and the carriers of culture.

Education was determined by what was natural to children, but the conception of nature was peculiar to the purposes it served. Knowledge was thought derived from things rather than people. Adults were assumed to create illusion through cultural devices such as language and art. Hence, young children were not to be taught how to read and write. While taught how to draw, Emile was 'not so much to imitate objects as to know them' [21]. He was not to study adult art, or copy drawings, the common practice for learning how to draw. For Rousseau, adult art was to enhance romantic love and define sexual roles [22]. Adult art was, in this sense unnatural, and therefore inappropriate for boys to see. Boys

74

were to learn to draw by observing natural objects and not to connect the activity of drawing to social life.

Many of the ideas reflected in these eighteenth-century perspectives of natural development were contained within nineteenth-century educational methods for young children. The conceptions of nature and knowledge represented in Rousseau's philosophy were fundamental to early kindergartens. Young children were to acquire knowledge of natural physical laws through a mystical and object-centred education [23]. Objects represented the physical laws' spiritual essence of the world. Through the manipulation of certain objects, children were to learn about what was basic in nature, and therefore what was basic in themselves. Through activities, such as sewing, constructing, and painting, children were not only to apprehend a certain conception of nature in general, but to reveal what was believed to be naturally within children.

Froebel claimed that he learned about educating young children by observing motherhood. All of nature was assumed in harmony with child development, and according to Froebel, education naturally required attributes of mothering in teachers. The women trained as kindergarten teachers were from upper-class homes and were expected to have the best 'natural' tendencies of motherhood. The training was to prepare young women with appropriate moral values. Inherent in the thesis that women were best qualified to educate young children, was the assumption that girls and young women were to be trained to reflect the 'natural' female role of maintaining the family unit.

The move of kindergarten methods to public elementary schools in the United States during the nineteenth century was part of a larger social shift which responded to cultural contradictions. A particularly important reform was the growing women's movement. Even in the early nineteenth century, the United States was a particularly favourable place to apply the eighteenth-century notion of human rights to women [24].

Through the women's movement, charity and public school kindergartens were used as a way of solving what were represented as social problems of immigration and industrialisation. Urban poor and European immigrants were thought threats to the 'natural' and democratic foundations of the United States [25]. The adoption of Froebel's system in public schools was viewed by some as a menace because it was formulated in European culture. Others saw kindergarten as promoting urban reform through a focus on individualism as well as social adjustment. Kindergarten in the United States was to instil national values in both girls and boys.

However, the contradictions of culture were apparent in the conception of individualism as it related to gender and family. While the family of the citizen was considered a valuable agent for instilling democratic ideals, there was a faith that public schooling could provide an escape from the socio-economic confines of family. Through a focus upon man's 'natural' right to freedom, which in the United States included economic competitiveness and personal drive, men could rise above a birth of low status through hard work; women could only improve their life through marriage.

Cultural contradictions were also evident in the demand for girls to have access to the education boys had received. Concurrently, women reformers sought to make schooling more humane by using the more 'maternal' kindergarten techniques and educational activities used before only with girls. Education was then criticised, because of the growing number of women teachers and students, for being too soft on boys who needed to develop strong characters.

Nature and social differences in educational science
Kindergarten art-making activities became common in other grade levels of schooling in the United States. As the activities became part of public schooling, they were influenced by scientific interpretations of child development. The activities lost their mystical quality and some of the aura of maternalism and became part of child study developmental testing.

Child study psychology maintained an enlightened perspective of human nature. The psychologists believed that human potential was determined by natural law. However, there were contradictions in this belief. Since human potential was assumed determined by nature, it was difficult to argue scientifically that people were free to improve their lives and that education could help. Eugenics, which was considered scientific at the time, supported the belief that natural potentials for intelligence and socio-economic success were determined by biological characteristics of gender and race. Ephemeral qualities like human will, individual drive and good character had to be evoked to explain differences within groups and to provide the possibility for schools to aid growth.

As a result, psychology was used in school to control students and teachers [26]. The scientific results of tests were used to differentiate groups and diagnose individuals as deficient. Psychologists sought to control curriculum development because measurement was considered beyond the capabilities of teachers. As child study psychology began to direct educational practice, the scientific conception of a child's natural self was internalised by children and accepted by adults.

The psychologists believed that the natural qualities of children would be discovered through quantitative tests and that scientifically established norms of development would improve schooling. 'Discovering' the natural characteristics of 'the normal child' through quantitative methods of research meant that normality would be tested, abnormalities would be revealed and children could be ranked in relation to the norm.

Shaped by child study, art education was consistent with the general socialisation purposes of public schooling in the United States [27]. Schooling was to prepare students with skills for work, to control and socialise those deficient in character and to maintain an environment for natural development to take place in those who would excel naturally. Public schooling was to be designed to give middle-class boys the best opportunities because they were thought naturally superior to other groups and would control the future of the nation [28].

Unlike Rousseau's conception of childhood, which represented boys as living in harmony with nature and girls as being socialised to serve certain purposes, the scientific conception of education allowed both boys and girls to develop 'naturally'. However, 'natural' development was limited to a range of norms presented as scientifically determined but laden with social meaning. It was assumed that boys and girls would naturally develop at different rates and that girls' potentials were inferior to boys'.

The differences between boys and girls were thought revealed through drawing tests. The tests became diagnostic tools for determining young children's personality traits as well as cognitive development: in a summary of drawing research, G. Stanley Hall reported that:

> boys distinctly excel girls of the same age. The latter more rarely
> draw figures in motion and still less often attempt humorous
> themes, are better in conventional classroom courses, but inferior in
> originality [29].

In turn of the century United States, which was generally anti-intellectual but valued innovation, girls were slighted even when they excelled.

By the 1940s, the perspective had not changed in developmental psychology; what was 'natural' to boys was valued and what was 'natural' to girls was not. Boys' drawings were viewed as efficient; containing no extraneous marks, wasted movements or time. Girls made more details and 'extraneous' objects [30]. Boys' efficiency was interpreted as resulting in drawings which displayed a selection of only the essential, rational elements of objects and greater capacity for rational abstraction, thought important in maintaining control of the social world.

In the twentieth century, there has been a strong undercurrent moving toward a reduction in gender differentiation in schooling. However, contradictions in the manner in which the reduction has been institutionalised has created other problems. One way gender differentiation has been reduced has been to focus on 'the individual'. This is a social ideal that discursively shifts attention away from the special opportunities for certain social groups and allows the areas maintaining discrimination to remain hidden.

A second shift in focus has been the conception of a natural democratic personality as being a particular national agenda. Art education after the Second World War sought the development of a democratic personality, as a reaction to national fears of totalitarianism and preparation for a new international role for the United States [31]. Developing the democratic personality in all school children through art was thought vital in a world divisively imposing unhealthy, anti-democratic principles.

The institutionalisation of nature as a scientific concept, as in earlier conceptions of nature, was to socialise children. Part of the socialisation was to adopt a certain gender role and conception of self as located within the boundaries of prevailing definitions. What was stated as natural remained a culturally constructed set of meanings attached to a discourse that has been part of the Enlightenment project from its beginning.

Conclusion

To become conscious of the 'absent totality,' or what unconsciously shapes our professional practice, may provide a way of understanding what we do. We may be able to develop that sense of awareness by studying past political purposes of education, projects of reform, and the ways intentions have been played out. It takes a complex analysis to see the larger, social and historical picture and to place ourselves within it.

The current reform movement is a good example of the problem because it has reinforced some of the dichotomies that have been with us since the Enlightenment. A fundamental contradiction is the assumed dichotomy between nature and culture. Rightly, the current reform seeks to move away from the focus upon the 'natural' child because it is both an illusion and excludes most social knowledge. However, wrongly, the reform maintains a sharp contrast between what is natural and social in a large sense, and what is defined as cultural by art community professions.

Like Giddens's notion of structure and agency, we must look at both nature and culture as constructed and transformed discursively. They are not real in an eternal sense; they are representations of two facets of the same structure that have been used to facilitate the institutional agendas of certain groups, while reproducing cultural contradictions that made their conceptualisation possible.

Notes and References

1   BRAUDEL, F. (1969, 1980), *On History* (Chicago, Chicago University Press), trans. Sarah Matthews.
2   *Ibid.*
3   GIDDENS, A. (1987), *Social Theory and Modern Sociology* (Stanford, Stanford University Press).
4   LAYDER, D. (1985), 'Power, Structure and Agency', *Journal for the Theory of Social Behavior*, 15, 2; pp. 131–49 (p. 142).
5   See BERGER, P., B. BERGER and H. KELLNER (1973), *The Homeless Mind* (New York, Vintage Books).
6   ROUSSEAU, J. J. (1762), 1979) *Emile, or on Education* (New York, Basic Books), trans. A. Bloom.
7   For an excellent analysis of conceptions of gender roles and sexuality in the eighteenth century, and particularly Rousseau's beliefs, see SCHWARTZ, J. (1984), *The Sexual Politics of Jean Jacques Rousseau* (Chicago, Chicago University Press).
8   ARONOWITZ, S. and H. GIROUX (1985), 'Radical Education and Transformative Intellectuals', *Canadian Journal of Political and Social Theory*, 9, 3, Fall, pp. 48–63.
9   DREYFUS, H. L. and P. RABINOW (1983), *Michel Foucault: Beyond Structuralism and Hermeneutics* (2nd ed.) (Chicago, Chicago University Press).
10 ALTHUSSER, L. and E. BALIBAR (1986) *Reading Capital* (London, New Left Books).
11 HABERMAS, J. (1979), *Communication and the Evolution of Society* (Boston, Beacon Press). See also HABERMAS, J. (1984), *A Theory of Communicative Action* (Boston, Beacon Press).
12 HABERMAS, J. (1976), *Legitimation Crisis* (Boston, Beacon Press).
13 PORPORA, D. V. (1985), 'The Role of Agency in History: the Althusser-Thompson-Anderson Debate', *Current Perspectives in Social Theory*, 6, pp. 219–41.

14 FOUCAULT, M. (1972), *The Archaeology of Knowledge* (New York, Harper Colophon) trans. A. M. Sheridan Smith.

15 GIDDENS (n. 3).

16 FOUCAULT (n. 14). See also FOUCAULT, M. (1970), *The Order of Things: an Archaeology of the Human Sciences* (New York, Vintage Books).

17 POPKEWITZ, T. S., A. PITMAN and A. BARRY (1986), 'Educational Reform and its Millennial Quality: the 1980s', *Journal of Curriculum Studies* 18, 3; pp. 267–84. See also WESTBURY, I. (1984), Review of *A Nation at Risk*, *Journal of Curriculum Studies*, 16, 4; pp. 431–45.

18 For example, see EFLAND, A. (1987), 'Curriculum Antecedents of Dis- cipline-Based Art Education', *Journal of Aesthetic Education*, 21, 2; pp. 57–94. See also KERN, E. J. (1987), 'Antecedents of Discipline-Based Art Education: State Departments of Education Curriculum Documents', *Journal of Aesthetic Education*, 21, 2; pp. 35–56.

19 See for example (i) FREEDMAN, K. (1987), 'Art Education as Social Pro- duction: Culture, Society and Politics in the Formation of Curriculum' in POPKEWITZ, T. S. (ed.) (1987), *The Formation of School Subjects: the Struggle for Creating an American Institution* (London, Falmer Press); (ii) FREEDMAN, K. (1987), 'Art Education and Changing Political Agendas: an Analysis of Curriculum Concerns of the 1940s and 1950s', *Studies in Art Education*, 29, 1, pp. 17–29; (iii) KORZENIK, D. (1981) 'Is Children's Work Art? Some Historical Views', *Art Education*, 34, 5, pp. 20–4; (iv) DUNCUM, P. (1982), 'The Origins of Self-Expression: a Case of Self-Deception', *Art Education*, 35, 5, pp. 32–5.

20 ROUSSEAU (n. 6). See also SCHWARTZ (n. 7).

21 ROUSSEAU (n. 6), p. 144.

22 SCHWARTZ (n. 7).

23 FROEBEL, F. (1967), 'The Education of Man' in LILLEY, I. M., *Friedrich Froebel: a Selection from his Writings* (Cambridge, Cambridge University Press).

24 CURTL, M. (1935), *The Social Ideas of American Educators* (New York, Scribner).

25 See for example HANDLIN, O. (1974), *The Uprooted: the Epic Story of the Great Migrations that made the American People* (2nd ed.) (Boston, Atlantic Monthly Press).

26 O'DONNELL, J. (1985), *The Origins of Behaviorism: American Psychology* (New York, New York University).

27 FREEDMAN (i) (n. 19). See also FREEDMAN, K. and T. S. POPKEWITZ (1988), 'Art Education and Social Interests in the Development of American Schooling: Ideological Origins of Curriculum Theory', *Journal of Curriculum Studies*, 20, 5, pp. 387–405.

28 HALL, G. S. (1907), 'Education: a Life-Long Development', *Chautauguan*, 47, pp. 150–6.

29 HALL, G. S. (1911), *Educational Problems*, Vol. 2 (New York, Appleton) p. 496.

30 GESELL, A. (1940), *The First Five Years of Life: a Guide to the Study of the Preschool Child* (New York, Harper).

31 FREEDMAN (ii) (n. 19).

Chapter Six

STUART MACDONALD Newbery and 'The Four': a School for Europe

A shock from north of the Border

It is undeniable that from 1900 to 1914 the Glasgow School of Art had a reputation in Europe such as no other British school of art has ever had. Firstly, students there had actually initiated a design style; secondly, its headmaster collaborated with a brilliant pupil to produce the most revolutionary public building of its time; thirdly, it was associated with the Glasgow School of Painters. Let us return to Saturday, 5 October 1896 to trace the School's sudden rise to fame. . . .

The visitors dismounting from their carriages in Regent Street, London, on that fateful day paused in front of the New Gallery, arrested by the words 'Death of William Morris' screaming from the bills of the evening papers. Another visual trauma awaited them at the private view of the Arts and Crafts Exhibition Society. Within the Gallery was a small collection of posters, murals, metalwork, furniture and needlework by some young products of the Glasgow School of Art, two of them mere lassies.

Brother of the mighty Art-Workers' Guild turned against brother. Most raged outwardly that the works were based on no traditional principle of design, but raged inwardly that they were artistic. Some brothers insisted that the young Glasgow rebels had copied the Japanese. 'Can it be that the bogiest of bogie books by Hokusai has influenced their weird travesties of humanity?' asked Aymer Vallance. One brother insisted on Egyptian, then recanted after a visit to the Museum. Others argued the malignant influence was Aubrey Beardsley, 'Daubrey Weirdsley,' as they called him. Some remembered that the public were inclined to regard the Arts and Crafts exhibitions as attempts to revive the aesthetic craze 'which born in *Punch* died in *Patience*,' and feared that the weird Glasgow group would confirm that prejudice.

> Probably nothing in the gallery has provoked more decided censure than these various exhibits, [wrote Aymer Vallance in *The Studio*] and that fact alone should cause a thoughtful observer of art to pause before he joins the opponents. If the said artists do not come very prominently forward as leaders of a school of design peculiarly their own, we shall be much mistaken [1].

The four young designers who gave chief offence were C. R. Mackintosh, J. H. MacNair, and the Macdonald sisters. Talvin Morris gave a little. Mrs F. H. Newbery gave none – her embroideries were spirited work but closer to the Morris tradition.

Gleeson White, editor of *The Studio*, disagreed with his brethren of the Art-Workers' Guild. He was so intrigued with the Glasgow movement that he crossed the border to investigate its source. Naturally he intended to call on Francis Newbery, headmaster of the Glasgow School of Art.

Before Newbery

In *History and Philosophy of Art Education* I abandoned my Glasgow diggings at the year 1863 when Charles Heath Wilson was forcibly 'retired' due to Henry Cole's machinations, leaving behind him a large residue of casts. Robert Greenlees, a landscape painter, took over in that same year, at which time the School's great accumulation of youth and Antique was still crammed into the Assembly Rooms in Ingram St. Six years later the title 'The Glasgow School of Art and Haldane Academy' was adopted as a condition for receiving contributions from the trustees of James Haldane, the Glasgow engraver. Classrooms for instructing the 1,164 pupils were then established at 3 Rose St where the School remained for the next thirty years.

If you gang west from Buchanan St along the north pavement of Sauchiehall St you presently find yourself outside a bonnie store by the name of Trerons. Interrupting its façade is the central doorway of the McLellan Galleries topped by the grey bust of young Victoria, the work of John Mossman, erstwhile modelling master of the School of Art. The façade fronts the block bordered by Rose St, Renfrew St, and Dalhousie St, the block known as Corporation Buildings. Into this block the School moved in 1869 to remain until the opening of the Mackintosh building in 1899. It was here that The Four studied and achieved their style; here that Gleeson White interviewed Newbery; here also that Sir John Lavery RA commenced his art career.

In 1856 Glasgow Corporation had purchased this block, which contained the McLellan galleries, dwelling houses, and ground-floor shops from the estate of Bailie Archie McLellan, along with his art collection, thus establishing the Corporation Galleries of Art. In 1869 the School of Art and Academy was granted the whole of the eastern section over the shops with an opening on to Rose St.

Sir John Lavery, who enrolled at Rose St for the evening drawing classes in 1874, left us this graphic description of procedure in those days when Scottish pupils had the enormous advantages of being subject to English art education policies:

> My first lesson occupied two hours drawing straight lines and
> curves, the second outlining a vase, the third in copying parts of the
> human face, and so on until a certain proficiency in what was called
> 'drawing from the flat in outline' was attained. [These exercises
> were] all done from copy-books, and in outlines which were much
> too small.... Complete heads came next, and then hands and feet.
> These were drawn in outline. After some weeks I was allowed to
> work on toned paper, using conte crayon and white chalk. It was
> pleasant to put in the lights and shade [2].

Most Glasgow students who survived the preliminary outline from the flat, or linear geometry, 'made either designs for fabrics or mechanical drawings', but Lavery, being apprenticed to a portrait artist and photographer, was allowed to follow the 'painting' course. 'Then the cast,' he related, 'and two whole years grinding at it, the life class and a sense of being on the road to fame and glory.'

Lavery then described the sequence in the Antique Room. It consisted of stages of South Kensington's Course of Instruction, namely *Stage 8a* (human figure from the cast in outline); *Stage 9a* (anatomical studies – bones or muscles), and *Stage 8b* (human figure from the cast, shaded). All started with an outline of the cast of Myron's *Discobolus*, and the bones or muscles had to be filled in within this outline. (The *Discobolus* had probably been acquired through the Department of Science and Art, where it was catalogued as *Example no. 459.*)

> The master chose an antique figure, the Disc Thrower, [wrote Lavery] then four drawings had to be made from it. Three were useful, though the technical methods were too delicate and pretty. One was outline drawing, another was a skeleton, and the third a tinted écorché, a figure without skin, for the study of the muscles. Then a shaded drawing, very elaborate and debilitated had to be stippled into existence, dot by dot until wasted weeks had become murdered months.

Lavery continued his studies in London, at South Kensington and Heatherley's Art School. Poynter, who directed affairs at South Kensington, had not (as some, including William Gaunt, have claimed) abolished the existing tedious methods for producing a drawing, which 'took many months to do'; so it was with joy that Lavery escaped to Paris to learn from Bouguereau at l'Académie Julian. Commenting later on *Stage 8* of the South Kensington Course of Instruction, he remarked, 'Abroad, in the same span of time, at least one large drawing would have been made every week, handled in a broad and square manner' [3].

In 1881 Greenlees retired as headmaster at Glasgow and the South Kensington authorities recommended Thomas C. Simmonds, head at Derby, for the appointment. The Derby man, as might have been expected, was keen on designing for lace and pottery, and in the words of the Glasgow School's committee 'raised the School to eminence in Design'. At the end of Simmonds's first session the School received a larger Department grant upon results than any other in the United Kingdom, and in the National Competition of 1884 only two Schools of Art won more medals. Simmonds had paved the way for Newbery.

Glasgow School of Art's most famous student enrolled at Rose St during Simmonds's last session. Charles Rennie Mackintosh was sixteen at the time, and newly articled to the firm of John Hutchison. The man destined to be Mackintosh's friend and patron succeeded Simmonds at the end of the session.

Fra Newbery takes over

Francis Henry Newbery (1853–1946), son of a Devon shoemaker, had studied at Bridport School of Art, Dorset, and from 1875 to 1880 had taught drawing in various schools in London. In 1880, at the age of twenty-seven, he had been accepted by the National Art Training School as a 'student in training' at South Kensington [4]. Here he had specialised in 'painting in oil, tempera, & water colours' and 'antique, life, & anatomy' under the direction of the headmaster, J. C. L. Sparkes, a survivor of the Cole/Redgrave regime. He was also required to teach the general students.

Newbery's three main convictions about art and art teaching were formed in London: his belief in the French atelier or workshop basis for art education, his faith in Whistler and the Aesthetic movement, and his respect for William Morris. During Newbery's stay in London the Ruskin/Whistler libel farce ran for two days, 'The Master' slew his academic enemies from his Fine Art Society and Society of British Artists bases, and Godwin built his White House. The engrossing subject of every young painter's conversation was 'Mr Whistler'. Thomas Armstrong, Newbery's chief at Kensington, Edward Poynter, the senior visitor and examiner, and Whistler himself were all products of a French atelier. Not that the South Kensington classrooms had any atelier atmosphere. Whistler rebuked Mortimer Menpes:

> Do you realise that I lifted you more or less out of the gutter,
> artistically? I found you in absolute degradation, studying under
> E. J. Poynter at the Kensington Schools [5].

The gods of Whistler's youth had been Velasquez and Rembrandt, and his companions in Paris had been Fantin-Latour and Legros of the French realist tradition. Newbery's inclinations followed suit. Equally important, he admired Whistler's 'aesthetic' interiors washed with lemon-yellow, white, and green; also Godwin's architecture. The architect's plain surfaces and the asymmetrical but exquisite placings of his wall openings were doubtless in Newbery's mind during his conferences with Mackintosh in the 'nineties.

Little was done to interest the student teachers in arts and crafts until Newbery's last session, when Thomas Armstrong invited Crane to give his lectures and demonstrations; but a London teacher, working next to the South Kensington Museum, in an institution examined by Morris, was in an ideal position to heed the meteoric rise of the Arts and Crafts movement in London. Morris tapestries were to decorate the Newberys' flat in Glasgow. Both Crane and Morris were to be invited to address Newbery's pupils in Glasgow. As he left for Glasgow, Newbery must have been encouraged by the recommendation of the Royal Commissioners on Technical Instruction that Schools of Art should produce 'applied art – workmanship in the materials themselves.'

Fra Newbery took up his duties at Rose St in September 1885 at the age of thirty-two. He was required personally to conduct classes in the Life and Antique, to lecture on Artistic Anatomy, and to direct the advanced classes. At the time of his appointment drastic changes were made. The deputy head went, along with three general assistants, and a design master and an architecture master were appointed for the first time, A. Aston Nicholas and Thomas Smith respectively. It was a move towards specialisation, surely on Newbery's advice [6]. As the new headmaster did his evening stint in the Antique Room on the first floor of Corporation Buildings he must have been struck by the rapid progress of a seventeen-year-old student. Glasgow University possesses one of the young Mackintosh's drawings of that session carried out in sepia wash from the Antique.

The Glasgow School of Art Club

The vital constituent of the ground in which *The Four* flourished was the Glasgow School of Art Club. When Newbery took up his duties at Glasgow he was singularly fortunate that already resident were a talented group of artists as smitten with Whistler and modern French painting as he was. James Guthrie was exhibiting at the RA for the first time in the year of his arrival. John Lavery had already achieved a reputation for portrait painting which was to lead shortly to a brief sitting, or rather standing, by Queen Victoria. The Glasgow School, sometimes called 'the Glasgow Boys,' was realist/impressionist, favoured direct painting and open air work; and rejected academic styles. Lavery wrote:

> Although we at Glasgow worked with a richer palette than Whistler, we recognized in him the greatest artist of the day and thought of his *Ten O'Clock* lecture as the Gospel of Art.

Joseph Crawhall was the artist most admired within the group. Vivid and detailed impressions of animals were painted from the memory of a mere glimpse. 'No artist I have known,' wrote Lavery, 'could say more with fewer brush strokes' [7].

During his first year as headmaster Newbery initiated open air sketching classes, monthly competitions for figure and landscape compositions, and vacation work – projects close to the hearts of the Glasgow Boys. These activities were organised so that past and present students, and anybody willing to pay a fee, could achieve ambitious work, learning one from the other. In October 1886 those taking part exhibited as the Glasgow School of Art Club. The annual report for 1885–1886 stated:

> The Glasgow School of Art Club, consisting of past and present Students of the School, has for its object the encouragement of the Fine Art section of the School's curriculum, more especially as regards Figure and Landscape Composition and Drawing, the means taken being the issue and criticism of set monthly subjects, both Advanced and Elementary. The Club is under the direction of the Headmaster, but is officered and managed entirely by the students themselves.

The fame of the School of Art and the emergence of The Four was due to this brilliant idea of a club. The regular competition subjects were of course based on the monthly *concours* of the French atelier. The Slade had already adopted the system [8]. What made the Glasgow scheme so different was that the Club involved past students and any adult who wished to join the landscape classes. This de-schooled the activities. The participants felt no longer pupils, but rather creative artists working with an important exhibition in view. Newbery saw to it that the Club's autumn exhibition was the School's social and artistic event of the year. When the School received money to set up 'technical art studios' in 1892 Newbery insisted that they were open to the School of Art Club both during term time and vacation. The members of the Club, past and present students working together, produced craftwork of a standard which confounded other Schools of Art. In this Club, in this manner, The Four raised themselves to fame.

A correspondent for *The Studio* complained after a visit to the School that 'the authorities rely chiefly for the material for their annual exhibition upon the work executed during the summer vacation' [9]. His words could mislead. The work done during the term in Newbery's time always secured a very high place for the School in the Government examination ratings.

'The Four'

In the autumn of 1890 the two Macdonald sisters were enrolled as day students at 3 Rose St, and in December were submitted as 'middle-class' candidates for *Stage 23c: Design for Tiles* on the List of Works for the South Kensington examinations of May 1891. Already enrolled were Charles Rennie Mackintosh and Herbert MacNair, the two evening students with whom the girls were to share fame and fate.

Within four years of enrolment the girls were mature artists and exceptional designers in beaten metals: within six they had shocked London with their fully developed 'spook style.' How was it possible for the Glasgow art students to progress so swiftly? What was their local source of inspiration? These were the questions that intrigued London art circles, and that Gleeson White set out to solve. The mature skill of the girls' work and its mystic inscriptions convinced some that its originators were frustrated Scottish hags 'weird sisters, hand in hand .... wither'd and so wild in their attire', but the gallant White on his return from Glasgow assured his readers that the Misses Macdonald were 'two laughing, comely girls, scarce out of their teens'.

Gleeson White could not establish a specific source of their inspiration. When he visited their Glasgow studio in the spring of 1897 the Macdonalds told him, 'We have no basis, that is the worst of it.' They told White they were quite willing to have their work jointly attributed, which was appropriate, for, as White said, it was 'impossible for an outsider to distinguish the hand of each on the evidence of the finished work alone' [10].

To discover the development of the sisters as designers it helps to return to their first session at Glasgow School of Art. In the South Kensington examinations for the session, held in summer 1891, both girls passed Second Grade drawing examinations, and were awarded 2nd Class in *Stage 23c* for designs for tiles. In the Local Examinations in the same year Frances was awarded 2nd Class in Plants from *Nature in Outline (Stage 10a)*, but, more significantly, the elder sister, Margaret, gained the top award in *Anatomy*, a 1st Class in the Advanced Examination and a ten shillings prize for a design for majolica. Professor Howarth was unable to find evidence that the sisters had any art education previous to their arrival at Glasgow, but it seems highly probable that they had, certainly Margaret. The girls told Gleeson White in 1897 that they had been 'denizens of greater London until a few years ago' [11]. The Macdonald family had quit their London home for Glasgow *circa* 1889. Margaret was twenty-four in that year, twenty-five when she enrolled at Rose St, so it is highly probable that she had previously studied in a metropolitan School of Art.

Howarth seems to have overlooked White's information that the sisters were London girls. He does mention that John Macdonald, their father, was consulting engineer at Chesterton Hall, Newcastle, Staffordshire, prior to the return to his native Glasgow [12]. Is it then pure coincidence that the Macdonald girls devoted themselves to designing for majolica and tiles in their first year at Glasgow? Did Margaret attend some classes in the branch School of Art at Newcastle, or in the School at Stoke during her father's stay in the Potteries? If so, Frances, nine years younger, may have accompanied her. She certainly shared the same interest in pottery decoration, indeed she excelled her elder sister in this field, for in the National Competition of 1892 she was awarded a Bronze Medal in *Stage 23d* for a design for a majolica plate. In the same year she was awarded a local prize of £1 for majolica. She was only eighteen. The South Kensington examiners for pottery design were Lewis Day, Fred Shields, and the great Morris himself. They reported:

> A bronze medal is given to Frances E. Macdonald of the Glasgow School. The award would have been higher but for the poor execution and very disagreeable colour, which mar an otherwise good design [13].

Morris and Day preferred strong hard outlines filled with bright colour in the Owen Jones tradition. Frances favoured soft line and sad pale washes of blue and green.

Howarth wrote that the few artists still living at the time he wrote his book, who remembered the arrival of the Macdonalds at Glasgow, emphatically denied that either showed more than average ability or any marked originality [14]. Their opinions are manifest nonsense. How could a lassie of eighteen win a National Bronze Medal in her second year and be average? How could her sister win a 1st Class prize in advanced anatomical drawing in her first year? In her third year (1892–3) Frances won the 1st Prize in the Design Section of the School for 'a tapestry hanging, bold and clever in conception' in Newbery's words. Margaret was commended for a design for a stained glass window. How could such girls have been average? As for lack of originality, what does 'bold and clever in conception' suggest?

Lest we think that the male section of The Four gave the girls a lead in matters of design we should note that in 1893 the young Frances passed 1st Class in the Honours Stage of the School's design examinations, and her future husband, MacNair, passed 2nd Class. Neither is it true that the Macdonalds' style was inspired by Mackintosh. The girls had already launched their particular brand of *l'Art Nouveau* when Mackintosh and MacNair were introduced to them. MacNair told Howarth that he and Mackintosh, who were evening students, were not aware of the sisters until the headmaster drew attention to the similarity of the work of all four at a criticism. Newbery confirmed that it was at his suggestion that The Four joined forces [15]. According to my calculations this advice must have been given at the School of Art Club's December exhibition of 1893. This was the first exhibition which included craftwork done in the new technical art studios at 264 Sauchiehall Street. It lasted five days and there was a *conversazione* and an 'At Home' reunion of past and present pupils.

The 'technical art studios'

Up to 1892, Design at Rose St was on paper, but during that year the governors managed to obtain £387–4s–8d from the City Council for technical education in art. It was the School's share of the government's surplus excise duties, that 'Whisky Money' which equipped many a craft room. From autumn of the same year three technical art instructors were appointed for glass staining, wood and stone carving, and needle-work, and the Museum and Galleries Committee gave up to the School some accommodation with an entrance from Sauchiehall St. A deputation from the governors then visited the Manchester and Birmingham Schools of Art, and consulted the authorities at South Kensington.

By the summer vacation of 1893 a large room split into various 'technical art studios' had been specially fitted up, and students and staff worked throughout the holidays. The Macdonalds worked there by day: Mackintosh and MacNair in the evening [16].

> Perhaps the most striking fact that confronts one at first [wrote Gleeson White of the Macdonalds' work] is to find that some comparatively large and heavy pieces of wrought metal were not only designed, but worked entirely by the two sisters [17].

The girls had not only acquired an original style, but also an ability to work metal which astonished the Victorian male. Some credit must be given to William Kellock Brown, their metalwork instructor in the technical art studios. Brown, who had been modelling master since 1887, had now taken over the additional areas of 'repoussé and metal work in silver, brass, copper and iron'. The Macdonalds also studied glass staining under Norman McDougall, and painting on china and earthen-ware under Aston Nicholas, the design master.

Technical art classes became a regular part of the School's curriculum from the autumn of 1893. At this time Newbery also organised a series of lectures by experts on arts and crafts. The atmosphere in the technical art studios was not that of a classroom, but rather an informal workshop. We can glean the mood in the studios from the words of Newbery's daughter, Mary Sturrock. She is describing the needlework class when her mother directed it (1894–1908).

> Everything was easier in those days and anyone interested in doing embroidery, besides regular students, could take this class in order to enrich their home [18].

The Prospectus for 1893–94 states 'Outsiders may join at £1-1s per term.'

Though the Macdonalds attended by day, and Mackintosh by night, they must have known him by sight and reputation before the School of Art Club exhibition of December 1893. Mackintosh had been recognised as a star pupil from the summer of 1885 when this entry appeared on the National Competition prize list:

Chas. R. M'Intosh, 2 Firpark Terrace. Painting Ornament in
Monochrome from the flat, lla (for 3).

In the following annual Competition he had won a 3rd Grade prize for
painting ornament from the cast in sepia, and in the same year the
second prize of the Glasgow Institute of Architects for 'Measurement
Drawings of the Royal Exchange (£2–10s)', also a book prize for 'Best set
of Lecture Notes, Building Construction'. In the Competition of 1888
Mackintosh had won a National Bronze Medal for 'Design for a Mountain
Chapel, 23b (for 2)', and the examiners reported: 'A mountain church,
simply but picturesquely designed by Charles R. M'Intosh, Glasgow is
worthy of notice.' He was also awarded a 3rd Grade prize for 'Measured
Architectural Drawings, 23a.' Next, in 1890, Mackintosh had won the
Alexander (Greek) Thomson travelling scholarship (£60 for two years),
and his trip to Italy had resulted in a series of sketches which gained first
prize in the School of Art Club exhibition of November of that year.
John Lavery, James Guthrie, and E. A. Walton adjudicated [19]. When
told the winner was an architect, Guthrie grumbled to the headmaster
'But hang it, Newbery, this man ought to be an artist' [20].

A night to remember

On the night of Monday 22 February 1892 the Macdonald girls witnessed Mackintosh receiving the Silver Medal he had been awarded in
the Competition of 1891 for his designs for a public hall and a science
and art museum. The sisters were in the Corporation Galleries that night
to receive their Second Grade certificates and awards for Design
Ornament from the hands of Sir George Reid PRSA. Margaret was also
due her local prizes for anatomy and majolica design. Perhaps it is the
sisters in the cartoon (Fig. 9) shown here?

The meeting, the annual meeting to report on the session 1890–91,
was a memorable one. The Glasgow School of Design's first session had
been 1840–41 and this was the Jubilee meeting. Indeed it was a night to
remember. Titanic were the *gaffes* of the guest of honour. The facial
expressions in the cartoon from the Glasgow *Evening News* record the
disdain felt by Fra Newbery and his circle for the grim High Art sermon
preached by Sir George. The Royal Scottish Academy had approved a
new charter and elected a new president, hence when Sir George had
been invited to present the prizes and certificates at the Jubilee meeting,
the Glaswegians had expected him to show the Academy's approval of
the Glasgow Boys and the School of Art, in short of Glasgow as the
centre of progressive art. But, alas, Reid managed obliquely to insult the
Glasgow Boys, the governors, and Newbery; also to digust the young
students with a Scotch 'porridge and persecution sermon' on the advantages of abstention and poverty. This from a prosperous portrait painter!

> The commercial spirit is entirely opposed to the artistic spirit [quoth
> the knight] . . . . . If only the old monkish vow of poverty, chastity,
> and obedience could only be observed for say the first fifteen or
> twenty years of the artist's professional life, it might prove of
> infinite benefit . . . . [21]

9 The prosperous Sir George Reid (centre) recommending poverty to the Glasgow art students. Fra Newbery is at top right. *Glasgow Evening News*, 23 February 1892.

A reply to Sir George came from a 'Dragon' in the *Glasgow Herald* (25 February 1892). 'A woman is not of necessity a drag upon an artist,' sighed the Dragon. '... Know, then, all beautiful women that we are with you.'

Sir George made a fearful *gaffe* by saying he had no belief in talk about art, and that people who had theories were often the least capable. All present knew that Newbery was an expert on theory and history of art, and often gave public lectures in the Galleries on both. Reid also denigrated the commercial artist, and said his business qualities would be more profitably involved in some other direction. Newbery always urged his students towards commercial art. For him a student selling his poster designs was just as much the artist as any other. As far as the Glasgow Boys were concerned, Sir George referred to them as followers of Impressionism and then quoted an attack on a great French Impressionist. As for the governors his remarks about commercialism and 'successful bagmen' were particularly insulting. Another letter to the *Glasgow Herald* voiced this protest:

> Both as a personality in art and as representing the Academy Sir George was hospitably, heartily welcomed by men whose virile enterprise in business has been but part of their all-round manliness – men who have successfully run an art school for 50 years by voluntary effort and who have annually shown to a great community what the wideawake world is doing in art, while the Academy was sleeping the sleep of senility. Yet the PRSA could find no better thing to do than flout to their faces these very men whose guest he was by east-windy, West-Endy sniffing at 'successful bagmen' and by insulting the art now growing from the seeds which these 'successful bagmen' have been sowing at their personal expense, while the RSA virtually innocent of 'commercialism' has been naively counting the money in her stocking.
>
> With the confidence born of knowledge, Sir George dealt with 'Commercialism in Art' . . . .

Glasgow's verdict was that Sir George, who hailed frae Aberdeen, was strong on commerce, but weak on art!

The *Evening News* cartoon (Fig. 9) is a mine of interest in the ceremony. Top left we see E. R. Catterns, who was secretary for many years, reading the annual statement of the School's achievements. Below him is James Fleming, chairman of the governors. Top right is Newbery, the spit of a French atelier master. At the pulpit is the grim Sir George. Bottom left we see the prize winners, including one in the 'aesthetic' robes favoured by the ladies of the School. In the background, just to the right of this lady, appears the chalk life drawing that has won a gold medal.

Mackintosh received his National Gold Medal at the next annual meeting in February 1893. The news of this award, for a design for a chapter house, was published in the *Glasgow Herald* on 10 August 1892 and it must have been the talk of the School of Art Club during the rest of the vacation. MacNair's memory might have been correct when he told Howarth that he and Mackintosh did not know of the existence of the Macdonald sisters until Newbery mentioned them at a criticism towards the end of their student careers, but the girls must have known of Mackintosh and his work at least from 1892.

What is certain is that by the year 1893, at the end of which the Macs joined forces, each had arrived at their own brand of Glasgow Art Nouveau. Of this year is Frances Macdonald's mystic painting *Ill Omen, or Girl in the East Wind and Ravens passing the Moon*. The year 1893 certainly was crucial, for in April appeared the first number of *The Studio* containing an illustrated article on Beardsley.

At the next School of Art Club show in November 1894 the volume and quality of work executed in the technical art studios was such that a separate room had to be provided in the Fine Art Institute to exhibit all the arts and crafts. In this show the work of the Macs was so removed from the other work both by its placing and by its striking originality that they were instantly recognisable as a group. I have the feeling that they themselves chose to be known as The Four, because of the mystic connotations of number.

A new feature of the November show was the lithographed poster work. Decorative posters, magazine covers, programmes, and mural panels were essential elements in the development of the Glasgow Style. At first the students' posters had appeared as advertisements for activities connected with the School and the Corporation Galleries, such as School of Art Club shows, *conversaziones*, and concerts. Their style owed something to Beardsley and to Japanese prints. It is interesting to note that Beardsley's poster for the Avenue Theatre, and Hardy's Gaiety Poster appeared in that year (1894). The bold strange designs of the School of Art posters startled the public, which of course is a poster's intention. Astute citizens recognised this, and began to employ their creators. The annual report of the School for 1893–94 states: 'In Lithographic Work some Art posters designed by students of the School have been accepted and used....' Newbery was not only promoting students' posters in Glasgow: he sent some down to South Kensington. But how could the authorities place them within their stages of design ornament? In the headmaster's words, South Kensington would have 'nothing to do with them'.

At the next annual meeting, in February 1895, a large collection of students' work was shown in the School of Art exhibition in the Corporation Galleries, and this was followed in March by an invitation to exhibit at the City of Liege Arts and Crafts Exhibition [22]. Howarth quotes a letter of 10 May 1895 from the secretary of L'Oeuvre Artistique, Liege, praising the exhibits. 'Many of us should like to have some of your posters which are very beautiful,' he wrote [23]. The following annual report mentioned that 'very favourable press comments were made upon the work, which consisted of examples in architecture, modelling, and design'.

Through Newbery's efforts The Four were now launched into the international Arts and Crafts exhibition circuit. The invitation to exhibit in the New Gallery with the Arts and Crafts Exhibition Society followed, next Gleeson White spread their fame and style to the Continent by his illustrated articles in *The Studio* from July 1897 to February 1898. The Four had arrived.

Newbery's contribution

First, a final word about one of Newbery's main contributions to the development of The Four, his open studio policy for past and present pupils. Both in Howarth's book and Macleod's *Charles Rennie Mackintosh* it is mentioned that Mackintosh and the Macdonalds obtained private studios in the years 1894–1895. Readers might assume that The Four ceased to work at the School of Art in 1894. This is not correct. They could hardly have afforded to equip their art studios to produce the various arts and crafts they exhibited at the School of Art, and later in the New Gallery. Much of it, excluding the furniture, was executed at the School. Newbery left no doubt on this score. The annual report for 1895–96 states:

> The Decorative Art Studios contributed work to the recent exhibition of the Arts and Crafts in the New Gallery, London, the exhibits receiving good places and being favourably commented on.

Next, a word about the man himself. Newbery, like Tonks of the Slade, was a strict disciplinarian. Anybody who was not would not have been highly recommended by the authorities at Kensington. The School's committee of management noticed the tightening up within a few months of his appointment, and commented on his 'strict and encouraging manner' and added:

> The Class Discipline is such that the Committee can give assurance of the Student's capacities and time being judiciously employed [24].

Newbery regarded himself as the director of a group of ateliers or workshops, and any idle students or dilettanti were, in his words, 'weeded out'. *The Studio* reported of the School, 'It is not only a school but also a workshop', and of Newbery:

> His unwillingness to tolerate anything merely conventional and commonplace, and his encouragement of original effort are most important factors in forming the taste and settling the convictions of his pupils [25].

How did Newbery achieve this? What was his concept of a School of Art?

In accordance with his workshop concept, Newbery did not put students through the usual mill, collecting their 2nd, then 3rd Grade certificates; nor did he insist, as most art educationists did, on all students doing the same number of years to reach a certain standard. Thus the Macdonald sisters were permitted to attempt the last stage of the Course of Instruction (23) shortly after their arrival in the School. Newbery directed entrants straight on to a drawing course they were capable of. No student was allowed to draw from the flat example. An interview Newbery granted to a Glasgow reporter in 1895 is informative:

> A young man or young woman comes to me and says he or she
> wants to be an artist. Well, I don't listen to that. I put them on to
> make an outline drawing of a cast selected by themselves in the
> Antique Room, and from that drawing I see what the student can
> do, and apportion for him work in accordance. He then goes
> through the course, learns to draw, and after that it lies with himself
> what special branch he will devote himself to.
> *Scarcely according to Kensington, that!*
> Kensington! I recognize no such thing as Kensington.
> *Yes, but Kensington exists and Kensington has methods.*
> No, Kensington has no methods. To the schools under it – or rather
> the schools examined by it – Kensington issues no set of rules and
> regulations saying 'You'll copy casts in this particular way' or
> 'You'll do your landscape in the style of this man and not the style

of that.' The schools where South Kensington is regarded as a bugbear are the schools where weakness at the top has necessitated refuge being taken behind what some people are pleased to call the South Kensington system .... South Kensington has more than once said it wasn't educated quite up to our designs, and we have replied that we never thought it was, but hoped it would be some day.

And your posters – the posters of Glasgow School of Art?

Are progressing famously. South Kensington, of course has nothing to do with them. The possibilities of the poster are great. Our early efforts (with which the public must be fairly familiar by this time) met with a show of adverse criticism. We expected that and were not cast down [26].

For Newbery to encourage original design style in architecture, graphic art, and craftwork was absolutely revolutionary by the standards of Schools of Art of the 'nineties. How far ahead he was can be judged from the fact that even eighteen years after he first sponsored The Four, a committee of the Board of Education described the style of work at the Royal College as 'mediaeval' [27]. Indeed Newbery was two jumps ahead. It was still the Classical and Renaissance casts of ornament that dominated design style at South Kensington. In 1896 'the very modern designer' in *The Studio* wrote:

I think that the cult of the Italian Renaissance with its queerly assorted local idols – Owen Jones, Moody, and the Rest – has come a cropper, and that South Kensington is trimming to popular opinion [28].

Newbery's students were turning out original designs in craft materials at least three years before Lethaby's Central School of Arts and Crafts opened.

Newbery shared Lethaby's view that an art school should not only be a workshop but 'a centre of civilisation' in the local community, but, unlike Lethaby and the Art-Workers' Guild, Newbery saw nothing wrong with advertising art work with maximum publicity, especially the work of his students. Guild craftsmen had a priggish dread of being thought commercial. The Glasgow posters were a product of Newbery's attitude. It was not possible for Glaswegians to ignore the activities of their School of Art, nor the institution itself, for Newbery had the lower portions of the windows fronting Sauchiehall street painted a bright Whistler yellow and inscribed in black with

LIFE CLASSES – TECHNICAL STUDIES – BUILDING CONSTRUCTION – HISTORIC ORNAMENT – PERSPECTIVE – SCIOGRAPHY – MEDIAEVAL ARCHITECTURE – MODEL DRAWING – GEOMETRY – ANATOMY AND PROPORTION – ADVANCED DESIGN – PRINCIPLES OF ORNAMENT – MODELLING – ARCHITECTURAL DESIGN – ELEMENTARY DESIGN.

Within his centre of civilisation Newbery sponsored public exhibitions, lectures, *conversaziones*, 'At Homes,' masques, and concerts. His own renderings of old English ballads were in demand. Tea was often 'hospitably served in the Life Room'.

Some elements of the South Kensington system, as interpreted by Newbery, contributed to this cluttered environment. The Four all did drawing exercises from ornament and plants in the Kensington manner of even continuous outline and filled given spaces with outlines from flowering plants, natural objects ornamentally treated, and arrangements of ornament. Attention to Beardsley and the Japanese refined their outline. In Glasgow Art Nouveau the limited areas or panels filled with intense linear pattern demonstrate the influence of the South Kensington ornamental exercises. In other Schools of Art these did not result in the continuous rhythmic outline characteristic of the Glasgow Style, because students were made to design and to copy with slow care. Newbery told his students:

> that method is the best, that style of work is the best, which best renders a drawing or painting a copy of the original, and which accomplishes this result in the shortest possible time [29].

He rejected the Stump and went for line. The clean economic outline Newbery encouraged in his class for Artistic Anatomy is revealed by the nude figures on designs done by The Four while they were still at the School. The figures are not costumed figures, like those in Japanese art, but rather nudes with drapery. Drapery arranged on the living model was a weekly event in Newbery's life classes, as was his lecture on *Figure Design and Composition*.

The Victorian drawing exercises contributed, but the main element in the artistic education of The Four was plant drawing. An artist can hardly fail to notice that the curves of the Glasgow Style, even of the drapery and figures, are the subtle living curves of growing plants, the feeling of growth often being enhanced by a proliferation of verticals. Plants were a life-long obsession with The Four. Mackintosh and MacNair had collected specimens from the early 'nineties, making use of their weekend breaks from the office of Honeyman and Keppie.

Today we tend to associate analytical and creative drawing from natural objects with modern art education. It is astonishing to find, as Howarth did, that on young Mackintosh's architectural sketch sheets and flower studies are drawings of this modern character:

> the delicate tracery of half a cabbage . . . the section of an apple . . . the grotesque fantasy of an onion gone to seed . . . the bulbous roots of subaqueous plants . . . a fish's eye seen under the microscope [and] strange patterns based on flower and plant motives – stalks, leaves and roots – reduced to their most elementary form [30].

It was significant that Mackintosh made special provision for flower painting when planning the new School of Art building. In their forties the great architect and his wife Margaret returned to flower pieces as he gradually abandoned architecture.

What places Newbery head and shoulders above other notable art teachers was his faith in the students he educated. He considered his graduates equal if not superior to the best professional of his day, and, as we shall see later, was willing to offend the most influential artists in defence of his students' original work. He was not the teacher who urges his charges to seek the fashion of modish elsewhere. Newbery declared that 'for a teacher with his heart in his work there is no satisfaction greater than the satisfaction that comes to him from the success of pupils' [31]. It was typical of the man that, when it came to the choice of an architect for the proposed School of Art building, Newbery preferred one of his own students.

The School of Art building

From an educational viewpoint the Glasgow School of Art building is of great interest because Newbery's schedule of accommodation made it the Victorian School of Art *par excellence*. Moreover it is a living, working museum, though perhaps I should not say so at a time when the word 'museum' arouses almost as much fury in fashionable circles as the word 'academic'. Up to the 'eighties Schools of Art were housed in classrooms of various institutions or in rented accommodation. From the 'eighties buildings were erected in the provincial cities specifically as Schools of Art, for example at Manchester (Cavendish St) 1881, Liverpool (Hope St) 1883, Birmingham (Margaret St) 1885. Of these the Manchester School would have approached Glasgow in accommodation if the governors had adhered to the original plan, which provided a second floor for masters' studios. As it was, Mackintosh's building was without a rival in the provinces. Its accommodation for studios and workshops was only matched by the LCC Central School building, opened in 1908.

At Glasgow, work on the central block and the east wing, siding on to Dalhousie St, was commenced in 1897, and this first stage was opened by Sir James King, Lord Provost, on 20 December 1899. A pause ensued while the Scots recovered from their extravagance, then in 1907 the west wing, siding on to Scott St, was commenced. Mackintosh's masterpiece was formally opened by Sir James Fleming, Lord Provost on 15 December 1909.

When the building was planned by Mackintosh to Newbery's schedule in 1896 its rooms were allocated to meet the requirements of the Course of Instruction of the Department of Science and Art. Hence the essential rooms which formed the basis of Newbery's schedule were those typical of every major School of Art under the South Kensington system, namely large Life, Antique, and Modelling Schools, and rooms for Ornament, Anatomical Studies, Still Life and Flower Painting, Architectural and Mechanical Drawing, a library, and staff rooms. The only other basic requirements, save those for nature's call, were that the Life School should be on an upper floor, and partitioned for reasons modest and segregational; also that the Modelling School should be in the basement to prevent clay and plaster dust percolating through the institution.

A main feature due to the Arts and Crafts movement is the Museum, which is placed in a central position, unlike the Schools of Art of the 1852–1885 period in which a collection of casts took precedence. The Museum was a gallery and workroom where the students could study and copy the collection of Arts and Crafts which the Glasgow School, like others, had amassed in the 'nineties. The 'School Museum of

10 CHARLES RENNIE
MACKINTOSH Glasgow
School of Art, 1907–9,
Scott Street elevation,
comprising fenestrated
Library and windowless
Museum; Annan, Glasgow.

Applied and Decorative Art' had been a prominent feature in the Sauchiehall St building in Newbery's time. The School Prospectus for 1893–4 stated:

> Through the kindness of the owners of private collections, by loans from students themselves and by the liberality of some of the Fine Art dealers of the City, a good selection of work can always be studied. By special concession a case of carefully selected Art Objects is on loan to the School from the Victoria and Albert Museum ....

The studios of the department of 'Design and Decorative Art' in the east wing were those most attributable to recent developments in art and craft education, namely the Design School on the first floor, and the Technical Studios and 'Living Animal' room in the basement. The craftwork, or 'Technical Art Work', carried out in the Technical Studios was extensive, consisting of bookbinding, printing, illumination, gesso-work, wood blocks and printing in colours, lithographic design, stained glass, mosaics, ceramic decoration, needlework and embroidery, furniture designing, wood inlay, wood engraving, wood carving, metalwork, and stone carving (in the sub-basement).

The basement studio for the 'Living Animal' was deemed essential by Newbery. Like Catterson-Smith, he regarded sketching from moving animals a vital part of a designer's training. Newbery was a pioneer in this field, and had introduced drawing at the Zoo, at the Veterinary College, and at the stables of the Tramway and Omnibus Company before Catterson Smith established his 'menagerie' at Birmingham School of Art.

Shortly before the completion of the east wing the Scotch Office took over the Science and Art education of Scotland. A short period of transition ensued during which the School completed current Kensington courses, then from September 1901 the Glasgow School of Art was established as the Central Institution of Higher Art Education for Glasgow and the West of Scotland. The governors were then authorised by the Scotch Office to issue diplomas and certificates bearing its imprint.

As a result of this transfer of control the School was now rid of the Course of Instruction, the National Competition, and the last vestiges of Payments on Results, thus Newbery was free to reorganise the curriculum and accommodation. The chief alteration in accommodation was the reduction of studio space for the drawing of casts of Ornament. The School was divided into the Upper and the Lower School, and the latter was given the ground floor studios originally provided for Elementary and Advanced Ornament. The space given to Still Life was taken over by the new School of Architecture. All elementary work was now done in the Lower School from which a student progressed into one of the Diploma departments of the Upper School, namely Drawing and Painting, Architecture, Modelling, Design and Decorative Art. The days of fragmentation, caused by the South Kensington exercises, were over.

As I have said, Mackintosh's building was the School of Art *par excellence*. It was not a School of Arts and Crafts in the sense that Lethaby's Central was, nor were design and crafts given the pre-eminence Catterson-Smith gave them at Birmingham. Despite his keen encouragement of craftwork, Newbery, first and foremost a painter with academic aspirations, believed that the French atelier system, which had produced Whistler, Lavery, and the French artists he admired, should be the basis, with Fine Art pre-eminent. His attitude was demonstrated by the appointment of professors from the Continent. Significantly the lofty Life and Antique Schools, occupying nearly all the north front on the first floor, were each as large as all the Technical Studios put together. The Design School was not allocated as great an area as the personal painting studios of Newbery and the professors.

Generous provision for Modelling was made in the west wing of the basement and sub-basement, for Modelling was a Fine Art subject taken to Diploma level. The subject was not Sculpture. Stone carving and wood carving were considered technical or trade subjects, their first stages being cutting letters and simple ornament. Neither did Newbery plan his School for industrial design. He believed strongly in Arts and Crafts. '.... the MACHINE IS A POOR APOLOGY for the hand,' he wrote. He did not condemn the machine, however, as Morris and his disciples did.

> The machine [Newbery argued] is a perfectly passive agent with a personality neither to mar nor make as far as art is concerned [32].

An unusual feature of the School was the provision and place of honour granted to the Flower Painting Room, but then one should have expected that of Mackintosh. This delightful roof-lit studio is on the top floor of the west wing close to the Professors' Studios, and is provided with a small conservatory, cantilevered some 80 ft above the ground, in Howarth's words:

> a most daring and exciting innovation unparalled, to the best of the author's knowledge, in architectural design at this time [33].

11   CHARLES RENNIE MACKINTOSH *Fritillaria, Walberswick*, pencil and watercolour 25.3 × 20.2 cm, 1915; Hunterian Art Gallery, University of Glasgow.

98

On my last visit I was enchanted by potted flowers flourishing therein as if to keep fresh the memory of The Four.

Newbery's requirements did have a slightly adverse effect on the artistic merit of the north elevation. The bases of Mackintosh's exterior style were solid cliff-like stone masses contrasted with light ingenious fenestration, delicate railings, and refined ornament. How could these be achieved on a front which required a series of enormous windows for the Life and Antique Schools? Moreover, for Mackintosh, as can be judged from the other three elevations and his other works, asymmetry was essential to exciting contrast. He had condemned buildings for their 'artificial symmetry' and now perforce had to embark on artificial asymmetry. Newbery's requirements for the north front made it nigh impossible to follow his natural inclinations, and his attempts to make the central block of that front asymmetric are slightly pathetic, likewise the rather unnoticeable variations in the large windows. If several small design or craft studios had been given pride of place on part of this front, Mackintosh could have been more positive in his contrast. Be that as it may, he provided Renfrew St with a daring expanse of glass that startled his contemporaries.

Mackintosh's genius is best grasped standing on Scott St slightly below the School, looking up at the soaring south-west corner, a surprisingly modern conception, yet full of the towering quality of the Scottish baronial. The library façade is particularly impressive. There is evidence that this lacks statues of Cellini, St Francis, and others, which were planned to complete the scheme. Maybe Mackintosh intended homage to his patron Fra Francis Newbery, but I doubt the saint would have relished the goldsmith's company.

Newbery versus the Art-Workers' Guild

The opening of the new Glasgow School of Art in 1909 marked the completion of Mackintosh's first major public building and his last. By that date modern tendencies, including *l'Art Nouveau* had been stifled in Britain by a revival of styles, a revival abetted by the senior members of the Art-Workers' Guild who, though now on the high road to 'success', had lost their way. The Guild and the Royal Academy wished to forget Mackintosh, moreover there were no Newberys on panels of assessors to encourage originality. The failure of Mackintosh to win the Liverpool Anglican Cathedral competition of 1903 was a personal disaster and a disaster for British architecture.

The deep resentment felt by the Art-Workers' Guild for the Glasgow school of designers had first been stimulated by Gleeson White's four articles in *The Studio* of 1897–1898. Up to that date the magazine had been regarded as a pillar of the Morris movement. Back in 1893, as Crane was preparing to take up his appointment at Manchester, *The Studio* had appeared for the first time. Owned and directed by Charles Holme, it was to prove the most successful art magazine of its time. Shaw Sparrow expressed this opinion:

Within his own sphere, Charles Holme was as important as Lord

Northcliffe; even more important, perhaps . . . he revolutionised the profession of art-editing. It was no easy thing to produce in London an art magazine that foreign countries would buy and imitate . . . a leader everywhere of arts and crafts, challenged in many lands by imitative rival reviews. . . . There was a French edition, an American edition, and the sales in Germany and Austria were larger than in France, Belgium, Holland, Italy, and Russia [34].

Existing magazines such as the *Art Journal* and the *Artist* were concerned mainly with the fine arts: *The Studio* was concerned with all arts and crafts – 'Art for the sake of everyday life among all classes' [35].

Holme's commitment to the Art-Workers' Guild was clear from the start. The first volume of *The Studio* (April–August 1893) includes articles by Walter Crane, H. Arthur Kennedy, D. S. MacColl, and C. F. A. Voysey; also illustrations of the work of R. Anning Bell, T. Erat Harrison, Selwyn Image, Heywood Sumner, and Voysey. In the second volume appears the magazine's first report on the Arts and Crafts Exhibition Society's show in London, in the third a report on the Home Arts and Industries Association.

Holme made a direct educational approach by the inclusion in each issue of articles on designing and techniques for various crafts. Students were encouraged by competitions organised by the magazine staff, the winning designs being published.

As a whole [wrote Shaw Sparrow] *The Studio's* competitions were very useful, disheartening students in the schools who had no talent, and encouraging those who had gifts for design . . . . Thanks in many respects to the widespread influence of this magazine, the applied arts are better taught now (1924) than they were in the nineties. Thus the LCC Central School of Arts and Crafts is a model institution [36].

Holme, like Gropius, believed all arts and crafts should be combined as the architecture the people lived in and frequented. For his own country house his chosen architect was one of the founders of the Art-Workers' Guild, Ernest Newton. Holme lost his early enthusiasm for the leaders of the Guild precisely when he began to suspect that they were losing contact with daily life and contemporary needs, because of their commitment to past traditions in design. This ran counter to his convictions. In Shaw Sparrow's words:

The Studio's policy, in brief, was to proclaim the urgent need of re-uniting the arts and crafts of daily life among all classes [41].

Close on the publication of Aymer Vallance's first comments on the work of The Four, on 3 April 1897 dissenters from the Künstlerhaus formed the Secession, and Holme became increasingly aware of the impact *The Studio* was making in central Europe. Josef Hoffman, and admirer of Mackintosh and the founder of the Wiener Werkstätte wrote of *The Studio:*

Those of today can hardly grasp with what eagerness the youth of those days awaited each new number. Amelia Levetus, a critic and designer in Austria at that time, said later that the Secession

12   CHARLES RENNIE
MACKINTOSH chairs, with
(background) gesso wall
panel by MARGARET
MACDONALD; Glasgow
School of Art.

movement learnt all about the London Guild of Handicrafts and the work of C. R. Ashbee and Charles Mackintosh from the pages of *The Studio*. [37]

In 1900 The Four received high praise from the Austrians for their furnished room in Olbrich's Secession House. Mackintosh's designs for the main buildings of the Glasgow International Exhibition of 1901 had been rejected. His designs for stalls, including the fine, strong, and simple School of Art stall, were carried out; but it was the work of Glasgow School of Art as a whole that impressed, particularly the needlework of Mrs Newbery, Anne Macbeth and their pupils in the Applied Art Division of Women's Industries.

The growing reputation of the School earned Fra Newbery an invitation to organise a Scottish Section for the International Exhibition of Modern Decorative Art at Turin to be ready for the summer of 1902. The overall scheme was prepared by the Mackintoshes who furnished one room. The second was divided between the MacNairs and the embroidery of the School. The third was occupied by the work of the Glasgow School of Art Club, i.e., past and present pupils.

This was the most crucial exhibition in the careers of Newbery and The Four. It ensured fame in Central Europe and exclusion at home. There was a direct confrontation between the Glasgow work and that of members of the Arts and Crafts Exhibition Society, who had excluded The Four from their shows since the furore of 1896.

Walter Crane had been invited to exhibit a collection of his own decorative art which had already toured Hungary, Austria, and Germany, and had seized the opportunity of appealing to the Arts and Crafts Exhibition Society to put on an exhibition of work. The resulting English Section shouted the decline of the Morris tradition. Compared with the Scottish Section, the room of the 'Arts and Crafts Exhibition Society, London', and Crane's own three rooms looked positively historic. As if to emphasise the funeral, Crane arranged for a Morris tapestry to be shown together with some photographs of Madox Brown's 'English Worthies'. The best-known designers in England were put to shame not only by the originality of The Four, but by the Scottish students.

For the Turin exhibition Fra Newbery was awarded the Grand Officer's Cross of the Order of the Italian Crown. The Mackintoshes received diplomas of honour and enhanced their Continental reputation. But all this was no substitute for recognition and major commissions at home. That was not to be. The two most influential art bodies in Britain, the Royal Academy and the Art-Workers' Guild, traditionalists all, wanted the Glasgow group forgotten. It is interesting that Crane devotes five pages of his autobiography to the Turin Exhibition, but omits not only all mention of Newbery and the Mackintoshes, but also all mention of the Scottish Section!

The refusal of the Guild, alias the Arts and Crafts Exhibition Society, to recognise the merits of the Glasgow style hurt the Guild as much as Mackintosh. Charles Holme became convinced that the Society was opposed to progress, and in 1903, the year following the Turin exhibition, an ominous review in *The Studio* declared:

> Much has been hoped from the Arts and Crafts Society in the way of raising the standard of public architecture and decoration; but the present exhibition reveals but a limited progress in that direction.... Broadly speaking the public is not far wrong in taking the leaders of this Society to be the custodians of the Morris tradition in art, rather than the founders of a living tradition of today.

The Studio's review of the Society's next exhibition (1906) sounded the death knell of the Society as an intellectual force.

> It has failed to participate in the great renascence of art which is now making such giant strides on the Continent [wrote the reviewer] and now especially in Germany and Austria; nor does it indeed adequately represent the best work now produced in the British Isles [39].

The Guild had bit British Art Nouveau a mortal bite, but died of it – albeit slowly.

The saga of The Four was to end as tragedy. The group first broke up when MacNair took up the post of instructor at Liverpool School of Architecture and Applied Art in 1898, marrying Frances Macdonald in 1899. Mackintosh married her sister in the following year and practised with Keppie in Glasgow until 1913. Then, deserted by clients, save Catherine Cranston, the Mackintoshes moved south to Walberswick in

Suffolk to stay next door to a house which the Newberys rented for sketching holidays. Final tragedy occurred in the 'twenties. Frances MacNair died in 1921 and Herbert abandoned art. Two years later the Mackintoshes moved to France to devote their last years to painting.

Glasgow architects then set about forgetting Mackintosh as quickly as possible, partly as a defence of their own dull work, partly in condemnation of the disappointed man's increasing addiction to alcohol. The authorities at the School of Art invariably referred to 'Honeyman and Keppie' as the architects of the School. As late as 1940 a comprehensive official history of the School, published as a centenary souvenir, gave no account of their greatest graduate. Only his name is mentioned, once with Honeyman & Keppie, once in a list of notable students. Fortunately in that same year Thomas Howarth, a young member of the staff, began to investigate Mackintosh and to seek out his work.

In May 1933 a Mackintosh memorial exhibition had been arranged in the McLellan Galleries, sponsored by W. R. Davidson and J. J. Waddell, and in that same year articles on the architect had appeared in *The Studio*, *The Builder*, and *The Listener*. Nikolaus Pevsner's *Pioneers of the Modern Movement* followed in 1936. This was the turning point. It began to dawn upon Glaswegians that their city had nurtured one of the few British architects of international stature.

War intervened, then in 1945 Glasgow University bought Mackintosh's former home, 78 Southpark Avenue, from the Davidson family, and, due to the resulting publicity Howarth was able to persuade Henry Y. Allison, acting Director of the School of Art, to start a Mackintosh Collection, which Howarth and H. Jefferson Barnes arranged in the old board room. The Mackintosh Room, as it is now called, was opened by the architect's sister Nancy in 1947. Five years later Howarth's *Charles Rennie Mackintosh and the Modern Movement* [44] appeared, followed in 1961 by Bliss's *Charles Rennie Mackintosh and the Glasgow School of Art* [45]. The Director, H. Jefferson Barnes, was responsible for selecting and describing the material for two superb booklets published by the School in 1968, namely *Charles Rennie Mackintosh: Furniture* and *Charles Rennie Mackintosh: Ironwork and Metalwork*.

Fra Newbery, who died in 1946, lived long enough to witness the belated recognition of his most gifted pupils, 'The Four'. Seldom can the staff of a School of Art have made such a contribution to the history of art.

References

1 VALLANCE, AYMER (1986–7), 'The Arts and Crafts Exhibition 1896', *The Studio*, 9, October 1896–January 1897, p. 204.
2 LAVERY, JOHN (1940), *The Life of a Painter* (London, Cassell & Co.), p. 32.
3 SPARROW, WALTER SHAW (1917), *John Lavery and his Work* (London, Kegan Paul, Trench, Trubner & Co.), pp. 27–30.
4 SPENCER, ISABEL (n.d.), *Francis Henry Newbery 1855–1946* (unpub. paper, Glasgow School of Art).
5 PEARSON, HESKETH (1952), *The Man Whistler* (London, Methuen & Co.), p. 101.

6 (1883–4) and (1884–5), *Annual Reports of Glasgow School of Art.*
7 LAVERY (n. 2), pp. 79, 108.
8 MACDONALD, STUART (1970), *History and Philosophy of Art Education* (London, London University Press), pp. 273, 286.
9 *The Studio*, 24, October 1901–January 1902, p. 284
10 WHITE, GLEESON (1897), 'Some Glasgow Designers and their Work: Part One', *The Studio*, 11, June–September 1897, pp. 89–90.
11 *Ibid.*, Part Two, p. 231.
12 HOWARTH, THOMAS (1952), *Charles Rennie Mackintosh and the Modern Movement* (London, Routledge & Kegan Paul/Glasgow University), p. 23.
13 (1891–2) *Annual Report of the Glasgow School of Art*, p. 12.
14 HOWARTH (n. 12), p. 24.
15 *Ibid.*, p. 25.
16 (1891–2) and (1892–3) *Annual Reports of the Glasgow School of Art.*
17 WHITE (n. 10), Part Two, p. 90.
18 STURROCK, MARY (1970), *The Costume Society of Scotland* (Bulletin 5).
19 (1885–1891) *Annual Reports of the Glasgow School of Art.*
20 EDDINGTON SMITH, R. (1933), letter to the *Glasgow Evening News* 17 February 1933.
21 *Glasgow Evening News* 23 February 1892.
22 (1894–5) *Annual Report of the Glasgow School of Art*, p. 7.
23 HOWARTH (n. 12), p. 37.
24 (1884–5) *Annual Report of the Glasgow School of Art*, p. 5.
25 *The Studio*, 19, February–May 1900, p. 51.
26 (1895) *Newspaper Cutting Book*, Vol. 1, Glasgow School of Art. Cutting dated 22 May 1895.
27 See MACDONALD, S. (1973), 'Articidal Tendencies', Chapter One of this book.
28 *The Studio*, 8, June–September 1896, p. 194.
29 (1884–5) *Annual Report of the Glasgow School of Art*, p. 17.
30 HOWARTH (n. 12), p. 17.
31 (1884–5) *Annual Report of the Glasgow School of Art*, p. 16.
32 NEWBERY, FRANCIS (1893), 'Art in Relation to Technical Subjects', *Glasgow Evening News*, 12 April 1893.
33 HOWARTH (n. 12), pp. 76–7.
34 SPARROW, WALTER SHAW (1925), *Memories of Life and Art* (London, John Lane), p. 240.
35 *Ibid.*
36 *Ibid.*, p. 249.
37 *Ibid.*, pp. 239, 250.
38 *The Studio*, Special Birthday Number, April 1933, pp. 241, 257–8.
39 *The Studio*, 28, February–May 1903, pp. 30–2, and 37, February–May 1906, pp. 48–50, 56.
40 HOWARTH (n. 12).
41 BLISS, D. P. (1961), *Charles Rennie Mackintosh and the Glasgow School of Art* (Glasgow School of Art).

Chapter Seven

DON SOUCY Without a National System:
Sheffield Artists Teaching in Nova
Scotia between the World Wars

In the first half of this century a number of Sheffield artists began to work and teach in Canada. This chapter [1] looks at three of these artists – Arthur Lismer, Elizabeth Styring Nutt, and Stanley Royle – who taught in Halifax at what is now the Nova Scotia College of Art and Design (NSCAD). It examines how economic conditions, the education system, Nova Scotia's artistic milieu, and the personalities and Sheffield background of the three artists affected the development and effectiveness of their NSCAD art programmes. Because Canada has no centralised system for art teaching, and because NSCAD's lay Board has always been partial to a 'strong principal/weak faculty' model for the school, the principals were free to determine their own curricula. I will suggest that this strong principalship became problematic in at least two ways. The first arose from the Board's ignorance of artistic concerns and the principals' ignorance of local economic conditions: this led them to devise programmes that trained students for jobs that did not exist. Second, although the strong principalship maintained organisational stability, it eventually impeded both the school's and the community's artistic advancement.

Nova Scotia is a small province on Canada's Atlantic shore that has always reached outside of its borders for the theories, methods, and personnel of its art training programmes. In this regard it was not unlike the rest of the country. From colonial days until the 1970s, most ideas and many of the people concerned with art teaching in English Canada had arrived there from Great Britain or, to a lesser degree, from the United States. During the first half of this century, a group of these British art teachers shared the same Alma Mater: the Sheffield School of Art. Ontario researcher Robert Stacey has pinpointed at least 14 Sheffield graduates who worked as artists, teachers, illustrators, or designers in Canada between the World Wars. Three of these, Arthur Lismer, Elizabeth Styring Nutt and Stanley Royle, taught in Halifax at the institution originally named The Victoria School of Art and Design.

The Strong Principalship

Halifax was not Sheffield: it did not have a strong industrial base to entice aspiring designers. Neither did the two cities share similar systems for providing art instruction. The Sheffield artists were trained in a British school that was historically part of a national system of art education, complete with centralised exams. These artists emigrated to a country that had no hint of such a centralised system. Indeed, Canada's schools were assured autonomy from federal regulation by the 1867 British North America Act, which assigned control of education in Canada to the provinces. Therefore, in designing art programmes in Canada, the Sheffield artists had fewer constraints than they would have had at home.

When the Halifax art school was founded in 1887, it hired a British immigrant for its first principal. His name was George Harvey, a graduate of the National Art Training School in South Kensington, London. Then, as it is today, the art school was directed by a lay Board, very few of whom had any art background. Rather, they were businessmen, members of the educational bureaucracy, or well-to-do citizens who wished to be associated with the fine arts. They therefore depended on the principal to develop and manage the school's programme. This dependence has, until recent decades, been reinforced by the weak networks that linked Nova Scotian artists and designers to their colleagues in other parts of the country. This isolation assured the scarcity of experts who could challenge the principal's authority on art.

At the turn of the century, a strong principal was, in the eyes of the art school's management, well suited to the circumstances. Faculty members were few, lowly-paid and inadequately trained. These factors, coupled with very limited options for other art-related jobs, rendered the school's teachers susceptible to authoritative supervision.

The autonomy and authority given to the art school's principals created at least two types of problem. The first arose because the school's Board of Directors were often ignorant of artistic concerns, while the imported principal was ignorant of local economic conditions. As a result, they worked together to create art school programmes of little vocational relevance. Second, although it was true that a strong principal could provide managerial stability and could, for a while, stimulate academic and artistic growth, continuous growth could become severely hampered. An authoritative principal, clinging to outmoded ideas, could refuse to allow in new ones.

Arthur Lismer

By 1916, when Arthur Lismer was hired to head the art school, a strong principal had become a necessity: the principal was the only teacher that the Directors could afford to pay. Enrolment had fallen to 30 pupils, compared to 282 when the school first opened. The province had established a technical college in 1907, stripping the art school of its role in training mechanical and architectural draughtsmen. Except for a couple of women Directors, most of the art school's Board had lost interest; they rarely met and accomplished little when they did. The Board's plan was to pay Lismer $900 a year and let him figure out the rest for himself.

Lismer was the first of Halifax's Sheffield artists, and is by far the best known. His education at the Sheffield School of Art (1899–1906) and the Academie Royale des Beaux-Arts in Antwerp (1906–1907), his membership of Canada's Group of Seven, and his work in children's art education have all been recorded in various books and articles – though many of these are hagiographic. His contemporaries at Sheffield included other artists who would eventually find their way to Canada, such as Nutt and Royle, Frederick Varley, Herbert H. Stansfield, Hubert Valentine Fanshaw, and William Smithson Broadhead.

Lismer arrived in Halifax in October 1916, after having spent five years in Toronto. In his first year at the Halifax art school, he was able to increase enrolment to 72 pupils. However, by his last year, 1919, he still had not succeeded in making the school a stable institution. In fact, Lismer's Halifax principalship is worth noting not for what he did then, but for what he did afterwards. His view of Halifax's artistic needs did not match the public's own, and he proved unable to reconcile the two. He proposed plans that nobody funded, set up exhibitions that not many saw, and organised art school programmes that few bothered to attend. Had he not become known as 'Lismer of the Group of Seven' and 'Lismer a pioneer in child art', history would have little reason to acclaim Lismer the Halifax art school principal.

Still, Halifax provided Lismer with his first major opportunity to apply populist ideas on art that he had developed in Sheffield. Lismer believed that the Halifax art school should not limit itself to providing academic training for the few who were capable of art careers, 'For the true purpose of art teaching,' he claimed, 'is the education of the whole people for appreciation' [2]. In an effort to draw the wider public into the school, Lismer organised a number of exhibitions – a task he had often undertaken in Sheffield as secretary of the Heeley Art Club [3]. But despite Lismer's attempts to publicise these exhibitions, the shows never attracted much of a crowd.

Although he would later be known for his work with younger children, Lismer's efforts in Halifax were restricted to high school students. Reflecting ideas of the arts and crafts movement, Lismer gave his students practical, applied exercises rather than abstract ones. He also set up courses in design and interior decorating to supplement the regular fare of perspective drawing and exercises from antique casts. Believing that working people could benefit from the art school, Lismer sought:

> the cooperation of employers to send such of their employees and workers in industrial trades, to whom a knowledge of Drawing and Design would be of value and equip them to be of better service to their employers [4].

Despite his efforts, class sizes remained small. Enrolment decreased to 60 students in his last two years at the school.

In truth, very few people in Halifax cared about, or even knew about, the art school. Furthermore, there is no evidence to show that Lismer was correct in promoting the school's value to the city's workers. When he linked drawing instruction to increased industrial productivity he was saying nothing new. The province's education officials had been hearing that argument for decades, and not many of them were still inclined to take it seriously. Few jobs in Halifax required drawing, and those that did could be filled by Technical School graduates. The 1921 census listed only 42 designers and draughtsmen in the city, and by 1931 that number was cut in half to 21. Even fewer were the city's artists and art teachers – there were seven in 1921 – and lithographers and engravers, who numbered five [5]. Although Lismer was sincere, his argument that 'the country's needs will demand a closer merging of Art and Industry' [6] was based more on passion than on a tutored assessment of economic conditions. Nova Scotia's industrial growth began its decline in the 1890s, and training labour for non-existent jobs would not reverse that trend.

Still, Lismer's education work in Halifax could have been more fruitful had he had at least a little help from the Directors. The autonomy and authority of the principalship had its toll. After his first year in Halifax, Lismer wrote the Board president that:

> I am willing and ready to do all in my power, but I would like to feel that my efforts were seconded & that I had the support of some organization to assist & advise in matters that it is beyond my power to undertake [7].

That support never came, so in 1919 Lismer left.

Elizabeth Styring Nutt

Lismer wanted to leave the art school with a fighting chance of survival. He believed his successor must be not only an artist, but also an educator with strong will and unremitting stamina. Elizabeth Styring Nutt was exactly that. It is not clear whether Lismer was particularly close to Nutt in Sheffield, but he knew her well enough to recommend her to the Directors of the Halifax art school. He gained their approval, wrote Nutt with an offer, and received her telegraphed, one word reply – 'Accept.'

Lismer never guessed how strong-willed and unremitting Nutt would actually be. To Nutt there was only one correct way – hers. And she saw only one correct role for anybody affiliated with the art school – absolute loyalty to the headmistress. She was the quintessential strong principal. Because of her resolute manner, and because of the autonomy rendered to her by the non-centralised system, the Halifax art school, sometimes for the better and other times for the worse, became, in part, a reflection of Nutt's ideas. This reflection continued for two and a half decades – and possibly longer. Of course, the art school also reflected contemporary social, artistic, and educational concerns. But Nutt can be seen as a conduit through which the effects of these concerns were transmitted to the school.

Nutt's background is less well known than Lismer's. Her painting generally followed an English landscape tradition that Tooby describes as 'watered down late impressionist' [8]. Her stated objective in painting was to achieve not only a naturalistic rendering but also, as she put it, to capture the more important reality behind the surface appearance. She had studied under John T. Cook at the Sheffield School of Art. She later did post-graduate work with Stanhope Forbes in Newlyn, England. A travelling scholarship allowed her a year's study in Paris at the Sorbonne, followed by two years with Professor Sim in Florence. Nutt then returned to Sheffield where she experienced some success in exhibiting her work. She had a miniature hung at the Royal Academy in 1908 and other paintings shown at the Women's International in Philadelphia. However, it was not her studio production that gave Nutt her real career success, but rather her work in art education. Upon her return to Sheffield, she became headmistress of the Firs Hill Branch School, where her main task was training teachers. She was, for a time, on the special staff of the School of Art, and did further work in art education at the Sheffield Training College for Teachers, the Pupil Teachers' Centre, and the University Training College.

Nutt, therefore, did not need the Halifax job. Indeed, she was being adventurous in accepting the position. She was almost 50 years old, she had a well established career, and her work had achieved recognition by her peers. In 1904 she had been accepted into the Society of Art Masters, a male-dominated organisation. In 1910 she was awarded Associate status and five years later she became a full Fellow of the Society – a distinction she gained upon completion of her Art Master's Diploma from the University of Sheffield, for which she wrote a thesis on the *Teaching of Colour in Schools*. In 1916 a series of her articles were put out as a book by J. W. Northend in Sheffield. In reviewing the book, the *Society of Art Masters Journal* reported that:

> Miss Nutt is well known to many of our members as a most
> enthusiastic teacher, and therefore this volume . . . will be welcomed
> by those interested in the teaching of children . . . . [It] should prove
> to be a great help and inspiration to those for whom it is written [9].

In 1921, after Nutt's arrival in Halifax, her book was reprinted under the title *'Significance' or Flower Drawing with the Children*. The book, which was illustrated with Nutt's adequate but unexceptional drawings, introduces some of Nutt's vague, spiritual rationales for art education. She was preoccupied with this type of rationale, a consequence, in part, of her religious convictions – she was a devout Christian Scientist. It was also an outgrowth of a Victorian upbringing. She cited moralistic purposes for art. She made ethereal claims of art's role in finding the truth of nature and oneself – and therefore finding the truth of God [10].

Parts of Nutt's book also reflected early twentieth-century notions about art. Although she emphasised a realistic representation of the artwork's referent, she urged teachers to cultivate individual expression of the self and also of the essence of the subject being drawn. Each element in the art work – the lines, the tone, the colour – should express the 'significance' of the subject's form and the character underlying its physical appearance. Here Nutt drew on terminology then in vogue. In 1913 Clive Bell had published his book *Art*, which introduced many to the notion of 'significant form'. In Sheffield, too, other theorists expressed ideas similar to Nutt's. In a lecture at Sheffield's Technical School of Art in August 1916, William Rothenstein, a portraitist who had been appointed to the newly created Chair of Civic Art at the University of Sheffield, told his audience:

> It is the artist's instinctive faith in the deep significance of all
> form . . . which make[s] the true value of his contribution to civili-
> sation. He . . . is able, through his faith in this exterior beauty, to
> interpret something of the reality which underlies it. [11]

13 ELIZABETH STYRING NUTT *Shape, the Alphabet of Drawing*, illustration from NUTT, E. S. (1916 [21]), *'Significance' or Flower Drawing with the Children* (Sheffield, J. W. Northend).

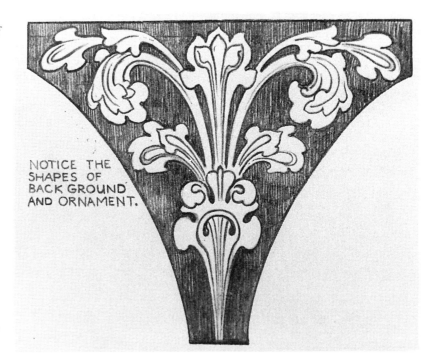

NOTICE THE SHAPES OF BACK GROUND AND ORNAMENT.

14 ELIZABETH STYRING NUTT *The Importance of the Lines of the Shade*, illustration from NUTT, E. S. (1916 [21]), *'Significance' or Flower Drawing with the Children* (Sheffield, J. W. Northend).

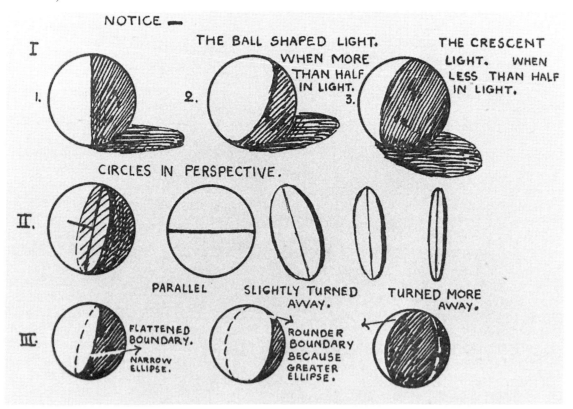

NOTICE —

THE BALL SHAPED LIGHT. WHEN MORE THAN HALF IN LIGHT.

THE CRESCENT LIGHT. WHEN LESS THAN HALF IN LIGHT.

I   1.   2.   3.

CIRCLES IN PERSPECTIVE.

II.   PARALLEL   SLIGHTLY TURNED AWAY.   TURNED MORE AWAY.

III.   FLATTENED BOUNDARY.   NARROW ELLIPSE.   ROUNDER BOUNDARY BECAUSE GREATER ELLIPSE.

110

Nutt would advance sentiments similar to Rothenstein's for the next three decades. Rothenstein was calling for a greater role for artist-craftsmen, an idea obviously arising from the Arts and Crafts movement, and one that was gaining credence in both Britain and North America. Nutt was to take such ideas, combine them with a particularly British landscape sensibility, her spiritual notions, and her theories on 'significance' and 'the world of appearance', and incorporate them all in a programme for Halifax's art school.

When Nutt arrived in Nova Scotia in October 1919, she found a school very different from those to which she had become accustomed. In the art school's dilapidated, century-old building overlooking Halifax Harbour, Nutt found a half dozen or so books, a few drawing boards, a couple of casts, several statues, an etching press, and only a handful of students. By the end of the year this had already begun to change.

Nutt made herself known in the community, with no prominent citizen or local business safe from her persuasive requests for donations. She used the money to recruit new students by offering subsidised tuition. Taking advantage of her free rein in curriculum matters, she initiated a variety of new craft courses, and then convinced the Board to hire a second faculty member to teach them. Other courses were added by designating the best pupils as student teachers, paying them a small bursary for their labours, thus expanding the school's offerings but not, to any great extent, its expenditures. She added prestige to the courses by instituting a diploma system. By 1921, the school could boast of 120 students and seven distinct programmes, each with its own diploma.

Nutt then convinced education officials to recognise the school's teacher's diploma and to compensate financially those who achieved it. The teacher's classes grew, and in 1924 there was money to hire a third faculty member to oversee them. Since the government did not dictate any standards for such courses, Nutt was able to set them for herself. She later incorporated some of her ideas into her third book, *The World of Appearance* [12]. Also in 1924, Nutt decided to require each student to study at least one craft, arguing that 'Crafts alone can make a design a real thing' [13]. Enrolment in craft courses consequently swelled, and a fourth faculty member was hired to help out with those.

Nutt also expanded the commercial art programme. She was very adept at finding projects with practical ends: students designed book plates and covers, theatre sets and costumes, Christmas cards, knitting patterns, and pages for the local newspaper. In all of this, Nutt was implementing art and craft theories brought with her from Sheffield.

When examining the art school's programme during the Nutt era it has to be borne in mind that Nutt rarely carried through with the described courses beyond the first few weeks of the fall. She spent each summer in Sheffield, returning to Halifax full of ideas and promises about reorganising the curriculum. The ideas found their way into the art school's publicity, but not necessarily into its classrooms. By mid-October Nutt was usually back to teaching in her pot-luck fashion, offering the students whatever she felt inspired to give them on that particular day. She rarely prepared her lessons, deciding on what she was going to teach just before she taught it. But she was an absorbing extemporaneous raconteur, and though the slogans in her lectures were always the same, the stories never were. She usually distorted history, depicting artists of the past as staunch strugglers for the artistic ideals and nebulous spiritual purposes that she herself espoused. She also tended to colour local events in a way that could promote her and the school's interests – the two being one and the same in her eyes.

Through all of her publicity and exertions, Nutt was able to put the art school on as firm a footing as it had been since its early years. Not that it was a symbol of opulence. It still received inadequate and insecure financing, and it was still housed in the same cramped fire trap that had been its home since 1903. Yet there was a renewed vibrancy in the school. In 1925, a legislative act elevated the institution's status to that of a college, changing its name from the Victoria School of Art and Design to the Nova Scotia College of Art (NSCA).

Dropping 'Design' from the school's name was by no means an indication that design was also being dropped from the curriculum. On the contrary, it was an indication of just how important Nutt felt design to be – so important that, to her, the word 'art' itself implied design. To include the latter in the school's name was now redundant. At that time three of the more influential design education theorists were Arthur Welsley Dow and Denman Ross from the United States and Walter Crane from England. Since the early part of the century, ideas from Dow and Ross had a small but recognisable impact on Halifax's art school. Lismer was to credit both Ross and Dow as influences on his early teaching. Nutt had at least second-hand familiarity with Ross's and Dow's designs ideas, especially as they manifested themselves in *School Arts* magazine, to which she regularly subscribed. But of the three design theorists, Crane's work seems to be most related to Nutt's NSCA curriculum. Such a situation is what one would suspect; Nutt had a strong attachment to the art of 'the Mother Country'. She also, of course, had a strong affinity with Crane's notions of the artist-worker, and the interpretations of Ruskin's romanticism that Crane represented. Crane's study of design was less analytical and systematic than Dow's, and certainly less so than Ross's. Crane's concerns centred around historic ornament, architectural details, overall patterns, and stylised floral, geometric, and animal motifs. Many of these same concerns were to be found in the NSCA course descriptions.

Nutt claimed that the College was 'really an apprentice school' that trained art workers who were capable of creating their own small businesses [14]. This claim had great cogency during Nova Scotia's economic depression of the 1920s. During that decade the number of workers in manufacturing decreased by 11.6 per cent throughout the province, while capital investment in manufacturing decreased by 5.57 per cent [15]. Instead of training workers for large-scale industries, then, the art school promised its students a path to cottage industries. For most students, however, the path turned out to be a dead end.

Nutt, like Lismer before her, was wrong: Nova Scotia's economy was not demanding trained art workers. In 1921, the census listed only 92 people employed in Halifax in art-related jobs – and that is if we use a generous interpretation of what constitutes such a job. Those 92 included 'artists and teachers of art'; 'decorators, drapers and window dressers'; 'designers and draftsmen'; 'engravers and lithographers'; 'photographers'; 'pottery, glass and china makers'; and 'printing and photography'. By 1941, this had increased slightly to 116 people, but this still constituted less than one half of one per cent of the civilian workforce. Furthermore, much of this increase took place in fields related to photography, for which the art school offered no courses. If photography were not included, art-related jobs actually decreased during Nutt's tenure, from 69 in 1921 to 63 in 1941 [16]. Not unlike many art educators today, Nutt's rationales for art education had more to do with merchandising a programme than with objective analysis. Training labour did not, in itself, create a demand for that labour.

Stanley Royle
In 1931 Nutt recruited Stanley Royle to come from Sheffield and teach at the NSCA. This was the first time since Nutt had taken over the College that somebody was hired who was not a former student of the school. Nutt knew Royle from Sheffield; before and after she moved to Halifax, she had spent each summer in Sheffield painting with him [17]. She boasted to the NSCA Directors that Royle's student days were 'a brilliant success of triumphs' [18]. He had been a scholarship student, was the recipient of the King's Prize in Design, and was awarded a silver medal in a lithography competition opened to all of the British Isles. Royle had been represented in the Royal Academy of Arts exhibition every year except two since 1913, and his work hung in collections in Britain, the United States, and Japan.

The Royles arrived in Halifax in December 1931. A charmer, Stanley Royle was quick to win over his new charges. His daughter, Jean, enrolled in the College's fine arts programme, and both artists had a good winter term. In Nutt's annual report, the principal told the Directors that:

> The College is indeed fortunate in securing [Royle] . . . we have secured a most loyal member of our staff, one whose ideals of both life and art are of the highest [19].

She would soon change her mind.

In November 1932 Stanley Royle was made Laureate of Art by the Montreal inter-department Art Association. In the previous month he had packed off two of his paintings and one of Jean's to the Royal Canadian Academy, which had accepted the works for its exhibition. Jean was one of the youngest RCA exhibitors that year, and the first NSCA student to have a large oil hung by the Academy.

A Weakening Principalship

The first major strains began to disrupt Nutt's school. After 13 years under Nutt's dominance, local artists were experiencing the limits of her ideas. Some artists were calling for new directions in the arts community, but Nutt was not about to let them stray from the path that she had set.

The Board had given her artistic control of the College, and that gave her control of government-sponsored exhibitions and art lectures. In her view, and in the view of most Board members, you either were loyal to the principal or you were cut off from the College network.

In 1933 Royle conducted a very successful summer school that was not given under the auspices of the art college. This, to Nutt, was insubordination.

Things immediately got worse. Local newspapers began comparing Royle's paintings to Nutt's, and preferring Royle's. Members of the Nova Scotia Society of Artists (NSSA) began comparing Royle's method of teaching with that of Nutt's, and preferring Royle's. A local gallery, Zwicker's, gave Royle a September exhibition of his summer work. In a newspaper review of the show, the gallery's operator made no attempt to disguise his weariness of Nutt's time-worn rhetoric:

> They are arresting canvases, suggesting consummate emphasis by the artist on technique rather than responsiveness to what might be called the subjective in 'the world of appearances.' . . . There is not a suggestion of the 'spiritual,' if one may so speak, in the collection of striking pictures [20].

Nutt, acting like a teacher who is challenged by her impudent charges, moved quickly and firmly to display her authority. She hauled Royle into the office and, as she put it, read him the 'Riot Act to pull his Life work together' [21]. She then took over his senior class. Under Royle, she claimed, the senior students had received poor teaching or no teaching at all. Worse, the senior students were being unduly influenced against the principal. When the less-timid seniors complained about Nutt's takeover, she accused Royle's daughter Jean of stirring them up, and suspended her from the school.

Then she charged that Royle had copied her style. Today that charge still remains unsettled. Michael Tooby notes that Royle's 'oeuvre is extremely close in style to the paintings of E. S. Nutt' [22]. Others point out that Royle's painting did undergo changes after he arrived in Canada, and that he may even have taken a few tips from Nutt's palette. But, they contend, any resemblance between Royle's Nova Scotia work and that of Nutt's is not a result of Royle copying the style of the College principal. Rather, Royle's painting, as with other English artists in Canada, was subject to natural influences, the most demanding of which was the intensity of light [23].

Nutt continued to harass and disparage Royle. Ignoring her earlier praise for his teaching, she wrote the Directors a letter that claimed Royle:

> is unsatisfactory as a teacher. He does not sufficiently know the *groundwork* of Fine Art to communicate the principles of the subject to his students. The need of the College is for *teachers* who are sufficiently educated in the subject, and who can communicate their knowledge, rather than for artists whose major energies are devoted to their own work [24].

Through all of this, most Directors stuck with their strong principal. Some Board members defended Royle – mostly those serving by virtue of their education background and not their business success. But they were outvoted. The Board's final decision came in May 1934. Although the charges alleging that Royle was instigating a rebellion and was incompetent as an art teacher were never substantiated, he was fired.

In the summer of 1934, both Royle and Nutt sailed to England, but only Nutt returned in the fall. However, Zwicker's Gallery regularly showed Royle's work, and he had paintings hung in the March 1935 NSSA annual exhibition. In reviews of the NSSA show, Royle's paintings often grabbed headlines, while discussion of Nutt's work was sometimes buried in the nether regions of the article. Later that month Nutt heard a disturbing announcement. Royle was returning to Nova Scotia to teach a summer art class. Nutt was further frustrated when Royle's class attracted students not only from Nova Scotia but also from other parts of Canada and the United States. It was better attended than the art college's summer programme. In fact, it was probably the largest summer art school in the Maritime provinces.

A year later, in March 1936, Nutt gave a speech to the Maritimes Women's Club in Montreal. She told her audience that she was convinced that the Maritimes, through the Nova Scotia College of Art, would soon produce its own style of art, different from central or western Canada. Her prediction was partly correct, since a notable Maritime art style did begin to emerge during Nutt's tenure as NSCA principal. However, it did not sprout from the art college. Instead, the centre for this Maritime school of painting was Mount Allison University in Sackville, New Brunswick. One of the earliest, and most prominent, leaders in this art movement was Alex Colville. On more than one occasion Colville has acknowledged his debt to his teacher at Mount Allison, Stanley Royle [25].

Royle had taken up his duties as head of Mount Allison's art department immediately following his 1935 summer art school in Nova Scotia. He headed the department until 1945, after which he returned to England, where he died in 1961. It was under Royle that, in 1937, Mount Allison instituted its Bachelor of Fine Arts (BFA) degree programme, the first to be offered by a Canadian university. In the following year, Nutt would propose that the NSCA also offer a BFA by affiliating with Halifax's Dalhousie University. That proposal, however, would not be acted upon until 1962.

The energy of most other 64-year-old educators would have been completely dissipated by the battles Nutt fought in the early 1930s. The art college principal, however, had the stamina to push forward. Except for occasional lapses, she put the Royle debacle behind her. In the 1934–35 school year she became the National Convener of Fine Arts and Letters for the National Council of Women. In that capacity she gave national radio broadcasts on art and lectured in different cities in eastern Canada. In the winter and spring of 1935, Nutt took part in establishing the Maritime Art Association.

The end began for the principal in the 1940–41 school year: the 70-year-old Nutt had a nervous breakdown. The next year was to be her last at NSCA, after 24 years as its head. Despite the problems of her principalship, it cannot be denied that, under her, the College went from a neglected institution with a handful of students to a viable school with an increasingly secure funding base. She was able to do this despite an economic depression and a traditionally indifferent community. It may be because of Nutt that the College is still around today.

Conclusions

Because they had no centralised bureaucracy to dictate their programmes, the Sheffield artists in Nova Scotia had to devise a curriculum of their choosing. Their lack of understanding of local economic conditions, however, often led to choices that did not meet their stated goals. Lismer and Nutt promised their students jobs as artist-workers when few such jobs were to be had.

Furthermore, the 'strong principal weak faculty' model may have suited the Directors, but it failed the art community. The same tough-minded, single-focused characteristics that allowed Nutt to keep the College administratively stable also kept it artistically stagnant. Nutt strove to make the College a centre for art that reflected her own beliefs. But she made little room for artists whose beliefs were independent of hers, regardless of the qualities of those artists. When Nutt first began putting her ideas into practice she made the College a dynamic place. But when those ideas began to reach their inevitable limits, Nutt resisted the new ideas required to sustain the dynamism.

It is difficult to say whether the College's history during the inter-war years was a result of the strong *principalship* or the *strong principals*. It is most likely that it was a combination of the two. Lismer's independent nature allowed the Board to fall asleep knowing that the principal would maintain watch. Nutt's autocratic nature was suited to the Directors' vision of how an institution should be run. Without a national system to fall back on, heads of art schools had to be confident of their convictions. The three Sheffield artists who taught in Nova Scotia between the Wars obviously were.

Notes and References

1   I thank the University of New Brunswick Academic Development Fund, which helped finance this research, and the British Council, which helped me attend the NSEAD Annual Conference, Bournemouth 1988, where this chapter was delivered in the form of a paper. I also thank Harold Pearse for his assistance.

2   LISMER, A. (1917), letter dated 20 April to Dr A. H. MacKay, President, Board of Directors, Victoria School of Art and Design (Collection of NSCAD). Lismer took this line from a book by design theorist Arthur Wesley Dow: Dow, A. W. (1912), *Theory and Practice of Teaching Art* (New York, Teacher College, Columbia University), p. 1. Lismer used it without acknowledgement. It appears, then, that when Lismer was principal he already knew of Dow's ideas.

3   TOOBY, M. (n.d.) 'The New North and the Old. Being a Study of the Early Years of some Emigrés from Sheffield' (Draft document, Mappin Art Gallery, Sheffield).

4 LISMER (n. 2).
5 (1929) *Sixth Census of Canada, 1921: Vol. 4. Occupations* (Ottawa, F. A. Ackland), Table 5. (1936) *Seventh Census of Canada, 1931: Vol. 7. Occupations and Industries* (Ottawa, J. O. Patenaude), Table 43.
6 LISMER (1917), 'Principal's Report, Victoria School of Art and Design' in (1918) *Annual Report of the Superintendent of Education for Nova Scotia* (Halifax, King's Printer), pp. 203–6 (p. 204).
7 LISMER (n. 2), p. 7.
8 TOOBY (n. 3).
9 Review of NUTT, E. S. (1916), *'Significance', or Flower Drawing with the Children* (Sheffield, J. W. Northend) in (1918) 'Books Received, etc.', *Journal of the National Society of Art Masters* (2nd Series) 3, 4, p. 204. National Society for Education in Art and Design (NSEAD) Archives.
10 These notions reflect what Stankiewicz describes as a romantic idealist strain in nineteenth-century art education. See STANKIEWICZ, M. A. (1984), '"The Eye is a Nobler Organ": Ruskin and American Art Education' *Journal of Aesthetic Education*, 18, 2; pp. 51–64.
11 ROTHENSTEIN, W. (1916), *A Plea for the Wider Use of Artists & Craftsmen* (London, Constable), p. 8.
12 NUTT, E. S. (1935), *The World of Appearance* (Sheffield, J. W. Northend).
13 NUTT, E. S. (1924), 'Principal's Report, Victoria School of Art and Design, Halifax, Nova Scotia' in (1925) *Annual Report of the Superintendent of Education for Nova Scotia* (Halifax, King's Printer), pp. 192–7 (p. 196).
14 NUTT, E. S. (1927), 'Principal's Report, Victoria School of Art and Design, Halifax, N. S.' in (1927) *Annual Report of the Superintendent of Education for Nova Scotia* (Halifax, King's Printer), pp. 127–34 (p. 128).
15 (1934) *A submission on Dominion-Provincial Relations and the Fiscal Disabilities of Nova Scotia within Canadian Federation* (Halifax, n.p.).
16 Sixth Census (n. 5). (1946) *Eighth Census of Canada, 1941: Vol. 7. Gainfully Occupied by Occupations, Industries, etc.* (Ottawa, Edward Cloutier).
17 TOOBY (n. 3).
18 NUTT, E. S. (1932, May), Report to the Nova Scotia College of Art Directors, MG 17, 45, p. 196. Public Archives of Nova Scotia.
19 *Ibid.*
20 ZWICKER, L. R. (1933), 'Stanley Royle', *Mail*, 21 September.
21 SMITH, N. (1933), unpub. Diary [1925–43] entry 14 November. MG 17, 5, pp. 2–4; MG 17, 44, pp. 7–8. Public Archives of Nova Scotia. Norma Smith was the art school's secretary and Nutt's closest friend. From 1925–43 she kept a daily diary of her, Nutt's and the art school's activities. The diaries are often referred to as 'Nutt's Diaries'. Nutt also kept her own diary for at least one year (1933–4), the year of her major confrontation with Royle.
22 TOOBY (n. 3).
23 LAURETTE, P. C. (1986), personal interview with Don Soucy. ZWICKER, L. R. and ZWICKER, M. (1986), personal interviews with Don Soucy and Harold Pearse.
24 NUTT, E. S. (1933), letter dated 13 December to Directors of the Nova Scotia College of Art.
25 HAMMOCK, V. (1978), 'Art at Mount Allison', *Arts Atlantic*, 1, 3.

Chapter Eight

JOHN SWIFT Marion Richardson's Contribution to Art Teaching

The name of Marion Richardson is known to most art educators either as a charismatic proponent of child-centred art education and 'child art', or for the linking of pattern forms to handwriting. She is mentioned in most standard histories of art education, but too often in terms as broad as the ones I have just used. There has been little probing research into precisely what she proposed, when and how she put her ideas into practice, and to what degree her aims and methods were successful.

The last fifteen years have seen an increasing move away from child-centred learning. It has been linked with Progressivism and criticised for lowering standards, not being cost-effective, and exhibiting *laissez-faire* teaching attitudes. There has been much generalised criticism, which may or may not have accurately described the situation in England's classrooms, but among those blamed are, by implication, educators who proposed and practised a non-traditional approach. Such a teacher was Marion Richardson. This chapter will investigate and clarify her aims and methods, and evaluate their current relevance. In order to reveal Richardson's significance, her strategies of teaching will be described, their relationship to her own training examined, her first school syllabuses analysed, the influence of powerful friends assessed, and her mature syllabuses and ideas evaluated.

Generally Richardson throughout her school art teaching used eight distinct but related strategies which were intended to arouse and maintain the learner's visual awareness and sensitivity, to develop skills and knowledge, and to apply these to everyday experience predominantly through the visual memory. The strategies could be listed as: Mind-Picturing, Word-Picturing, Beauty Tours, Observation Studies, Experimental Studies, Classroom/Studio Environment, Pattern and Handwriting, and Pattern and Crafts.

Mind-Picturing involved the learner closing the eyes and allowing images of any type – figurative, non-figurative, ornamental, etc. – to appear in the 'mind's eye', whereas Word-Picturing consisted of carefully worded descriptions of actual events or paintings recalled by Richardson, or poems read by her, acting as stimulants for pictorial work. As in mind-picturing, the product was not predetermined, indeed the word-picture might or might not relate directly to the described image. Beauty Tours were guided walks through places of visual interest in the locality with an emphasis on the 'unexpected' beauty of the local urban environment. Specific qualities would be discussed *in situ* and recalled from memory in the studio. Observation Studies usually consisted of working from a posed model or still-life, and were frequently lit or staged to enhance their visual impact. They also consisted of coloured studies from

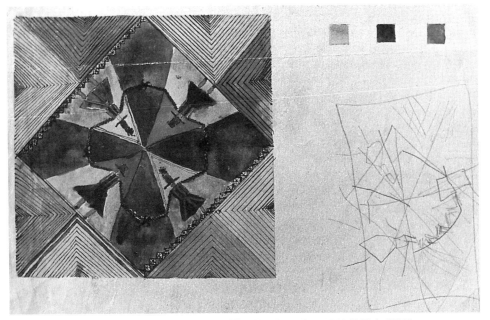

15 G. STANLEY (age 14) *Mind-Picture with Shut-Eye Drawing*, 1919 [MRA 4051].
Richardson began mind-picturing by borrowing the shut-eye techniques that she
had learned under Catterson-Smith at Birmingham Municipal School of Art.
However, rather than use the shut-eye drawing to replicate the essentials of
observed phenomena, she used it to capture involuntary images (which were not
necessarily representational) brought to consciousness through relaxation. The
shut-eye drawing acted as a rapid study to outline the subsequent mind-picture;
Marion Richardson Archives, School of Art and Design Education, Birmingham
Polytechnic.

artists' paintings, ranging from early Italian to contemporary reproduced
work. Experimental Studies were mostly concerned with either the
qualities and treatment of pigment, *viz.*, opacity, translucency, wet-in-
wet, dry brush work, etc. [1], or with colour, e.g., colour matching from
memory, colour exercises related to hue or chroma [2], and work
involving artists' use of colour, e.g., Neo-Impressionism [3]. The
classroom/studio environment was enhanced by the work of children and
reproductions of artists' work mounted and arranged, along with objects
to stimulate curiosity and colour memory. Pattern played an important
part in her teaching of both Handwriting and Crafts. In the former,
freely developed patterns using line, mass and colour were intended to
develop handwriting through the consideration of balance, symmetry,
and rhythm; in the latter, relief printing on paper, cloth and objects
(mostly from wood or linoleum), and occasionally decorated furniture in
the style of the Omega Workshop [4], related pattern to craft practices.

Mind-Picturing is arguably the most central and unusual part of her
teaching, although the different strategies should be seen as reciprocally
enriching. The term can be found in art educational texts, but its origins,
use and implications are usually left undetermined. This is in part due to
the mythology that only Richardson could teach and evaluate 'visions', or

16   F. TURLEY (age 13)
Beauty Hunt; Dudley, 1922
[MRA 7194].
Beauty hunts were either
guided or suggested by
Richardson, and
emphasised the unusual
aspects of the customary —
in other words, seeing
familiar scenes afresh or
anew. Having found and
memorised a suitable
subject, the pupil recreated
it from memory in the
school art studio; Marion
Richardson Archives,
School of Art and Design
Education, Birmingham
Polytechnic.

17   ANON (age 14) *Word-Picture: Russian Ballet Series: The Midnight Sun* n.d.
[1919] [MRA 4443].
Word-pictures were stimulated by oral presentations by Richardson. The pupils
began work when a retainable image began to form, even if it differed from the
input. The Russian Ballet series is a particularly strong sequence of paintings
where the power and freshness of Richardson's descriptions may have dominated
pupils' reactions; Marion Richardson Archives, School of Art and Design
Education, Birmingham Polytechnic.

120

that its contemporary scarcity as a teaching method rendered it idiosyncratic. Such a lack of attention demands a remedy where the antecedents, introduction, and development of its potential are examined.

Richardson's early education began at home, followed by a private school and a boarding school. In 1906, at fourteen years of age, she attended Milham Ford School in Oxford where she came under the influence of the headmistress, Miss Catherine Dodd, author of books on Herbartian principles of teaching which she had studied in Europe [5]. Dodd thought highly of Richardson [6], and the art mistress recommended her to sit for an open scholarship to Birmingham Municipal School of Arts and Crafts [7] in which she was successful. The principal of the Art School was Robert Catterson-Smith, who had originally trained as a fine artist, but had become an advocate of, and practitioner in the Arts and Crafts Movement. His book *Drawing from Memory and Mind Picturing* [8], published at the end of his teaching career in 1921, gives a clear if uncritical account of his teaching aims and methods. He was an advocate of training the visual memory, following and extending the earlier work of Lecoq de Boisbaudran in France.

In 1903 Catterson-Smith had taken over the Art School from Edward R. Taylor, another Arts and Crafts supporter, who also believed in and taught memory drawing. The type of visual memory training was essentially replicatory, i.e., the criterion for a successful memory drawing was the precise recovery of the initial stimulus. At the time, *c*.1900, the memory stimulus was usually a drawing or engraving, a set of geometrical figures, or details of ornamental casts. On his appointment Catterson-Smith continued using the same methods, but began to extend the subject-matter. His friend Henry Wilson, a noted silversmith and examiner of Birmingham Art School, had more far-reaching claims for the memory. Wilson reiterated the concept of the memory as the storehouse for the imagination, but further argued that it was the route to the unconscious area of the mind where the deeper, more profound spiritual values of each individual lay untapped [9]. Influenced by the range and persuasiveness of the claims, Catterson-Smith attempted to find a means to verify them, and developed the practice of 'visualisation' or what was more commonly called 'shut-eye drawing' around 1910 [10].

Typically in this activity, the learner was shown either a projected glass-slide, a drawing, or an object. Attention-directing comments were made before the learners were asked to close their eyes and visualise, or mentally picture, the stimulus. When the mental image was 'secure' the learner drew it on a small piece of paper with closed eyes. Then, with both the original stimulus and the shut-eye drawing removed, the learner drew the same stimulus with open eyes. While the claims made by Catterson-Smith paralleled those of Wilson, the practice and results did not. The relationship of the shut-eye drawing to the open-eye drawing was never clearly articulated or understood by Catterson-Smith or his staff, although he was aware that the shut-eye drawings were livelier. The overall purpose of the various memory and visualisation activities was to equip Birmingham industries with competent and able designers – designers who had heads stuffed with visualisations which they could emit on request, thus saving time and money. However, the criterion for success used by Catterson-Smith was almost always that of verisimilitude, so that claims for individual, unconscious, and imaginative powers, even if possible in theory, were mostly contradicted in practice. Catterson-Smith had 'discovered' visualisation *c.*1910, midway in Marion Richardson's four year studentship for art teaching. He was passionate in his pursuit of visualisation [11] and extended its use to almost every area of the Art School syllabus. It is highly probable that Richardson as a teenager would have been increasingly affected by the theories and various practices of visualisation. She would also have been aware that not all the staff agreed with the method and that some students found it problematic. Nevertheless, Catterson-Smith was an important influence on her, and they continued to exchange letters for many years after her studentship. Having completed her Art Pupil Teacher studentship, achieving the qualification of Art Class Teacher's Certificate, she gained employment at the newly rebuilt Dudley Girls High School in June 1912 to teach drawing throughout the school plus embroidery and lettering to some classes [12]. It should be remembered that at this time, the teaching of 'art' was rare; the customary term was 'drawing'.

Marion Richardson's first known *Drawing Syllabus* of 1915–1916 is particularly interesting in that mind-picturing is not mentioned, although the 'visual faculty' is. The overall aims were to allow each child to develop 'art as a means of expression'; to develop 'good taste'; to 'differentiate between the essential and the non-essential . . . to train the memory and the visual faculty'; and to 'give to those able to receive it, the power of accurate and skilful drawing'. The syllabus consisted of drawing from nature, drawing from geometrical models and common objects, drawing from life, drawing scenes out-of-doors, illustration, pattern-making, embroidery, colour washes and colour mixing. Apart from the last two activities, all the work was done from memory. Thus the syllabus was, in terms of titling, very like a standard Board of Education drawing programme: it is only when we realise that almost all work was produced by visual memorisation, that we see a different embryonic approach.

> The visual faculty is most directly trained in the making of patterns,
> but the girls are encouraged to visualise by a special time in each
> lesson being allotted this, before any work is begun [13].

In order to stimulate self-criticism and reveal that different age groups responded in different ways, each class in the school worked with the same syllabus. Thus within three years at most, Richardson had introduced the idea of visualising to all her art classes, but it is not absolutely clear from this just how Richardson used visualisation. That visualisation took place 'before any work is begun', could mean that she used visualisation as a type of exercise but that the mental pictures were not converted into paintings, or that visualisation of the idea preceded every piece of work.

It is relatively difficult to define precisely how one recognises a picture derived from visualisation, but much easier to recognise a mind-picture. This is because mind-pictures (at least those produced under Richardson's tutelage) tend to appear in a standard format, have the learner's comments under the image, and do not closely resemble any other form of work. In many cases, usually for exhibitions, Richardson has written something on the painting which also aids identification. Of the 568 mind-pictures in the Marion Richardson Archive, 529 are named by author and 199 are dated. The dating of many others can be approximately deduced from other dated work by the same pupil. The earliest dated examples are from 1916 (2). The numbers from the following years are 1917 (2), 1918 (9), 1919 (12), 1920 (25), 1921 (42), 1922 (8) and 1923 (20). The mind-pictures from her part-time teaching were also collected and retained, but in a more erratic manner.

The typical Richardson mind-picture developed from her use of shut-eye drawing learned at Birmingham School of Art. However, there are important changes in her use of it. The archive holds a small number of items where a shut-eye drawing is in evidence – two mind-pictures dated 1916 and 1919 [14] and one undated mind-pattern [15]. The evidence of her 1915–1916 *Drawing Syllabus* states that for mind-patterns a preliminary shut-eye drawing was made [16]. But this type of shut-eye drawing differed from that of Catterson-Smith. In Richardson's case there was no overt source – the idea was mentally induced. It would appear that from 1915 at the latest, she had continued to use the visualisation technique, but she had divested it of two of its former elements: its basis in direct observation, and its criterion of replication. Instead she had extended visualisation towards the qualities of imagination and the unconscious extolled by Henry Wilson.

Mind-pictures tend to fall into recognisable groups. Many are non-representational, some having soft, unfocused imagery, while others reveal hard-edged angularity. Some contain a mixture of both features. Some have what appears to be a random, accidental quality of colour and shape, while others tend towards a deliberate, pattern-like, decorative form. The minority are representational, showing views, people, and evidence of other paintings. Despite the relative orthodoxy of her *Drawing Syllabus*, in 1916 Richardson's pupils were producing non-figurative paintings and commenting on their quality both orally and in writing. Within one year of using this syllabus, Richardson wrote a brief introduction for an exhibition of Dudley Girls High School art work held in December 1917. This is worthy of close study, because it appears to show that she had developed sufficient confidence to ignore some, if not most of the requirements of the Board of Education examinations. Visualisation, memory and personal expression are emphasised in a way that finds no equivalent in statements by other art teachers of the period.

> The drawings in this exhibition are all the work of children who receive no help but the encouragement to draw. They are taught that drawing is a language that exists to speak about things that cannot be expressed in words.... It is these ideas and not literal and photographic representation of appearances that the artist seeks to express, and as the children are working with this motive ... their drawings must be considered as tiny works of art.
> There is no fixed syllabus ... as far as possible each child decides what she will draw and comes to the studio with her ideas ....

There is no emphasis laid upon mere skill and no direct teaching of mechanical, technical methods.

The force of an idea is of itself sufficient to find means of expression . . . if any such help is needed it is better given individually when the child is ready to ask for it.

The point most insisted upon is clear thinking . . . never begin to draw until they feel that they have grasped the idea . . . the greatest factor in attaining this clearness is the visual power. To attempt to teach visual drawing, and at the same time to reject any genuine visual effort is both contradictory and dangerous.

All art must reveal to us something of which we were not aware, we must not reject them [sic] for what seems to us queerness – queerness which we mostly accept in primitive or foreign art.

Look at them and try to receive the message . . . often simply an idea of space, colour, volume, contrast, etc . . . [17].

Suddenly, within a year, drawing from natural forms, geometrical models, life, etc., are no longer mentioned; the elements of instruction are reduced in significance; and the work is deemed 'tiny . . . art'. The syllabus as such is done away with, and the 'queerness' of the work is recommended and justified. From the 1915–1916 *Syllabus* that reached a compromise between her ideas and the requirements of the Board of Education, she appears to have become an advocate of children producing art, and of little, if any, instruction. What could explain such a shift of self-confidence and emphasis in the space of two years, and was Richardson's statement really accurate, or more a reflection of the Progressive reaction to traditional teaching?

The shift of emphasis may be explained in two ways – a growing confidence in her methods of working as the results confirmed her theories, and the influence of significant figures in the art world, especially Roger Fry. Richardson had seen one of the two Post-Impressionist exhibitions early in her career, probably the second one in 1913. She may have been recommended to attend by Margery Fry (Roger's sister) who was the warden of Birmingham University House where Richardson lodged from 1910 to 1912. Margery Fry had visited both exhibitions, bought one of Roger's paintings, and a little later furnished her rooms with the products of the Omega Workshop. As warden, she used to discuss the dreams and aspirations of her students and talk about pictures and books [18]. However, there is no evidence that Richardson met Roger Fry by arrangement. Richardson had been unsuccessfully interviewed for a post in London in early 1917, and had happened on a notice for an *Exhibition of Children's Drawings* at the Omega Workshops and met Fry there. She had shown him the Dudley girls' work, and he was sufficiently impressed to retain some for exhibition. Richardson's book *Art and the Child* indicates the nature of Fry's comments and their impact on her [19]. Fry was also impressed, and attempted to persuade the Minister of Education, Fisher, to employ her, and wrote an article about her work for the *Burlington Magazine* [20]. Fisher admired the work, and mentioned her in an annual address to Stockwell Training College in June, 1917 [21].

Roger Fry, like his ally and collaborator Clive Bell, had little patience with the customary teaching of drawing/art in schools. Bell had castigated the Royal Academy, the art schools, the private drawing masters, and the teachers of drawing in schools three or four years earlier in *Art* [22]. Fry had strong reasons for linking what he considered to be the 'natural' work of the Dudley children to that of the Post-Impressionists and his colleagues at the Omega Workshops. If he could establish that the qualities of 'primitivism' – directness, expressiveness, simplicity, spontaneity – were identifiable in the work of 'untaught' children, the recurrence of them in artists could be argued to be a continuum, rather than a break in tradition or an adult aberration. In other words, in order to explain the modern painters' work as a normal phenomenon, he had to be able to show that it derived from natural sources. Whereas badly-taught children lost their 'naturalness', evidence was still needed that the art of 'untaught' children epitomised the sought-for qualities. Richardson's pupils' work offered Fry the evidence and link he was seeking. Fry's 1917 *Exhibition of Children's Drawings* had shown the work of relatively untrained children of artists, but it was the Dudley work that contained the qualities of simplicity and directness that he valued. Obviously he would have speculated on how the work was achieved, and would have sought confirmation from Richardson that it resulted from a lack of directed teaching. How would Richardson as a young art teacher have responded to the magnetism of Fry's personality, and his well-articulated recapitulation theory?

Richardson's syllabus of 1915–1916 had already hinted that all children were capable to some degree of making art as 'a means of expression', that technical skill alone was insufficient, and that the memory and visual faculties were fundamental to her teaching. There is also little doubt that her reasons for using memory work and visualising techniques were to tap some of the more deep-seated, individual qualities within each pupil. Such qualities could not be taught as such, but could only be made apparent through encouragement and the giving of self-confidence to the learner, (although it should be noted that the means by which they would be represented certainly could be taught). To this extent at least, Richardson would have been susceptible to Fry's ideas. It is likely that he found her a willing listener, and that her shift from thinking of childrens' drawings as developing via teaching, to recognising 'natural' development without any formal teaching was readily made. Maybe she was ready for such a conversion, or perhaps Fry's theories offered her a reinforced and rational outcome for her practice: whatever the case, the 1917 exhibition notes for Dudley Girls High School reveal factors that reverberate with Fry's beliefs. They also make explicit the connection between the images of the young 'natural' and the 'primitive' artist, by drawing attention to those properties that Bell had argued were central to all art [23].

Two years later, in February 1919, in the introduction to an exhibition of drawings by the girls of Dudley High School at the Omega Workshops, Fry wrote:

All children who had not been taught had got something interesting and personal to say . . . with keen and unjaded visual appetite. Further . . . most educated children infallibly lost much, if not all, of this power when they reached the edge of complete self-consciousness.

Richardson's success was explained as developing:

a special system . . . without ever giving instruction or interfering with the free development of the individual vision . . . without setting them given tasks or modifying their means of expression . . . the children . . . have been encouraged to criticise their own and fellow-pupils' work and so to build up a common tradition . . . [24].

Fry's summary, whilst to some extent capturing the spirit of Richardson's teaching, passes over the fact that she did give instruction, set 'given tasks', and 'modified their means of expression'. It also implies that any teacher, who merely stood back and allowed children to behave 'naturally' would achieve identical results.

Certainly Richardson's aims were to reject the traditional drawing emphasis on externally agreed, skill-based replication and copying, and replace it with an experience that involved the learner in taking responsibility for the quality of work produced through working from visual memory and visualisation. In this experiential sense, each individual's responses at the level of ideas were encouraged and endorsed rather than altered, but the pupil still had to convert the idea or mental picture into physical reality. Despite Richardson's statement that the idea's force was generally sufficient [25], an examination of the work produced suggests that considerable time was spent in exploring media, varnishes, natural dyes, etc., and that extensive colour and pigment experiment was undertaken. The *Russian Ballet* series mainly produced in late 1919 could not have been produced without extensive pigment experimentation, and a sophisticated knowledge of how colours react against each other.

My contention is that around 1919, Richardson had acknowledged the importance of the teacher's role, and attempted to articulate it through publication. In 'Childrens' Drawing' [26] published as two articles, she goes some way to reinstate the importance of the teacher and the particular skills needed. The articles clearly show what she disliked most about contemporary art teaching, and what she considered essential in her own teaching. Whether Richardson considered these views to be counter to Fry's earlier claims and her own 1917 Exhibition statement is unknown, but a change of emphasis is clearly discernible – 'merely to refrain from teaching is not enough' [27].

The two articles examined five models for the teaching of drawing: Drawing as a Manual Discipline, Drawing as a Grammar of Art, Drawing as a Means of Training Observation, Drawing as Accomplishment, and Drawing as Free Expression. She rejected every one. The rejection of the first four is no surprise, but the fifth, 'free expression' is a term frequently linked to Richardson over the years. However, her dislike of the theory is absolute and clear – she considered the position to be riddled with loose terminology, it confused 'free' expression with lack of technique, and its notion of 'freedom' was usually more conditioned by the teacher's rather than the learner's view of 'successful expression'. In place of the five discarded models, Richardson erected a system which made the learner the ultimate arbiter, developed inner vision, and aided learning to express vision. The achievement of the system depended on the development of self-confidence, and eventually self-reliance of the learner, to enable the personalising of experience to occur. The teacher's positive and constructive assistance was needed here. Richardson did not anticipate literal correctness in the work, which she dismissed as external, standardised conventions, but expected the learner to recognise a truly realised image, worked to its proper resolution [28].

She argued that the teacher's role was fivefold: to be a provider of external stimuli to aid and develop individual impulses; to encourage the childs' efforts in a constructive and positive manner; to avoid offering artistic formulae; to act as a technical instructor in order to help and give incentive to self-discovery; and to guide, rather than impose, taste and aesthetic judgement. She did not mention several other aspects of her methods. She encouraged children to study the work of adult artists by making paintings based on their work, and she required children to talk and write about their images, and to act collaboratively in evaluating their work, although this may have been implied in the teacher's fifth role. It is also worthy of note that Richardson marked the children's work. Many of the paintings, word-pictures, and mind-pictures are graded, often with a series of marks relating to separate stages of the work's progress [29]. In line with her belief in a positive and constructive stance, most of her marks are high, invariably 'B' and 'A', although occasionally there is a comment by the pupil on the work 'to make up for a 'D',' [30] and in at least one case, her mark was altered by the class outvoting her.

It is apparent that by 1920 Richardson had rethought her position, and I would suggest that her consciousness of her own teaching practice had obliged her to re-emphasise the priorities of *teaching* art. She could not help but see her own role as central to her pupils' progress and achievement. Her later teaching methods, at Dudley Girls High School and elsewhere, do not appear to deviate much from the 1919 exposition of her practice. Her methods of relaxing the child and bringing 'inner visions' to the fore through suggestion via the spoken word or by mind-picturing, the development of these through technical exercises, 'beauty tours', colour and pattern memory, are established as early as 1915. Her methods are also evident in her notes for lectures, and in the work she retained which now forms the Marion Richardson Archive. The relative importance of each to the success of the whole is evident, but centres on the role of mind-picturing or visualisation in my view. Although Richardson herself believed towards the end of her life that the mind-pictures were preliminaries to the real work, I would argue that they were more than this, and that without them the other works would not have been possible. It is the process of realising mind-pictures in practice that is the basis of the relative success of each pupil in terms of confidence, awareness of individuality, and the means physically to realise mental ideas.

The mind-pictures may not be the most spectacular examples of the work although they are certainly the most unusual. They are mostly small and square in format. The necessary requirements to render a mind-picture qualitatively inform the word-pictures, beauty tours, and patterns. The children, with their eyes closed, faced with the request to relax and allow anything to 'appear', might have been expected to find this difficult. They usually sat in a circle on the floor, relaxed physically and mentally, and awaited some manifestation. Once something appeared and seemed fairly secure, the child went straight to a desk and painted. Richardson was adamant that she did not expect any 'forced', or artificially concocted images by physical or mental means.

Some information is available on how pupils reacted to Richardson's request [31]. This suggests that images when they did arrive, could be vague, unfocused, pulsating, moving across the field of vision, partly stable and partly mobile, flashing, or fading. Some were readily retainable, others more fugitive. Apart from the problem of retention, the quality and complexity of the colours, light, and textures were of a kind that normal observational painting practice did not encompass. Thus a programme of sophisticated technical exercises became necessary in order to assist the pupil to externally realise her internal image. The examples of colour charts, colour mixing, colour flooding, wet-in-wet, dry-in-wet, veiled washes, textural applications with a variety of tools, glazes, etc., were all attempts to find effective ways in which the pupil could parallel the intensity of the mind-picture. Not only were these exercises useful, they were a necessary set of skills needed for any hope of restating the force of the mental image. The techniques discovered were used with considerable skill and sensitivity in the mind-pictures, and in turn, were used in all other aspects of the pupils' work.

The mind-picture was not important merely because of its impetus to technical experiment and the consequences of that; it was also important for its own sake. A mind-picture by definition is not available to public scrutiny unless the 'owner' can replicate it in physical terms. Thus the only person who knows whether the physical replication and the original match each other, is the original 'owner' of the mental image. It follows that the 'owner' must be scrupulously honest in the assessment of success in rendering the mental image – thus, of necessity, confidence is placed in the learner by the teacher. The mind-picture required the owner to recognise that each and every such image was 'of the self', and in that sense, was a unique offering on a unique occasion. The pupils became adept at recognising the fake, forced, or contrived mind-picture. Richardson's work demonstrates that the pupils could be fair and self-critical, confident, technically adept, and aware of their individual uniqueness. It is upon those qualities, required by the mind-picture, that the rest of the visual work stands. Her continued use of the method throughout her teaching, lecturing and inspecting career supports this argument.

The muddle and confusion between the theory and practice of believers in child art, free expression, and the like have both distorted Richardson's views, and led to a re-evaluation of child-centred learning.

The re-evaluation has tended to typify the child-centred movement as undisciplined, lacking clear objectives, essentially untaught, profligate with time, and leading to lower standards. In addition it has been linked with Modernism, in a way which already prejudges Modernism as deservedly moribund [32]. Much of the above is arguable, but rather than making a full case here, I am merely sounding a note of caution against any too ready belief in the rationales of the excessive reaction that has already taken place. If the issues that have occasioned the swing have been misinterpreted and in part wrongly identified, a swing away from them may have moved to equally mistaken alternatives.

Richardson acts as a useful case study. The belief that child-centredness, as identified with Richardson, indicated a *laissez-faire* approach has been and is being challenged [33]. The evidence that Richardson's teaching of art enhanced and developed each learner's potential is relatively uncontroversial, as is the evidence that ex-pupils and students have recorded their indebtedness in some form or other to Richardson's direct influence. The hypothesis that Richardson's art teaching succeeded because it was based on sound educational theory, has been retested and found to be valid [34]. This is not to suggest that one can merely lift Richardson's theories and practice out of one context into another, but it is to suggest that there is proven value in what and how she taught. There are valuable qualities achievable through Richardson's methods which are no longer observable in the art rooms of junior or secondary schools, and which will be unlikely to be seen as long as the current obsession with predicted outcomes informs the content, and therefore the manner of art and design teaching.

Notes and References

1   Marion Richardson Archive (MRA) 4014–4021 and 4043. The MRA at Birmingham Polytechnic is part of the National Art and Design Education Archives (NADEA) Network.
2   MRA 4022–4029.
3   MRA. Unnumbered item dated 1919.
4   Examples of cupboards painted in this manner are on loan from the Dudley High School to the National Arts Education Archive, also part of the NADEA Network, Bretton Hall College.
5   See HOLDSWORTH, B. (1990), *Marion Richardson and the New Education* (unpublished M Phil., Birmingham Polytechnic).
6   MRA 895.
7   (1947) 'Marion Richardson 1892–1946', *Athene*, p. 6.
8   CATTERSON-SMITH, R. (1921), *Drawing from Memory and Mind-Picturing* (London, Pitman).
9   SWIFT, J. (1978), *Robert Catterson-Smith's Concept of Memory Drawing 1911–1920* (unpublished MA, Birmingham Polytechnic), pp. 31–2. See also SWIFT, J. (1983), *The Role of Drawing and Memory Drawing in English Art Education 1900–1980* (unpublished PhD, Birmingham Polytechnic), pp. 303–4.
10 Deduced from earliest dated examples and student register, Birmingham School of Art Archive (BSAA), Birmingham Polytechnic.
11 SWIFT (1978) (n. 9), p. 34.
12 Dudley Public Library: Staff Appointments.

13   MRA. Unnumbered *Drawing Syllabus 1915–1916.*

14   MRA 4033, and MRA (unnumbered item).

15   MRA 4056.

16   Syllabus (n. 13).

17   MRA. *Dudley Girls High School Art Exhibition*, December 1917.

18   HOLDSWORTH (n. 5).

19   RICHARDSON, M. (1948), *Art and the Child* (London, London University Press), pp. 30–2.

20   MRA 3203, June 1917.

21   HOLDSWORTH (n. 5).

22   BELL, C. (1913), *Art* (London, Chatto & Windus), p. 253.

23   MORAN, F. (1984), *The Impact of Children's Art on Art Criticism and the Fine and Decorative Arts in Britain 1900–1945* (unpublished MA, Courtauld Institute, University of London) pp. 3–13.

24   FRY, R. (1919), 'Introduction', *Exhibition of Drawings by Girls at Dudley Girls High School.*

25   *Ibid.* (n. 17).

26   RICHARDSON, M. (1921), 'Children's Drawings', *Child Life*, Froebel Society, March–June 1921 (first published *Cambridge Magazine* 1919).

27   *Ibid.*, March; p. 25.

28   *Ibid.*, March; pp. 27–8. June, pp. 48–50.

29   MRA 4031, 4125.

30   MRA 4096, 4125.

31   The MRA comprises letters, tape-recordings etc. Some letters were originated by Richardson, later letters and recordings by D. CAMPELL, P. ADAMS and J. SWIFT.

32   For example, see BRIGHTON, A. (1982), 'Ill Education through Art', and FULLER, P. (1982), 'Art Education: Some Observations', both in *Aspects* 18, n. p.

33   This view has been challenged by all Marion Richardson Teacher Fellows, whose reports are housed in the MRA. Reports are listed as dated: HART (1984); CIESLIK (1985); KINCH (1986); KEANE (1986); LARKIN (1987); and ADAMS (1987). A major exhibition of the first three MRTFS findings was held in Manchester in 1986.

34   SWIFT, J. (1986), 'Marion Richardson and the Mind Picture', *Canadian Review of Art Education Research*, 13, pp. 59–61. See also SWIFT, J. (1989), 'The Use of Art and Design Education Archives in Critical Studies' in THISTLEWOOD, D. (ed.) (1989), *Critical Studies in Art and Design Education*, Vol. 1 of the Art and Design Education Series (Harlow, Longman/NSEAD) pp. 158–70.

Chapter Nine

SUZANNE LEMERISE A New Approach to Art Education in Quebec: Irène Senécal's Role in the School System and the Art Field 1940–1955

For almost three decades Quebec has been a centre of the large art education movement advocated by the International Society for Education through Art (INSEA). This chapter describes and probes some of the conditions that enabled the emergence of this new trajectory in Quebec between 1940 and 1955, in which Irène Senécal is considered to have been a pioneer [1].

Irène Senécal was born in 1901, the oldest child in a low-income family. Her father (a tailor, in process of climbing the social ladder) differed in outlook from most Francophones of the time in his open-mindedness: he encouraged his children to study and obtain an education. Senécal entered the newly formed École des Beaux-Arts in 1924 and graduated in 1929. She was active in art education from 1930 to 1968, and influenced an unusually high number of young people because she always carried a triple teaching load – in the public schools; at the École des Beaux Arts de Montréal; and in Saturday morning classes. A painter by training, she exhibited her work until around 1955. She was a member of the *Association des Anciens des Beaux Arts* and of the Association of Women Painters.

An occurrence in 1987 prompted my research for this chapter. A colleague of mine, having learned of my interest in Senécal, said to me: 'Senécal was part of a reactionary group that fought against the artistic avant-garde.' He produced 'incriminating' evidence [2] to the effect that although Senécal was greatly appreciated as an innovator in the *art education field*, she was among those who resisted changes in the Quebec *art field*. This apparent contradiction demanded clarification in respect of her acknowledged innovations. From what position, and how, did she negotiate with the authorities for changes in art education? Was Senécal the only Francophone to advocate such changes? Were there others, and if so from what context did they speak? What theoretical considerations underpinned the proposed changes to traditional methods?

The first part of this chapter will briefly describe the social and institutional context within which Senécal started to teach (1930–1940). The second part will present Senécal's position and method, juxtaposed against the debates taking place in the art field and in the public schools regarding art education (1941–1950). The last part will deal with the first phase of implementation of a programme conceived by Senécal which aimed to change the paradigms for teaching art in the public schools (1950–1952).

Senécal began to teach in the public schools and at the École des Beaux-Arts de Montréal [3] in 1930. It was the beginning of the Depression; in Quebec this was a period of ideological conservatism. Church and state shared power. Education for Francophones, controlled by the Church, had a double structure: private schools led to universities and public schools led to the workplace.

In public general education, primary and secondary programmes were organised around polarities: the omnipresence of religion and the utilitarian character of lessons. The Drawing programme, with French influence, reflected the latter, and aimed to develop talent in industrial design and, particularly, the decorative arts. Art appreciation, in which taste in art was to be developed, featured in the higher grades. Geometrical drawing was the theoretical and practical basis of classes, and imitative drawing from the model and still-life encouraged a naturalistic, replicative aesthetic.

In art, the Canadian landscape and Quebec regionalism were the dominant themes. During this time, Senécal took part in group exhibitions, her paintings dealing with daily life, landscapes and religious themes. A number of Montréal artists questioned 'official' values and called for an art that was more contemporary – in its treatment of formal problems as well as in its themes. In 1939 a group of artists, declaring their devotion to 'living art', formed the Contemporary Art Society.

Lay teacher-specialists had great difficulty over integration into schools. In 1993, in a speech to colleagues at the École des Beaux-Arts, Senécal voiced her anxiety about difficulties she faced:

> Why don't these children like drawing? What are the causes, and how do we fight them? [4]

She felt that professional competence and a tolerant attitude towards children's mistakes would help in developing their memory and imagination, thus avoiding an evident lack of stimulation in the uniformity of their work.

Against the backdrop of the Second World War, many artists who had been in Europe returned to Canada, and a number of French intellectuals (including such eminent visitors as the Surrealist poet André Breton and the painter Fernand Léger) left their occupied homeland and came to Quebec. Father Marie-Alain Couturier, who was interested in the stylistic replenishment of religious art and architecture, was invited to the École des Beaux-Arts. Conflicts between him and the Director, Maillard, were immediately apparent, and he noisily left the school [5].

In 1941, Father Couturier organised, in Quebec City, an exhibition of a group of young artists entitled *Le Salon des Indépendants*. Maillard saw evidence of a conspiracy in this title, and attacked three of the artists in the exhibition, since they had not mentioned in their curricula vitae the fact that they had graduated from the École des Beaux-Arts. He saw this omission as a personal affront [6]. The artists released a statement condemning education in the art schools as deplorably academic. A month later, Irène Senécal, who was secretary of the *Association des*

Anciens des Beaux-Arts, published a declaration, signed by 55 persons, endorsing Maillard's position. Senécal thus placed herself on the side of those the young artists were fighting. The artists and intellectuals who attacked the École des Beaux-Arts in 1941 also rejected methods of teaching art practised in the public schools. During this debate, a newspaper article reported the following remarks by Father Couturier:

> [He] declares himself struck by the richness of our talents, especially among our children. But, he continues, these precious talents are wasted in the academism and false classicism that are taught to students. They are stifled, because their sense of liberty is taken away [7].

In 1945, Maurice Gagnon, art historian and critic, recorded the debates in a book entitled *On the Present State of Canadian Art*, an entire chapter of which was dedicated to art education. Gagnon took a position opposing drawing by observation, utilitarian drawing, and strict imitation. He endorsed free expression, paid homage to a number of pioneers from both linguistic groups, including Paul-Émile Borduas, cited a 1941 children's exhibition from England, and praised educational institutions that were open to new concepts. Bordaus, the leader of the avant-garde group of painters called the 'automatists', who, by use of abstraction, laid claim to being 'superrational surrealists', stated, in an autobiographical text:

> Children's drawings are the only confirmation that the road we are following will one day lead to victory, even if it is a hundred years after my death. Everything else presents itself as dreams, illusions, false and unrealisable hopes. . . . The children who have stayed with me have opened wide the door to surrealism by automatic writing. Finally, the most perfect condition for painting has been revealed to me [8].

For Borduas and Gagnon, as for many in the modernist movement, the child was a poet, and children's spontaneous expression formed the basis for the aesthetic conception of the avant-garde.

Léon Bellefleur was a primary school teacher who had a passion for painting; in 1946, in his first exhibition, he presented his paintings accompanied by paintings by his own children. A year later, he wrote an article denouncing 'copies' and 'academic tricks' [9]; however, in spite of his involvement with painting and his declarations on children's art, he did not in any way modify the way he taught art in his classes, because, in his view, it was impossible to do so in the context of the time [10].

Bellefleur had a point. The intellectual milieu reacted violently to the automatists and to abstract artists, who advocated not only a new art but a new art education. The traditionalists used an arsenal of terms to condemn, socially and intellectually, all practitioners of this disruptive form of art: madness, anarchism, communism, Bolshevism, and materialism [11].

Those within the school systems did not stand on the sidelines during the debate. Maurice Lebel, director of art education at the Montréal Catholic School Commission (MCSC) (to whom Senécal reported in her capacity as art teacher), mentioned on a number of occasions the necessity to reject the influences of surrealist and abstract artists. In 1943, in his annual report to his superiors, Lebel wrote:

> There is a reaction against certain ultra-modern aesthetic influences from the outside, which are trying to insinuate themselves into our teaching. Certain admirers of modernism (none of whom are on our staff) are advocating theories that have questionable value to our programme, for they are aimed at a unique artistic culture. They invoke the 'subconscious', 'originality', 'personality', and 'pure ingenuity', and even propose suppression of all methodological techniques, which will take us straight down the road to anarchy and absolute graphic freedom . . . . Our official art programme tends toward utilitarian applications, but 'training' artists is not our mandate. [12]

Lebel used instrumentalist arguments to respond to attacks levelled at art teachers. He avoided the issue of training in art appreciation and development of artistic tastes, which were an integral part of the official art programmes. He denounced modernism and automatism, because they broke the alliance between academe and utilitarian production.

In 1948, a new art-education programme for primary schools was approved by the Catholic Committee of the Department of Public Education. This programme was divided into two sections: psychological directives and pedagogic directives. In the first section, the development of artistic expression in children was delineated: from involuntary drawing, the child progressed to voluntary drawing, which had three stages: lack of reality, intellectual reality, and visual reality [13]. In the pedagogic directives, drawing was defined as 'an ensemble of shapes, lines, and colours that represent the exterior world'; observation, memory, and imagination exercises allowed concretisation of the mental image of the model. This document presented two conceptions of drawing, one relating to children's graphic development and one relating to the traditional definition of drawing. A 'domestication' of nature or 'instinct' was proposed which submitted expressive, spontaneous drawing to 'rational teaching'. The programme was evidently responding to detractors by advancing a scholarly theory of shape which could better guide children towards visual realism and geometricisation of forms.

Irène Senécal's progress: experiments and official recognition

Senécal, caught between Maillard's polemical battles with young artists and Lebel's watchdog attitude toward his teachers, was regarded as a teacher who was docile and respectful of authority.

> Starting in 1942, I was categorised as a figurative painter, that is, an academic painter . . . . I was never able to join the avant-garde painters, partly because they never asked me, and partly because I was working too hard as a teacher – what's more, as a teacher in the official system [14].

This quotation clarifies retrospectively the situation at that time. It contextualises the debate at two levels, stylistic divergences and institutional positions: young artists embraced cubism, surrealism, and abstraction, and attacked academicism. Senécal painted landscapes, portraits, and scenes of daily life – paintings which in no way broke with official art; besides, she occupied an official teaching position and publicly supported institutional positions. Her comment thus raises a number of questions: how did Senécal come to terms with this conflict and become the leader of a new school of thought? What were her influences, her progressions, and her guides, and where did she innovate?

In 1942, Senécal was invited to organise Saturday classes to awaken children to art (*'éveil à l' art'*) in public libraries in Montréal. Liberated from the supervision of the school programmes, she supplemented presentation of works of art with activities where the children expressed themselves freely:

> Seeing the interest and enthusiasm of children visiting the library
> when they were in the presence of works of art, Miss Senécal
> decided to try another experiment. She started to get the children to
> draw freely. She furnished them with crayons, water paints,
> brushes, and large sheets of paper, and asked them to give their
> imagination free rein [15].

Senécal's interest in children's spontaneous expression was confirmed in the discovery of an archive she carefully kept of drawings by her niece, dated 1942. These experiments outside of the schools coincided with Senécal's discovery, in 1944, of a small book by Tomlinson, *Children as Artists*; the Saturday courses allowed Senécal to discover through personal experience that which had been known in the Anglophone and automatist communities for a number of years. Examination

18 Irène Senécal's Saturday art class in a children's library; first evidence of her pedagogy based on spontaneous expression. Photograph from *Le Samedi*, 1944.

of Senécal's course-preparation books reveals that in her teaching in the schools, she conformed to the requirements of the programme and of her Director; however, she was constantly attempting to improve her pedagogical methods, and she tried, tentatively, to increase the amount of work produced along themes drawn from the daily lives of the children and adolescents she taught.

Numerous documents attest to the fact that the drawing programme of 1948 profoundly outraged Senécal, and filled her with bitterness. The Director of art education of Montréal reported the reactions of teachers to the new drawing programme:

> The ladies were of the opinion that the new primary school art program is too bookish and has too much technical terminology, that it could paralyse children's sensitive and imaginative concepts, and that it is too far away from modern, up-to-date trends [16].

At any rate, Senécal's Saturday programme was noticed: in 1948, J. G. Chassé, Director of Studies at the School Commission of Lachine, a

19 IRÈNE SENÉCAL *Still-Life*, oil, 1941; Suzanne Lemerise.

20 PAUL-ÉMILE BORDUAS *Abstraction verte*, oil, 1941; Collection of the Montreal Museum of Fine Arts, Purchase Contribution of the Government of Canada under the terms of the Cultural Property Export and Import Act and Harry W Thorpe Bequest.

suburb of Montréal, invited her to develop a series of art exercises for primary school teachers. In 1949, she went to the Seventh Annual Conference of the Committee on Art Education, organised by Victor d'Amico, at the Museum of Modern Art, in New York, taking a number of documents with her. In 1950, Senécal obtained from the Director of Studies of the MSCS, Trefflé Boulanger, authorisation to experiment with her new methods in a Montréal school.

Between 1942 and 1950 many things happened in Senécal's career: new pedagogical experiments in courses outside the school system, new references confirming her views and ideas regarding innovation, and, especially, new support from Anglophone colleagues and various authorities. At this point, Tomlinson, Read, and Van Moé Laforest were Senécal's inspirations as she planned her themes; after 1952, Read, Lowenfeld, and Piaget became her unquestioned references. Booklets published by Sanborn in 1950, *Growing with Art* and *Art for Living*, fed the wide range of experiences she promoted in the classroom. Senécal was impressed by English and American writers, and linked her work to new research in psychology, particularly Piaget's.

'A New School': types of lessons developed by Senécal 1950–1952

Senécal prepared for her primary-school teachers in Lachine a series of sample lessons. This documentation indicates that Lowenfeld's stages were broadly explained to teachers in meetings, but do not appear in the sample lessons. Exercises in discovery and interpretation preceded each creative project; these exercises consisted of experimenting freely for a few minutes with a technique (dry pastel), a procedure (crumpling paper), or a notion of visual language. It was suggested to show to the students at this time reproductions of non-figurative works of art.

This familiarisation with new ideas, new materials, and new procedures was then put to use in thematic creations, which varied according to the age of the child. Senécal suggested themes related to the child's school life, family life, and social life [17]. There were more exercises in memory and imagination than exercises in observation and decoration. Emphasis was placed on three-dimensional and relief work, collages, and collective work, sweeping aside the old hegemony of two dimensional work executed in one format, the drawing book. Works of art from different periods were to be integrated into the presentation of such themes as portraiture and still-lifes.

One notes a wild vacillation between terminology of the official programme and that proposed by Senécal to meet its requirements and to prepare students for examinations. By using different curricular and pedagogical strategies, and at the price of certain contradictions, Senécal was trying to change the old paradigm of teaching children's expression; at one level, she was trying to reconcile respect for the official programme with individual expression by the child. One also notes a differentiation between evocative memory and replicative memory [18]. Certain proposed 'technical' and 'decorative' compositions dealt with geometrical abstraction of shapes and colours, without measurements or references to functional objects or applications. Finally, she tried to harmonise instruction and expression by the use of explicit pedagogical directives and a way of teaching appropriate to children's development: 'We must remember that all adult concepts paralyse and destroy the precious gift of *children's spontaneity*' [19].

Implementation of the 'new method' was not without resistance; letters to Senécal from several young teachers attest to difficulties relating to classroom discipline, changes in criteria for evaluation of students' work, and the coexistence in the same school of traditional and new methods [20]. A letter from a provincial inspector to J. G. Chassé, in 1956, makes this laconic statement: 'Generally, the official study program is well applied, except for the teaching of drawing.'

After 1950, Senécal received increasing support. In 1952, Lowenfeld's *Creative and Mental Growth* was accepted by the MCSC as a reference volume. In 1955, Senécal created, at the École des Beaux-Arts, a programme of artistic pedagogy, which complemented its programme of studies in fine arts. She trained her adherents, which permitted her to disseminate the new art education. In 1955, she participated in the founding of the Canadian Society for Art Education, an organisation affiliated with INSEA. In 1956, a visual-arts programme replaced the drawing programme for secondary schools [21]. In the slow process of legitimisation of 'innovative' education in Francophone Quebec and the professionalisation of its teachers, Senécal remains the dominant figure.

Conclusion

In 1942, Irène Senécal was among the representatives of academic education; ten years later, she was working to implement a new definition of art education, a definition which prevails today and which, indeed, is now the orthodox definition. I have sought to identify the conditions under which a new trajectory emerged in the Quebec school system. The teaching positions that Senécal occupied at different academic levels contributed to this emergence, as did her determination to solve problems in learning that she encountered in the 'thirties, her intuitive discovery of children's expression, confirmed by the theories of Lowenfeld, Piaget, and Read, her contacts with the Anglophone milieu, her capacity to conceive a practical teaching methodology and to play a leadership role. In 1976, she commented on her involvement:

> I didn't choose to do only painting or only teaching. I was caught up in teaching, because I knew that children could not follow the programmes that were being taught. It was within teaching that I attempted to deal with problems of innovation, because it was of primary importance to me [22].

Senécal's rapport with the art milieu diminished gradually; there was no explicit relationship between her personal imagery and her pedagogical involvement, though Borduas and other artists of the modern movement considered children's spontaneous drawing the foundation of their aesthetic ethos. The avant-garde was not able to modify the approach to art education, because it aroused too much aggressive opposition, but one can easily imagine that Senécal was indirectly touched by it. At the beginning of her career, she played by the rules of the educational milieu, and it was through negotiation with the authorities and compromise with the official programmes that she was able to change pedagogical methods in art education.

The influence of the Anglophone milieu and the pre-eminence of American and English thought were the determining factors of the content of the new trajectory. Armed with these theories, Senécal expanded the network of forces, previously dominated by French thought, brought to bear upon art education in Quebec. Between 1950 and 1960, no French texts appeared in the lists of suggested documents for new pedagogical approaches. To trade in the old French and Québécois models for the American and English models was almost a sign of liberation, a way of registering rebellion. Many intellectuals, artists, and politicians in the 'fifties felt that Quebec was backward and that France was imposing its cultural values, hence the desire for other models, which were generally American.

This Québécois allegiance to American thought, especially under the aegis of Lowenfeld, could be interpreted as proof of the overweening expansionism of the ideology of the United States, which was seen as the paradigm of liberty and democracy [23]. The present chapter explores an example of how certain dominant theories were received in and appropriated by relatively small communities [24]. In Quebec in the 'fifties, these appropriations became part of an ideology whose aim was to modify the political and cultural climate of Quebec and bring it forward into the modern era [25].

Another path is indicated in the following quotation: 'What is going on in art education is that which teachers are doing in the elementary schools, the secondary schools' [26]. This observation is pertinent to the present article, because between 1950 and 1952 Senécal installed a concrete curriculum for the school system in Quebec, which gained legitimacy in the 'sixties. At this time, the practice of art education referred to Senécal's theories in a way that was more implicit than explicit. Senécal started to write in the 'sixties, and so it became easier to discern the true effect of certain influences on her actions and her thoughts.

Seen globally, the emergence of a new trajectory in art education highlights the conflictual relationships between different factions in the art and education fields. In the decades covered here the stakes were double: the academic artistic tradition was reconciling with the utilitarian function of art and the school programmes in the reproduction of values and usages. Senécal – like Borduas and the automatists – subjugated the representation of nature and the teaching of visual arts to 'natural laws' of the genesis of creation, and distanced herself from the representative and utilitarian societal functions of art. This rupture between expressive art and functional, utilitarian art took the debates on art education to the level of autonomy of artistic practice. As this chapter reinforces, the links between modernism and children's expression are fundamental – especially if one takes into account the conflictual relationships between the art field and industrial society, that is, between the autonomy of the aesthetic sphere on the one hand, and scientific rationalism and materialism on the other.

Notes and References

1   This chapter is a product of research with Leah Sherman on the role of two innovative women, Anne Savage and Irène Senécal, in art education in Quebec. We compared the American and European influences that bore on their thinking in different ways, and were interested in their relationships with the art field. We also noted the numerous uneasy relationships between English and French linguistic groups in Quebec. LEMERISE, S. and L. SHERMAN (1987), 'American and other Influences on Art Education in Quebec 1925–1960' paper presented at the NAEA Conference, Boston, April 1987.
2   SÉNECAL, I. (1941), 'Les Anciens des Beaux-Arts', *Le Devoir*, 14 June, p. 14.

3   The École des Beaux-Arts de Montréal was founded in 1922 to train artists, architects and art teachers. See COUTURE, E. and S. LEMERISE (1980) 'Insertion Sociale de l'École des Beaux-Arts de Montréal' in *L'Enseignement des Arts au Québec* (Montréal, Université du Québec à Montréal), pp. 1–73.
4   SENÉCAL, I. (1933), unpublished paper, p. 24. Senécal Collection, Université
    du Québec à Montréal (SC UQAM).
5   COUTURE and LEMERISE (n. 3).
6   BOURASSA, A. G., J. FISETTE and G. LAPOINTE (1987), *Paul-Émile Borduas* (Montréal, Les Presses de l'Université de Montréal; Édition Critique).
7   *Ibid.*, p. 555. The cited article is: (n.a.) 'Truer Art Stays Simple – Father Couturier, o.p., asks for Respect of Artistic Liberty', *La Presse*, 8 May 1941, p. 34.
8   BORDUAS, P-É. (1949), 'Projections Libérantes', *La Barre du Jour*, January–August, pp. 5–45.
9   BELLEFLEUR, L. (1947), 'Playdoyer pour l'Enfant', *Les Ateliers d'Art Graphique*, 2 (n.p.).
10 Interview Lemerise/BELLEFLEUR, 2 June 1987.
11 See LABERGE, D. (1945), *Anarchie dans l'Art* (Montréal, Éditions Fernand Pilon). See also BERGERON, R. (1946), *Art et Bolchévisme* (Montréal, Fides).
12 LEBEL, M. (1943), letter dated 23 December 1943 to Trefflé Boulanger, Director-General of Studies, Montreal Catholic School Commission, p. 5 (MCSC Archives).
13 These ideas were probably drawn freely from LUQUET, G.H. (1927), *Le Dessin Enfantin* (Paris, Delachaux & Niestlé).
14 Interview Lemerise/SENÉCAL, 24 January 1976.
15 SAINT-PIERRE, J.M. (1975), 'Irène Senécal et les Bibliothèques pour Enfants de Montréal', *Vision*, 19, Summer, pp. 32–3.
16 LEBEL, M. (1948), Report to the Inspectors, Montreal Catholic School Commission, 10 November (MSCS Archives).
17 In the Senécal Collection (SC UQAM), which contains 16,000 items, religious themes are largely dominant.
18 As elaborated by SWIFT, J. (1987), 'The Role of Visual Memory in Art Education 1880–1980: a Re-evaluation', paper presented at the Canadian Society for Education through Art (CSEA) Conference, Halifax, NS.
19 SENÉCAL, I. (1950–1952), 'Division of exercises for classes from 1st grade to 9th grade', *Direction des Études*, Lachine.
20 Letters D. BROSSEAU-TOUCHETTE and L. PARENT to SENÉCAL, 1951, 1952 (SC UQAM).
21 A similar change in primary schools was not made until 1968.
22 Interview Lemerise/SENÉCAL, 24 January 1976.
23 See COCKCROFT, E. (1974), 'Abstract Expressionism, Weapon of the Cold War', *Artforum* 12, pp. 39–41. See also FREEDMAN, K. (1988), 'Art Education and Changing Political Agendas: an Analysis of Curriculum Concerns of the 1940s and 1950s', *Studies in Art Education*, 29, 1, pp. 17–29.
24 See SOUCY, D. (1985), 'Present Views on the Past: Bases for the Future of Art Education', *Canadian Review of Art Education*, 12, pp. 3–10.
25 RIOUX, M. (1968), 'Sur l'Évolution des Idéologies au Québec, des origines à nos Jours', *Revue de l'Institut de Sociologie*, 1, pp. 95–124.
26 LOGAN; in Soucy (n. 24).

Chapter Ten

LEAH SHERMAN Anne Savage: A Study of her Development as an Artist/Teacher in the Canadian Art World, 1925–1950

Anne Douglas Savage (1896–1971) was a Canadian artist/teacher who made a significant impact on both Canadian art and art education in Quebec. She was one of the first women to participate actively in the creation of a school of Canadian painting; she was also an early exponent of child art. From 1922–1948, she taught at Baron Byng High School in Montreal where she developed an exemplary and avant-garde art programme and influenced some prominent Canadian artists and art educators. Her careers as an artist and as a teacher were closely related and interdependent. A study of her development provides insight into a germinal period in the history of Canadian art and art education.

In this chapter I will deal with the relationship between her painting and her teaching, and explore the ways in which she reconciled the aesthetic notions of the Canadian landscape movement with the pedagogical ideas of the day. Anne Savage was trained as a painter and was a self-taught teacher. As an artist, she was part of the vital Canadian art movements of the 'twenties and 'thirties with close links to the landscape painters who worked in the Northern Symbolist Landscape tradition to establish the first identifiably national school of Canadian painting. In her teaching, she was influenced by American and British developments in teaching methods and the new ideas about child art and 'creativity'.

Development as a Painter

Born in Montreal in 1896 to a well-established English Canadian family, she was brought up in a religious (Presbyterian) and cultured home. As a child, living in the countryside near Montreal, she developed an early attachment to nature and the visual world. She attended Montreal High School where art had an important place in the curriculum, and her early role models as art teachers were a Miss Stuart, who as art supervisor, 'put up her work', and Miss James who fought the academic structure of the high school to get time for 2 hour art periods [1].

Unable to pass the technically oriented drawing examination for entrance into McGill University, she enrolled in the school of the Art Association of Montreal, which she attended from 1914 to 1918. There she received an academic training in drawing, oil painting and (art nouveau) design and was also introduced to Impressionism and the new European developments by two of her teachers, Maurice Cullen and William Brymmer. Maurice Cullen, who had studied in Paris, was instrumental in bringing Impressionism to Canada. Savage recalls his influence:

The . . . thing about Maurice Cullen that . . . influenced me was his complete absorption with what he was doing and his great love of the outdoor world . . . . He loved the skies and the trees . . . he had a very sensitive reaction to moods . . . the lovely spotted feeling of the impressionist group . . . he freed us very much . . . for work [2].

William Brymner, Director of the school of the Art Association, was an influential painter and teacher. A fine draughtsman, he was a demanding teacher and imbued his students with a strong sense of purpose. Savage remembers Brymner as a man of great character and personality who was able to give his students a feeling of the importance of the world of art [3]. It was through Brymner that she was first exposed to the Canadian artists who were to inspire her painting, the Toronto-based painters called the Group of Seven who were to break with European tradition and develop a school of painting inspired by the Canadian environment.

Savage's generation of Canadians felt a new sense of nationalism and pride in their country. She identified closely with the developments in painting and became an early exponent and ardent supporter of the Group of Seven, following their exhibitions and their writings. She met them on trips to Toronto where they gathered at the studio of her friends Florence Wyle and Frances Loring. A. Y. Jackson, a Montreal painter who moved to Toronto, was a link between the artists working in the two cities, and he and Savage maintained a lifelong correspondence, sharing their discoveries. Jackson supported Savage who, as the younger of the two, often felt she worked in isolation [4].

In the introduction to his autobiography, Jackson recalls the pioneer spirit of the Group:

Things were different forty years ago; then a little group of embattled artists found itself in opposition to nearly everybody in the country. Through their efforts, the restraining hand of convention was loosened and new life was breathed into the arts in Canada [5].

The energy and excitement generated by these artists can be felt in the foreword to their third exhibition held in 1922. In it they wrote:

Artistic expression is a spirit, not a method, a pursuit, not a settled goal, an instinct, not a body of rules . . . Art must take to the road and risk all for the glory of the great adventure [6].

Savage must have internalised this message. Although teaching became her vocation, painting remained a central and centring force in her life. Her painting was influenced by both the ideology and the painting techniques of the Toronto painters. Although the Group of Seven struggled to find new ways of painting to suit the new Canadian content of their work, Mellen thinks that they did rely on European techniques. Their work was influenced by Impressionism, Post-Impressionism and Art Nouveau. The Art Nouveau aspect was clearly motivated by an exhibition of contemporary Scandinavian art held in Buffalo in 1918 [7].

From a historical perspective, the Canadian painters can now be seen as part of a movement which affected painters in North Europe and North America between 1890 and 1940. Roald Nasgaard, in his catalogue to the exhibition called *The Mystic North*, describes the movement as 'Symbolist Landscape Painting' and traces its roots to the Symbolist movement in art and literature in the late nineteenth century, and to Post-Impressionism, especially the painting of Gaugin. He defines the subjective aims of the 'true symbolist' as the:

> investing of given [subject matter] with subjective and transcendental meaning... [in an attempt] to achieve seamless continuity between external forms and states of inner feeling, freely transforming their subjects and reorganizing their forms and colours in the belief that meaning and form are inseparable [8].

He quotes Gaugin's advice to his friend, Emile Schuffenecker,

> Don't copy nature too closely. Art is an abstraction: as you dream amid nature, extrapolate art from it, and concentrate on what you will create as a result [9].

Savage's development as a painter encompasses many of the concerns of Canadian painting in her time. A study of her work reveals tendencies common to the landscape movement in general as well as definite ways in which she personalised its influence. Alfred Pinsky, her student at Baron Byng High School, and now a professor of painting and art criticism at Concordia University in Montreal says:

> For an English Canadian... in Montreal at that time, nature was revealed as an ideal state of joy, perfection and beauty... Anne Savage's attitude towards nature is one of gentle sweetness. She endows nature with a lot more design than nature ever had... she worked perfectly in a pre-abstract art situation... she was never a photographer or a realist; she was a designer of nature.... It seems that... she was saying that nature in its fullest is a perfect relationship of elements, of colour and shape and design and rhythm... and one thing Savage knows to almost a point of perfection is the relationship of colours that are muted... she can take a pink and a green and a muted yellow ochre and with fantastic sensitivity... work them together [10].

Savage transmitted her love of nature and her sense of design to her students. Pinsky goes on to say that:

> she gave us enough of specific information about colour, rhythm, form, picture composition so that combined with this enthusiasm, this love, you had a... remarkably good basis to work from [11].

On another occasion Pinsky amplified the philosophy behind her painting and described some of the problems inherent in her work.

> Savage's view of nature was essentially romantic... her ideal was the St Francis image of nature... man and nature are one, the birds and the animals are our friends... God's creatures to be loved. Love infused her attitude towards the landscape. Her self-image was humble and she was uncertain about her own talents.... She borrowed from other painters who were her contemporaries. The ongoing conflict (in her painting) is evident between the function of form as three-dimensional illusion and the two-dimensional decorative treatment.... She imposed a flat pattern on the three-dimensional image she was drawing from.... The conflict and

21 ANNE SAVAGE *Autumn Fantasy*, oil on canvas, 74.0 × 58.5 cm; Hamilton Art Gallery, Ontario.

difficulties of the art of the period seem evident. The art nouveau flattening out, an overall pattern which simplified and organised nature, leaving out light and shadow and emphasising rhythmical movement, dominated her work, and yet she was tied to the locale and its content. She often got involved in some volumes and flattening out in the same painting without being able to resolve the contradiction in spatial terms [12].

Like other landscape painters of her time, Anne Savage painted in oils directly from nature on small wooden panels which she then used as notes for larger studio paintings. These oil sketches and drawings in the sketchbooks in the Concordia collection reveal a keen perception of essential forms and a strong sense of place and mood. She could be selective and spontaneous at the same time and her sense of colour and fluency in drawing resulted in an immediacy and life which seemed to flow from her sentimental and spiritual attachment to the landscape.

Due to her involvement in teaching art, there were long gaps between painting periods, preventing her from having the continuity and concentration necessary to solve the painting problems that occurred in working out the large canvases. The immediacy and time span of the small panels seemed to suit the limitations under which she worked and perhaps account for the conviction and authenticity of the best of them.

In her studio she struggled with the problems of space and place and the contradictions between formalism and romanticism. As Pinsky recalled, she carried the emphasis on design over into her teaching, and during the time when she was doing both, it seemed that the pedagogy got in the way of the painting. She seemed to be self-consciously arranging forms on the canvas and often resorted to decorative devices. About the time she stopped teaching she began to paint more regularly. During those years I visited her studio often and we had many discussions about her painting process and the changes it was going through.

She changed from painting on stretched canvas to gessoed masonite. The white surface of the gesso was stimulating, suggesting an internal source of light. She talked about wanting to do 'pure' painting and often referred to the paintings of Cézanne. She became more experimental and the paintings took on a searching quality. She began to use a scraping technique in an attempt to retain the lightness and spontaneity of her outdoor sketches, and the familiar linear rhythms gave way to an overall surface treatment. She seemed more conscious of the contradictions between form and mood and tried to deal with space in a more abstract way. I sensed that place became more of a memory and space now was the two-dimensional space of the painting surface.

Although the demands of teaching and the need to structure learning experiences for her students had some inhibiting effects on her painting, there were also ways in which the teaching enriched and inspired the painting. The content of her painting carried over into her teaching, and she found support for her intuitive solutions to painting problems both in the pedagogical writings of the day and in the theories of contemporary art.

Development as a teacher

In 1922, when Anne Savage began her teaching career at Baron Byng High School in Montreal, she had no formal training as a teacher. A fellow painter and member of the Group of Seven, Arthur Lismer, introduced her to child art and encouraged her in her early teaching with positive feedback [13]. Lismer, an Englishman who had migrated to Canada in 1911, was an international pioneer in child art. In 1927 he brought Cizek's exhibition of children's art to Toronto, and was one of the first teachers in North America to implement the new approach to art education. Funded by the Carnegie Foundation, he ran an innovative educational programme at the Art Gallery of Ontario [14]. Inspired by Cizek's teachings, he believed that children could express their experience through drawing and painting. The theme of art as experience was basic to Lismer's approach, and consistent with the spirit of the times in which Canadians, including Lismer, were making new art inspired by direct experience with the land. He encouraged children to draw from their imaginations and replaced copying exercises with projects in which groups of children were engaged in researching, drawing, painting and constructing. His goal was to 'turn children on' to art through art experience. By 1932 he was travelling and lecturing on 'education through art' [15].

Savage recalls visiting Lismer's classes in Toronto around 1923:

> I would go up on a Saturday morning to see this demonstration, and I learned a great deal . . . I owe Arthur Lismer a very great debt . . . . I'll never forget the impression going into that gallery and seeing it just filled with children, with the most extraordinary feeling of enthusiasm going right through the group [16].

In 1937, Savage started Saturday art classes for children at the Art Association of Montreal. She had adopted Lismer's goals with the addition of her personal reasons for making and teaching art. In an information sheet sent to parents in 1940 she wrote:

> Our aim is to encourage and develop creative expression in children and to cultivate an early contact with art . . . the intensification of life, to perceive not merely to see, to give children a love of all things that grow . . . and to find interest and delight in just looking [17].

Other notes (in her handwriting) found in the archives reveal the concern with design which was to dominate so much of her teaching:

> The aim of this Saturday morning class for boys and girls between the ages of 10–15 is to encourage in them an interest in things of the art world. Their creative imagination is at its liveliest, and by stimulating them to use and apply the principles of design and form as found in any great work of art – they learn to understand the language of the artist – which seeks to express its feeling for life in terms of line – form and colour [18].

During the 1930s and 1940s, Quebec teachers were exposed to a wide variety of influences, both British and American. Books found in Savage's library included works by Belle Boas, Leon Winslow, Victor D'Amico, Morris Davidson, Ralph Pearson, Marion Richardson and Herbert Read. In addition it is certain that she read the *Quebec Educational Record* where articles by American and English educators were published. There is evidence from catalogues found in the archives that she saw travelling exhibitions of child art circulated by the British Council and the National Gallery of Canada and that she was aware of Marion Richardson's tour of Canada in 1934.

Savage was selective in her adoption of ideas and theories. Examples of her students' work and her pedagogical notes indicate that she evolved a successful method of teaching and then found the theories to support it. Her instructional devices and her subject matter were closely linked to her own painting concerns which centred around the reconciliation of the visual world with the demands of the flat surface, and the cultural move from representation to abstraction. Her sketchbooks reveal that she imposed a flat pattern on three-dimensional subject matter, eliminating light and shadow and emphasising rhythm and colour.

It appears that Savage found certain American writers confirmed her intuitive approach to teaching and helped her make the link between her painting and the necessity to structure a series of art lessons. In 1924, Belle Boas, a teacher at Horace Mann School in New York and a student of Arthur Wesley Dow's, published *Art in the School*. I found a well-worn copy of this book in the library at Baron Byng High School. Boas provided Anne Savage with a course of study 'built on principles of design as adapted to children's needs'. Savage's early curriculum follows Boas's ideas very closely. She taught design principles through subject matter which included, as Boas suggested, figure study, imaginative illustrations, still life compositions and landscape. In addition there were colour exercises and decorative design projects with motives taken from the museum [19]. Boas emphasised the use of works of art to illustrate design principles and picture study to learn art history. To this programme Savage added the story of the Canadian painters with whom she identified so personally.

In Morris Davidson's *Painting for Pleasure*, Savage found a more conceptual approach to the teaching of painting, placing it in the context of modernist aesthetics. She copied excerpts from the book in one of her sketchbooks:

> It is not the poetry of subject matter which is the legitimate poetry of painting – it is the artist's organization of the canvas . . . the sense

22 *The Snowstorm*, painting by a student of Anne Savage, Baron Byng High School, Montreal, *c*. 1940; Anne Hirsh Collection, Montreal.

of space is not the same thing as the illusion of distance . . . a good
painting must have a good deal more power than the object
represented . . . a painting of an object is an abstraction [20].

Savage incorporated these concepts into her teaching. In the Calvin
interview she recalls:

> I would suggest that they [the students] go ahead for the big
> motif . . . get the big shapes in and then look for the dark shapes and
> the light shapes, and try to get rid of the extraneous detail so that
> they look for the structure . . . looking for the basic thing [21].

In 1948, Anne Savage was given a copy of Ralph Pearson's *The New
Art Education*. Pearson's book was popular with art educators of the late
1940s who were looking for ways to link abstract design with subject
matter. In addition, he invested the teaching of 'creative design' with
meaning and mission. He saw art as important for the spiritual life of all
people, 'a kind of spiritual language with universal meanings' [22]. This
spiritual aspect of art education had always been important to Anne
Savage. She was a deeply religious person and often turned to the Bible
and the scriptures as a source of content and inspiration. In 1938, she
said to the teachers of the Art Gallery school:

> One of the finest things we can teach young people is this, that each
> of us has the possibility of some new discovery in him . . . . Perhaps
> in no place do we read [more] of the high esteem in which the
> designer is held than in the accounts of the planning of the
> Tabernacle in the wilderness. Over and over it repeats how the
> workers were filled with the spirit of God . . . God hath put it in his
> heart that he may teach others these crafts [23].

In these words, we find indications of Savage's view of the artist and the
teaching of art. The artist is inspired and the teaching of art is a form of
service to God.

Two British books are quoted extensively in Anne Savage's notes.
They are Marion Richardson's *Art and the Child* and Herbert Read's
Education Through Art. In 'Art in the Elementary Grades', a booklet
written for teachers in 1951 when she was art supervisor for the Pro-
testant School Board, she calls Richardson 'the great inspired teacher in
England who brings the poetic approach to the spiritual values (of art
education)' and quotes from Richardson's *Art and the Child*: 'the teacher
frees the artist's vision within the child and inspires him to find a
completely truthful expression for it' [24]. According to Herbert Read,
Richardson revolutionised the methods of teaching art by changing the
role of the teacher from that of giving specific instruction to the creation
of an atmosphere of suggestion which would induce the child to exte-
riorise the rich imagery of the mind [25].

Anne Savage had always used descriptive storytelling to motivate
imaginative illustrations. Although highly visual, her 'mind-pictures'
lacked the emotional content of Richardson's descriptions. She was
inspired by Richardson's poetic quality, identified with her enthusiasm
for visual experience, and shared her confidence in children's artistic and
creative potential, but stopped short of the psychological introspection
that Richardson's method implied.

Savage was often called upon to give public talks and lectures. It was in Herbert Read's *Education Through Art* [26] that Savage found a philosophical rationale for art experience that she could share with other teachers. For her, art experience was centred around the enjoyment of the visual world. She could now reconcile the education of the senses implicit in her teaching with larger goals for the individual in society. By taking Read's social goals a step further, she was able to incorporate her religious mission as well.

Among her papers was a small packet of notes for a talk to teachers. She wrote:

> Those teachers here all agree, I know, with the essential need of art in the programme ... to show the point of view that the attitude of the artist to life is one that should be striven for and appreciated in all areas of learning ... as H. R. says in *Education Through Art* 'the purpose of education is to preserve the uniqueness of the individual and to integrate him with society' ... education discriminates between good and evil .... H. R.'s contention is that the development of good positive qualities eliminates the opposite negative poor qualities .... My contention is that ... we avoid hate by loving. We shall not need to repress because we have made of education a process which prevents us in the ways of evil – because the impulses which God will release precede the anti-social impulses [27].

Conclusion

The success of the teaching programme at Baron Byng can be attributed to several factors which coincided in time and place. Savage had the support of a sympathetic and tolerant principal and the freedom to develop her own curriculum. The students found her to be a strong and attractive role model. As first generation Canadians and as adolescents, they were rejecting the values and attitudes of their parents who were in transition from European to Canadian culture. Anne Savage provided them with an image of Canada which was humane, creative and exciting. She gave them a sense of self-worth through the identification with the artistic process. Her own relationship to the art of Canada was authentic and vital and she believed in the importance of the artist's role in society.

In the catalogue to her retrospective exhibition at Sir George Williams University, I recalled the special quality she projected in the classroom:

> as her student, and later as a fellow teacher, I was conscious of being a partner to discoveries which we shared. In her company, the visual world became an endless source of stimulation and pleasure [28].

Most significantly, she inspired confidence in the students' ability to make pictures and gave them strategies derived from her own art-making experience. Through the use of flat, linear and rhythmical pattern, the elimination of light and shadow, and an emphasis on pure colour, they were able to achieve satisfying pictures without resorting to the representational skills adolescents so often lack. As a result, there were very few students in her classes who experienced 'the crisis of adolescence'.

Anne Savage found herself in the centre of one of the most stimulating periods in the history of Canadian art and art education, both growing out of the same spirit of discovery, romanticism and humanism. Along with other artist/teachers, she was aware of the lack of cultural and human values in Canadian society and made it her mission to educate through art. Rather than accepting the role of art as (then) defined by the educational system in the service of a materialistic and industrial society, she would, in Arthur Lismer's words, see it 'as a creative force in the self-development of human beings' [29].

Notes and References

1 CALVIN, A. (1967), *Anne Savage, Teacher*, unpublished MA thesis, Sir George Williams University.
2 *Ibid.*, p. 21.
3 *Ibid.*, p. 3.
4 McDOUGALL, A. (1977), *Anne Savage: the Story of a Canadian Painter* (Montreal, Harvest House).
5 JACKSON, A. Y. (1958), *A Painter's Country* (Toronto, Clarke Irwin).
6 MELLON, P. (1970), *The Group of Seven* (Toronto/Montreal, McLelland & Stewart), p. 102.
7 *Ibid.*
8 NASGAARD, R. (1984), *The Mystic North* (Toronto, University of Toronto Press/Art Gallery of Ontario), p. 4.
9 *Ibid.*, p. 5.
10 CALVIN (n. 1), p. 8.
11 *Ibid.*
12 Interview Sherman/ALFRED PINSKY, 1980.
13 McDOUGALL (n. 4), p. 63.
14 YANOVER, S. (1980), *The Gallery School: 1930–1980: a Celebration* (Toronto, Art Gallery of Ontario).
15 *Ibid.*, p. 21.
16 CALVIN (n. 1), p. 24.
17 File 45, Item 12.5, Savage Archives (SA), Concordia University.
18 File 10, Item 3.5, SA (n. 17).
19 BOAS, B. (1924), *Art in the School* (New York, Doubleday, Doran & Co).
20 DAVIDSON, M. (3rd ed. 1938), *Painting for Pleasure* (Clinton Mass., Colonial Press), p. 38.
21 Interview Calvin/ALFRED PINSKY, Montreal 1967, SA (n. 17).
22 PEARSON, R. (1941), *The New Education* (New York, Harper).
23 File 10, Item 3.10, SA (n. 17).
24 RICHARDSON, M. (1948), *Art and the Child* (London, London University Press).
25 READ, H. (1943), 'Introduction', catalogue of the exhibition *British Council Exhibition of Children's Drawings* (London, British Council), p. 8.
26 READ, H. (1943), *Education through Art* (London, Faber).
27 File 12, Item 3.30, SA (n. 17).
28 SHERMAN, L. (1969), catalogue of the exhibition *Anne Savage: a Retrospective* (Montreal, the Art Gallery, Sir George Williams University).
29 LISMER, A. (1937–38), 'Foreword' catalogue of the exhibition *Pictures by Children* (Ottawa, National Gallery of Canada).

Chapter Eleven

DAVID THISTLEWOOD A Continuing Process: the New Creativity in British Art Education 1955–1965

The aims and objectives underlying a post-school art education in Britain changed utterly during the working lives of a generation of teachers. What prevailed before the 1950s was a system devoted to conformity, to a misconceived sense of belonging to a classical tradition, to a belief that art was essentially technical skill. What came to exist is a general devotion to the principle of *individual* creative development. There is no compromise between these two states; and so it is appropriate to describe the succession as 'revolutionary'. For decades there had been a preoccupation with drawing and painting according to set procedures; with the use of traditional subject-matter – the Life Model, Still-Life and the Antique [1]; with the 'application' of art in the execution of designs; with thorough knowledge of selected precedents, such as historical ornamentation; with, above all, the monitoring of progress by frequent examination. Now the validity of these began to be questioned in the search for a valid alternative.

Or rather *alternatives*, for in the early 1950s there were several. There had for a while been one – among the earliest, though generally unknown – shaped by Olive Sullivan at Manchester School of Art: this was inspired by an understanding of the Bauhaus, gained at first hand and from such sources as Herbert Read's *Art and Industry* [2]. There were other Bauhaus-like courses taught by Albert Halliwell at Camberwell and the Central Schools of Art from *c.* 1930 until the mid-1950s [3]. A range of alternative approaches was encouraged by William Johnstone when, as Principal of the Central School, he brought Victor Pasmore, Richard Hamilton, Eduardo Paolozzi, Robert Adams, William Turnbull, Alan Davie and others into his studios, giving them free rein to impart creative attitudes in previously moribund departments. And there was the approach first determined in a series of summer schools organised by the North Riding of Yorkshire Education Authority, which resulted in courses at Leeds College of Art and at King's College, University of Durham (at Newcastle-upon-Tyne). This latter approach came to dominate the alternative educational agenda for at least a decade.

The principal innovators here were four – Victor Pasmore, Richard Hamilton, Tom Hudson and Harry Thubron. This chapter, however, makes only limited reference to Thubron – not because he is thought to have been less important (in fact he was inspirational and his efforts were formative) but because his philosophy merits the separate consideration provided by Norbert Lynton in Chapter Twelve. Pasmore was knowledgeable about the Bauhaus and identified closely with Paul Klee's description of an ordered process of learning, beginning with considerations of mark-making, and progressing via linear exploration towards planar construction in space. Hamilton knew the theories of Klee, and also those of another prominent Bauhaus teacher, Laszlo Moholy-Nagy, who in his influential book *The New Vision* [4] had been concerned to identify certain principles common to all the visual-plastic arts. Hamilton, too, was a member of a group of artists, architects and critics, the Independent Group of the Institute of Contemporary Arts (ICA), which was committed to the idea that popular imagery and culture were worthy of respect. Hudson and Pasmore both had commitment to the subject of child art: Pasmore was fascinated by the power and richness of the work of the very young; while Hudson was trying to find ways of extending this state into the teenage years, when it was usually stifled. And Hudson had made studies of those modern art movements which had exploited principles of construction or assemblage, to bring these to bear upon art education as a counterpart of the expressive. They thus possessed distinct but overlapping interests, each of which held current 'organicist' theories in special regard.

Arguments about a fundamental connection between art and nature were being aired regularly at the ICA (of which Hamilton and Pasmore were members); and there was a brief period in which Goethian principles, in particular, seemed to underlie many of its presentations. Organic form could be said to be present 'not only in the crystal and the bone, in the leaf and in the cloud, but also in the painting and the poem': the form discoverable in nature would be said to be the very form revealed by art: a single creative process would be admitted – formation and transformation [5]. Such speculation led to the Institute's symposium *Aspects of Form* (1951), when a variety of views were presented of formative processes at work in art and in microscopic and macroscopic nature [6]. And it also prompted this attempt to maintain the relevance of Goethian arguments in the presence of modern science:

> The increasing significance given to 'form' or 'pattern' in various branches of science has suggested the possibility of a certain parallelism, if not identity, in the structures of natural phenomena and of authentic works of art . . . . The revelation that perception itself is essentially a pattern-selecting and pattern-making function . . . that pattern is inherent in the physical structure or in the functioning of the nervous system; that matter itself analyses into coherent patterns or arrangements of molecules; and the gradual realisation that all these patterns are effective and ontologically significant by virtue of an organisation in their parts which can only be characterised as 'aesthetic' – all this development has brought works of art and natural phenomena onto an identical plane of enquiry [7].

An exhibition entitled *Growth and Form*, organised by Hamilton, was held in conjunction with the symposium. This partly paid tribute to the scholarship of D'Arcy Wentworth Thompson, whose standard biological text *On Growth and Form* [8] had been appreciated for the insights it offered into artistic formation; and it partly put forth the suggestion that artists might take inspiration from the objects of a new visual environment, made available by microscopy.

Thompson's general thesis, elaborated in numerous studies of the growth of a vast range of living things, was that natural form was the product of growth and that this, stated simply, was conditioned by protoplasms responding to internal energies and external forces to produce *unique conformations*. In a very few simple organisms the results of growth were reasonably predictable; but in organisms having several 'growth points' (organisms, for example, composed of flesh, liquids, bone, cartilage and other tissues, each of which would exercise varying rates of growth), though generalities might be anticipated, the *precise* results of growth were individuated, complex and unpredictable. In all cases healthy growth was manifested in equilibration, unhealthy growth in aberrations which contributed to imbalance. There had been obvious temptations to seek analogies between such arguments and others relating to the growth and development of works of art. Hamilton had been astonished at the possible consistency, for example in passages such as these:

> The form, then, of any portion of matter [*of a work of art*] . . . and the changes of form which are apparent in its movements and in its growth [*in its development*] may in all cases alike be described as due to the action of force. In short, the form of an object is a 'diagram of forces', in this sense, at least, that from it we can judge of or deduce the forces that are acting or have acted upon it: in this strict and particular sense, it is a diagram – in the case of a solid [*in the case of a finished work of art*] of the forces which *have* been impressed upon it when its conformation was produced . . . in the case of a liquid [*in the case of a work in progress*] . . . of the forces which are for the moment acting on it to restrain or balance its own inherent mobility. [9]
>
> [And] . . . symmetry is highly characteristic of organic forms and is rarely absent in living things – save in such few cases as *Amoeba*, where the rest and equilibrium on which symmetry depends are likewise lacking. And if we ask what physical equilibrium has to do with formal symmetry and structural regularity, the reason is not far to seek, nor can it be better put than in these words . . . . 'In every symmetrical system every deformation that tends to destroy the symmetry is complemented by an equal and opposite deformation that tends to restore it. In each deformation, positive and negative work is done . . .' [10].

Acceptance of such ideas as being relevant to art carried important implications, the most obvious of which opposed the traditional rehearsal of pictorial form, in sketches and cartoons, as preparation for the accomplished execution of a final work. Now each *unrehearsed* act of 'allowing a work to develop' represented and extended the present limits of an artist's experience, as Hamilton's contemporary work demonstrated. Each of his studies began with a point, the simplest mark, its location made in considered relationship (as were the positions of all subsequent marks) with elements already existing (in the first instance, with the dimensions of the surface). As the number of elements within the composition increased, so did the complexity of the problem of arranging each point or part in satisfying relationship with all the others. He said that he took a blank canvas and after considerable thought placed a mark upon it: then he made another addition in significant relationship with the first and with the boundary. The marks in this way accumulated; but at each stage there had to be a reasoned contribution to the growth of the idea [11]. On other occasions, as he conducted the 'balancement of growth' of the developing image, he would reduce or even obliterate existing marks if this assisted the greater cohesion. Whereas the former process of simple accretion could be said to be analogous, for example, with the growth of a snail shell, in which the resulting form would contain a complete record of its development, the latter could be regarded as comparable with D'Arcy Thompson's scheme, in which biological formation produced corresponding deformation, and in which positive and negative work was done.

Although he would later explore the ramifications of a morphological approach to art *teaching*, these painterly experiments were of passing interest to Hamilton; and in retrospect it is seen that the most sustained examination of art as a developing process was Victor Pasmore's. He respected an obvious precedent of developmental art – the work of Paul Klee. According to Klee's essentially dynamic theory, the meeting of medium and surface (say, pencil and paper) established a point, which set creative exploration in motion. The moving point generated line, which in turn moved laterally, generating plane, which also moved to generate volume. In an ICA debate [12] Pasmore was a principal speaker against the motion that Klee's practical application of this theory in his late works reflected the decline of creative powers. He identified with Klee's anti-academic stance; and he recognised close parallels between Klee's discourse on a dimensional progression, and the development of his own painting over the period in which he had been familiar with Thompson's thesis.

A decade earlier, his work had flirted with impressionism and a kind of cubism: from his rejection of these two tendencies, however, had emerged an intention to devise more efficient ways of manipulating (initially two-dimensional) space, which he later interpreted as a wish to free painting from its two-dimensional context, ultimately to examine confrontations of real and illusory space [13]. At first his aims were realised by engraving the painted surface or by using paper collage [14], which techniques respectively worked beneath and above the supporting picture plane. Eventually he found that he could succeed only by working more deliberately outwards and backwards: he made the picture plane transparent, so that painted reliefs could be built before and behind and be seen in juxtaposition [15].

For a while his 'painterliness' seemed to vanish, and he realised that to continue the logical development would be to sacrifice a reputation as a lyrical handler of paint. Then he began using transparent materials, such as perspex and glass, to replace the picture plane, and lyrical qualities returned. Transparency served two objectives: it articulated construction behind the plane, which had previously been implied rather than stated;

and by its reflective nature it introduced softening influences. The observer was permitted to see mirror images of himself and of surrounding objects in conflict with the real image of the construction. The whole became an essay in contrasting or fusing real and apparent, the precise and the diffuse, the intended and the accidental.

As a succession, Pasmore's constructions clearly were 'organic'. They were stages frozen within the development of a creative sensibility – 'units of emergent value', not embodying a visible record of process (as, for example, Hamilton's works did), but constituting moments in the development of a process itself. They were Gestalt formations: indeed, there was little in the gauntness of construction to entice an observer into Gestalt-free perceptivity. And yet the later works did provide for the wandering or the particularised attention by registering every fluctuation of environmental conditions. Some accepted that Pasmore could anticipate the future 'accidents' of illumination and perspective that would bring his utterly plain constructions to life. More to the point, perhaps, was Herbert Read's observation: Pasmore had achieved, by process-dominant means, an advanced condition of art in which the rational construction and the irrational effect were synthesised [16].

Taking a successive-dimensional model towards logical conclusions, Pasmore speculated about connections between constructive art and environmental design. His belief was that when painting and sculpture were representational they did not share organic relationship with architecture: unity then was established by the use of similar materials or common techniques, and the whole conditioned by an obvious unifying idea or *style*. Today, however, by virtue of their purity, abstract painting and sculpture might act as strengthening forces, intensifying or reinforcing the environmental design concept. And if pure, abstract form might strengthen architecture, architecture in its turn might vitalise pure form. Representational art was said to refer to an imaginary environment, and its relationship with the actual forms and spaces of its surroundings was consequently ambiguous. Pure form, however, expressing itself as an actual physical reality, shared real relationship with its surroundings. In its space-creating capacity, therefore, architecture was said to bring pure form to life [17].

In practice this belief enabled Pasmore to describe a theoretical creative process, and maintain that it was sound in practice, beginning with the origination of the germ of an idea in the first dimension, progressing into the second and the third dimensions, and ultimately moving towards environment-scale construction in space. This had been the structuring of his own creative development: and it shaped his part in the efforts, with Hamilton, Thubron and Hudson, to devise a sound preparatory teaching.

Tom Hudson's art-school training had been interrupted by the war, and he returned to it determined to concentrate upon aspects he thought relevant – the subject of children's creativity (inspired by Herbert Read's *Education through Art*), which he studied for a year while at the Courtauld Institute, and, rather daringly, the subject of 'modern movements', principally Constructivism and de Stijl, which had been concerned with assemblage and construction. In 1951 he was appointed Painting Master at Lowestoft School of Art where, at his insistence, he was permitted to spend a proportion of his time extending his research into Child Art. He organised a research centre, and worked for one week of each month with children from the local schools. He found that if perceptual or constructive 'problems' were framed slightly outside the scope of the youngsters' abilities they would quickly put together an experience necessary for coping. Young children, in particular the under-sevens, had great appetites for creative learning which noticeably declined as they grew older and began to imitate adult expressions. Hudson reasoned that if the child could somehow be persuaded away from a preconceived approach to 'mature' art, it might be possible to prolong the creative, learning-by-doing stage of his or her development (previously thought to end naturally at around the age of seven) into early adolescence and beyond. He realised that if his ideas were to dent the current complacency (the Festival of Britain was now proclaiming to the world the successful end-products of a British creative education) they had first to be seen to be working in an art school.

Hudson, therefore, looked to Child Art for principles he might employ in his commitments to adolescent teaching; and there were precedents in Britain which he chose to ignore. Notable among these was the work of Marion Richardson, which had had wide acclaim and the compliments of imitation for thirty years [18]. This had been styled by its devotees 'The New Art Teaching'; and among its aims had been to ensure that there should be a minimum of damage when natural abilities met with mannerisms in the awkward stages of a child's development, and that *expressive* abilities be allowed to play a full part in the shaping of personality.

Superficially, this seemed to be what Hudson was engaged in; but he was actually quite opposed to something he saw as essentially repressive, concentrating as it did in the formative years upon expressive tendencies alone. His encounter with Read's theories had convinced him that there were differing aspects of creativity, expression being but one, and that it was the teacher's responsibility to provide for all of them. Read had generalised about three of these:

A. *The activity of self expression* – the individual's innate need to communicate his thoughts, feelings and emotions to other people.

B. *The activity of observation* – the individual's desire to record his sense impressions, to clarify his conceptual knowledge, to build up his memory, to construct things which aid his practical activities.

C. *The activity of appreciation* – the response of the individual to the modes of expression which other people address or have addressed to him . . . [19].

Hudson's research had led him to conclude that Read's activity B, which had been virtually ignored by the New Art Teachers, was of fundamental importance. Emphasis upon expression and appreciation, he believed, had cultivated the narrative and the subjective. This had fostered preconceived notions which thwarted true creative discovery; and the prevention of such discovery, to complete a vicious circle, had prohibited firsthand expression. Activity B, on the other hand, which Hudson retitled *Construction*, a piece-by-piece assembling of awareness, was precisely the way in which children learned by trial, error, and the storing of resulting experience.

It seemed obvious that constructive abilities were instinctual, and easily destroyed by misguided advice about rules and methods, or by insistent exhortations to 'express'. For a while he found himself questioning whether art should be taught at all. Then he decided upon a principle of minimal interference with the child's explorations: at the stage where an 'expressionist' teacher, observing an imperfect aping of adults, might have demanded *more expression* in the belief that this promoted greater experience, Hudson saw it as his responsibility to steer the child back to natural creative processes. And he applied this principle at all levels of art education. His problem at Lowestoft, though, was that while it was a simple matter to achieve good results with children, it was difficult to encourage childlike attitudes in students, corrupted as they were by assumed sophistications. A short-term compromise was the direct involvement of his adolescent students in the work of the Research Centre, in an expectation that they would perceive the vital qualities of the children's creative explorations. In fact they were asked to perceive ways of perceiving. (Hudson was not concerned so much with *how* children perceive, as that they be allowed to do this for themselves instead of receiving predigested information.) So the children experienced visual memory tests, involving simple shapes and colours. They played games in which they were encouraged to 'hold' the memory of a certain arrangement of coloured shapes, and to rearrange it, or to make omissions, according to instructions. They were shown projected images of simple black shapes on white and asked to draw them in reversal; or they were asked to select identical images out of many which were closely similar. These activities, in the students' eyes, emphasised the *real* properties of imagery rather than its capacity to reflect a subject. And they fuelled the child's discovery: instinctual 'scribble' led to the recognition of images, to material exploitation and the evolution of visual structure. The images and symbols the children used in their creative inventions afforded limitless comparisons with their surroundings (when the image was real), as opposed to the only possible comparison (when the image was that of a particular subject) [20].

Pasmore met Hudson in 1954, partly as a result of their common interest in Child Art [21]. Pasmore also met Harry Thubron, a consistent attender of his lectures and exhibitions in the north east. And Hudson and Thubron had known one another for some time, having regularly compared notes on their teaching at, respectively, Lowestoft and Sunderland schools of art. In 1954 John Wood, of the North Riding Education Authority, asked Thubron to run a summer school at Scarborough. When it was repeated the following year Victor Pasmore took a leading part; and on the third occasion, in 1956, when Hudson and Wendy Pasmore participated, it had assumed a form which may now be recognised, with hindsight, as typical of the fundamental revision of art education which was to follow. Great credit must be apportioned to Wood for his insight that such a revision was needed, and to the others for recognising an opportunity not merely to modify but completely to revise existing practices. The series of summer schools in effect were prototypes in which ideas were forged prior to their incorporation within full-time courses. Pasmore introduced a basic course into the Painting School at King's College (the first full-scale course in the context of Fine Art), where Hamilton already had his own basic course supporting his Design teaching. First Thubron then Hudson were appointed to posts at Leeds College of Art, and there in 1957 they initiated their own basic course, assisted by Wendy Pasmore, as well as Alan Davie, Terry Frost and Hubert Dalwood, who were Gregory Fellows in Fine Art at Leeds University [22].

The categories of study at Scarborough are indicative of certain influences: Point; Line; Plane; Area; Space; Volume; Tone; Colour; Drawing from Nature; Technique. The first six derive from Moholy-Nagy and Klee; Tone and Colour are partly traceable to Johannes Itten's *Vorkurs* at the Bauhaus (as it was represented by Moholy-Nagy in his book *The New Vision* [23]; and Technique related to Pasmore's assertion 'Construction is both Technique and Aesthetic' [24]. Emphasis was placed upon a programmatic learning, echoing both the morphological theories examined at the ICA, and the sequential attitude of the Bauhaus teachers. When a detailed history of modern British art education comes to be written, John Wood and the modest beginnings at Scarborough will assume their proper significance. So too will the SEA Conference *Adolescent Expression in Art and Craft*, held at Bretton Hall, Yorkshire, in April 1956, when the chairman, Herbert Read, gave his unequivocal support in the face of wide predictions to the contrary. The time will be seen to have been right for change, and the coming together of complementary talents fortuitous. For very many years Read had been representing abstraction to the surrealists and surrealism to the abstractionists in the hope of encouraging a synthesis of these polarities, and by this means an advancement of the general condition of art [25]. Hudson, Pasmore, Hamilton and Thubron created just such a synthesis, in the form, in Pasmore's view, of a four-dimensional approach embodying, respectively, technical, constructivist, surrealist and irrational creativity. In his view Thubron was the one who checked most against a strict process-dominance, with decisive insight and a tactical immediacy. In this sense the combined approach will be seen to have been not merely process-dominant but *organic*, that is, accommodating leaps of inspiration.

At King's College and Leeds the process began with experience of 'designing' at its most elementary: nothing more was done, for perhaps several days, other than the making of dots with charcoal upon paper. The barest directives were issued, and little advice was given about how to proceed. Students were merely urged to find themes and explore them. This had the temporary effect of bringing everyone, no matter what his or her accomplishments had been in previous art education, to similar levels of competence. After a period of embarrassment, students would begin to confer about the nature of the exercise and the underlying intentions: out of a common necessity a language of co-operation would quickly develop about the intangible properties of simple graphic marks.

23   *Developing Process*,
1959. Point, line and plane
exercise; The Hatton
Gallery, Newcastle
University.

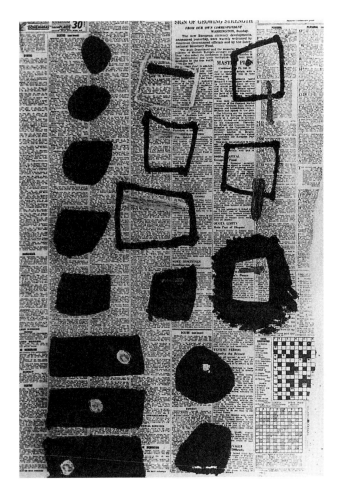

24   *Developing Process*,
1959. When line moves
laterally it generates plane;
The Hatton Gallery,
Newcastle University.

Preoccupied with such matters, students would unwittingly, but no less positively, achieve three objectives of the study. They would establish the beginnings of a visual and verbal communication; in the absence of a spirit of competition they would begin to work co-operatively; and they would define a basis for subsequent study.

Multiples of dots (actually connected or their connections merely implied) inevitably describe lines; and such linear qualities were next for close investigation. This had more facets: whereas the essay in simple graphic marks was mainly a locational exercise, the linear project offered possibilities of exploring 'length', 'width', 'change of direction', 'spatial interval', and so forth. Permutations were infinite: at this early date in his or her art school education the student became absorbed in an exploratory *process*, in spite of *product*-oriented expectations.

If line is a record of the movement of a point, then lines which touch may represent collisions of movements, a diagram of forces (if movement is implosive); or alternatively they may represent a branching outwards, a diagram of organic growth. Depending upon the speed with which decisions are made and the lines are drawn, it is possible to charge drawing with characteristics of vigorous activity, or with those of careful, deliberate balancing. Resulting images are documentary records of ideas originating, developing according to the 'demands' of marks, media and constructive technique, and either leading naturally towards other possibilities of study, or terminating. There are rhythmic and other organic-analogous qualities in dispositions of lines which, although perhaps not actually touching, express some positive relationship. Such qualities may be effected by differences of thickness, an exhibition of vigour or deliberation in each execution, contrasts of sharpness and softness, and variations of interval. And such organicism is consistent in other dimensions.

When line moves laterally it generates plane: when line moves linearly and changes direction it similarly generates plane. This two-dimensional exploration is the beginning of three-dimensional, plane-by-plane construction in space. This progression from one to two to three dimensions – the removal of traditional distinctions between painting and sculpture, and between sculpture and 'architecture' – was the fundamental principle of the new approach. Had it not been for examination requirements, the three-dimensional activity of carving would have been discouraged because of its lack of direct connectivity with two-dimensional ideas, and also because, by the nature of the discipline, carved results tended to be predetermined. Casting was more acceptable, for the need to think 'in reverse' foiled preconception: *construction*, however, was the most legitimate activity because it embodied the systematic growth of creative ideas. As a result of this emphasis 'Basic Design' [26] came to be characterised by the use of space as a positive design element, and by the ultimate aim of creating works of substance by insubstantial means.

The two main areas of study extraneous to the dimensional progression were Colour and Drawing from Nature. Although principles of colour-mixing, the accurate reproduction of colour spectra, and the exploration of such as hue, intensity, harmony, discord, complementary contrast,

25 *Developing Process*, 1959. Planar development is the basis of construction, embodying the systematic growth of creative ideas; The Hatton Gallery, Newcastle University.

were all pursued, as with Drawing from Nature more importance was attributed to the trains of thought they might initiate. Great value was placed upon the use of natural materials – flowers, fruits, barks, geological samples, the life model – as objects to set creative exploration in motion. This kind of study was presented as the means of understanding nature's colour forms, those combinations of colour and form which best fulfil certain functions (of, say, attraction or of camouflage) in nature. The student was urged to observe the rhythms of growth coupled with colour change, to see the principles by which they were linked, and 'to allow his work to grow, as in nature.'

When such broad introductory considerations of points, lines, planes, spaces, volumes had been made (after perhaps a term of study) much of the ground already covered was re-examined. It was realised that certain properties overlapped the dimensional categories. There was the property, inherent in series of progressively changing forms and shapes, of linking into types or 'families': there was that of 'polarity', caused by like forms attracting, different forms repelling, and the resulting visual tensions: all design elements were conditioned by 'positive' and 'negative' effects, which were caused by optical hierarchies of visual dominance. Exploring such second-stage phenomena had the result of developing quite sophisticated language about otherwise intangible properties, ensuring that the processes of design remained at the centre of attention, yet providing for individual expression. As Pasmore said on the occasion in 1959 when these principles were represented to the ICA [27]:

> something more is required than a ready-made repetitive course of abstract exercises. It is essential that [the course] is one which is capable of extension and development. The idea of a static system which every student must copy is not compatible with the dynamic aspirations of modern art. A modern 'basic' course, therefore, should assume a relative outlook in which only the beginning is defined and not the end . . . .
>
> For the sake of practical organisation it is necessary to divide a course of studies of this kind into categories; but these categories ought not to be regarded as isolated studies. On the contrary, each category should be presented as part of a developing process. All categories, therefore, overlap . . . .
>
> A foundation course of this kind can no longer be divided into the separate departments of painting, sculpture and architecture . . . .
>
> An exercise in the partitioning of space, for instance, begins in the division of two-dimensional area (drawing) and develops into actual three-dimensional structure (architecture). Similarly a project in shape making and shape relationship begins in two dimensions (drawing or painting) and ends in three dimensions (sculpture or construction) [28].

Richard Hamilton gave his own basic design teaching at King's College from 1953 to 1958 and from 1961 until he left in 1966: in the intervening period his teaching was coordinated with Pasmore's in an amalgamated preparatory course. Though this suggestion surprised him [29], in his own teaching Hamilton, too, was concerned with values reminiscent of some of Read's. The earlier preoccupation with organic growth and form was reviewed in his lectures: if matter could be analysed into coherent patterns analogous to 'its design', then it could be valuable for students to be aware that one approach to designing might begin with establishing an appropriate 'coherent pattern'.

Though Hamilton did not adhere to a single developing process, he was concerned that creativity should be understood to be an organic, evolving phenomenon. So far as he was concerned, the ideas to which Pasmore was committed were appropriate for application to some problems, inappropriate for others. Thus he made a significant contribution to the consensus – notably the principle that the student's work should be a diagram of his or her thought processes and also exhibit the grammar, the logical framework of the chosen rules (for which Hamilton coined the composite term *Diagrammar*) – without identifying too closely with the specific ideology [30]. The effect of this attitude combined with Pasmore's (as Hamilton noted, one-man teaching eventually became limiting and repetitive [31]) was that studies became programmatic but open-ended, with highly disciplined beginnings, yet encouraging eventual research of the most personal kind.

At the start of the collaboration exercises tended to be framed in aesthetic terms (for example: Arrange linear graphic marks in relation to one another and to the boundary formed by the paper's edge, until the positioning is felt to be satisfactory: at the same time explore a wide range of graphic qualities). Later, work would either begin with a non-aesthetic directive (such as: Examine by carefully observed drawing the convolutions of string) or with a simple proposition or question: (A point may move so that it leaves a residual path, which is a line; Lines may retain their separate identities and also, under certain conditions, cohere as a group; Lines may generate apparent forms; When does line become shape? [32]. A sharpening of observation and an understanding of elementary design principles would, it was thought, develop naturally as by-products of the student's other-directed work. He or she would produce an enormous volume of responses; and out of this vast production there would emerge discernible patterns of reaction and selectivity, bearing evidence of individuality [33].

Hudson, though a member of staff at Leeds, was theoretically close both to Pasmore's constructivism and to Hamilton's free-ranging explorations. And he was impatient to progress beyond what he saw as primary objectives. Once it was accepted that there might be at least *one* equally valid alternative to accepted methods of teaching [34], he argued, it was time to progress further towards an entirely unrestricted education. In this he was inspired by Read's advice that in the pursuit of radical objectives it was not necessary to wait for the general but gradual converting of others to the ideal. Dynamism at the nucleus would be irresistible by the mass; and the chief priority, at the centre of events, would be to maintain momentum. When he moved to Leicester College of Art, therefore, he proceeded to decategorise the curriculum he found there. While work obviously had to be categorised afterwards for the purpose of criticism, he was careful always during creative exploration to emphasise the individual's ideas, and to encourage the expansion of these across dimensional, material and technical boundaries. In the *Developing Process* mark-making had been protracted into painting, painting into construction: in authentic open-ended education, he now began to argue, there could be no anticipation of the student's future creative forms because of differing perceptions and preferences and the resulting, infinite range of formal languages. Because individuals could invent their own languages, it was not the teacher's responsibility to determine whether the work should be abstract or realistic or related to a given project. For the student, then, the ease of passive learning was to be replaced by difficulties of self-motivation; and the teacher's need to work one-to-one would mean that he would have to be familiar with perhaps twenty or thirty programmes of learning instead of the traditional one.

> To improvise and control a flexible structure requires more wit and enterprise than devising an administrative and artistic trap [35].

Hudson's 'flexible structure' was a loose envelope of experimentation which gradually unfolded as the course proceeded, being propped into shape by various discoveries. For example, a brief introductory talk about colour would initiate experiments with a vast range of techniques, materials and phenomena – colour juxtapositioning and the assessment of visual and psychological effects; observation and recording of colour forms in nature; work with light beamed through various filters; analysis of optical effects and retinal after-image; systematic and intuitive colour-mixing; the grasping of verbal language with which to compare opinions and responses. Only after a protracted period of visual experimentation (*Visual Adventure* was the term which was coined) came the criticism, and the propping into place of the two principal definitions of Additive and Subtractive Colour and other established theory [36]. In this more liberal scheme 'the mark' no longer defined a precise element of constructive use but, through the students' observations, it came to embrace parts of patterns found in nature, as well as a range of imprecise and unrefined man-made marks including accidental daubs and splashes. The lack of clinical control inherent in the using of these would have placed them well outside the context of the *Developing Process*: because there were no accepted procedures for their deployment, however, they were ideal vehicles of an entirely exploratory approach. Morphological systems could be considered when appropriate; but in the absence of an overall 'point into line into plane' directive other devices, such as mathematical or random sequences, were used as determinants of form. It was realised

26 *Visual Adventure*; invention of visual language; Tom Hudson, Leicester Polytechnic.

that permutations of shape, location, character, accident, system, material property, visual energy, growth, gesture . . . were infinite.

Sooner or later in the development of a creative theme it became necessary to use other than simple technology, and to employ machines, efficient extensions of the human form. Read had been aware of this latter necessity, and of the ease with which the individual might become the passive minder of the machine: it was held to be difficult to incorporate the erratic or intuitive act within a primarily mechanical sequence of operations. Hudson therefore encouraged the individual's *creative* participation in such matters: he urged him to 'invent his own technology' and to devise appropriate machine processes. He maintained that if he were to teach students accepted practices of, for example, joining materials (jointing wood, riveting sheet metal, using mortars and adhesives with stone and plastic) they would then tend to design only those things they could realise by the 'proper' means. If, however, they were asked simply to analyse for themselves problems of 'joining' it was probable that many of their discoveries would later be confirmed in existing craft-practices, and also possible that, as a result of exploiting materials beyond normal limitations (not merely 'going along with the nature of the material' [37], new techniques might be invented. In the group-criticism of such inventions, necessary skills (to magnify or simplify a link in a chain of events for purposes of clarification and decision-making; or to use symbols, diagrams and other equivalents in order to communicate critical details to others) would be developed which would enable the user to be active and imaginative in his or her correspondence with the machine.

In Hudson's work at Leicester, then, and later at Cardiff College of Art (where he went as Director of Studies in 1964), there was to be found an array of machined and polished forms as precise and crystalline as any in the world of industry. And, paradoxically, there was also to be found an affection for discarded rubbish, 'used' and 'spoiled' artefacts of all kinds – an array of loose and imprecise objects, the three-dimensional equivalents of accidental daubs and splashes. To some these extreme preoccupations seemed mutually destructive, but to Hudson they were reconciled in a simple aim of projecting creativity into everyday life. At the one extreme this was satisfied when conventional ideas about machine production were challenged. At the other it was realised when the familiar trappings of everyday life were brought into unfamiliar contexts, enabling them 'to be seen for the first time' – changing, by however small a degree, general views of the world of which they were a part. And, far from being irreconcilable, these extremes were considered eminently capable of resolution by means of an attitude Hudson termed 'combine-construct' – an intermixing of real, unreal and surreal, only given full expression, perhaps, in the four-dimensional art of performance [38].

The constant factor in all the work of Pasmore, Hamilton and Hudson was a resolution of opposites – in its simplest and most obvious form a combination of intellectual and intuitive faculties within entirely fresh approaches to creativity. Their experimentation as a whole is seen as having been concerned with minutest technicalities of grammar, and yet as having pursued implications of even the smallest creative act upon the realms of three-dimensional construction, of 'architecture', and of the real world presented in popular culture and in performance art. Their images were not conceived as isolated from the real world: such images, to paraphrase Klee's famous dictum, were to make the world real.

Notes and References

1   See MACDONALD, S. (1970), *The History and Philosophy of Art Education* (London, London University Press).
2   READ, H. (1934), *Art and Industry* (London, Faber).
3   See THISTLEWOOD, D. (1987), 'ALBERT E. HALLIWELL: Educationist in Contemporary Design' in THISTLEWOOD, D. (ed.) (1987), *The Bramley Occasional Papers of the National Arts Education Archive, Bretton Hall*, Vol. 1, pp. 1–6.
4   MOHOLY-NAGY, L. (1929), *Von Material zu Architektur* (Munich, Langen), translated D. M. HOFFMAN as (1932) *The New Vision: From Material to Architecture* (New York, Brewer, Warren & Puttnam); 2nd ed. (1938) *The New Vision* (New York, W. W. Norton); 3rd and 4th eds (1946), 1947) *The New Vision* (New York, George Wittenborn).
5   READ, H. (1950), 'Goethe and Art', *The Listener*, XLIII, p. 13.
6   For a record of the symposium see WHYTE, L. L. (ed.) (1951), *Aspects of Form* (London, Lund Humphries).
7   READ, H. (1951), 'Preface' *op. cit.* (n. 6).
8   THOMPSON, D. W. (1917, revised and enlarged 1942), *On Growth and Form* (Cambridge, Cambridge University Press).
9   THOMPSON (n. 8), p. 16 (my bracketed additions).
10 Ibid., p. 357.
11 MORPHET, R. (1970) catalogue of the exhibition *Richard Hamilton* (London, Tate Gallery) p. 18.
12 ICA, London, December 1953. See BANHAM, R. (1954) 'Klee's Pedagogical Sketchbook', *Encounter*, April 1954, p. 57.
13 See EHRENZWEIG, A. (1957), 'Victor Pasmore's Architectural Constructions', *Quadrum 4*, pp. 51–60.
14 'The Importance of Collage' was the subject of an ICA debate, 21 October 1954.
15 EHRENZWEIG (n. 13), p. 52.
16 READ, H. (1964), 'Victor Pasmore' in DORIVAL, B. (ed.) *Les Peintres Célèbres* (Paris, Masenod). Republished (1965), catalogue of exhibition *São Paulo Biennale* (London, British Council).
17 PASMORE, V. (1957), 'Connections between Painting, Sculpture and Architecture', *Zodiac One*, p. 66.
18 See RICHARDSON, M. (1948), *Art and the Child* (London, London University Press).
19 READ, H. (1943), *Education through Art* (London, Faber), p. 208.
20 See HUDSON, T. (1964), 'The Language of Structure', catalogue of exhibition *National Exhibition of Children's Art* (London, Sunday Mirror).
21 Pasmore was a member of the National Committee on Children's Art, to which Hudson was co-opted after his success at Lowestoft.
22 See REICHARDT, J. (1959) 'Form, Space, Dimension and Colour', *Art News and Review*, XI, 7, 29 April.
23 See n. 4. Little was known directly of Itten's work until his book *Design and Form: the Basic Course at the Bauhaus* was published in Britain by Thames & Hudson in 1964.

24 PASMORE, V. (1957) catalogue of exhibition *Statements* (London, ICA).

25 For a detailed discussion of this aspect of Read's work see THISTLEWOOD, D. (1984), *Herbert Read: Formlessness and Form: an Introduction to his Aesthetics* (London, Routledge & Kegan Paul).

26 *Circa* 1954–9 when there was most agreement about aims.

27 In the form of the exhibition *The Developing Process*, ICA, London, April–May 1959.

28 PASMORE, V. in PASMORE, V., R. HAMILTON, T. HUDSON, H. THUBRON (1959), *The Developing Process* (Newcastle, King's College University of Durham), p. 3.

29 Interview Thistlewood/HAMILTON, August 1975.

30 HAMILTON (n. 28), p. 19.

31 HAMILTON, R. (1961), 'About Art Teaching Basically', *Motif 8*, Winter, p. 17.

32 *Ibid.*

33 HAMILTON, R. (1961), 'First Year Studies at Newcastle', *Times Educational Supplement*, May, p. 1234.

34 It was sufficient to have gained the support of an informed body of educationists (e.g., L. Gowing and K. Rowntree at King's; E. E. Pullée and E. Taylor at Leeds; J. Wood who had been inspirational; and H. Read).

35 HUDSON, T. (1969), unpublished address to the World Congress of Art Education, New York.

36 See catalogue of exhibition *The Visual Adventure*, Leicester College of Art, 1962.

37 HUDSON, T. (1969), *Creative Technology* (London, Schools Council Bulletin).

38 See (1975, 1976) transcripts 'Guernica' and 'Matisse Lecture: an Academic Performance'; Cardiff College of Art.

Chapter Twelve

NORBERT LYNTON Harry Thubron: Teacher and Artist

Towards the end of 1979 I got down to the preface of my book on modern art. A lot of time and agonising had gone into the book, and there seemed to be a lot of thoughts left over, clamouring to get into that opening. In fact, it wrote itself quite quickly and turned out quite brief. It is no more than a couple of paragraphs of acknowledgements: to students because they force one to rethink one's ideas, to a couple of Sussex University colleagues, to the publishers, to my wife, and, much more prominently, to two 'truly great teachers' – the one who had got me hooked on art history at Birkbeck College, then called Professor N. B. L. Pevsner (I had never heard of him when I started), and the other one: Harry Thubron. It was at his suggestion that I crossed the narrow road between the School of Architecture and the main body of the College of Art in Leeds, and found myself in touch with living artists and live art.

When *The Story of Modern Art* came out the following year I sent Harry a copy. Some time later I got a phone call. 'Harry here. About what you wrote...' (I had stressed his infectious way with students and his energising effect on colleagues, as well as having called him a 'truly great teacher') 'Quite right! Quite right!' I don't think he said anything else. He certainly did not go on, as so many others did around that time, to ask why I had not discussed his work as part of the history of modern art. Writing a history of something involves all sorts of decisions at the conscious level as well as external and internal limitations.

Of Harry Thubron's historical importance as a teacher there can be absolutely no question ('Quite right, Norbert'), and of the quality of his work as artist I have no doubt. But his historical role as artist is yet to be acknowledged. As a teacher Harry was a public figure, locally and nationally. As an artist he was more private than most, though not, I must stress, lacking in his own certainty that what he was doing was good. But he never jumped on to the art world's pater-noster lift, that brings artists up and down again, exposing them to the world. It may be that the time for Harry's art to work its power is right now, when we are recoiling from art commerce's passionate embrace of large-scale, clumsy but rhetorical figurative painting. He could never see any necessary division between abstract and figurative art, but found opportunities where others see barriers and contradictions. In that respect, as well as others, his art corrects the false priorities of the moment.

It was in 1956 that I crossed that road to join Harry on the other side, a year after he had arrived to be Head of Fine Art. My ignorance of modern art was almost total. I had got to know Tom Hudson (who had spent some time at the Courtauld Institute where I got my art history degree), and then also Harry; they must have thought me educable and somehow congenial. What mattered was their support. Harry, who could be dismissive of pretentious books and scholarship, had no doubt at all that students needed information and the stimulus of ideas. He and Tom both insisted that students should attend my art history lectures – fumbling as they must have been, as I discovered the great moderns and held forth about them a week later – and that they should write essays and generally take their studies seriously. Harry also encouraged me to set up a liberal studies programme by means of a lecture and discussion series using people from Leeds University, all of them famous names now. In talking about Harry we tend to linger over his free spirit and mobility, his emphasis on intuition and the personal response; we should not forget his leadership and authority. At Leeds he rebuilt instruction in and beyond the fine art area, and my work greatly benefited from his guidance and his support.

I must try to suggest the image he presented at that time, inside and outside the College. Looking back at my time there, I recall events that struck me as significant then even though I was not able to see them as part of a larger picture, and that now reveal themselves as markers along a path that was not as straight and predetermined as people have thought. His image inside the College, at first, was that of a fierce and wild man, full of missionary fire and ready to condemn old ways. It seemed to me, as I watched from across the road, that the pre-Harry staff were cowering in corners, hoping the storm would blow itself out and things would return to normal. The problem was partly one of communication. Harry called meetings. I remember attending one of them, in one of the painting studios, attended by College teachers from all departments. I listened hard, but I don't recall what Harry said. As we dispersed a lot of people said to each other that they had not understood him. We got a sense of energy, and of urgency, but no clear statement of what was wanted.

Harry had no formula with which to unsettle the staid conventions that ruled the College. Of course the old faculty was suspicious of this newcomer and his two disciples (Tom Hudson and Ricky Atkinson). He was not even a clubbable man from the south or with southern ways (whatever veneer two years at the Royal College had given to Harry had been rubbed off by five years service in HM forces). He was Bishop Auckland, West Hartlepool and Sunderland, and perhaps it is no wonder that people hid from him. In fact, the same people came to work with him very successfully in time, some getting there quite quickly, some more slowly: Harry could win one over with kindness and sheer human respect for what one could do. But this did demand a change of tempo, and a loss of status and the comfort of divisions. Barriers between departments were ignored. Even the barrier between faculty and students crumbled as intenser activity made for mutual regard. Teachers' and students' work alike became an urgent, priority business.

What was Harry bringing into art education? What he seemed to be bringing becomes clear if we study the report of the *Easter Conference of the Society for Education through Art*, held at Bretton Hall in April 1956 under the title 'Adolescent Expression in Art and Craft'. In summarising what went on I shall do my best to avoid caricaturing it, though I cannot help emphasising contrasting attitudes represented there.

Herbert Read, president of the Society, chaired most of the sessions during three and a half days. Barclay-Russell, vice-president and art inspector to the LCC, gave the first talk. He spoke of 'abstract expression through pattern' and how this could strengthen pictorial work, of Marion Richardson, of intuition and play, and simple harmonies. Key phrases in his talk, concerned principally with the work of pre-adolescent children, were of the 'spontaneous inner development' sort. The talk by the leader of the Cheam Group of art teachers, Miss Wallis Myers, spoke of the adolescent child's needs. She weighed up the dangers and benefits brought by various degrees of 'interference' in 'the child's own type of art expression' and concluded that this should be minimal, just enough 'to keep the creative will alive'. The only guidance available to the teacher would be his intuition. The only area where direct teaching was advisable was in craftsmanship; it was here that the adolescent often found a basis of security that art work could not offer. The discussions that followed on that day, and reference back to them subsequently, confirmed this as a general belief: in speaking about crafts, teachers clearly felt more secure about what could usefully be said.

Harry Thubron spoke on the morning of the third day, Friday. His subject was 'An Experiment in Basic Art Education', but we do not know what he said. The report does not offer a listener's summary but a text provided subsequently by Harry. He had written to say that what he said that morning had ignored the notes he had prepared. These provided the material for the written report he offered – which, since others too had preferred to write up their own reports on what they said, or had meant to say, was accepted and appears in the conference report. I presume that on that Friday morning, stimulated by what he had seen and heard during the preceding sessions, he spoke freely and fiercely.

Maurice de Sausmarez spoke immediately after Harry. He had transferred from Leeds College of Art to the University. He spoke of the three faculties that art education must develop in a pupil: 'the emotions, the capacity for feeling'; 'the promptings of intuition'; 'and the desire to know, the intellect'. He emphasised the last of these, asserting that

> there is in art theory today a thinly disguised conspiracy against the
> intelligence. . . . The denigration of intelligence has serious
> consequences in art education, showing fully at adolescence.

He called for awareness of science, quoting Bronowski, and spoke of Paul Klee as an artist who worked and taught on the basis of objective knowledge and methods. 'Adolescence should be the age of experiment', he said, 'yet the work in some Training Colleges is debased mindless activity.' Notions of art were still dominated by romantic ideas that gave exclusive rights to painting and sculpture, and to folk values in craftwork, and permitted 'powers of feeling to oppose powers of knowing'.

The discussion that followed related to both talks. It is reported very briefly. The signs are that it was a very uncomfortable session. What the report offers relates only to three contributions. The first of these was by the chairman of the SEA, John Morley. He took grave exception to this talk of science in relation to art. Science meant destructive powers developed to new levels and the erosion of human values. Art education should turn its back on it. Barclay-Russell spoke of the work in abstract painting done in a number of schools; he felt that 'the abstract quality of the child' needed more attention from teachers. Miss Audrey Martin spoke of the value of craft work in developing children's sensitivity and imagination, but associated this with work in materials 'lovely in themselves', not the cardboard and balsa wood used by them 'in the constructional work Mr Thubron had shown'.

It is clear in retrospect that these positions relied on a misunderstanding of what Harry and Maurice de Sausmarez argued for. It is interesting that Morley's references to science expressed a fear that art might lose its innocence. Miss Martin's emphasis on the inspirational role of materials and making could have shown her to be Harry's ally, had she not gone on to reserve this to time-honoured materials. Barclay-Russell's attempt to build a bridge between that morning's speakers and their reluctant audience by stressing that abstract art work was already being done elsewhere illustrates a difficulty that still inhibits art debates in this country and which still serves as a false stimulus to critical squabbles.

Harry had presumably shown slides of work done in his classes by children of New Earswick Secondary Modern School and students of the Sunderland School of Art. I can imagine him speaking of this work with warmth, revelling in its energies and its quality as work actually superior to the paintings, drawings and sculpture illustrating the talks of other speakers. He is likely to have spoken of 'the kids' in terms that implied their superiority to others. No doubt he was dismissive of the emphasis on 'spontaneous inner development' and teachers' nervousness in approaching the whole subject of children's 'expressive powers'. Were they not to be allowed any contact with the real world, the world that so obviously attracted many of their enthusiasms?

His written report can only have caused further pain to many of his readers. It asserted that the art of today was experimental and required 'the study of space-form and space-time and also a wider use of materials'. He wanted emphasis placed on: (1) the development of a form of professionalism in the students; (2) 'the removal of any woolliness of thought which sustains the romantic isolation of the artist'; (3) 'a more intellectual training incorporating modern technological research'; (4) acceptance of painting as a central activity that had to recognise its relationship to contemporary design; and (5) the artist proving himself as a constructive force in a world dominated by science. He praised the children's appetite for knowledge and for technical processes; they should have access to tools and machinery and a great range of materials, because what needed to be developed in them was 'an aesthetic and plastic experience that would have distinct value in the matter of living' and was not directed only to the production of artists and of art. The stimulus offered by materials and processes would carry the adolescent across the all-too-familiar gap created by the ending of childhood's unselfconscious expressivity: the adolescent thrives on 'the discipline of making and the exploratory nature of the work'. Constructive work develops new ways of seeing as well as new ways of making, and can feed organisational and formal elements into representational drawing and painting, though this alone was not its justification. The work he recommended was not the enemy of intuitive practice; it represented a 'heightening of the intuitive'.

The conference was startled to find Herbert Read, introducing the final session on the Saturday morning, giving his backing to Harry on several points. His words were moderate, but he too said that painting and drawing were not necessarily the most productive forms of activity for children and young people if one was concerned to develop mental powers and meet psychological needs which tradition had ignored. Art could neither avert its gaze from modern technology, nor hope to function as a 'fifth column' to work against technology. The essential thing was to show that art could match any other aspect of education in providing a base for technological development.

The discussion that ended the conference showed passions flaring again. I'll represent the kind of thing that was said symbolically by referring to Mrs Veronica Zabel's previous talk on 'Adolescent and Pre-Adolescent Art' and then to her contribution to the discussion.

In her talk she had reported on the work of her girl pupils in high-minded terms that contrasted sharply with talk of technology and a partnership with science. She spoke, with evident feeling, of her pupils' productions, especially 'those, perhaps the rarest and most precious of all, who, like beauty itself, remain mysterious and (fortunately perhaps) beyond all explaining', and of 'that fragment of the human spirit which is captured and preserved on the paper'; this alone really mattered. She had evidently been profoundly upset by the tone of Harry's contribution. 'If you impose any "techniques" or "principles" on "troglodytes" (I use Mr Thubron's own words), they will remain "troglodytes" for ever'. Children may put up with it but there is 'certainly nothing original, let alone genuinely childlike' in the work Harry had shown: 'it is all pastiche – of Mondrian, Klee and Pasmore'. Children needed delicate and individual guidance. 'I very much suspect that Mr Thubron despises the children as much as he despises all of us in this room.'

Clearly it was the manner as well as the matter of Harry's declarations that produced such a response and such misunderstanding. Certainly he could be harsh. Undoubtedly he spoke with the urgency of one who, ten years after the war, saw everything going on as before. The young he did not despise – I would argue that in his rough way he treated them with truer respect than those who hoped to protect their sensibilities against any confrontation with the world outside the art room. But he could and did despise adults who defended convenient *laissez-faire* views in senten-tious but polite phrases. He despised above all southern-English habits of false affability.

But his contribution – his written statement – shocks me too. I do not recognise him in it. I never heard him speak of 'space-form' and 'space-time'. He certainly looked for access to modern tools and machines for his students, and to the materials suited to them, so that the work done might have some relationship to the world everyone lives in outside the art room and the art school, but his opinions were never as one-sided or as exclusive as the statement suggests. Sent in after the conference, it was, I suspect, produced with the help of Tom Hudson (who attended the conference) and perhaps Victor Pasmore. Whatever Harry said spontaneously at the conference, the statement was probably a group effort. Pasmore was teaching in Newcastle (at King's College, University of Durham). At the end of the 1940s he had abandoned finely constructed and delicately touched in landscape and *intimiste* painting for abstract painting and then constructing that relied on a vocabulary of geometrical forms. Tom Hudson, whom I came to know and admire when we were colleagues in Leeds, was passionately committed to an updated machine aesthetic, and taught it with energy and resourcefulness. Harry delighted in what machines could be made to do and the widening range of possibilities machines and, especially, new materials offered to everyone. Above all else, he delighted in the mental mobility and physical adaptability shown by students moving between drawing and painting and turning metal, vacuum-forming plastics, laying up reinforced resin, soldering and welding. (This was of course before Caro's example made welding equipment a standard sculptural tool.) But he never turned away from art's old materials nor from the endless stimulus to be got from new and old materials of every sort. The Tom Hudson I knew was a man in the mould of Moholy-Nagy, driven by a splendid appetite for technology and especially for technology's delight in renewing itself as it led mankind towards omnipotence. If Harry had a dominant model (I think he had several models, none of them with exclusive rights to his attention), it was Paul Klee.

My own interest in Klee made that one of our bonds. Nonetheless I recall being puzzled, even shocked to hear him speak of Klee's preciousness. I misunderstood him because in those days 'precious' was a dirty word, as bad as 'illusionistic', a red rag to the avant-garde bull. There was also an all-over clumsiness to Harry's actions. I never saw him at work on his own paintings or reliefs. I am thinking of his way with his stacks of student work, gathered in because so much in it delighted him and got out often and spread around the floor because it helped him make points in a discussion – and I see him, we all saw him, walking all over it, almost intentionally destroying it as though he cared nothing for it. In a way he was right. The 'kids' did marvellous things, became articulate on paper in most surprising ways, and within given exercises could demonstrate strong individualities. But that is all it was: studio exercises, and there would be plenty more and probably even better. But precious?

It would be difficult to imagine two men less alike than Klee and Thubron, the Swiss-German all bourgeois and correct, demanding formal behaviour, wearing formal clothes, assertively highbrow, and the English Northern, unnervingly informal and shockingly careless in his dress, at a time when students expected to call one Sir or Mr and we wore ties, and capable of language, often humorous language that was earthy and often unforgettably accurate. Yet the preciousness he saw in Klee was important because it was his own. It had to do, first of all, with responsiveness to visual data and with husbanding the materials of the moment, leaving nothing unemployed, uncherished in the end product. And though he could walk all over students' work (and his own) he brought a similar kind of preciousness to his working with them. He could be hard – equally hard on the adults who came to his short courses as on the 'kids' – if they were reluctant to invest the right intensity and persistence. But he could also fire them with enthusiasm by offering his own and by helping them to discover within themselves individually the nugget of creative power that few guessed they had. He loved them for their commitment and for the talent they discovered.

The 1956 conference implies a defined and wholly antagonistic attitude – it has been said to you of old: self-expression, mysterious beauties to be happened on in a lucky moment; but I say unto you: brains, calculation, disciplined technology, rejecting the beauty of the visible world in favour of abstraction, industrial methods rather than the old means of art. That is how he must have seemed also to his new colleagues in the College of Art. In his teaching he gave his first attention to the newly arrived students, and I presume they accepted his ways as the sort of thing one meets in adult education. At any rate they did not recoil.

I spent what time I could in the studios, watching Harry and his team developing what the outside world called the *Basic Course* or *Basic Design*. But I also attended three of the short courses Harry taught on, at Scarborough in the summer of 1957, in Leeds during the Christmas vacation of 1958–9 I think, and at Boxford in the summer of 1961. I have never thought of being an artist of any kind. I went on these courses as a student (participated in others as an occasional lecturer) because I felt that there was something to be learnt about art in general through the kind of work that went on there. It did not seem odd, as it would have done a couple of years earlier, to join College students on these courses, any more than joining the rich mix of students and professionals, and occasional amateurs, who came to the Boxford summer school. The combination of informality and intensity wiped out questions of status.

Four people taught at the Scarborough course: Victor Pasmore, Wendy Pasmore, Harry and Tom. Victor Pasmore was quite obviously the leader of the team. He set the day's work and led the 'crits' in the evening, and we followed his didactic system, point and line leading to plane and three-dimensional work. Harry spoke very little. Wendy Pasmore and Tom perhaps helped us most to understand what Victor wanted us to do, because he too was more ardent than comprehensible. It is generally said that Victor was well informed of the Bauhaus's methods in 1920s Germany. I saw no evidence of that, beyond an awareness of Kandinsky's Bauhaus book, *Point and Line to Plane*, and perhaps only the title of that. We were to explore the plastic action of these elements, using charcoal and black poster paint on cheap off-white paper. It was a limited sequence of experiences, and seemed related to predetermined goals, with praise given to those who reached them. I felt I learned a lot, scarcely ever having made a mark on surface for visual purposes before and so able to be wholly surprised by the life of abstract forms. I suspect that for many of the Leeds students who came the course was far too prescriptive and limited.

The winter school was quite different. Victor came only for the last two or three days out of ten, so that it was Harry's course. I must here interject something relating both to Harry's teaching and to my developing understanding of it. I had seen Harry's students in the College on first-year courses not unlike the Pasmore programme of point, line, plane and black on white. After the Scarborough experience, thinking about it during what remained of the vacation, I found myself questioning that programme. The first day of the new term I ran up the College stairs to try to say to Harry that it was wrong to treat the blacks of charcoal and poster paint and the whites of various papers as things to be taken for granted, as non-contributors to be used without scrutiny. I was too late. The new students were already hard at work, and they were working with and on colour. The winter school was about colour. I had asked what to bring and had been told to arm myself with Windsor red, Windsor blue and Windsor yellow plus black and white. I was lent some brushes. Paper would be provided.

We worked long days. The first one dragged a little for me; the rest shot by until Victor arrived, seemed cross with Harry, and tried to stop us doing what we were doing and to restart us on his programme. We refused, carrying on as before. It was a curious moment. I think it was also an historic one, since Harry and Victor never worked together after that time. Harry had been getting us to do extremely simple things, it seemed. Do the primaries provided in the tubes show the same clarity of hue and intensity? Are they true primaries. Try adjusting them to see if you can end up with a trio of equals. Make black by mixing them together. Add white to see what black it was, and try again. Make secondary colours out of the primaries, and arrangements of primaries and secondaries and, having understood their interrelationship, explore the heady land of 'discords' (difficult to understand, that, but very thrilling in the end). Harry had us bent over our tables hour by hour, pursuing these things with a concentration of a kind met traditionally in well-run life rooms but very rarely outside them. I, the absolute beginner, came away feeling I had never seen before, neither colour nor form. For the amazing thing was that Harry, having kept us giving all our attention to these particular tasks, and coming around to make us look harder and warn us off coarse solutions, talked to us at the end of the day about the miraculous things we had done by accident: about clusters of forms, about the haloes of oil around our hard-won patches of colour, about what the materials had done to us. This added an unexpected dimension to the learning process, a response to peripheral elements that awarded them central value. It strikes me now that this brought us close to the essence of Harry as artist.

Though all this remains very clear, I still find it hard to describe Harry's teaching method. He was there a lot of the time; he was absent a lot of the time, and one sensed his absence. Sometimes he said quite a lot, on occasion interrupting work to redirect us if he felt we had gone wrong. Sometimes he said very little. Coming round and speaking to us individually he could, with a few words and gestures, bring illumination and joy. One knew he was intensely interested, and this knowledge recharged one's own batteries. I felt I was working for him, and at the same time doing myself proud, giving myself the best experience the world had to offer. The words seem excessive, perhaps, but, in effect, after years of art history I was discovering art.

The broader picture had changed very little. As far as national art education was concerned, there was something going on in Newcastle and Leeds, with Victor Pasmore and Richard Hamilton up there, and Thubron and Hudson in Leeds, that threatened mimetically-based art teaching and seemed to propose abstraction as the only worthwhile means and product. I have referred to a sudden change in Harry's Basic Course teaching, and the surfacing of differences between himself and Victor Pasmore, but to the wider world they were one art mafia, with Pasmore the boss. An essay of 1959 by Barclay-Russell represents a typical response. It is entitled 'Consideration of claims of an approach to art education which should be through the learning of the grammar of abstract design as a basic and comprehensive course in education at art schools and in secondary education'. Barclay-Russell's points are quite clear, though embedded in sentences of amazing length.

First, he refuted the claim (whose?) of novelty. At the Central School and elsewhere, he said, work had already been proceeding 'as a result of the vital contribution of the Bauhaus'. Secondly, he argued that this 'training in the grammar of abstract art' amounted to imposing 'a new aesthetic' and that this, in narrowing the possibilities put before the child and the student, undid all the liberalising work of those who had striven to free art education from the routines enforced by Victorian pedagogy. Art done for the sake of artistic development was being replaced by a supposedly more up-to-date notion 'of an art dictated and conditioned by the outlook of science'. Art was being subjugated to 'this scientific sovereignty', and he identified this product of 'the orientations of Bauhaus philosophy' with 'contemporary scientific interpretations'. Here was an intelligent and concerned man completely misconstruing Harry's intentions as well as the multiple and changing aims of the Bauhaus. He named 'Messrs Victor Pasmore, de Sausmarez and Thubron' as those eagerly 'finding ways to propitiate science' and 'to perpetuate the scientific domination of man's mind through an art that is subservient to or conditioned by science'. He was also misconstruing Pasmore, and certainly he went too far in his insistence on this subservience to scientific ideas, but I do suspect that Pasmore was consciously or unconsciously teaching a grammar of abstract art. Harry was not. What may have added to Barclay-Russell's passionate feelings in the matter is that he was writing during or shortly after the exhibition in which the teaching in Newcastle and Leeds was given a London showing. Moreover, the exhibition was at the Institute of Contemporary Arts, the old ICA in Dover Street, whose president was Herbert Read.

It was the ICA's first exhibition of art school work and consisted exclusively of Newcastle and Leeds productions. I suspect that Richard

Hamilton, who worked a lot with the ICA, made the original proposal. In Leeds I recall Tom Hudson's enthusiasm for it. It would be a great and overdue opportunity to stand up before all the world and show it what was going on. There would be discussions, press reports, all sorts of opportunities to address and change the art education in the country on the model of Leeds and Newcastle. Foreigners would come, perhaps readier than anyone in the country to honour what they saw.

Harry, I was shocked to discover, was not keen. He did not seem to have clear reasons: there was something wrong about it all. I certainly could not understand what held him back. Was it some sort of modesty and shyness? In my admiration for him and his teaching I added my pleas to Tom's and in the end we persuaded him. Leeds would join Newcastle in this undertaking. I think Harry provided the title for it: *The Developing Process*. The result was an exhibition in which the more programmatic work of Newcastle dominated in quantity and impact, and the Leeds section was dominated by Tom's display of constructions, whereas the two-dimensional work sent from Leeds was relatively sparse and looked tentative beside the rest. This struck me at the time, but I could not then say to myself that perhaps first-year art work should look tentative and not as though every problem had been solved. The public response – art reviews, art-education reports – was cool. The exhibition was seen as quite an interesting demonstration of abstract art work by students in two Northern art schools. ICA-goers reckoned they had come to terms with abstract art; this exhibition could not teach them anything. Commentators lumped Newcastle and Leeds together and implied either that Leeds was an off-shoot of Newcastle or that there was total unanimity between them.

I now think that Harry, in his instinctual wisdom, knew that this is how it would be. The exhibition would not be able to show how far he and his teaching had moved away from the supposed Bauhaus model, and how little of a system, let alone a grammar of abstract art, was being imposed by him. He had never accepted the general conviction that abstraction and figuration were opposites (no Klee admirer could). Neither had he developed a system of teaching. What he had was an ever-changing repertoire of starting points to propose to his classes. What followed would grow out of a symbiotic relationship between teacher and student in situations that were never the same twice. No one exhibition, no display of end products, could do other than misrepresent that, and the ICA had the worse effect of identifying Leeds' emphasis on open-ended teaching – awkwardly encapsulated in its title – with Pasmore's much more routine course. Might a book do it?

Maurice de Sausmerez' *Basic Design* of 1964 was a well-intentioned attempt. Maurice had a very good relationship with Harry and, with his adroit verbal ways as well as southern manners, might have been a good PR man for Harry. Moreover, he had strong views of his own about the need to bring new energies into art education and, as we have seen, insisted on the need for an intellectual base as well as for skills and sensibilities. I am not sure whether Maurice thought Harry would welcome the book. My guess is that he wrote it without consulting Harry too much. He may have mentioned the project to Harry and found him reluctant to have anything to do with it. So Maurice went ahead, prefacing what was in effect just his own presentation with a firmly worded acknowledgement to Harry. In his text he said things that Harry surely would have approved of: he was not recommending a method but an attitude, the actions described in it were not to be imitated but could suggest a host of new activities, the work illustrated was not to be mistaken for 'art'. All that is good, but if you publish a book that, whatever you said to the contrary, appeared to be offering a complete set of exercises and the results they lead to, people will receive it as a 'how to' book and reckon they can all do it as long as they have got it open at the right page.

Again, Harry's instinct was absolutely right. No book, not even Harry's own book, whoever would have done it with him, could have failed to have this unwanted didactic effect. Perhaps the only way of doing anything of the right sort, assuming a very idealistic publisher, would have been to present a visual and verbal diary of what was done at Leeds, going on for three or four years lest anything like a closed system emerged. Perhaps I should have done it. I did not think of it then: it was all just beginning and would surely go on for ever, getting more productive all the time. I had neither realistic foresight nor the ambition that might have primed such an undertaking. I was standing too close to sense what was needed.

Harry Thubron is dead now; I nearly said 'safely dead'. We who loved him and sincerely admire his work as artist – perhaps aided by the countless many who benefited from him as teacher – must bestir ourselves to get him recognition before the work is more widely dispersed. But I think that we have tended to misrepresent him, with the best of intentions. We express our delight at his keen eye and ironic mind, at the wit as well as the visual acuity with which he responded to colours and textures, and brought an infinite range of found bits and pieces into telling juxtapositions as *papiers collés* and relief compositions. We should of course go much further, and give our attention to the meaning of these works, to the many 'woods' (carved pieces), to the drawings and prints he did. We don't because no one asks us to, whereas other work is waiting for us. But we must also set our sights higher. We must attend to meaning, as I have said, and that will soon have us recommending Harry's visual sharpness and his essential seriousness, his *gravitas* much more. There was much he did in the later '70s and the '80s, often in Spain, that is intensely serious and represents a wise and sensitive man's response to the world as well as to his personal drama – deeply felt, deeply poetic art that at times touches heaven and hell.

Chapter Thirteen

DAVID THISTLEWOOD The Formation of the NSEAD: a Dialectical Advance for British Art and Design Education

The National Society for Education in Art and Design has two distinct lines of descent. One comprises the Society of Art Masters (est. 1888), which became the National Society of Art Masters in 1909, and the National Society for Art Education in 1944. This began as an association of art school principals, who were exclusively male, and its interests were predominantly hierarchical and subject-centred. The second line of descent comprises the Art Teachers' Guild (est. 1900), The New Society of Art Teachers (1938), and the organisation they combined to form in 1940, the Society for Education in Art. The ATG was formed to give voice to the large proportion of classroom teachers who were women, and its interests were predominantly egalitarian and child-centred or individual-centred. After the 1944 Education Act the perspectives of these two main parties, now the NSAE and the SEA, each broadened to accept alternative ideas. But their two ingrained characteristics, the polarities of the history of creative education in Britain, did not fully synthesise until the NSAE and the SEA amalgamated in 1984, requiring the fusion of their inherent philosophies. What I wish to argue, while also celebrating, is that this fusion of ideals has represented a dialectical advance for British art and design education as a whole.

I am conscious of using the term 'dialectical advance' in the sense in which it would have been used by Herbert Read who, as Chairman and President of the SEA for twenty-eight years [1], was the longest-serving officer, and one of the most distinguished policy-makers, of either branch of this Society. In his terms it signifies a synthesis of opposites, creating a resulting condition that somehow comprises much more than the sum of its two original constituents [2]. In Read's book *Education through Art* (1943) [3] the opposed constituents of creative education are called 'didacticism' and 'originating activity' (today we should perhaps use the terms 'subject-centrality' and 'individual-centrality'). When we realise how mutually exclusive these were held to be by the two distinct factions of art education, and when we then consider how curiously old-fashioned these factions have become in the past few years, we may in fact accept that each constitutes considerably less than half of our present conception of our subject.

The SAM/NSAM was subject-centred, didactic and hierarchical in the following respects. It naturally addressed most of its pronouncements to the Board of Education and the Local Education Authorities [4]. If it had one *paramount* dedication, this was to the preservation of drawing as an academic discipline. It instituted systems of examination in order to preserve the discipline of drawing in general education, and, through the NSAM Teaching Certificate, to maintain an involvement in the control of standards of drawing on entry into the profession. Possession of its certificates signified competence in classical draughtsmanship, and in design allied to the industrial arts. After 1911 the NSAM opened its membership to uncertificated teachers of drawing, design or art; but because these were offered a form of junior associateship, and because many potential recruits were already members of the Art Teachers' Guild, the NSAM did not become truly representative of the entire profession – that is, as we conceive of it today.

For there was an ill-defined, but nonetheless real, distinction between the 'higher' discipline of teaching drawing and design, and the 'lower' discipline of teaching art. The former was associated with national purposes and aspired to academic respectability; the latter was hard to dissociate from 'play' and rather modest learning. The former had historic justification for calling itself Art (with a capital initial), and a sense of belonging to traditions of Classical scholarship. The latter had the kind of romantic outlook that, along with such things as simple dress, vegetarianism, and a belief in the spiritual value of craftwork, had been a by-product of the English Arts and Crafts Movement.

It was not an accident that the Art Teachers' Guild was formed as a guild: it belonged in the same ambience as those other, more famous, associations – the Art-Workers' Guild, the Century Guild, and the Guild of Handicraft. As such it was committed to the socialisation of art and the widespread dissemination of creative competencies throughout the community. By contrast, the contemporary vested interests of the Art Masters lay in arguing the case for academic exclusivity, and in elevating the significance of its didactics (to match the significance afforded to Science). These aims were effected by encouraging ever higher levels of technical excellence in teachers as individuals, while also demanding that the authorities respect the academic and professional standing of members who had devoted their lives to perfecting conventional competencies. Guild members, on the other hand (while many subscribed privately to this academic strategy as applied to themselves) were much more concerned with tactical approaches necessary for encouraging an essential creativity – or an 'originating activity' – in people who were not specifically destined for, or committed to, an aesthetic way of life. The first Chairman of the ATG, Lucy Varley, made oblique reference to this difference, and to the SAM, when she said:

> Some associations exist primarily to secure for the teachers better
> salaries and shorter hours, but it [is] the main object of the Art
> Teachers' Guild to secure better methods of teaching [5].

In pursuit of this object the Guild's chosen models were all child-centred. Whereas the Art Masters tended to honour academicians, politicians and members of the establishment, the ATG honoured educationalists and writers who were arguing for child-centred and individual-centred creativity. Ebenezer Cooke, Franz Cizek, Clive Bell and Percival Tudor-Hart were all made Honorary Fellows (coincidentally the Guild was opened to male membership but for many years this did not amount to more than a few per cent), and it became the Guild's prime purpose in its conferences and publications to propagate Cooke's and Cizek's arguments concerning means of expression, invention and imagination peculiar to childhood.

These arguments, of course, centred on the principle that art was more than merely *comparable* to other educational disciplines in the curriculum, but was an aspect of human development whose absence impaired mental growth and diminished social fitness. All perceptible ills of society – from the expansionism and aggressive competitiveness of nations to the tastelessness and boorish behaviour of their citizens – could be attributed to the suppression of free creativity in children and the encouragement of a substitute, pseudo-creativity in the form of conventional art. In Britain this conventional, or 'industrial', art and the international competitiveness it engendered, were most closely identified with the Art Masters.

The views of Tudor-Hart (who is now less well remembered than Cooke or Cizek) were admired by the Guild as the voicing of extreme opinions. For him childhood creativity was *superior* to that of adults through its immediate perceptivity towards events in all their vividness that was invariably lost in later life. The essential need of adult art was to regain contact with naive perception, and Tudor-Hart's own academy in Paris (the Paris of Post-Impressionism, Cubism and Futurism, which of course themselves were devoted to precisely this objective) became a centre of pilgrimage for members of the Guild, stimulating a strong Guild commitment to avant-garde art [6]. He moved his academy to London in 1913 – probably due to the worsening political climate but also no doubt because London's members of the ATG, if not the public at large, had positively welcomed Roger Fry's expositions of Post-Impressionism [7].

London, along with Cizek's Vienna, for a brief time became exceptional as a centre of association between avant-garde art and the spontaneous, expressive art of children. It was therefore extraordinary but *explicable* when Marion Richardson, a member of the ATG, exhibited the work of her children beside that of leading abstractionists at Fry's Omega Workshop in 1917 [8]. With Clive Bell, Fry had originated an aesthetic theory, featuring a special 'emotion' sensitive towards line, form and colour, stimulating inner vision and design in the connoisseur and artist [9]. It is not hard to imagine this doctrine giving impetus to the proceedings of the Guild, and to the classroom work of members' pupils as it replaced submission to instruction.

I hope I have indicated enough of their objectives to suggest that the Art Masters and Guild Members were fundamentally opposed in philosophical outlook and practical purposes. However, there was constant contact between their two associations on consultative and regulatory bodies of various kinds. There were intermittent initiatives to amalgamate from as early as 1925 [10], but these invariably came to nothing. The reasons were often caricatured as reflecting the mutually exclusive differences of a trade union and a learned society, or of conservatism and radicalism. These prejudices took sixty years to reconcile.

Now one faction – let me call it the *classic thesis* of twentieth-century art education – came to the fore in the early years of this century and predominantly shaped the provisions for art that followed the 1918 (Fisher) Education Act. This was the initiative of the NSAM, and what it achieved was the formalisation of a system of drawing and design education that had prevailed 'unofficially' in art schools led by many of the Society's most prominent members. In general, this approach had emphasised drawing (both conventional and observational) and design (the realisation of artefacts through *practical involvement with materials*) – drawing and design – as the twin features of a specifically modern industrial education. The recognition and adoption of this British (that is, the Art Masters') approach by the Deutscher Werkbund in 1907, it was accepted, had given rise to German industrial success, enhanced national consciousness, and cultural revival.

The Art Masters' values were imprinted on the Fisher Act, the superior motive being the complete reconstruction of British industrial education (in order to meet anticipated post-war German competition). The Act enabled local authorities to provide extensive, post-school continuation classes and training for young workers entering art industries, and also to admit apprentices-in-training to half-time courses in the art schools. As might have been expected, these trainees had special courses devoted to their crafts and industries; but their diet also included substantial amounts of drawing, and this often meant sharing classes with general students.

Thus, depending on their vocations, they would take part in Figure Drawing, Drawing from Nature, Architectural and Ornamental Drawing, and so forth. This fulfilled one of the NSAM's prime objectives in linking drawing expertise to the health of manufacturing trades and industries, and thus directly to the national well-being. This enlarged the scope of the subject, suggesting a normal progression from art in the early years of education, via design in the later years, towards the provision of continuing education and training in tandem with trades and industries. Above all, it demonstrated the national, strategic importance of art and design. This overtly subject-centred principle, when won, was considered by the NSAM one of its worthiest achievements, only slightly marred by a failure to attract the sort of royal approval that had been bestowed on industrial art in the reign of Queen Victoria.

I now move on a couple of decades in order to observe events towards the end of the 1930s that were forming conceptions of art that would figure in the 1944 (Butler) Education Act. The ATG is to be seen as having persisted through (for it) a most unfavourable period in which its principles had been generally acceptable only in the field of early learning. It recognised the New Society of Art Teachers, on its inception in 1938, as having identical objectives for adolescent pupils. It saw, moreover, that the NSAT was pursuing these objectives energetically and commercially (by marketing publications and operating a picture circulation scheme) – that is, in ways which seemed to the ATG to signify an enviable confidence. Members of the NSAT were invited to a Guild seminar entitled 'The Teaching of Art to Children over Fourteen', and it was in response to a challenge from the floor, on this occasion, that the two bodies affiliated [11]. They did not fully amalgamate until 1946, but in the meantime were associated as separate organisations possessing a joint Council, a common journal, *Athene*, and a single umbrella title, the Society for Education in Art [12]. As a result of adopting the NSAT's assertiveness a Consultative Council was appointed, composed of some of the most eminent, independent persons in the arts and education – including Herbert Read, Sir Michael Sadler, R. R. Tomlinson, Sir Fred Clarke, Eric Newton, Misha Black, and William Johnstone – whose dual role was to act as a think-tank and also lobby government on the SEA's behalf.

A rather curious situation existed in this interval, there being a cohort of (mostly women) ATG members, a much smaller cohort of (predominantly male) NSAT members, and a growing number of joint members consisting of all enrolments after 1939. In spite of the two organisations having identical short-term ambitions, there was a strong distinction between ATG-inspired and NSAT-inspired *long-term* objectives that were adopted as SEA policies, and because many NSAT members entered the armed forces and most ATG members did not, the officials of the latter were the ones who ran the SEA throughout the Second World War. This resulted in ATG policies persisting into the late 1940s, by which time they had become firmly characteristic of the SEA. This offers a unique case study in policy-making because the SEA records reveal, side by side, detailed agreed policies that were implemented and equally detailed agreed policies that were deferred indefinitely.

The *combined* objective was to convince educationalists in general of the value of 'imaginative and emotional education' throughout the whole of compulsory education. The ATG faction of SEA believed this could best be achieved by encouraging piecemeal development of teaching initiatives allied to specific learning circumstances. The NSAT faction of SEA believed that a prime requirement was the establishment of a research institute, the function of which would be systematic curricular experimentation involving artists, teachers, psychologists, the adult public and the other arts, as well as international cooperation [13].

Substantial funding – a grant of £2000 from the Goldsmiths' Company – was obtained for the realisation of these aims. Under ATG management, this money was expended in the most democratic fashion, on the development of the journal *Athene* from which all members gained benefit, and on the nurturing of discrete, individual initiatives to originate new principles of expressive learning [14]. Alexander Barclay-Russell, who had been NSAT Chairman until called up for war service, however, had believed this funding to have been granted expressly to establish a research institute. This prompted his resignation shortly after his return [15], but this is incidental. The interesting thing for historiographic purposes is the obvious fact that the SEA had sidelined a subject-centred enterprise (an agreed programme for research into the nature of art education) in favour of developing, and lobbying for, a logic of individualism – what might be called the *romantic antithesis* of twentieth-century creative education.

As the SEA's Consultative Committee members had been appointed because of their eminence and capacities to influence statutory bodies including, ultimately, the government, it is not surprising that it was this logic of individualism that so positively shaped the provisions for art in the 1944 Education Act. This was the SEA's strongest moment – when its Consultative Associates so expertly drew out the Society's prime concerns, gave them persuasive form, and argued them so convincingly that they came to characterise the democratic and optimistic tenor of the time. Even the NSAM was affected by this propaganda: its general evidence to government was broadly in line with the SEA's, even to the point of arguing, for the first time, that true democracies are founded on genuinely creative early learning [16]. The NSAM, too, revised its constitution, and symbolically transformed itself into the *National Society for Art Education* in 1944. But as the instincts of this organisation were unchangeably didactic, the way that *it* responded to the new ideals was to support the liberalisation of art and design as *subject*, and to work for overall curriculum reform.

Two episodes in the 1950s illustrate perfectly the differences of outlook that continued to affect the two Societies in spite of their apparently converging philosophies. One was the SEA's declared commitment to the 'naive' creativity of the untutored (an anathema to the still didactic NSAE); the other was NSAE's support for what appeared to promise a new didacticism for the art schools, in the form of Basic Design.

The earlier of these occurrences was the SEA's contribution to the *Festival of Britain* (1951), in the form of an exhibition presented at the Whitechapel Gallery, London, entitled *Black Eyes and Lemonade* [17]. This was the first comprehensive exhibition of British traditional and popular art to be shown in the country, and the accompanying special issue of *Athene* [18] was the first publication to argue the relatedness of popular home decoration, vernacular crafts, the peculiar conventions of shop and market display, public house interiors, fairground imagery, and the naturally expressive art of the untutored. This major exposition represented a determined effort to be definitive about the Society's values in an age that promised a genuinely egalitarian future. It had one principal objective – to promote the vitality of creativity manifested in 'ordinary' taste and timeless customs – supporting Herbert Read's adopted argument that every individual could become a special kind of artist. However, an emergent objective became more memorable – to demonstrate that popular creativity was not some imperfect aping of the refined arts, but on the contrary an authentic alternative, constituting a set of practices with its own standards, conventions and enduring symbols. The exhibition and, in particular, this message are now recognised as having been of seminal importance in the origination of Pop Art in Britain and America [19].

At the same time as the SEA was becoming involved in avant-garde art at the romantic extremity, finding itself unexpectedly associated with the modern gothic world of science fiction and popular horror movies, the NSAE was engaging avant-garde art of the opposite polarity, constructive abstraction. The NSAE did not initiate an educational interest in this aesthetic, as the SEA had done with regard to popular art, but embraced it after it had been highlighted in a famous public disagreement between art educationists.

This occasion was the 1956 SEA Conference at Bretton Hall College, into which Herbert Read had speculatively infiltrated the prime subject-centred influence of the day – what became known as the Basic Design approach of Tom Hudson, Harry Thubron, Richard Hamilton and Victor Pasmore. Read's intention, I think, had been to precipitate a crisis of thought in art education that would result in a synthesis of the two equal and opposite philosophies, such as he had demanded in *Education through Art*. But clearly the time was not yet right, and it caused only a crisis. SEA stalwarts were offended by Basic Design's 'point into line into plane' abstractionism and its apparent impersonality. They detected a conspiracy to deny young people one of the few remaining avenues to spiritual beauty still available to them in the modern world – expressionistic realism [20]. For their part, those teachers who identified with Basic Design became more and more convinced of an underlying SEA objective to retard adolescent creativity in an aspic of romantic sentimentality.

Basic Design naturally received its most tangible support from the NSAE, for it was seen as providing a new didactic framework to replace outmoded practices [21]. Tom Hudson and Herbert Read deprecated this academisation of Basic Design, insisting that its methodological structure was meant to support *individual* aesthetic experience and originating activity. But as Basic Design became trapped, despite their best efforts, in one half of the great debate, it must be assumed that the moment was wrong for the kind of synthesis Read had expected to influence in his lifetime. When he died, in 1968, the SEA and the NSAE were as polarised as ever.

Today, however, more than twenty years on, a Readian synthesis has taken place. By this I mean that the SEA and NSAE have not merely amalgamated to form the NSEAD, but have subsumed their respective policies within a vision of the future of art and design education that makes earlier objectives appear dated and curiously factious. To illustrate what I mean by this I should like finally to describe two areas of concern in which the NSEAD has taken positions that, to me, seem obviously the results of dialectical advances. The first area is 'Art, Craft and Design in the Primary School', and the second is 'Critical Studies'.

Primary Education was formerly the province of the SEA, of course, and Critical Studies (in its 'art history' mode) that of the NSAE. In the painstaking preliminaries prior to amalgamation, each organisation sent delegates to the other's seminars and conferences. Now initiatives for change are always the efforts of individuals, and what happened was that innovations posited by such respected educationists as Keith Gentle, Ken Baines, Eileen Adams, Rod Taylor, Robert Clement, Arthur Hughes, Maurice Barrett – and many, many more to whom I apologise for lack of space to do them justice – these innovations were shaped in the same collision of forces that was also creating the NSEAD. These individual initiatives were tempered by audience reaction that was often partial and sometimes philosophically hostile. The great benefit of this was that theoretical resolution took place in the cross-representation before amalgamation, and there has been no noticeable nostalgia for former independence such as that which certainly effected the ATG/NSAT amalgamation for at least six years.

Therefore when we read Keith Gentle's reminder in the NSEAD publication *Art, Craft and Design in the Primary School*, edited by John Lancaster [22], that art teaching, in this as in other phases of education, is as much about art as it is about the individual, we know this is a coded reference to innumerable differences of agreement now resolved. It signifies that the former NSAE concerns for subject definition have percolated through the age ranges, and that it is now legitimate to imagine very young children acquiring a discipline with its attendant techniques and aesthetic concepts, and becoming proto-practitioners, besides fulfilling their expressive potentialities in ways demanded by the SEA. John Lancaster suggests – elsewhere in this book – that it is as legitimate to ask children if their work has taught them what they wanted to know of representational appearances in the external world, as it is also to ask what it has taught them about a grammar of aesthetics – line, form, plane, texture, volume, tone and colour. This heresy of 1956 is today's accepted truth.

Critical Studies has also benefited from the collision of SEA and NSAE convictions. This domain of creative education has always been dominated by conventions. The NSAE, as descendant of the SAM, held onto the Classicist belief in the establishment of cultural principles at notional centres of scholarship, and their gradual dissemination throughout a more or less receptive population. In this sense the Classical draughtsmanship of the Renaissance, and the Elementarist influences of Basic Design – to take two radically different phenomena – were compatible at least in suggesting that critical principles were subject-centred, that is, inherent in an *authorised* art history.

The SEA, on the other hand, had conventions of its own that were derived from an equally idiosyncratic tradition of Art Appreciation. According to this, works of art were regarded as communicative of aesthetic values by their presence (without much teaching intervention apart from selection of works for appropriate ages). The original referents of this belief were the 'aesthetic emotion' of Roger Fry and Clive Bell, and the associated aim of replicating for the child-observer *in appreciation* the emotional creative impetus of each work as experienced by its originator *in realisation*. Few of the inherited principles of our discipline today seem as naively old-fashioned as this, suggesting that all that was wholesome in the motivation of a van Gogh or a Gauguin (for example, their palpable delight in uniquely perceived chromatic relationships) could be apprehended by pupils while disregarding less wholesome motivations (for example, mental instability and lust).

Again the resolution of two traditions has taken place in the same philosophical reaction that produced a fusion of the SEA and NSAE. The result is a principled consensus [23]. Critical Study is didactic and subject-centred in its reference to existing scholarship in art history, aesthetics, economics, sociology, psychology, and all other contextual phenomena that leave traces of themselves in works of art. But it is also originative and individual-centred in the ways in which it encourages those who engage in it to find patterns of feeling and logic which may be used to reinforce, measure or supplant conventional wisdom. As one of the most complex of cultural phenomena it must be taught exhaustively, but it generates sparks of understanding that defy methodical teaching. It is both 'didactic' and 'individually originative'. Herbert Read was not referring to Critical Study when he wrote the following words in *Education through Art*, but to the wider concept 'creative education'. His remarks, however, apply equally to this domain and demonstrate its identity of purpose with the other essential disciplines of art and design education. His words also summarise the principal argument of this chapter:

> It is evident that the distinction between 'didacticism' and 'originating activity' has become clear . . . . The imaginative does not stand over against the logical, the originating against the didactic, the artistic against the utilitarian, as a claimant to which a concession must be more or less unwillingly made; the two processes are in absolute opposition, and though the end we desire may be called a synthesis, our contention is that the basis of all intellectual and moral strength lies in the adequate integration of the perceptive senses and the external world, of the personal and the organic . . . [24].

I do not think it inappropriate to extend the context of these remarks to embrace the 'personal-perceptive' concerns that traditionally inspired the SEA, and the concerns to maintain and enhance the 'external organism' of art and design education as a body of scholarship that traditionally preoccupied the NSAE. Almost fifty years after Herbert Read wrote this passage, the NSEAD has achieved more than an 'adequate integration': it has achieved the synthesis of 'originating activity' and 'didacticism' he so fervently desired, and it is this, as much as government policy, that will shape the provisions for our subject in the foreseeable future.

Notes and References

1   Herbert Read's record of service is as follows: Patron of *Athene* 1939; Chairman of the SEA Advisory Panel of External Consultants from its inception in 1940; Member of the Editorial Board of *Athene* from 1941; President of the SEA from 1947 until his death in 1968.

2   For a detailed analysis of Read's dialectics see THISTLEWOOD, D. (1984), *Herbert Read: Formlessness and Form* (London and Boston, Routledge & Kegan Paul).

3   READ, H. (1943), *Education through Art* (London, Faber).

4   For a survey of this see: THISTLEWOOD, D. (1988), 'The Early History of the NSEAD: the Society of Art Masters (1888–1909) and the National Society of Art Masters (1909–1944)', *Journal of Art and Design Education*, 7, 1, pp. 37–64.

5   CARLINE, RICHARD (1968), *Draw They Must* (London, Edward Arnold), p. 139.

6 *Ibid.*, pp. 138–9. Miss Collins, the ATG's first Secretary, studied with Tudor-Hart in the Rue d'Assas, proposed him as Honorary Member, and thus initiated the association between Guild and Academy.

7 *Manet and the Post-Impressionists*, Grafton Gallery, London, November–January 1910–11. *The Second Post-Impressionist Exhibition*, New Grafton Galleries, London, October–December 1912.

8 For a description of how this arose see RICHARDSON, M. (1948), *Art and the Child* (London, London University Press), p. 30 *et seq.*

9 See BELL, CLIVE (1914), 'The Aesthetic Hypothesis' in *Art* (London, Chatto & Windus), pp. 3–37. See also FRY, ROGER (1920), 'An Essay on Aesthetics' in *Vision and Design* (London , Chatto & Windus), pp. 16–38.

10 NSAM Council Minute 421, 20 March 1925 [NSEAD/C/1], NSEAD Archives.

11 This was initiated by a letter dated 7 March 1938 from the Secretary of ATG to Alexander Barclay-Russell, Chairman of NSAT, welcoming the formation of NSAT and inviting its members to the proposed Seminar (on 20 or 27 May 1938). Barclay-Russell agreed to recommend approval to NSAT Executive. By 10 December 1938 a Joint ATG/NSAT Finance Committee had been formed preparatory to amalgamation. In *Athene*, 1, 2, Summer 1939, the Editor, Erik Sythr, reported that the affiliation of ATG and NSAT was now virtually completed. However, the separate designation *President ATG* and *Chairman NSAT* did not disappear from the list of officers of SEA until 1946.

12 The SEA changed its name to the Society for Education *through* Art in 1953.

13 See position paper entitled 'An Institute of Art Education', especially Section 1, 'The History of the Institute Proposals', prepared for Extraordinary General Meeting of SEA, 4 March 1950, NSEAD Archives.

14 This was defended and also proposed as SEA's continuing policy. See position paper entitled 'Alternative Proposals', signed Audrey Martin, Vice-Chairman, February 1950; prepared for EGM, 4 March 1950, NSEAD Archives.

15 See letter Alexander Barclay-Russell to Nan Youngman dated 29 July 1952: NSEAD Archives.

16 'Art is not one aspect of life: it is the whole of life seen in one aspect': PULLÉE, E. E. (1945), 'Presidential Address', *NSAE Journal*, XV, 2, October 1945, p. 7. It was widely acknowledged that three of the Society's wartime publications [*Art Education after the War*; *Art in General Education after the War*; and *The Curriculum and External Relations of the Art Schools*] had helped shape both the 1944 Education Act and the cultural agenda.

17 Whitechapel Gallery, London, 11 August–6 October 1951 (organised by Barbara Jones).

18 *Athene*, 5, 3, August 1951.

19 See ALLOWAY, LAWRENCE (1966), 'The Development of British Pop' in LIPPARD, LUCY R. (1966), *Pop Art* (London, Thames & Hudson) pp. 31–2, and especially p. 200.

20 For an account of this public disagreement see NORBERT LYNTON, Chapter 12.

21 For example, see the subject featuring in the NSAE *Journal of the Conference, Brighton, 1960*, especially GODWIN, ARTHUR (1960), 'What Should Constitute a "Basic" Art Course?', pp. 53–8, reproduced in *NSAE Journal*, VIII, 2, November 1981, pp. 17–18.

22 LANCASTER, JOHN (ed.) (1987), *Art, Craft and Design in the Primary School* (Corsham, NSEAD).

23 See THISTLEWOOD, D. (ed.) (1989) *Critical Studies in Art and Design Education* (London, Longman/NSEAD).

24 READ, *Education through Art* (n. 3), p. 220.

Index